Usurper

Wayne Schreiber

CW00863689

The Tanarian Chronicles – UK Edition

Book 1 – Arise A Hero

Book 2 - The Crystal King

Book 3 - Usurper of the Gods

Visit my website www.ariseahero.com

Cover design by Wayne Schreiber

MAP

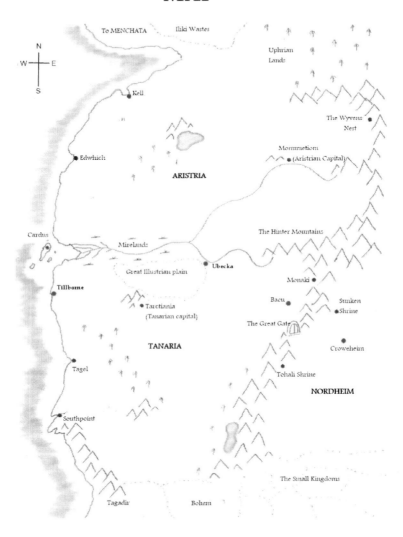

To MENCHATA   Iliki Wastes

Uphrian
Lands

N
W — E
S

Kell

The Wyvens
Nest

Momnnetiom
(Aristrian Capital)

Edwhich

ARISTRIA

The Hinter Mountains

Cardus

Mirelands

Great Illustrian plain

Ubecka

Tillborne

Monaki

Taretiania
(Tanarian capital)

Bacu

Sunken
Shrine

The Great Gate

TANARIA

Croweheim

Tagel

Tehali Shrine

NORDHEIM

Southpoint

The Small Kingdoms

Tagadir

Bohem

Prologue

"A legend finishes and a story begins"

The Aristrian soldier nervously stepped forward to stand by a great ram's horn that hung from a post swaying gently in the wind. The herald felt the burden of his duty this day, as he prepared to relay his Lord's signal. Thousands of heads turned anxiously to face him, watching him eagerly in anticipation of the order yet to come. The detail of the watching crowds was lost to the herald, who wet his lips preparing to relay his orders, one soldier's face merged into another as the sea of men stretched away from him as far as the eye could see. Lord Banok mounted his warhorse and after a minor adjustment of his reins he nodded at the Herald; it was time. Taking in a great lung-full of air he pursed his lips about the cold brass mouthpiece attached to the great horn, it had hung for months like a relic from the past facing out towards the enemy, unused and redundant dangling from a roughly-cut wooden post. At last the order had been given and he blew the long harrowing blast that signalled the overdue advance of the Aristrian army. They had bided their time on the desolate grassland plain that led towards the small border town of Ubecka. Each day had been laboriously filled rehearsing battle formations or spent oiling their steel against the rust that was slowly working its way through their stagnant ranks. The once green fields of their vast camp had turned into a dark and muddy stain that had annoyed all that had cause to struggle across it. The mud had been the talk of the camp for months. However, now they readied themselves for war, its annoyance was pushed far from their minds as talk turned towards the possibility of victory and finally returning home. Their ranks had swollen to the point of being so vast that several relaying horns were necessary to pass on the signal to begin their assault across the rippling sea of men; at last their months of waiting were finally over. Lord Algar commanded the left flank and Banok the right. The army was now too large for any single man to control its mass, so both men held the position of command, an undisputed right given to them by the countless years of service in the elite order of the Su-Katii. A grin of pleasure unwittingly spread its way across Lord Banok's face as he watched his troops advance across the open field like an endless stream of ants, this was the moment he had been waiting for since leaving his God's temple years before, a chance to destroy a nation and become a legend amongst his Order. He had initially been disappointed with his urgent reassignment from Tagel. The coastal town was already under siege and with a guaranteed fight of epic proportions on his hands Tagel was one party that he did not want to miss, but like every good soldier he had followed orders and taken up his new joint command and was rewarded with the surprise that he had underestimated the scale of the glorious battle about to begin. This battle would make Tagel look like a side show and the bards would sing of his victory in days to come… but through the clouds of his elated sensations he sensed that something about this day was wrong. In his repeated dreams leading to this moment he had been embracing the final victory in a different way, he had been leading the slaughter of the enemy from the front, not commanding them from the rear. For some unknown reason he needed to experience this moment exactly as he had seen it in his dreams, the moment needed to be savoured and enjoyed, it had to be perfect. Today he controlled his dreams and would carve them into the flesh of any man who dared to stand in his way. Lord Banok drew both of his blades and spurred his horse forward, now was his moment. It would be best

4

enjoyed with the screams of the dying playing as his anthem; he needed to get to the front immediately. Riding low in his saddle Banok raced towards the front ranks of his men, it must be him who drew the first blood of the day; his ego demanded it.

Delanichi, the trickster and accomplished magician, stood on the opposing side to the menacing swarm of the Aristrian army; the strong wind blew his long brown robes irritatingly about his face, their soiled fragrance reminding him that they desperately needed a wash. Rubbing the offending smell from his nose he watched the mass of men advance from his vantage point within the fortified town. A lesser man's legs would have weakened at the fearful sight of the approaching army, but Delanichi considered himself to be a foolish man rather than a fearful one and just watched on with awe. The great waves of Aristrians surged forward to the increasing beats of the battledrums and they were met with a storm of arrows that fell upon them as they broke into a full charge to reach their first objective, the outer rampart of the town. Delanichi watched the drama unfold from the domed roof of the town's temple of worship. The structure had seen little use over the past months, for even the most pious men in the Tanarian army were convinced that the gods had deserted them. With the loss of their commander and the expanding ranks of their enemy it was difficult to argue otherwise; but at least it had a commanding view of the surrounding plains. The sun was still low in the sky struggling to crest the crimson horizon as the Aristrian force chose to attack in the twilight of the dawn. Delanichi was an unkempt soul, he ran his grubby fingers through his greasy matted hair with nervous indecision, struggling to pull his fingers free of the tangled mess; there had been greater matters afoot to worry about than his own personal hygiene. Against

5

such a vast force the men stationed around the town would undoubtedly rely on his help today, but he was still just one man and would need to make some tough and perhaps unpopular decisions on where and how he should use his gift of power to its best effect? If only Tamar and the General were still with him. 'If only' would not do for today.

Under the shade of an arrow-filled sky, darkened by the vast exchanges of fire between the two armies, the Aristrians poured over the outer trenches and barricades to meet with the thin line of defenders. The outer wall to the town of Ubecka was without doubt undermanned on its long perimeter in the face of such an immense force - at best it would only serve to slow the enemy down, buying a fraction more time for the Tanarian garrison to muster and fully man the second higher and final wall. With the months of stalemate between the two camps, an inevitable reduction in the Tanarians' readiness had occurred. Delanichi uttered the ancient words of power he had been forced to remember by his Bohem Spell Master years before. Until now he had never needed to use such powerful and dangerous magic and the months of monotony forced upon him as a young apprentice perfecting the spell's use would at last bear fruit. He finished the spell and a wide arc of lighting forked out across ground to the nearest group of Aristrian soldiers that crested the outer wall. The electrical storm passed from his outstretched arms and jumped from man to man conducted by their armour and weapons frying everyone in its path as it snaked its way across their line with terrifying effect. Delanichi raised his eyebrows, he had surprised himself with his own power; throughout the years he had always tried to steer away from being a destructive force and had just spent his years using his magic as a source of amusement to himself. As a result of his lifetime spent meddling with the composition of spells and magic his experimentations had developed a level of understanding rarely seen in one so young; well one so young for a magician whose lifetimes could span centuries. His head swam with the addictive sensation that only raw power could bring and he immediately ceased the spell as he realised that he was actually beginning to enjoy his destructive work. He recoiled with disgust at the use of such magic, but knew that he would do worse before this day was done. Within seconds a new group of men clambered over the ramparts and replaced the fallen line of charred and smouldering men. The men on the outer wall fought desperately against the unstoppable wave of Aristrian soldiers that flooded around them, struggling on defiantly against the relentless tide until the desperate realism of their situation struck home - only death would meet them on this wall. The sudden panic of their realisation spread through their thinning ranks in seconds. Men fled their posts as the Tanarian defenders broke the line and begun to dash backwards across the two hundred yards or so of open ground to the second and final stone wall. Several short ropes were lowered in anticipation of the arrival of their fleeing comrades, but few would actually make it back to the refuge of the higher stone wall. Most of the retreating men fell with their backs exposed to the many arrows that darted across the sky. The only obstruction that slowed the Aristrians rapid advance was a series of well concealed spike pits. It was only after a group of pursing soldiers fell to their deaths, impaled on the well hidden spikes that their shocked comrades begun to slow their pace. Delanichi tried his best from his distant position to help the retreat; he once more rained down lighting bolts but not all fell on their intended targets. He could feel the mounting toll of exhaustion from his continued efforts, so he slowed his rate of attack to a more controlled manner, instead using his powers with surgical precision where they would count the most and bringing death to the lead men who pursued the fleeing Tanarians like a tsunami. One figure suddenly stood out above the sprawl of the approaching chaos, a mounted knight who surged forward to cut down any defenders that trailed behind. It was not his splendid gleaming armour that caught Delanichi's eye, nor the savage blows with which he split the skulls of the fleeing men; it was the twin silver swords that he waved about in the air indicating where his men should go. Delanichi knew this marked the man as one of the Su-Katii generals and a prized target for his magic. Delanichi dashed down from the shrine's roof and ran the short distance to the defenders' stone wall to bring him within a more accurate and lethal range for his magic, he may only get one shot at this prized target. He was quickly out of breath from the dash, which did nothing to help utter the words to the powerful spell; the years of reliance on magic had made such physical exertions an alien experience to him. After gathering his breath he ciphered the magical powers in the air around him, managing to master the new theories explained in the book of Magnus that he was several chapters through and he unleashed the deadly force in one great burst at the unsuspecting rider. The swirling mass of magical power flew across the battlefield and hit the rider, knocking him from his saddle. Delanichi smiled with delight as the rider was unhorsed, but was unpleasantly surprised when the rider pulled himself back up onto his feet and brushed himself down as if he had fallen off on his own accord, the last flickering traces of his magic were absorbed by an unseen barrier protecting the armoured rider. Delanichi realised that only another magician's hand could have stopped such force. A dozen dark-robed Brotherhood magicians crested the gangplanks of the rampart close behind the Su-Katii general, they chanted their protective spell in unison; this man was far from unprotected. Lord Banok was visibly angered by his fall and lifted one of his swords pointing it directly back at the wall where Delanichi stood; the general yelled at his Brotherhood magicians for action. Delanichi could not hear his words over the din and clatter of the raging battle but knew their meaning all too well. A cold chill washed over Delanichi and he felt himself wishing that Tamar were standing with him shoulder to shoulder once again. He had called out for his help many times over the last few days, yet nothing but an empty breeze had returned. Deduction led him to the grim and saddening reality that the Brotherhood had already dealt with him. He suddenly felt as if every set of eyes on the battlefield were upon him and many were, he began to feel very alone and particularly vulnerable as the members of the dark Brotherhood began to summon forth something nasty to deal with him.

Chapter 1 – A Time Long Past

'The life of a child was one of such innocent bliss,' thought Myridin, as he watched his baby son's eyes sparkle with joy as his little hands repeatedly smacked a wooden spoon against his chair leg. 'Just look at him, so easily pleased with such a simple object, if only we could maintain that same level of satisfaction in later life,' he sighed to himself as he considered the deeper thoughts of his memory, remembering the lust for conquest in every king that he had served with. He watched his youngest son's eyes sparkle; absorbing every new experience, giggling to himself as he repeatedly smacked the chair with annoying regularity. As Myridin looked on with rosy cheeks he found himself wondering if his son would be just as content with something other than the spoon, perhaps something less pleasing. Unable to stop the inquisitive and meddling nature of a Magician he cast a small illusion on the spoon. Suddenly the wooden spoon transformed into the image of a wriggling snake in the boy's hands. There was no chance of harm to the little one, it was just a simple illusion – he was merely intrigued to see his son's reaction. Who was he kidding? It would also be a test to see his son's reaction to magic. The discontented snake hissed and spat at the toddler as baby Ambrose continued to bash it against the chair, he was unbothered by the creature wriggling in his grip, except that now his laughter had become hysterical. He heard the approach of Niviane his wife, who called out to him, wondering what all the laughter was about and not wanting to miss out on a single second of her son's upbringing, she hurried in. Myridin quickly dispelled his illusion before she entered the room; she would not approve of such a frivolous use of magic. Like him, Niviane was also well versed in the ways of magic yet she was a lot more conservative in its application than her husband. In fact most people who met her would not have the slightest inclination that she knew anything about the ways of magic and she preferred to keep it that way. That was where she and Myridin differed, he had always sought recognition for his accomplishments… *he was a legend*. It seemed strange to him that now in his later years he sought the opposite to that which he had craved for as a youngster. As always on entrance, Niviane captivated his gaze, such beauty was rare and he considered himself a lucky man to be waking up to her every morning. For a man of maturing years and brandishing a distinguished but full head of gray hair, he considered himself lucky to have married his younger bride for no other reason than their love. Niviane was no spring chicken herself, but compared to him, she was more of a middle aged dove. She bounced into the room gleefully with her long blonde hair waving behind in tow and placed herself on the edge of his chair. She wrapped an arm lovingly around him, so they could both enjoy watching their youngest son's amusement at the wooden spoon episode. He placed his arm easily about her petite waist; she was still incredibly lean for all she had been through, providing him with three beautiful children over the years and he didn't know how she maintained her figure so well without magic? He had suggested several times after childbirth that she should use magic to speed up her recovery, but he knew all too well that she would never be so vain as to use magic on herself to maintain her perfect figure. He decided not to mention the first grey hairs that he had spotted in her hair as she nuzzled in close to him. Had the tables been reversed, magic would have been his very first call; a woman should always look good, he considered it was her duty.

'It's nice to have the place to ourselves again; I thought your visitors would never leave,' she said in little more than a whisper. Myridin stroked the beard protruding from his chin as if he were grooming a domesticated pet. It was a trait he would often mimic when deep in thought,

'As did I my love, as did I.'

Niviane closed back in on him and kissed Myridin gently on the cheek,

'Well I'm pleased that you refused their outrageous demands, I didn't want to see you return with them, though for a moment I thought you might. Who do they think they are, issuing you with demands? *Really!* Besides I don't know what I or your children would have done without you here.' A bell rang and Magnus, the head of their household, drifted into the doorway. He was a man of few words and had a knack for coming and going without being noticed, even with his tall slender figure that you would expect to normally stand out; the first sign of his appearance was often his shadow looming over you. They had all forgotten about his presence at one time or another in the past. You could easily have just walked into a room and not noticed him standing there like a tall unmoving coat rack or have passed him in the street and not recalled his face. For all his oddities, however, Myridin would have none other in charge of his villa and had even introduced him to the ways of magic in his spare time, teaching him several minor spells. With his gentle, unassuming nature and his willingness to attend to their needs, Magnus was always ready to help and was regarded almost as one of the family.

'Lunch is served,' he simply stated and then drifted away to find the other children.

Soredamor sat outside the villa rocking gently in the swing that had been constructed for her as a child. At seventeen, she had far outgrown the swing, but with her slender figure, she prided herself in the fact that she still managed to somehow fit into its saddle. Her gaze was as downtrodden as her mood and her frown extended down as far as her pouting bottom lip. She was lost in that moment, to her it was as if her entire world had just fallen apart. Two nights before, shrouded in the secrecy of her father's stables she had made the passage from girl to woman, submitting herself to the charms of Gorran, the son of her father's visiting guest. None had noticed their departure from the feast, not even the ever watchful Magnus and she intended to keep it that way. They had momentarily split up and left alone to avert attention; then when the coast was clear met up outside. To say father would not approve was an understatement and she had hidden the memory deep within her mind and used fathers very own magical teachings to secure them away from him. She suspected that such a crafty man may also have a backdoor into the magic that he regularly taught them, but this thought only depressed her further.

Gorran was her first and only love and her painful and awkward first experience was not at all how she had imagined it should feel, yet she had been drawn back to him with a new, unlocked craving. They had once again met in the secrecy of the stables the following morning to discuss if anyone had noticed their disappearance from the feast the night before. Their impromptu meeting had been early, but then she had not slept a single wink after her hurried departure the night before. She had been buzzing from their encounter; it had been so physical, both tender and rough at the same time, it had replayed in her thoughts until dawn. Gorran couldn't have been able to sleep either, for he had sat gazing out of the window of the guests quarters, watching the sun rise when he noticed Soredamor passing back to the stables, it was as if she were compelled to return to the scene of the crime. He had quickly dressed and silently slipped out of the villa to meet with her; there was little chance of their detection, the villa echoed with drunken snores. Their conversation did not last long as she crumbled to his first embrace and discovered the deep pleasures of his touch once again. This time their excitement in the hay had been exactly how she imagined it.

Magnus repeatedly ringing the lunch bell brought her out of her daydream and she felt only the present despair, with Gorran departed from her life and returning to the old world, there was a gaping hole that yearned for his touch once more. In that moment she hated her father for sending their visitors away, she knew little of their business here and only wanted him back. She dragged herself away from the swing stamping on a passing beetle and dragged her feet slowly back into the villa.

Lunch was a quiet affair, with the only noise being made by Hadrak, Soredamor's younger brother, as he slurped loudly at his soup. He held his head with one hand as he shovelled down the hot liquid with the other; the liquid seemed to suck between his well spaced teeth with annoying regularity and produced a sound that made her feel sick. He was still feeling the effects of the wine from the heavy feasting with their guests and just wanted to return to his bed. After moving about the hall, draining the dancing or departed guests' cups, he had collapsed onto a table and had been carried off to bed by Magnus, who unusually wobbled as he walked. He was not quick to learn his lesson and on the second night of their guests' stay he had been found crumpled in a heap outside his door covered in his own vomit. He had failed to find the door handle and had crawled about on the floor before finding a comfortable spot. He bore a bruise on his forehead and father refused to heal it as a lesson to the boy. It was not often they entertained guests and the children had been left to their own devices, although at sixteen Hadrak considered himself a man. He had never learnt when to give up, but then Soredamor was no better – it must be a family trait. Soredamor's mood grew more agitated as the rhythmic slurping of her brother further annoyed her, she heard every inch of the soup's journey to his gullet. She looked across the long table at her parents hoping for some form of intervention, but they were engrossed in feeding Ambrose with a bowl of milk and bread. She glanced behind her, Magnus had pottered off somewhere. It was a perfect time to strike. The children ate on a smaller table from their betters, as was the normal way of things. Their table had a wobbly leg which had been repaired more than once over the years. All that held the damaged leg in place was a single loose peg, a peg that Soredamor now stretched to grab as she slumped across the table to conceal her other hand searching beneath it. She had been tempted to use the magic that father had taught her to dislodge the peg, but she had been caught out by her father too many times before with her pranks in the past. Her father had an all seeing eye for magic and could always tell when it had been used to meddle or interfere with anything she touched. So instead she strained to reach the protruding peg under the table and with a slight tug pulled it free.

'*Soredamor*, stop slumping – a lady should maintain her posture at all times,' suggested her mother as she finished feeding Ambrose. She followed her instructions and sat upright, several moments later with only her brother's weight on the wooden top, the table collapsed on top of him, sending hot soup all over Hadrak's arm. He frantically brushed off the burning liquid as she gleefully watched his pain,

'That shut him up,' she thought to herself. It was the first thing that had cheered her up since the departure of Gorran. Hadrak glared back at her, knowing that she would be in someway connected to his little accident, she always was. They were normally at each other's throats in one way or another and he would pick the appropriate moment for his revenge. As if from nowhere a head appeared at Hadrak's feet and Magnus picked up the broken bowl,

'I'll send a maid in to clear up the rest, would you

like another bowl young master?'

Hadrak waved him off, his head pounded far too much to worry about soup,

'No, no thanks Magnus.' He looked up, his menacing gaze fixed on his sister and Magnus was nowhere to be seen. Soredamor made her excuses and got up to leave, she just needed some dark quiet place to hide away and console herself. On passing the window she froze, her jaw dropped to her frock in shock; could it be? Yes, her father's visitors were returning, yes there was Gorran amongst them riding behind his father; they all looked splendid riding in through the open gates, dressed in their dazzling silver armour. Her heart fluttered with a surge of excitement and she called out to her family that the riders had returned in an excited tone, a tone that her father did not share.

'*What?* They should be back in their own world by now?'

Soredamor watched from the open window, hopeful of another glimpse of Gorran, she couldn't help but notice the thirty or so armed men that followed,

'Father?' she said with an air of indecision. A rider steered towards a passing servant, a gardener by the name of Miles; he was kicked to the floor, as he attempted to rise an armoured boot was delivered to his arse from the dismounting soldier, hastening his departure. Myridin rushed out from the room to the villa's main entrance. Its stern wooden doors smashed against their stoppers as he catapulted them open with both his arms raised aloft in mounting anger.

'*What is the meaning of this, Elic Black-tooth? You should be back in the Weithiel by now!*'

Sir Elic dismounted as his men-at-arms continued to file into courtyard before the villa; the courtyard was barely large enough to contain the milling riders.

'I'm not sure I like your tone Myridin the Deceiver. Did you really think I would take 'no' for an answer, let us forget the niceties of my last visit - you are still bound to my service.' Elic spat out his words in a deliberately slow manner to let them better sink in, revealing his blackened canines in the process. Myridin's face reddened at his last comment,

'The king that I served now lies dead, slain by his nephew. My obligation was to him and him alone. My time meddling in the affairs of kings and men is over, I have learnt my lesson. If you want his crown, do as he did and go fight for it.'

Sir Elic laughed,

'Look around you, I have already taken your advice,' he indicated towards the soldiers behind him. 'It would have been more pleasant had you accepted my proposal the other night. You see I have one distinct advantage over the other players in this game – I know that you are still alive. The charade of your staged death may have given you a chance to slip away and start afresh in this strange new land, but it will only be a matter of time before the others also work out that you are still alive and come looking for you and the sword. I just can't risk that …*Take him!*' he commanded his men.

Myridin whispered three words and a loud explosion cracked in the air above their heads, panicking the mounts of the men who had just started to dismount. Horses reared and flailed the air with their hooves and some flung their riders to the floor to be trampled in the crush of their panic. One of the men was dragged off screaming across the courtyard, his foot still entangled in his stirrup and he was dragged out through the open gates. Amid the initial confusion that he had created, Myridin prepared his second, more powerful spell, these people would soon regret the day they had tracked him down and found the Portal of Worlds. A clear voice suddenly rang out behind him halting his actions.

'I would hold your tongue Wizard, if you hope to keep your lady alive.' A group of warriors had entered the villa from the rear and one large soldier now held a long dagger to Niviane's throat.

'It would be a crime to slit such a pretty throat,' said the man giving him a toothless smile. Myridin felt his advantage slipping through his fingers like sand; he had no choice and immediately ceased his spell and held high his hands in a sign of submission. A thin and pasty looking soldier appeared from behind the larger man that held Niviane, he was holding baby Ambrose awkwardly in his arms. Myridin's heart sunk further in his chest he was a resourceful man but he would need to get his family out of this fix, for the lives of his family he would do anything.

'What do you want me to do with this thing?' the pasty man asked his triumphant commander, he looked as if he had never handled a child before in his life.

'You must treat it well and look after it, as if it were your own – for it will help make master Myridin here calm and compliant, won't it old friend?' Myridin answered his words with only a glare. The soldier looked somewhat disappointed with his new assignment as the smile dropped from his face; Sir Elic continued,

'...Because if he does not comply, you will have my blessing to dash the poor child's head against the nearest rock.' The soldier's smile returned and Myridin gave a shudder at Elic's words as he could see the terror etched in Niviane's eyes as he spoke.

'Do I have your total undivided attention to my orders and tasks now Wizard, or do I need to give your wife and daughter to the men to assure you of the lengths I will go to?' Myridin felt the surrounding men's minds begin to race with Elic's suggestion and disgusted he drew his attention back to the man who had recently been his guest. Why had he been so polite as to not delve into his guest's minds days before, perhaps with the usual meddling he was renowned for he could have foreseen their intentions and avoided this whole situation? He replied to Elic with little emotion and with a quiet and defeated voice,

'I am your man now Elic. Leave my family be,'

'Good, then let's keep things as civil and businesslike as we can from now on, serve me well and I will see no reason to harm anyone.' Elic looked down his long nose at the magician; he was suddenly filled with distrust as a small commotion occurred outside. Myridin's daughter and elder son were shoved into the courtyard by several soldiers; Hadrak bore an obvious mark around his eye where he had been cuffed.

'The little bugger thought he could get away,' commented the lead soldier as he realised that everyone was staring at him,

'Now get down on your knees you little shite or you'll get another.' He raised his arm as if to strike Hadrak and the youth quickly obeyed, kneeling on the floor shying away from the raised hand.

'Good, this one learns fast …lets hope the father does too,' commented Sir Elic with a faint smile. The remaining staff of the villa were soon rounded up into the yard and were quickly herded up at sword point and Sir Elic made a short statement to the small crowd.

'Listen up, I'm in command of this place now; you will take orders only from me. Disobey me and I will see that you meet with a slow death. If Myridin plays his part I will soon be gone from your lives, so your fate lies solely in his hands.' Sir Elic swung around to face Myridin. He really hadn't wanted to take this course of action, but with his string of offers being refused he had little other choice. He was responsible for the defence of his own kingdom and thousands of other lives, an important and trusted position. However like all nobility he was a blood sucker, a leech to power and he had a large appetite. 'Now then old friend,' Elic used the word 'friend' to give the illusion that they could work together with a hint of respect. 'I know that your powers are without equal and you have the rare cunning and wit to match.' He had watched Myridin when he had accompanied his father, the Baron, at the battle of Celyddon, Elic had been no more than a boy then, but he had watched the magician as he had used his magic to weave a spell to mislead the enemy, guiding them through a thick cloud of fog and into a deep marsh bog beyond. The survivors met only with the High King's swords. They had waited concealed in the dense forest that bordered the bog, ready to carry out their grim work as the enemy pulled themselves out of the freezing waters. He could have sworn that Myridin hadn't aged a day from that distant memory.

'I will be separating your family Myridin and placing them under house arrest until my orders for you are complete – each will be going to a hidden location, just in case you decide to get any plans for escape or disobedience. Should you attempt to rescue them or consider not following my orders to the letter; then I can assure you that you will not be able to reach all of them at once. The way I will have them spread out widely apart, at least one of them will die.' Sir Elic smiled coldly at Myridin and raised his hand giving the signal for the men to depart. Four groups of men led their horses forward, three further mounts were led forward by Gorran; they were saddled and ready to go. The men rode off in groups of five, with Gorran selecting his own group to lead away. He stopped before the men that held Soredamor and gave a quick wink at her before selecting her group. Gorran proceeded to man handle her onto the waiting horse. Only she noticed his hand linger on her foot as he eased it gently into a stirrup, it was the smallest of signs, yet it had the desired effect of easing her nerves. She knew it would be too dangerous to exchange any words of affection between them. The thin soldier with Ambrose had looked less than enamoured as he attempted to work out how exactly he was supposed to sling Ambrose about himself and ride? The riders rode out through the gate and went their separate ways as Myridin's gaze remained fixed and emotionless, although his grip did tighten to a clenched fist as he grasped the open door, more for his own support than through anger. His new world was tumbling away from him and his dreams of a fresh start and a new life had just come to an abrupt end. Inside the mounting turmoil of his mind, he cursed himself for not sealing the Portal of Worlds once and for all. At the time he had chosen to hide it instead of close it, deception had been the easiest route; but then when fleeing from a land where the power of magic was dying he had little choice, his resources were low.

Sir Elic waited for the clamour of the departing riders to die down before speaking again. He turned as if nothing had happened between them and patted Myridin's shoulder.

'Come on, let's talk over some wine.' The ten remaining soldiers split into two groups, some followed Elic into the building whilst the others began to direct the house staff.

Soon they were seated in a reception room, Myridin listened intently to Elic's words and some wine was brought by one of the soldiers, but it did little to help stomach Elic's ambitious demands. Days before he had originally requested that Myridin accompany him back to the old world and aid him in his attempt for the throne, the High King was dead and the numerous barons now circled his throne like crows. Myridin had seen a similar occurrence years before when the High King's eldest son had challenged him for the throne. He had been slain by the King himself in personal combat and his younger son had fled the land, thinking that he might meet with a similar fate, but Myridin had known the reality - he just didn't have the stomach to rule. Now with no bloodline for the transferral of power it was a dog eat dog world where only the strongest would conquer. Sir Elic held a sizable command of both men and land, he was a baron of high standing, but like the others – he was without a legitimate claim to the throne. People would only fight for his cause with the correct amount of coin. If the Baron was to return with the High King's mystical advisor and perhaps the last real magician in the land, then it would provide him both a powerful ally in battle and would also represent a direct association to the former King. For Myridin, when he had left there had been no going back, he knew it would not end there. He had already feigned his own death to get away from his old life, allegedly at the hand of Niviane of all people; the world had been so gullible then; he could have feed them anything and they would believe it. Men's minds were simple – he could plant a seed and they would believe every ounce of gossip he spread. His sudden reappearance could cause far too many questions, or perhaps he may even be hunted down as an abomination – the undead returned; who knew what their simple minds would conjure up? He had left for many reasons and would return for only one – the lives of his family. If only he had the strength to close the Portal of Worlds on his last passing, but then after all this time he had hoped that the gateway would have simply burnt itself out. It had been a severe case of out of sight, out of mind, and based upon the fact that it still remained open it proved the magical elements of this world to be massively abundant. With no magicians to consume its powers, this new world held thousands of years' worth of raw magical power ready for the taking. Some would call his kind parasites or leeches to the world's powers, but others would call him a god. For now, he would have to settle as a slave to Sir Elic's will.

Lord Elic smashed his fist on the table, making the deep red wine spill from the goblets and soak into the delicate carvings of the wooden surface. The action drew

Myridin's attention quickly from his thoughts.

'The sword, god-damn it ...I need it Myridin, the sword will make me king. I understand you have it ...or at least know where it is?' *I want it ...I need it ...don't deny it.'* Myridin flinched at Elic's raving words. How had he known that the King's sword had also made the journey into this world? The dying king had ordered it put beyond use. Niviane had played her part well in their deception and been seen by the army casting the sword deep into the lake. She had successfully made the switch with a standard great sword of an identical design after holding up the original blade before the men and then wading out into the shallows of the lake, deliberately tripping and falling into the icy cold water to the exact spot where she had earlier placed the duplicate sword. The switch was easily made and after several steps further in the water up to her waste, she dragged up the switched sword and flung the heavy blade into the reputed bottomless depths of the lake. The deception was carried out without the use of any magic; they had needed to improvise, for magic was all but dead in the old world. With the deed competed, the king's wishes would appear to be satisfied. Later that night she returned to the lake and retrieved the sword under the cover of darkness. The secret of its passing from the old world to the new was still thought to be unknown to all.

Myridin looked into Elic's mind; it was filled with a desire for the sword and the power it would give him. He knew of its existence but to trace his thoughts would take concentration and time, both things that he lacked. He quickly recoiled from the seething mass of greed that leaked out of Elic's thoughts and threatened to overcome him.

'How did you find out about the sword Elic?' he asked, knowing well that sometimes there were quicker routes than magic. He added,

'Such things should be beyond your knowledge.'

Myridin glanced behind the high-backed chair in which he sat; two swordsmen stood ready, but in a relaxed position resting their weight on their drawn blades. He sipped at his wine gauging the reaction of his captor who gloated at him as he spoke.

'You don't need to be a magician to find out these things, you just need people in the right places. You see Myridin, I have discovered things that for all your might and magic you have missed – the truth is, people are the real magic of the world, not your hocus-pocus arts.' Elic finished his wine and threw the goblet to one side. 'Now the location of the sword, first, if you please, or you will force me to set my men to work on you, and let's not forget, your family.' Myridin heard an excited shuffle of feet behind him as his guards prepared to dish out a beating. Myridin's finger traced the outline of his wine goblet as he sat in thought of his family. He knew that every problem has a solution; he just needed to think of it and quick.

'Before I reveal its location, tell me, what have you done with my house staff, are they unharmed?'

Elic rolled his eyes wondering why this magician would care about his underlings when his family were being whisked off to some unknown fate.

'They are locked in the stables, they will be held there to cool off for a while. *Now, the sword if you please, Wizard!*'

'Good,' Myridin replied dipping his finger into the wine.

'Your world has nothing but people like you left in it, its magic is gone. You have obviously forgotten the power of magic or you would not have come here. My dwindling powers back in your realm are but a distant memory. Here, I am more powerful than you could have ever imagined – you should have gone home when you had the chance.'

Myridin flicked the wine from his finger and with a

single word uttered from his lips it accelerated faster than a shooting arrow into the Lord's eye. Elic recoiled in agony as Myridin shoved his chair backwards into the two men behind, unbalancing them as they had stood to close, although one still managed to extend his arm in a sideways swipe at the magician as he leapt from the discarded chair. Myridin evaded the wild blow; he had gained himself the vital three seconds that he needed to utter the spell of protection. After regaining their footing, the men advanced, striking low at Myridin's legs – their Lord had given them strict instructions that this man was not to be killed and a cripple could still talk. The soldiers' eyes widened in fear as their swords hit an invisible barrier that surrounded the magician. They rained down blow after blow against the unseen barrier as their frustration grew. Lord Elic eventually recovered from the agony of his blinded eye and through the blurred vision of his one good one he noticed that the magician was mumbling away in some unknown language.

'No …Stop him,' he roared at his frustrated men.

'What the heck do you think we are trying to do,' snapped one of the men.

'…My Lord,' the man hastily add, suddenly remembering his place. Myridin's mumbling stopped and directing his comments past the men towards Sir Elic he spoke without any trace of emotion as he calmly stated.

'I have seen your future. *You will run.*' Myridin's body shivered and contorted wracked with pain and a glowing light filled the room. The swordsmen stopped their hacking and slashing and backed away from the outline of a growing form behind the translucent shield and eye-averting light, one tripping on the discarded chair as he backed away to the door. Long talons extended from what was once Myridin's finger tips and a mane of rough fir sprouted from around his neck partially concealing his now demonic face and lolling jaws. The invisible barrier was dispelled and the beast leapt forwards raking its claws through the back of the fleeing soldier, his leather and ring mail armour split leaving four bloody lines across his back, as he desperately made it to the door he dashed through and disappeared. The nine-foot beast rose before the doorway blocking any further escape. Elic fumbled for his sword and the other soldier who had fallen raised himself on very weak legs. The monster jumped forward and enveloped the man in fur and claws, its mighty jaws circled the man's head and crunched down loudly. The man instantly went limp and the beast lifted its bloody snout from the corpse and howled at Sir Elic. The advancing creature blotted out the light as it towered over the lord. A loud scream rang through the rooms of the villa.

Chapter 2 - Judgment

Two riders left the villa against the backdrop of the setting sun, the constellation known as 'The Eyes,' to the locals was clear in the sky; it consisted of two brightly shining stars spaced closely together. It was said that the eyes could only be seen on a clear night and was a bad omen; but few of the locals believed the old wives' tales. Tonight they looked down from the night's sky almost disapproving of the riders as they left the villa in panic. The riders whipped their mounts and stayed low in the saddle, riding at such speed during the night was dangerous to both rider and mount, but what was still behind them was far worse. They split directions on leaving the gate; one soldier's blood-soaked back stung him with every step of his galloping horse; he winced with pain as the ripped links of his armour flailed at his exposed flesh. The other rider had only the salty taste of fear in his mouth from the vision of the creature that they had left behind them. He was intent on doing his duty and warning the others; he was heading for the town of Kell. Amsden, the first and bleeding rider knew that he would soon need to find a place to stop and tend to his wounds as best he could, or else he may fall from his saddle through blood loss. Even as he weakened he dared not to stop for some time with the image of the beast of fur and fang in close pursuit. It was enough to suffer the pain that drove him on. With all things considered and his life in peril, Amsden decided to abandon his lord's orders to alert the four groups of men – unlike the other man, he had seen Elic slain and he cared not for his son, Gorran. Amsden cared only for his own life in this moment and if he was being pursued his best chance of survival would be to head for the great forests that they had passed on their journey to the villa. This land was unfamiliar to him and there were few paths to guide his way, he would just have to wind his way through the bright yellow and red bushes that vibrantly dotted the way ahead. Still if they slowed him down they would also slow any would-be pursuers. He just wanted to get as far away as possible from this bad episode. His horse had now slowed its pace, panting heavily from its mad sprint away from the villa, its eyes had been as wide as his own when it had smelt the beast. He needed to let it recover; it was his lifeline, although the gait of its methodical trot only served to bring further pain to his back.

Carter the second rider had a different agenda to his peer, he had been lucky enough to be stood watching the horses when the beast emerged from the villa. Foolishly he had at first dismissed the crazed ranting from Amsden as he had run from the door for his horse. Three of his fellow men-at-arms had engaged the beast. They had been brave men, but he had not stayed long enough to look back at the screams that followed his departure. With just his initial fearful glance at that thing he could guess the result of their battle. Where had that thing come from? It was not that he was a coward in riding off so fast; he was just following orders as the others should have done. The four men were told to wait ready at their horses to deliver their news to the hostage holders. Carter prided himself in his ability in following orders. Only two of the four messengers made it out of the villa alive.

The beast circled the villa grounds, its long wolf-like snout sniffing the many new scents that scattered the ground. It scampered up to the stable door that now had a long wooden beam locking the two large doors; it could smell human flesh inside. The horses inside grew skittish as they sensed the shadow at the door, as did the villa staff; Magnus had found a pitchfork that had been missed by the soldiers in their hurried imprisonment in the barn. He raised the fork protective of the handful of people huddled behind him as the whining of the horses caused them to further retreat from the doors. A large clawed fist smashed down snapping the locking plank cleanly in two and making everyone inside jump with fright as the doors slowly creaked open. The beast raised itself onto its hind legs further extending its height and field of view into the shadows of the barn and then it turned, looking out into the surrounding fields, crouching back down onto all fours and with a forceful snort it sprinted off through the gate. Myridin had managed to master the animal instinct of the beast to kill and kill again; although he still felt its barely controllable rage burning within him as he departed the villa. Myridin had learnt the spell of the Vargulf in the old world, from a foreigner, when there were still a handful of others who held the power of magic in the land. The man had traded the knowledge of the deranged spell in exchange for a cure to the spell's curse; for it was more a curse than spell, but then that's what can happen when the caster is not ready for the power of the spell. Many a new spell had actually come about through an accident or inability to control the magic, but only if the caster lived long enough to recall the spell. Fortunately he knew exactly how to control the spell of Vargulf, but until now he had never dared to use it on himself, or anyone else for that matter. The magic was complex and the hunger of the beast became near unstoppable once it had tasted flesh; but the spell could be dispelled with magic or accepted by another without the use of magic. This was a more dangerous element for it could spread without the control of magicians if the person would willingly give their soul to the beast. Even worse the magic could sit dormant for years before being triggered by a violent event. He really had not wanted to use such volatile magic, but it was the only thing he could think of that would fit his desperate needs to hunt men.

The first hundred yards of following their scent had been easy to follow, two riders – horse and man, both held the stench of fear about them, but the beast now circled in indecision at the point where the two riders had separated. One rode east, the other south, which was it to follow? The beast smelt blood, the rider to the east was wounded, he would be the quicker to take down, and then he could hunt down the other. The beast broke into a run on all fours to the east.

Amsden had stopped briefly, shortly after daybreak on a small hillock, which had a good view of the ground he had just covered as well as the surrounding area. He had tethered his horse to a bush as he checked on the large blood-soaked cloth pad that he had stuffed into the rips in his armour. He had patched up his wounds as best he could manage when he had stopped for a few moments during the night. The cloth was now held securely by the dried blood of his wounds and he winced as he gave it a quick tug of adjustment. He had only allowed himself a ten-minute break through the cold night to tend to the immediate need of his wounds. He had been spooked by the slightest of noises that the night carried and had quickly set off again. Now that the sun had warmed the morning air he thought it wise to make use of this vantage point. Amsden half-emptied his water sack, hurriedly gulping it down as he surveyed the land. He had somehow known that this venture into the unknown land was going to end in blood, but what could he do – he was only following orders. A thought suddenly occurred to him. If he could make it back to the Portal of Worlds, Elic's army was camped on the other side, there would be safety in those large numbers, but without his Lord or son he would run the risk of being hanged as a deserter. No, he would stick with his first thought; his mother had always said that,

'Your first thought is always your best, son.' Perhaps she was right, his first thought as a young man had been to be a miller – there was good money in flour, but instead with the pressure of the invaders to the east, he had done as most other young men had in the region and given themselves to the service of the crown.

'Bloody fool. You should have followed your mother's advice,' he said to himself as he observed the ground. To the north he could clearly see a great field of large jagged crystals jutting from the ground and, even at this distance their structures stood out like great giants exposed and defiant. Riding to the north was out of the question. Traversing the hulking crystals would slow him down far too much and this was where he would be expected to go. He knew this, for he had already ridden through the visual spectacle of the crystal fields when he had pasted through the Portal of Worlds. The predictable route home would get him killed for sure. To the east, the land flattened which would make easier going and the dark green tips of the tall pines could just be made out on the horizon. A distant wolf-like howl instantly drew his attention back to the ground that he had just covered, his eyes seeking for signs of movement. He couldn't make out anything. Unnerved by the howl he quickly remounted and spurred onwards towards the distant trees.

The beast stayed low, it could cover the ground better on all fours. The mid-day sun warmed its shaggy flank increasing the perspiration of its efforts to close the gap on its prey. It knew it had been closing in on its prey all morning and scrabbled up the high ground weaving through the coloured bushes to reach the summit where it came to an abrupt halt. This place was strong with the man's scent and a blood-soaked rag attracted the beast. It stood once more on its hind legs surveying the land as Amsden had done hours before, yet its eyesight far surpassed that of any man. It spotted the movement of the rider far to the east; he was close to reaching the tree-line. The beast growled in a low tone to itself, yet instead of stopping, the growling changed pitch several times and the creature circled where it had stood. Eventually the beast lay down and its growl grew into a monstrous howl as a magical light enveloped it and it changed shape back into the form of a man. Myridin gave out a great gasp of air, the brutal rage of the beast began to fade from his mind as he stretched his arms and brushed down his robes before focusing on the distant point of the rider, which his human eyes could now hardly make out, but as the beast, he had seen its location as clear as day. He rubbed his face, clearing the savage thoughts from his mind, repeating his name to give himself clarity of who he really was. Satisfied that he was himself again he then prepared a spell of transportation and focusing on the distant point, he uttered the required words. In the blink of an eye the air was heavy with the buzz of magic and he appeared on the tree-line several leagues forwards of his original position; the great distance travelled in a fleeting second. He turned to face the approaching rider, with his back now facing the shadows cast by the giant pine trees behind. At first the exhausted rider did not react, a second ago the ground ahead had been clear – now Myridin stood in his path. With the sudden realisation as his mind absorbed the information that his eyes supplied, the vision of being confronted by the wizard made him immediately rein his horse to a halt, almost falling from his saddle in his effort to stop. Amsden made no move for his sword; he knew its use would be futile after attempting to cut through the magician's magical shield back in the villa. He realised his end was near and he dismounted, better to die on your feet like a man, he thought. In a way he was pleased to be met with the magician's human form rather than the beast; his death should be less savage. Myridin was yet to speak his first words; he just stood there, stark and tall blocking the man's path.

'I …I wasn't going to warn them and I ain't gonna.' Amsden stuttered unable to take the silence between them. 'You still have time to catch them, I'll tell you where they are.' He played the only card he had and prayed it would be enough.

'Go on,' suggested the wizard with a cold and emotionless gaze.

'Your baby son goes to our camp at the Portal of Worlds, but waits on this side of it. Your eldest son and daughter have been taken to two separate camps in Kell and your wife to Ember Creek. Oh yes and if you wish to see your wife alive again I would suggest you go for her first – that's where Carter was heading. Once they get news of the Baron, they'll be gutted for sure.'

Myridin stroked his beard, there was blood matted in it from where he had been the beast.

'And I suppose that I am to reward this information with your life?' he replied.

'I would not protest if you did, I am but a soldier dragged into other men's ambitions and really, I bear you no harm. I would make promise to any means?' Amsden replied. Myridin started to chant some words of magic and the soldier waited with his gaze tilted towards the ground for his end.

The magician finally stopped his chanting and spoke again,

'It appears that you are telling me the truth Amsden …shame, I was just getting the taste for blood again,' he lied; he had needed to retake human form before the beast consumed him. He slowly walked around Amsden as he continued to address him,

'They used to call me mad in your world and now I'm going to prove them right. I will be merciful for a change, you are what you say which is rare, so I will release you if you swear by all the old gods to receive the gift that I give. You will take the beast or else be consumed by the beast. *Do you swear it?'* Myridin questioned.

'I do,' replied Amsden who would have agreed to any thing in that moment.

'Good, now go on home, off you go now - back to your own world with you,' Amsden stood frozen to the ground for a moment, half expecting a lightning bolt to strike him down. But none came. He took his first tentative steps back towards the crystal fields and froze when Myridin voice boomed out sending the nearby birds of the forest flying.

'Amsden Quatermain ...I would suggest that you treat the people of this world with more respect. You have been marked by the curse of the beast. Should you ever draw blood from just one single person – the beast will return. Now go and live the remainder of your life in peace, if you are careful the beast will see to it that you have a very long and careful life.' Myridin turned and placed a small chunk of crystal on the ground and stepped back invoking the magic needed to create a transportation portal, the type of magic better used for longer journeys. Amsden was shocked at his full name being used and quickly led his horse back onto the grassy plain before his luck changed. A swirling vortex of power erupted from the crystal opening up a portal to another place, Myridin stepped through and disappeared.

Myridin was not usually the forgiving type and for every action he calculated a reaction, the release of the soldier and the curse of the beast had addressed two areas of his calculations. Firstly when he had inspected Amsden's thoughts, he had planted a suggestion deep into the man's mind, the man did not know it was there but when he would arrive back at the Portal and the group of soldiers that held Ambrose, the suggestion would play out. He would give a wonderful account of how the Wizard was assisting Lord Elic and that all was well, putting the men to ease and buying him the time that he needed. Secondly he sent the curse of the beast back to the old world as a parting gift, but the curse would depend on the man. By having the man accept the curse he had also saved himself the enormous drain on his powers of removing the curse. He would need his strength in the days to come. Now that he was prepared for them he would not invoke the spell of Vargulf again. He could deal with them in other ways.

Ember Creek was peaceful apart from the song of a bluebird calling out for a mate. The soldiers had just settled in after their first night in their riverside tents, which lined the creek that flowed down from a large lake above. The lake several hundred yards higher had formed in the crater of a long dead volcano that dominated the lands. The creek had formed over time from the constant spillage of the crater; eventually it had eroded its banks and enticed a plethora of greenery to smother the long inactive black volcanic rock. They had ridden to the point of exhaustion to get here and had set up their tents in the black of night. Why Elic had chosen this location nobody knew, the reason had died with the man; but he had personally decided on each of the four locations selected for Myridin's family to be held.

'We'll have to loosen her bonds soon Terrel – what if she needs to pee, she hasn't gone since we got here.' Terrel gave a wide smile at the bound and gagged woman as Yedd spoke. He was a thickset man with a face as grubby as his hands.

'Not everyone needs to piss as much as you do Yedd, I tell ya boy there's something wrong with you.' Terrel never took his eyes off the woman as he spoke. Yedd went over and checked Niviane's bonds, her hostile eyes glared at him as he did so.

'Don't you worry about that son; she won't need her

hands free if she needs to go. I'm sure I'll be able to fumble my way through the folds of that dress to bring some air to her arse.'

Yedd, the younger man of the two gave a short approving laugh and he continued to mock the older man,

'I'm sure it is a very fine arse at that, but I fear that should it meet with your ugly old face glaring down at its nakedness, she may instead shit herself with fright.' He followed his comment by blowing a raspberry at Terrel.

Terrel shoved Yedd out of the way and leaned over to prod Niviane and she struggled against her bindings, her mouth was gagged and she made a muffled sound as she attempted to respond to his annoying prods,

'I'm willing to find out,' he leered at her and ran his hand over her soft skin, running his fingers a few inches up her dress.

'Are you willing to lose your head? Lord Elic said she was not to be touched.'

Terrel withdrew his hand. Niviane continued to make muffled noises struggling to form words with the gag so tight.

'What's that missy, are you trying to tell me something? Have you really got to take a leak?' Terrel lifted her gag a little.

'Anall brock tol de hellic,' she said immediately.

'What? What kind of weird speech is that?' He quickly replaced her gag.

Behind Terrel, Yedd's eyes glazed over, he drew his belt knife and cupped Terrel's mouth with his left hand pulling the man backwards and off balance, the point of his dagger plunged into his comrade's throat again and again. Terrel soon went limp in Yedd's hands, ceasing his brief struggle. Those few magical words were all that she had needed to take control of his feeble mind; Myridin was not the only person with an understanding of magic in their household, yet it pained her to use her powers in such a way. She was actually surprised at the potency of her magic, for it had been the first time that she had used magic in anger in this new land and felt its power was heavily magnified in comparison to the old world. Yedd cut her bonds and removed her gag, then slowly ambled over to the entrance to the tent, as if standing guard. Niviane hopped from foot to foot as she was cut free,

'Heavens, I didn't think I could hold it in for much longer,' she said to the corpse at her feet and squatted down by the side of the tent to relieve her full bladder.

'Ah, that's better,' pulling up the folds of her dress she kicked the corpse, 'You see – you waited all that time for a glimpse of my bum and then you go and get yourself killed before you get your chance to see it. Ah, life is a bitch and now your comrades are about to find out just what a bitch I can be.' She cast a short spell of vision and her head swum with the images outside the tent. One man slept in the second tent and the other two were out walking the perimeter chatting casually.

'Where have my children been taken?' she asked Yedd who was firmly under the power of her control.

'Kell and the Portal of Worlds, mistress,' he replied dully.

'Thank you, now if you would be so kind as to go outside and kill the others for me, starting with the one sleeping in the tent.' She asked him politely as was in her nature but the fury of a mother's instinct boiled beneath the surface of her otherwise pleasant demeanour. She did not care about such notions of honour when the lives of her children were at stake, that feeble notion was reserved for the men.

Yedd replaced his knife and drew his long sword as he moved between the tents; the sword rose and then fell with ruthless efficiency splitting the sleeping man's skull. The canvas of the tent was suddenly dashed red. There was no sound other than the snapping of bone at the man's execution; Yedd moved out from the tent and began to follow the creek to where the remaining men walked. As he approached, one of the patrolling men challenged him, why should Yedd have his weapon drawn?

'Yedd, there's blood on your sword, what has happened?' Yedd continued his deliberate walk towards them.

'The woman had better not be harmed? ...*Yedd.*' Yedd suddenly dashed forwards the last few steps and ran the man through his guts, he had known the man for years and yet he watched through his eyes helplessly as his body did things that his mind would regret. Blood gurgled from the man's mouth as Yedd jerked violently in an attempted to withdraw his impaled weapon. The second man could not believe his eyes and fumbled for his sword. Yedd gave up on withdrawing his sword and pulled his belt knife, leaping on the man as he just managed to free his sword. They rolled on the ground in a desperate struggle before Yedd bit the man's sword hand and his own dagger stabbed down several times. They both lay still for a moment before Yedd regained his feet; he was covered in the other man's blood. He stood up and awaited his master's next command, but after regaining his feet a shimmering bolt of energy punched through his chest burning his leather and ring-mail vest into tiny shards. Yedd's body silently tumbled to the ground, coming to rest on the man he had just slain, the blue sky changed to the darkness of the void. High on the volcanic crater stood Myridin, the breeze ruffling his hair and his hands still pointing down towards the man he had just killed. He relaxed and felt the energy flow back into him after casting his last spell. Without lingering he ran down the slope towards the tent, several small black volcanic rocks followed him down as he scrabbled to meet with his wife. Niviane left the tent to meet with her love, her long golden hair flowing with her dress. After a short embrace Myridin looked about the camp with an air of disappointment,

'Oh, I thought I had come here to rescue you but it would appear that you have beat me too it. I didn't know that you still practiced the arts with such proficiency?'

'I don't any more, but I guess if you've just got it then you don't need to practice every day ...as you do?' She gave him a cheeky wink. He withdrew from her and surveyed the scene before admitting defeat,

'Indeed so.'

The galloping of a rider made them both swing around in unison. The man was tucked low in his saddle as he guided his horse towards the tents. The shouts of the rider could be heard long before the man could be seen,

'*Kill her*, by Elic's command, kill her,' yelled the rider as he frantically rode into the camp. The nostrils of his horse flared with exhaustion as his horse fought to catch its breath. The rider stared wide eyed at the two figures standing before him and the blood soaked tent.

Myridin turned to his wife, 'Could you repeat that? I think he wants me to kill you, or perhaps you could just clarify?'

'Oh shit,' gulped the rider.

Chapter 3 – Rescue

Gorran's face nestled into Soredamor's chest. The previous night's wine was still on his breath but she didn't mind, they had shared the bottle and retired early to the bedroom. As long as she was close to him she felt complete and when nestled in close the troubles of her situation were forgotten. Gorran had occupied a farmhouse on the outskirts of Kell, the dwelling was far enough from the town as not to be bothered but near enough to easily re-supply. The owner had been an old widow and she was unable to work the land any further since her old man had passed away. The rental had been paid in silver ingots and the owner would live well enough with her relatives in Kell for some time. A small advance party had secured two locations for their captives; Hadrak had been taken to a hired vessel moored in Kell's harbour. It was a vessel of some size that had been storm-damaged and ripe for hire. Gorran and Soredamor now exclusively occupied the main farm building, whilst his men had been assigned to walk the grounds and take shelter in the surrounding barns and outbuildings. They all knew their little lordship's game and had heard their noises throughout the night, though none would make comment to the young nobleman. He was Elic's first son and when pushed he had a temper to match his father's. They all knew that he was not to be trifled with, not even in jest, for one day he would also become their baron. Three nights had passed and there was still no word from his father. He had expected some form of instruction by now, even if it was only that they needed to sit tight. He already knew deep down that he would not obey any order to slay Myridin's daughter, but hopefully the magician would just comply with his father's demands. These thoughts led him naturally to his next dilemma. If he could no longer follow the commands of his father – where did this leave him?

Back over at Ember Creek some twenty leagues away, Myridin and Niviane had discussed their next move at length; the safety of their children was not a trivial matter. The urge to rush head-long to their rescue had been overwhelming, but Myridin had repeatedly assured his wife that they needed to take a different course of action. The immediate threat at the villa had been eliminated, as had Sir Elic, but an army waited to pass through the Portal of Worlds, and if the gateway was not shut, how many more would be foolish enough to come seeking his power and the sword? This was not just about them; the people of this world could be dragged into a stupid war, and for what - a sword? It was all happening again.

Myridin had made only one attempt to close the Portal, shortly after his arrival, but realistically he had never stood a chance. After the trials he had faced in his old world, he had been far too weak and needed more time to digest the facts and regain his strength. He now knew that it would take much more than just his own skill to close the mighty rift, but if his calculations were correct, there may be a chance to close it. They had as good a chance as any – for he had spent several months working them out long before Sir Elic and his band ever darkened his doorstep. He had arrived at one conclusion. With the combined strength of his family and the magic of the sword they may be able to close the portal once and for all and perhaps finally enjoy the privacy that he had sought all along. He would create such a spell that both worlds would have never witnessed before and hopefully would never again. Myridin had fled the old world as a hunted man, he had used up the last of the old world's power to open the great portal, but his magic had backfired in an unforeseen way, like a forest fire it had caught hold of the fresh and abundant magic at his destination. He had at first lacked the strength to extinguish the Portal and had diverted his attention to the mounting challenges he faced, but as time had passed he had just ignored the problem; there had always been other more immediate problems to solve rather than the one large one; that was until the first visitors had appeared a year ago. The Portal was kept open with the massive self sustaining fields of power contained within the crystal fields. Maybe over several hundred years it would eventually suck every ounce of magic dry from this region and then collapse the portal on its own? Myridin was not prepared to wait that long to find out, besides it would also be a useless waste of a great resource, one that he could use to fashion this world as he had done with less success in the last. In the last world his resources had been lacking and his problems had been confounded by starting too late – mistakes he would not make again. He ran through a checksum of his calculations again as Niviane made the most of the camp's ample supplies, preparing a hot broth and come the night they both sat together on the banks of the creek watching the sun go down. She looked up into his eyes with sorrow,

'You know I trust you, if you are absolutely sure that this is the best course for our future, but is it the safest course for our children? They must remain safe - what use is a future without them?' She rested her head on his shoulder. Myridin held her hand to reassure her, gently caressing her fingers, eventually bringing her hand to his lips and kissing it lightly.

'You know I would do nothing to harm them, they are my life, as are you and I would never put them in danger. My calculations suggest that to maximise the power needed to close the Rift between the worlds, it must be distributed evenly about the Portal. A triangle of power around the Rift will indeed be the best way to surround it and close it, but I have only one magic sword with which to harness the power?' After a moment she patted his knee,

'Stop thinking like a magician and just use your head – just break the sword into three,' she shrugged her shoulders at him, he had seen the face that she pulled many times before, it was the one she used at him when he was being a little dense.

'What possible use could you have of a sword again?' she added to reinforce her logic. He kissed her lightly on the cheek,

'I knew you would be worth saving and become useful to me one day,' she jarred him in the ribs for his comment before he could continue,

'Hmm you are as ever correct, well almost - but not break it, re-forge it, there is a family of skilled blacksmiths in the village, they have made all manner of things for Magnus in the past; we will get the sword in the morning and prepare things before we retrieve the kids, once we strike out we will need to act fast and be in a position to close the Portal. We must prepare the sword first.' He made it all sound like nothing more than a day trip out, but then he had read the mind of the rider before he had died, there was no way the men would risk killing their children without the order from Elic or the discovery that he was dead. For now they would be quiet safe. Two messengers were set to rotate through the three camps and back to the villa to carry instructions, but as they were so spread out it could be more than a week before their return. If any of Elic's men dared approach the villa they would not make it out alive. Over the years Myridin had coached Magnus in a little of his art, he was not his best student, Soredamor had taken that honour, but when prepared he knew enough to be dangerous. Myridin wondered at how long the army would wait before passing the Portal to find their Lord? This was an unknown factor, but his planted suggestion in the fleeing man should buy him more time and if it came to it Myridin could always attempt to mimic the image of Sir Elic as a deception, it wouldn't be the first time he had done such a thing. The only problem with this was that he had not yet worked out how to reproduce his voice, with the illusion of magic he could only make the image of the man and Sir Elic had a very deep and distinctive voice. Myridin wished for a moment that he had not been in such a hurry to slay the Lord; the fit of madness had taken him like a storm, he knew that he needed to keep a handle on that repeating trait in himself, it had landed him in trouble in the past. In hindsight it would have been better to just break his will and control the man. Oh well, what is done is done.

After a brief and restless sleep the two had risen early and decided to get a head start on the day and travelled by Portal back to the village of Milton, several leagues from their villa. It was a small settlement, as most places were in this region and the blacksmith's had been easy enough to find. They were a trio of brothers and Myridin had met them only once in the past. He normally left the daily tasks to Magnus, but with his own reputation far larger than life, most people would often remember him and indeed fall over themselves to gain his favour. The three brothers, Thulnir, Taric and Sum did not share that same joy when disturbed with the morning larks. Myridin's shouted greetings and repeated knocking on their bolted door was met with the brother's furious reply,

'What the hell time do you call this, were shut, now piss off,' shouted Thulnir, a great ox of a man from behind the bolted door. He had been the first to awake from a drunken slumber with the racket. Each of the three brothers had arms the size of tree trunks and they were not used to any annoyances so early in the morning, especially after the amount of mead they had consumed the night before.

'It is I, Myridin from out of town, let me in. I have

desperate need of your skills gentlemen,' he raised his voice loud enough to be heard.

'Did you not hear me? Piss off, we're shut, come back when my head stops pounding and I can be bothered to open.' Thulnir turned and headed back from his half-risen position back to the comfort of the rug, where he had slept all night.

The splinters of the imploding door showered the room as the thick wooden door flew off its hinges and barely missed the thickset man on the rug. The electric presence of magic in the air sobered the man up as if his face had been dunked in a bucket of icy cold water.

'What the…' Taric and Sum knocked over a string of empty bottles as they quickly scrambled from their slumped overnight position sitting at a large oak table to stand with their brother, Sum quickly grabbed a nearby smith's hammer to hand.

'Easy men, do not hasten to a foolish action, I am here to make you rich men.' Myridin quickly threw a large bag of coins into the room, which landed in front of the three groggy-eyed men to reassure them of his words. Several of the coins spilled to the floor from its open drawstring. Taric knelt down and inspected the bag.

'Bloody hell, you've got my attention, there's enough coin in there to make us all rich, well at least me …which leads me on to asking what exactly have we got to do to earn it?'

'Only what you do best,' Myridin replied and Niviane came around to her husband's side dropping a small crystal to the floor.

'Step back,' she commanded as the magic of the Portal began to grow. 'If you want to become rich for a day's work …then follow me,' she stepped into the crackling oval Portal and disappeared. Myridin cleared his throat,

'Gentlemen, if you would be so kind as to gather

your tools and follow me.'

Taric looked back at the destruction in their dwelling and muttered under his breath, 'I hope your also paying to replace our bloody door.'

Myridin led his group of followers up to the top of the small hill that overlooked the villa. Magnus was already there with three other men from Myridin's household, a lively wind swept through them and their hair blew into their eyes as they worked. Each man had a spade in hand and had been digging for over an hour. The steel of the spade's head hit something solid, something that had been buried years before on their arrival in this land and all four men focused on digging out the object. Sum, the blacksmith, perched himself on a fallen log and took a long swig from the wineskin that he carried. Over the years it had become his favourite travelling companion and it provided fantastic company.

'I must admit, there's nothing like watching men work to give you a thirst,' he commented to Niviane before remembering his manners and offering her a drink. She refused and moved off to take a closer look at the men's work. Magnus and the others had struck iron and after stripping a soft leather cover from the object, they found themselves struggling to lift a great anvil which they had uncovered from the ground. The large lump of iron had been buried there for years and as the soil was brushed off it revealed a great-sword protruding through its centre. It looked as if the sword had been thrust directly into the iron so it stood impaled vertically. An unnatural blue and sliver reflection came from its sharp steel clearly marking this as no normal blade.

'Hey, we need some help here, this thing is bloody heavy,' Magnus cried out and the three blacksmiths reluctantly came to their aid still arguing about a disagreement from the night before.

'It was her mother.'

'No, it was her sister I tell you.' Their bickering was cut short on seeing the blade.

'I've never seen anything like it before,' commented Sum,

'It is the crown of swords,' stated Thulnir, Taric just gawped.

'Indeed it is,' Myridin replied. 'And this sword is the reason for your attendance here; you will have a chance to add your names to history today.'

Taric laughed out loud,

'We are good at what we do, but I don't think we will be able to copy a blade like that, if that's what you are after?' confessed Thulnir.

'No, no – I don't require a copy. I expect you to melt it down and make three smaller swords from its steel for my family. I don't require a masterpiece, just three swords; make them large, small – however you like or as far as the metal will stretch. Can you do this for me?' The three smiths nodded in unison, 'But it would be a sacrilege to destroy such a masterpiece,' suggested Thulnir.

'And we will need a fire hotter than will burn in this wind, that is no normal sword – it may not even melt in fire?' added Sum.

'Oh it will melt, my magic will see to that, I shall create a fire for you that will burn brighter than the sun and I will weave further ancient and powerful magic into the steel, magic from the old world and when we are done you will be three of the richest men in the kingdom.' The three men hovered in indecision, their minds were in turmoil – some in thinking it a sacrilege to destroy such an object of beauty, the sword was one of a kind; others thinking how they should best go about their task, but none of them were in any doubt at wanting to be rich.

'I think you will be hard-pushed to make three out of that,' Sum said scratching his chin. 'Don't be an oaf Sum, that's a solid steel great-sword, its not like the long-blades that we have made in the past, the metal extends from point to hilt – it's one solid piece. We can make three long-swords out of that thing, just hammer them out a little thinner, you see how thick that blade is.' Taric suggested, still shaking his head at the size of the weapon, 'Anyway, who the hell had the strength to wield such a thing in battle?'

'Oh there was one,' Myridin recalled, 'He became the king of our people.'

Sum shrugged, 'I'm not bloody surprised, if he could swing that thing - I for one would not want stand in his way.'

Myridin got back to business; he needed the men to come to a decision,

'What of it men? I need these swords made today.'

'You are both wrong …probably still pissed from last night, they will need to be made into three different designs,' suggested Thulnir.   Sum scoffed at his suggestion,

'What the hell do you know you dumb hammer oaf? You couldn't even shoe Eta's horse without my direction last week.'

'I'll shoe you if you don't shut up; you all know that I'm the best blacksmith here.' Thulnir punched Sum in the back.

'Hey, I think you're forgetting that I normally deal with swords.' Taric protested. The three men broke into a full blown argument, as was their way.

'*Gentlemen*,' Myridin's voice boomed out regaining their attention,

'I'm not paying you to bicker, you shall have from me whatever you need and I think you will find the sword lighter in the hand then you would expect,' Myridin looked down at the sword jutting out from the anvil,

'Oh, sorry about the anvil – but I had to make the

sword difficult to just run off with and it will take my hand to free it,' he reached down and tugged the great-sword free, handing it over first to Thulnir.

'Now, to work, time is of the essence.'

Thulnir marvelled at the lightness of the steel, he had never seen it's like before, he decided to take the initiative.

'Ok people, its time to follow my lead I'm in a hurry to get rich. Let's get to work.'

Soredamor had not found her captivity as difficult to tolerate as her brother, in fact she had been making the most of her time together with Gorran. The week had past as quickly as a breeze but the memories of their repeated exploration of each other would last until her dying breath. Gorran had become growingly frustrated throughout the week. His mood was confounded by his mixed emotions and the mounting pressure of explaining himself to his father. He had sent away one man to check with the group that held Hadrak hostage, he had returned stating that all was well, but still there was no news of his father. His worries had been further increased with his growing love for the girl, he had toiled in thought most nights as she slept in his arms. Their shared warmth was special to him and he wondered at what he would do in the worst case, if Myridin did not comply with his father's will. His father was strong-willed and far from being easy to get along with, something he had found out for himself as they had locked horns over the years. Even worse, he dreaded to utter the words to his father that he loved her; he already knew what his father thought of that. '*Love?* Love is for poets, boy – *Duty*, now that's what makes you a man,' he would repeat at such times. Whichever way he turned he was hemmed in and the constant battle between his head and his heart consumed his thoughts each night, yet like Myridin himself he realised that every problem has a solution if you can think hard or long enough. Eventually the solution came to him. She had to escape. If the order came to kill Soredamor, she would not be here to slay. He would take a beating for his failure but at least she would be alive. If he could convince her that she should return to his world then he may even be able to utilise the powers that she bragged of to help their cause against the invaders and be reunited with her once again. He told her of his plan and although she did not favour the thought of leaving him, she was swayed in agreement. Gorran thought it strange at the time, that she made no plea for either of her brothers' safety, but then he guessed it would show his hand in the matter if several of the hostages were released. The last problem to be ironed out in his mind was that the men with him were loyal to his father, only Sebian who was from his household bodyguard could he truly trust, the rest here were soldiers of the barracks – they would follow their liege's orders to the letter. He would have to try and keep the whole thing secret, but he would wait until Sebian was on shift. Should he be spotted aiding her escape it would be easier to smooth things out with Sebian. Hopefully it would not come to that, but tonight he would find out. His father's messenger was now overdue and the chance of his 'Kill' order being received was growing more and more likely, so it must be tonight. He had been unusually generous with the men's meal that night, breaking out several dusty bottles of wine he had found in the cellar. The local vintage was both fruity and potent. Later, Gorran led Soredamor out into the night. Shortly after the evening meal as the men relaxed, with full bellies of bread and stew washed down with the rich wine the bulk of the men became like a group of old men after the meal and retired for a little snooze. Tonight only two men walked the grounds during their shift and Sebian was one of them. Gorran had waited until he passed before slipping out; he led Soredamor down the track and directed her path of travel towards the town. He handed over several silver ingots with his parting embrace to see her good.

'Take this and stay low, I promise you - I will come back for you when this is over.'

She took one backwards glance and whispered,

'You had better.' With a final kiss they sadly departed.

Gorran crept back inside and decided to take a nap like the others, yet sleep did not come easy. His thoughts were far away.

Chapter 4 – The Portal of Worlds

Myridin looked out across the moonlight lit harbour, his gaze fixed on the deep hulled barge that swayed gently at anchor some way out. From this distance he could just about make out the lone figure constantly walking rings about the deck, obviously the lookout. He began to formulate his plan to free Hadrak, Sir Elic and his band really had no idea whatsoever of the extent of his powers. Had they had the slightest inclination of how powerful he had become in this world, they would have abandoned their insane plan immediately. Men were such foolish creatures they only judged on the past. Today had already provided him with enough excitement to last a lifetime yet he had several lifetimes to fill. Only one last task stood in his way; to free his family. He had been busy since the time spent with the blacksmiths and the forging of the swords. He had moved directly to the Portal of worlds and freed Ambrose from the soldiers that guarded his youngest son. He had first placed a protective shield about Ambrose and then systematically eliminated his guards at his leisure. His following task had been to locate and secure Soredamor's release, he had scoured the land around Kell and been drawn to her life-force, unexpectedly he had found her hiding in the town on her own; a very delighted Niviane was reunited with two of her children and now only Hadrak remained captive. Soredamor had explained Gorran's part in her escape and reassured her father that she had been well treated during the whole ordeal. It would seem to Myridin that Sir Elic's son had a little more sense than his father and so he had left them to return to their own world unhindered; a courtesy that he would not afford to the men holding his teenage son. Ambrose's release at the Portal had been a brief and bloody affair, but then as the people on the vessel before him were about to find out - anyone who would dare to do harm against his family had forfeited their right to life.

A cool sea breeze blew across the water into Myridin's face as he begun to utter the spell that would carry him across the water to the boat, even at night it was an easy task with the direct line of sight. He held 'Sum' the newly created sabre in his hand and intended to test the enchantments that he had worked into the blade. In the blink of an eye he was teleported onto the deck of the moored vessel and he tuned his mind into the magic of the sword, calling upon the power inside the enchanted blade. Concentrating he pushed out a bone chilling suggestion from his mind and the sword immediately glowed as its power took hold and amplified the blood-curdling terror that he projected across the boat. The man who had been walking the deck spotted the sudden arrival of the newcomer but he quickly changed his expression from one of surprise to that of utter panic. The man went screaming into the darkest cubby hole he could find scrabbling to get away from the chilling demon that his eyes perceived. Several other men came rushing past him from below deck, they were delirious with fear, they weren't stopping for anything and went charging straight over the side of the boat in their desperate effort to escape their own fears, not even the icy cold sea water could clear the men of their delusions and their heavy padded armour soon carried them under the water after several minutes of thrashing. Myridin approached the cowering sentry who was now insane with fear and attempting to hide in the darkest corner of the boat; he glanced back down at the glowing blade in his grasp - he was quietly impressed with his work. Myridin quickly ran the sabre through the man's exposed back; the blade's steel was as finely crafted as his enchantments and passed through the man with ease. He had cleared out the larger infestation of rats from the boat, now to find his son; he descended down the squeaky steps to take him below. Myridin passed through the unkempt living areas that he found and headed towards the bow; the air was thick with the smell of unwashed bodies and stale food. The compartments were dimly lit with several lanterns that annoyingly grated and creaked with the sway of the boat. An open door led into another compartment at the far end of the room. The open door squeaked annoyingly as the boat moved, but his frown was soon replaced by a large smile which spread across his face. He could make out Hadrak through the doorway, he was slumped on the floor, bound and gagged but his body moved as he struggled at his bindings. Myridin moved rapidly to his son, his ordeal would soon be over. He moved into the next compartment and bent over his son pulling free his gag before he cut his bindings, but as he did so a shadow moved out from its hiding place behind the open door, Myridin half turned as he heard a noise – but it was too late, a half-full wine bottle came smashing down onto the side of his head. The bottle shattered with the impact and the lady who had delivered the blow quickly fled for the deck. Myridin only caught a fleeting glimpse of her half-naked back in the last seconds of his consciousness.

After some time, Myridin slowly came around with the tapping of a foot on his shoulder, the smell of cheap wine filled his nose and a sticky wetness smothered his face.

'*Wake up father*, wake up.' Hadrak's tapping foot stopped as he begun to show signs of life. Myridin pulled himself up onto his shaking legs, he placed his hand to his head and it came back red – a mixture of both wine and blood. Hadrak's words took a moment to sink in through the pounding of his injured skull.

'Father, can you reach the sword? Cut me free and I will help you.' After he had regained his full focus he followed the simple instructions and quickly sliced through the ropes.

'*What* …what happened?' Hadrak gave his father a quick account,

'All of the men on the boat suddenly went crazy as if they were possessed, but their whore from the town was unaffected, she calmly went about her business and gathered up anything that wasn't nailed down, then when you came along she was spooked and hid until she whacked you one then legged it. You've been out for so long she has probably swum back to the shore or drowned by now.' Hadrak explained.

Myridin continued to pick at the drying blood in his scalp, finding the odd fragment of glass that had remained in his lacerated head. Myridin appeared more concerned with his magic than his wounds,

'I don't understand it, she should have been affected by my spell …perhaps I will need to modify my enchantments before I pass the sword on to Soredamor. Anyway, the main thing is you are safe,' he reached across and hugged his son,

'It's damned good to see you again son.'

Later that evening the family was reunited in a guesthouse in Kell, Myridin had rented the entire top floor at a very reasonable rate and the remainder of his family had anxiously waited here for his safe return. His head still pounded from his injury and he had no desire to strain it further by using his magic to rush them all back to his villa, it would be better to rest for he would soon require every ounce of his strength for the mammoth feat before him. Even in Kell he was well recognised by many of the townsfolk and he had received a friendly welcome; after all he was something of a celebrity. Nearly twenty years before, he had aided with the construction of the town wall. It didn't sound like much now, but back then it had been a time when there were more menacing things that roamed the surrounding lands and the tall wall had saved many lives. It was no ordinary wall that protected the town and no ordinary man that had overseen its construction and soon after Myridin had stepped outside its protective gates to deal with the carnivorous beasts once and for all. The bards still sang of his exploits in the streets today. Now with Sir Elic's men eliminated he no longer had any need to conceal his whereabouts in the land. Well, almost all of Elic's men – Gorran and his small group of guards were making their way back to the crystal plains and the Portal of Worlds with their tails between their legs. He had permitted them to leave in peace for their part in freeing Soredamor and once they were through he would close this doorway of the worlds and at last enjoy his retirement the way he intended.

'Ah yes, the gifts, go and get the gifts Niviane,' Myridin motioned her off with a quick wave of his hands.

'I almost forgot, before I call it a night and retire. We have decided to welcome you all back with a little present, you could call them practical gifts for you may need them in the days to come, but after I close the Portal I hope you will never need to raise them in anger again.' Niviane returned with a grey blanket that clanged as she put it down. Ambrose came crawling across the floor for a closer look. She unwrapped the cover to reveal the three swords of varying sizes and Hadrak's eyes widened at the bundle of swords. For years he had fashioned his own play swords out of sticks and been told not to play with weapons by his mother; now they were giving them away by the bundle. He never could understand the logic of grownups, but was not about to complain. He would often leave the villa on his little camping expeditions with his friends or sometimes even alone for days on end. They would hunt and explore, he had spent many an evening sat around a campfire whittling a pretend sword with the one knife that he was allowed. His father had encouraged him to have a healthy amount of adventure and now he was overcome with excitement at seeing the blue steel of the swords before him. They looked different from the other swords he had seen.

'Hadrak – that big one is for you,' Myridin handed over the largest of the swords to his son, the youths eyes lit up and he wasted no time in grabbing the sword in a warrior's stance and enthusiastically started to swing the two-handed weapon about in mock combat, luckily there was ample clear space in the room.

'*Hadrak*, not in here please!' demanded his mother. He was right, he would never understand grownups, why give him it if he was not allowed to use it?

'Soredamor, this one is for you – it is called Sum, after the man that forged it for you,'

Myridin's voice reduced to a whispered as he noticed his daughter's expression drop.

'A rather drunken blacksmith at that,' he said to himself.

'Do all of the swords have names father?' Hadrak enquired, his voice was a high pitched shrill with his excitement.

'Yes, you will find the name on the blade – yours is called Thulnir.' A wide grind spread across Hadrak's face. '…Awesome,' he added.

Soredamor was a little unsure of what to say to such a gift? When the word 'gift' had been mentioned she had been rather hoping for some nice jewellery or a broach, but a sword? What could she say? It was certainly well made and shiny. She half shrugged her shoulders and replied with an appropriate but deflated,

'Thank you,' she then found an appropriate use for the sword by using the highly polished blade as a mirror to inspect her reflection in its steel; she adjusted her hair then placed it to one side. Myridin lifted up Ambrose,

'And you, you little rascal – you will have to wait a

few years, it's to sharp for your little fingers, we'll let Magnus look after it until you are a bit bigger.'

With the strain of the last few days and a pounding headache Myridin took his leave early and retired to the bedroom. Before turning in he reminded Niviane to set the protective wards tonight, whilst there were still foreigners in this land there was no need to be too relaxed.

His dreams were not the most relaxing; they were filled with the troubles of the old world, things that were better left there too. When he woke he thought it strange that he should find himself worrying about such things in his dreams at a time like this, it was the first time he had been troubled by such thoughts and he didn't like it. The night's sleep had provided little refreshment and come the morning his mood was short as his head still throbbed. Judging by the height of the sun that projected through the nearby window, he realised that he had unusually slept in late into the morning. His family had been sneaking about the rooms all morning, trying to remain quiet, realising he deserved the extra rest. Hadrak came into his room first and after the usual pleasantries they got onto the subject of the last few days. He had been bound up and kept below deck nearly all of the week; on reflection he appeared quiet shaken up from the whole experience. The only time he had been moved or exercised was when he was frog-marched top side to do his business over the side. Then when taken on deck he had been leashed to a pole like a dog to ensure he was never tempted to jump over the side.

'I'm sorry we did not come for you sooner,' Myridin admitted, 'But it was imperative that we split the power of the sword, I knew that its powers would aid with your rescue and also be needed to surround the Portal of Worlds and close it.' Hadrak scratched his head, thinking over his father's words,

'It's alright dad, I understand. I guess you will need

to move really quickly with the army already sending press-gangs through the Portal?'

'*What?*' questioned Myridin.

'…The army, Elic's army? Soredamor told me of it this morning,' judging by his father's shocked look, he quickly realised this was news to him.

'Gorran told her that his father's army was to bolster its ranks with the people of this world. I was surprised you let him go? They will take who they please as slaves or recruits and once he discovers you killed his father you could have a thousand soldiers marching through that Portal for revenge?' Myridin scratched his chin before replying,

'Or I guess he could just be thankful of his promotion?' Hadrak snorted at the comment,

'Hmm, I wonder which it will be – maybe both, I reckon he will be close to arriving at the Portal soon and then we will find out?' Hadrak had calculated his words well.

'Never you mind about the Portal, I have plans for that thing.' Myridin rose and walked rapidly into the next room and called for his wife.

'*Niviane*, I need you to go back to the villa and get the things we talked about, then meet me with the children at the Great Portal, I'm going to go on ahead, I will need to keep an eye on that Portal, we wouldn't want any more marauders coming through; now there is not time to lose, I must get going and I think it would be a good time for some cherished father and son time – it will make up for our time apart, Hadrak prepare yourself – you are coming with me. Oh yes Niviane, if you happen to pick up some of those nice rolls that I like on the way, I wouldn't be disappointed.' Myridin whispered several words as he dropped a crystal to the floor then as soon as the Transportation Portal opened the pair stepped through and vanished.

Later that day Niviane shepherded her children through the jagged crystal fields that led up to the Portal of Worlds. Each of the children carried a pack and wore their newly crafted sword on their belts. Magnus carried Ambrose, nursing him in his arms and wore the dagger 'Taric' on his belt; he would look after it until an age when the little man could carry it himself. Soredamor spotted her father in the distance and went running to his side. Today even Niviane wore a sword; although hers was just standard steel – Myridin had ordered everyone to be carrying arms when being this close to the threat of the Portal.

'Father, I know it's only been two days but it's great to see you again.' Without the distraction of Gorran, Soredamor had started to realise just how much she had missed her family. Myridin moved to each member of his family in turn giving a brief hug of greeting; they were not the only ones who had been affected by the strain of the last week. His action made Niviane realise that things were about to get serious.

'I'm sorry that I had to rush off, but I needed to get things in place, closing this Portal is no easy task and I won't be able to do it with out the aid of you all. If you could drop the gear over the back there and get a brew going …Magnus, I could murder a hot drink and a roll.'

'What do you need us to do?' Niviane asked. Myridin scratched his head,

'Where to start now …this spell will be complicated. Well, gather round; I suggest we have a dry run through so you all know your tasks.' He placed a large chunk of crystal from the ground behind into a clear space before him. Everyone gathered around.

'Your mother and I will need to stand in front of the Portal and focus our energy towards the Portal, Soredamor you will be to the right, Hadrak to the left and we will need Magnus to take little Ambrose to the rear of the Portal. Each of you will need to place the sword into the ground and hold onto it at all times,' he placed several small pebbles around the crystal chunk to mark their places.

'I must stress this is very important, fail to keep contact with the sword and there will be dire consequences. Magnus, be sure to sit with Ambrose and keep his hand pressed against it at all times.' Magnus nodded back understandingly.

'The spell should not take too long and whilst I'm channelling the spell, Niviane will need to repeat it, amplifying the magic out around the Portal and into the swords, it will be quiet an impressive show, so Magnus whatever you may see try to ignore it and just keep Ambrose's hand pressed tight. With our combined strength I am sure that together we can close this threat forever. Now I will need a little more time to infuse the surrounding crystals and then we will begin. If you would be so kind as to prepare us a good meal Magnus, we will need all of our strength later, for once we start on with this spell we cannot stop until the portal is closed.' Everyone nodded their heads in unison.

As Niviane went off to walk the crystal fields, Magnus begun to prepare a pot of food for them all, he was a good cook and quickly rustled up some rolls to tied them over until the hot food was ready. Soredamor who was forever inquisitive about magic, sat scratching her head at some of her father's words, it just didn't sound as if it would work to her and she sought more details of the spell's workings,

'Father I don't understand? How can you direct the magic around the Portal? Surely the power of the surrounding crystals will divert and absorb some of your magic?' Myridin was delighted at her astute observation and was pleased to see that his years of coaching Soredamor in his art had not been a total waste.

'Ordinarily yes, the crystals would absorb our power instead of evenly distributing it exactly where I need it, but I have taken special measures to stop that, I have found a way to link the magic of my spell to our bloodline and on through the swords. It will actually flow directly through us to place it correctly around the Portal where I need it and then its power will be focused into the centre of its mass. I will take you through the finer points of the enchantments when we are done here, if you can understand this spell you will manage anything in life. Now if you would excuse me, I must go over some of the spell's details with your mother. He whispered to her,

'She is not as bright as you, but don't tell her.' Myridin stalked of to join Niviane in the crystal fields.

Soredamor took herself off to a quiet spot as she begun to digest her father's words and began to ponder the ramification of the Portal being closed. The growing panic of her thoughts spread from her stomach and the taste of bile filled her mouth. Gorran had left her to return to the old world and meet with his father's army on the other side; if the Portal was closed it would mean that Gorran would be forever lost to her. She had not revealed to her family just how close they had actually become, in fact father had been so engrossed in the dramatic events of the last week that he had not the slightest inclination of her new affections. He was not in the habit of looking into his family's minds; well not any more after Niviane had caught him in the act last year and given him such a tongue-lashing and lecture which he would not forget in a hurry. On meeting with her family from after the abduction she had simply explained that she had not been harmed in any way by Sir Elic's men and given them the truth about her escape, well some of it – just the part that Gorran had wilfully freed her. Father had been relieved at her safe return and that had been enough for him, but mother perhaps had a better handle on things. Soredamor had deliberately attempted to calm her quickened speech and beaming smile when talking of the man to her mother, but perhaps she had her suspicions. She had noticed her mother's gaze aligning on her when she thought she was no longer paying attention. She had renewed the spell of protection that her father had taught her, just in case anyone decided to get too nosey about her business.

Now she sat alone, upset at the prospect of losing the one thing that had brought her more pleasure in one week than a life time in that stuffy old villa. She tried to logically think through her options but her thoughts were quickly abandoned, she would do anything for Gorran's gentle touch caressing her body once more, their warmth together was as special to her as the memory. But what were her options? She could leave this land before her father cast his spell and join with her love on the other side, but if the Portal was still open she knew that her father would only pursue her and retrieve her, wherever she may be – he would never permit her to leave. She considered her father's recent words,

'Once we start, we cannot stop until it is closed.' Well, perhaps if she bailed out through the Portal half-way into the spell, they would not be able to follow her. She liked this thought, for it took her closer to her lover as she pondered upon it, but there were two evident problems with this plan. One – she had no idea what would be half-way into the spell, or at which point her father would be fully committed to complete his magic. She knew enough about magic to know that there was always a climb before you hit the peak of no return. Besides, if she left the magic being channelled through her it may cause the spell to fail, or perhaps harm her family. There were so many possibilities that her head swam, but the reality was that even if the Portal was closed behind her, father had the power to open up a new one and she knew he would stop at nothing to get her back. After all he had originally opened up the Portal in a land where magic was all but dead. Either way

Gorran would soon be beyond her reach. Tears formed in her eyes as the reality dawned upon her. Hadrak came upon her sobbing which brought a large toothy grin to his face, he did so enjoy the moments when his sister was at her most vulnerable and just couldn't hide the gleeful look in his face as he made his sly comment.

'Frightened of father's magic are we?' he said sarcastically.

She hardly heard his words, until moments later when his mocking tone sank in.

'Don't bother me, you foolish little boy.' She waved her hand at him as if to shoo him away like an annoying fly, although she could tell by just his very stance that her apparent misery intrigued him all the more. After his initial excitement faded, he readdressed her with a new attitude.

'What's the matter then, really?' he asked in a more serious tone.

'You wouldn't understand, you're just a boy,' Hadrak pushed out his chest a little further, obviously irritated by her comment, at sixteen he considered himself a man. He noticed the tears in her eyes, just before her hand came up and rubbed them away.

'Now then, what could you possibly be crying about big sister? I have rarely reduced you to tears over the years. Perhaps they are tears of joy? No ...tears of sorrow?'

Soredamor quickly swung around as his prying words struck home. Hadrak smiled at her reaction, knowing that he had just struck gold,

'Ah, perhaps I have struck a sore point? Now then big sister, what could bring your hard face to tears? Perhaps you are scared for father,' he carefully judged her reaction thinking of the possibilities, 'No, maybe scared for somebody else? Goddamn it, you can't hide it from me sis. Why, if it is not your own family that you worry after, it only leaves the villa hands or who else have you mingled with?' A gaping grin crossed his face. 'Surely not ...it can only be one of Elic's men; yes you have been in their company – no, perhaps not the men, you would never lower yourself to the common men, you are too stuck up for that, but Gorran perhaps?' he trawled through the possibilities eventually finding his mark.

'Don't you dare whisper a word of this to father?' She snapped back at him realising that the game was up. He was smug, pleased at working out her dilemma. She instantly reached out in retaliation, using her magic to dredge his empty mind for any ammunition. She soon found some.

'I would not be in such a hurry to mock my feelings my dear brother, perhaps father would like to know of your little adventures through the Portal?' she sneered back at him.

'I ...I only wanted to see the things that father had told us about in his bedtime stories,' protested Hadrak.

'You bloody fool, it was you who led them straight back too us,' fired back Soredamor in disgust.

'*No I didn't.*' Hadrak was infuriated with her accusations. She delved deeper into his mind and could sense his distress was growing as he desperately sought to bury his thoughts. Hadrak had never shown any interest in learning their father's arts in the same way that she had; he preferred the more physical pursuits in life such as athletics or sword play. His mounting anger opened up the gateways of his mind, making him even easier to read. Soredamor soon wished that she had not delved so deep. At first she saw the image of her beloved Gorran and his small band of men riding back towards the Portal in his thoughts; then a dark shade crossed his path.

'*No*, no ...*No*.' She screamed repeatedly in blind rage.

'*It can't be*, Gorran is dead and father killed him.'

Without thought, her hand snaked out slapping Hadrak across the face in a fit of rage.

'How could you keep this from me? *Why?* He freed me?' Her tears overwhelmed her. Hadrak stood straight as a board unmoving during her outbreak; he showed no emotion at her grief.

'You didn't really think father could let him live did you? He was the enemy and was far too dangerous to leave alive, can't you understand you stupid girl; he had an army waiting in the old world to invade us. Had he returned seeking revenge for his fathers death they could have marched through the Crystal Cave with their entire army; you don't think father would allow that to happen before his spell was ready, do you? They were already starting to send through small groups to raid the local villages.'

She continued to sob in a state of shock, struggling to form her words,

'But father …wouldn't do that, I loved him.'

A smarmy smile spread across Hadrak's face, he agreed with his father's correct decision and had helped to steer his course of action.

'Oh my god, you really did it with him – didn't you? …You stupid slut, this is war. How do you think father got his nickname in the old world, '*The Merlin*' just like the bird of the same name, he flies low and lets events happen, then when he has clearly identified his prey he strikes with incredible speed and sharp talons. Gorran was a fool for following his father into our world, he only freed you to save himself; he got nothing less than what he deserved.' Soredamor halted her sobbing, her mounting rage had squeezed out the last of her grief and she moved to strike him again; but with more force this time. He was prepared this time and caught her blow, turning her arm and shoving her to the floor.

'*Grow up* – it was never going to work between you.' He stalked off as she screamed into the ground; he headed towards Magnus and for some food, all this excitement had made him hungry.

Myridin and Niviane came sprinting back at the sound of Soredamor's screaming, weaving rapidly through the crystal fields, the intensity of her noise had made them think they were under some kind of attack. They were surprised to find just Soredamor crying on the ground.

'What's going on here? Is everyone alright?' called out Myridin as he approached.

Soredamor lifted her head from the ground; dirt was stuck to her face as her tears had mingled with the soil to give her a more primeval appearance. Her contorted and soiled face hid her normal beauty like an evil mask,

'How could you father?' She screamed as they innocently approached. Myridin actually had the grace to look embarrassed, as he realised that his actions had been made.

'It was necessary my dear, I took no pleasure in it – but it had to be done to protect us all.' Niviane went to her side and comforted her but was quickly shoved away.

'But I loved him …*I hate you, I hate you.*' She screamed again.

'Oh dear, I was afraid you would say that. *Atominus Baraknid Slouman,*' he chanted the words several times and Soredamor's face went blank and her tears ceased, as did her memory of Gorran and the words that had just passed between them.

'And that was that,' he sighed with a hint of regret at his daughter's pain. Then as if the last comment and events had never occurred he announced,

'Good, we are all ready then? Let's eat and then get this Portal shut once and for all.

Let's get going. Soredamor pulled herself from the ground as if nothing was wrong and moved off towards the Portal,

'Ah the wonders of magic,' Myridin said under his breath as Niviane passed.

Niviane glared at him with open hostility,

'You really can be a bastard some times,' she shook her head and walked off.

Myridin brushed off the comment. Later as Hadrak sulked passed him knowing that he had done wrong he avoided his father's glare and took his position; Myridin had known that the kid would be the weak link in his actions but Hadrak needed to see such things – the killing of men should never be relished but sometimes it just had to be done; in such circumstances the kid needed to learn that one should never hesitate. Hadrak would be a man soon and needed to harden up to the harsh realities of life. He would speak with him later about this, but first there were bigger issues to deal with at hand. Myridin did not underestimate the complexity of the magic needed today; it had been one of the reasons that he had put this spell off for so long and could well have done without this little family drama before such a draining and challenging event. The Portal had been infinitely easier to open than it would be to close. He was certain that the power in the swords would help give the extra boost that was needed, they held the last of the magic from the old world; it was all that was left. It was the time.

Everyone had taken up their assigned places and Myridin began a low chant of magic almost like a song as he paced about in front of the great vortex that joined the worlds. A circle of rippling light spread out from him to reach his family and envelope the great Portal as they clutched their sword handles pushing the tips of their weapons ever deeper into the ground.

The pitch of Myridin spell lowered and the air began to tingle with magic, Niviane stood behind Myridin repeating his words parrot fashion as he spoke them, the air shuddered and clouds of power formed about his hands as he commanded the magic from the swords. The sky reddened around the Portal and a crack of lighting ruptured the sky with a giant thunder-clap directly above the growing magic, as Myridin's spell began to crush the Portal in on itself. The air about Myridin buckled, throwing him staggering backwards to the ground, his impact with the floor narrowly missing one of the large crystal shards that jutted up defiantly from the ground. He shook his head in shock; he had not expected such a violent reaction,

'That wasn't meant to happen, something is wrong.' He scratched his chin in disbelief as his magic continued to gather and mutate without its master to channel it in the right direction. Niviane came rushing over and touched his shoulder as she sensed his mounting indecision and tension,

'What's wrong? The magic is growing, you can't stop now,' she questioned.

'*You think I don't know that!*' He ran through the calculations again in his head as the magic continued to grow. Static discharges' of raw energy forked randomly out around them, expanding ever outwards from the Portal. Niviane sensed a change in the air, the sensation was intoxicating at first as the tingle of magic washed over her, but soon it seemed to claw at her skin like a corrosive gas as she and the others begun to experience the acceleration of time,

'*Mother what's happening?*' screamed Soredamor as she watched her fingernails visibly grow.

Niviane also felt that something was desperately wrong; she looked about her and soon noticed the difference. She was aging, no – they were aging. It had started very slowly but within the field of magic growing in the rift the passing of time was beginning to build up in momentum. She looked across at her children with fearful eyes, Hadrak was growing noticeably taller and the first signs of stubble began to sprout from his chin;

she twisted her head to behold the changes in her daughter. Soredamor's figure was growing noticeably fuller, her waist slimed to an hourglass shape and her full breast strained against her smaller robe constricting her chest.

'Myridin, quickly do something – my children are aging, *if this magic continues to grow it will kill us all.'* She ran over to Hadrak, who following his father's instruction had not moved from the spot, still grasping the sword for all he was worth.

'Keep hold of those swords whatever the cost or else we will all be finished, shouted Myridin from across the way as he rapidly reworked his calculations. As he had already guessed, his previous calculations were correct; it had to be the delivery that was wrong, the magic was not compressing the portal at the exact points he had expected. It pointed to only one possibility, his magic was not flowing entirely through his own bloodline; his own progeny had to be the conduit of the magic - one or more of the three vessels magnifying his magic was not of his bloodline. Impossible Niviane was his loving wife, she would never have betrayed him? The situation was desperate, he knew that he did not have the time to recalculate or double check - years would be shaven off their lives. He looked about at his children, trying to keep the sickening thought of betrayal from his mind; reassuring himself that a magician should be clinical and logical in every task. Which one was not his? Ambrose was already growing into a young boy and the others approached adulthood. For a moment he was blinded by his own rage, kicking over a nearby crystal jutting from the ground; he had to just let his anger consume him like a huge passing wave for a moment before he could focus on the immediate threat at hand. The realism of her betrayal hit him like a hammer. He screamed out a curse releasing the last of his rage,

'*You whore, how could you?'*

He snatched out his long belt knife and looked around at his three children.

'Which one of these children is not mine?' he bellowed at Niviane deliriously. He had made his calculations to the problem as swiftly as he could; it would only be down to his best guess which one of his children was not his own. He needed Niviane to tell him immediately …his actions would force her hand if she did not. Soredamor had always showed a natural aptitude for magic, as had his father before him; it was a trademark of his line. This left Hadrak or Ambrose. Hadrak had never shown any interest in magic and Ambrose was too young to tell, but unless a solution was found quickly he would be old enough to ask him himself. *Which one is the bastard?* He had to destroy the half-blood or they would all be consumed by the growing spell, it was the only way to release the magic. He would take no pleasure in the task, he had raised them all with a father's love, but the calculation was simple – one life to save everyone. His hands trembled as it became clear in his mind what had to be done.

'Quickly Niviane, I demand you tell me …which one is not mine – *tell me now or we are all done for,*' he yelled as his mouth curled into a snarl of hatred. Niviane approached him pleading for his forgiveness. She clung to his arm dragging him back as he took a step towards Hadrak and her sword came defensively to hand, as if to guard her children.

'No Myridin, I …I never betrayed you' she pleaded 'I …I was raped.' There were some things that magic should not be used to stop and others that she would not use to stop, shame, guilt, a young life growing inside her and the love for her children; they were all a part of her. She had also returned back to the old world on more than one occasion herself.

'I can't let you do this. There must be another way; I will not let you slay our child.' She replied as the tears filled her eyes.

'Which one is it woman.' He demanded coldly. She searched her mind to the depths of her memory for a solution to the growing spell that surrounded them; she had a wealth of skill and ability from a different school of thought to her husband. A possible solution surfaced in her mind.

'Use your magic to retune the spell to my bloodline.' She demanded. He kicked over a nearby crystal in rage as he pulled his arm from her grasp; his mind was so full of anger that he had not considered this.

'*Yes*, yes it might work, but it will take time and we may all die of old age before it is done. Time, yes – that's it, it can be altered,' he raved almost as if mad.

'He began to cast a new spell; her two children were now fully fledged adults and Magnus struggled to hold onto the growing Ambrose.

'Can you do it? Is it working?' She questioned. He could not stop now to reply, not mid-flow as he worked a new magic, instead he just gave her a single reassuring wink. She listened to his words, studying them with mistrust as she sensed that they were not recalibrating the original spell. She knew her husband and he was an addict to deception, he had threatened to kill her children moments before and the new magic he was creating was forming into a great mass of power above them. Assuming the meaning in the words of power that flowed from his mouth was near impossible. She strained to interpret the possible meanings; he was gathering a huge force from the crystals surrounding them all, perhaps strong enough to annihilate them and he was directing this force at their children. Her mind raced, she knew in her heart that he would stoop to any level to survive this.

'*No, not my children*,' screamed Niviane. Myridin did not hear her; the thick buzz of magic enveloped him as he raised his arms in the final throes of his spell. In a sudden flash of panic she swung the sword and thrust it straight through Myridin's back. She knew enough about magic to know that the magic could also be stopped if the source of the power was eliminated. He sunk to his knees in disbelief at the length of iron that burst out through his chest and he felt the tumble of his wet innards as they trickled down his front to his groin.

'You will not kill my children, your magic dies with you.' She declared through tear filled eyes. She had made her own calculations and came to a different resolution to that of her husband. Myridin toppled to the ground and reached out for her foot, panting out the last words to end his spell with his final faltering breaths. He had only sought to protect his family from the ravages of time with this spell, protecting them whilst he adjusted the magic in his original spell. With his last breath he finished the spell and uttered a dying curse.

A brilliant arc of light shot out from the portal enveloping the three children in a blinding light. Soredamor whispered a lone word as she was smothered in a dome of magic, 'Gorran.'

A colossal explosion shock the world as the Portal of Worlds collapsed moments later.

Chapter 5 – The Storm Begins

The morning had a distinct chill to it; this was not entirely down to the weather. Delanichi jumped down from the battlements just in time as a cone of raw power was projected from the opposing Brotherhood and smashed into the spot where he had been standing. The blast of power rocked the wall and sent large fragments of rock flying into the air felling several nearby men. The Aristrians troops pushed forward into a tight crush of men against the second wall, the Tanarian garrison had now fully mobilised and had manned the eight foot wall in strength, short ladders and grapples clattered against it's length as the Aristrian infantry attempted to breach their defences. Pike men on the walls thrust down at the iron clad mass that fixed the wall with their hateful glare upturned. Rocks, arrows and flammable oils held back the tide of men that attempted to push forward and climb the wall, soon the defenders started to throw anything that they could find to hand as the their supply of projectiles ran low. Wooden planks, helmets and the dead rained back down on the men as they continued to send men up the hundreds of short ladders that lined the wall. Delanichi was no military man but he realised that the wall gave them the best advantage in the defence of the town, should it fall their casualties would be higher and nothing else stood between them and the town of Ubecka. He had felt the power of the Brotherhood gathering in the camp of the enemy over these past days and with the use of his magic he had called for aid. He didn't know how many of Tamar's agents still lived or even if the man himself still drew air. All that he knew was that his messages for aid were soon cut short by a shroud of magic that smothered the entire area, no doubt the Brotherhoods work. After feeling their combined strength he had decided to save his strength for the battle to come. Despair had quickly set in; he knew that some of his repeated pleas for help had reached the world beyond and he also knew that none had come.

On the opposite edge of town a Su-Katii warrior charged forwards with a small assault force to secure the town's bridge that led from Ubecka over the rapid flowing river to the bleached rocks of the Aristrian shore. His bright crimson cloak fluttered behind him as he dashed forward cutting down several men in his way to secure his objective. With over a hundred Aristrian skirmishers and archers at his back they presented a major threat, blocking an escape route and squeezing them on two fronts. Delanichi had prepared for an assault on the bridge and had stockpiled a large supply of green crystals beneath it, the weighted wicker crates could just be seen deflecting the surf of the river in the shadows of the bridges stone arches. The crystals were massed together and prepared in such a way that he could quickly focus his magic upon them, to detonate with explosive results. Yet another trick he had learnt from the study of the book of Magnus. He drew upon his powers as the invaders were just over half way across the bridge and with his chanted spell he forced the green stones to quickly expand releasing his focused magic in one great pulse. The ground shook and the sound of battle was instantly muted as the bridge erupted in a shower of rubble, the shocking action halted the last of the advancing Aristrians in their tracks as their leader and the bulk of the skirmishing troops were pulverised in the blast. The flying debris scattered across the banks and landed in the fast flowing waters. The rubble quickly sank and the dark silt was carried off down stream.

The wall above Delanichi's head shook again with the bombardment of the brotherhoods magic, they were concentrating their magic at the centre of the stone wall that blocked their armies path and the breach that was sure to come would quicken their end. An archer in the centre, who had stood a little too high on the battlements was vaporised by their fiery blast as he tried to find a better angle to shoot from. Delanichi felt the wall bend and strain against the heat of their magical assault and chanted a spell of protection on the central segment of the wall; he needed to stand exposed to better deflect their attempts and several nearby shield men assisted with his call for protection. His efforts were rewarded, the fiery beams of light that arced across the battlefield were only the work of the acolytes and not the Masters, they were deflected away from the central section of the wall to randomly burn alive both Aristrian and Tanarian alike. Delanichi felt the combined magic of the Brotherhood with genuine fear and knew that, against their continued assaults, his spells would not last long. The Brotherhood of Keth had also prepared and allowed for this rogue magician, their acolytes' would keep him entertained whilst the Masters prepared him a rare treat.

The demon did not take kindly to being summoned into this world; it had just started to enjoy a feast of blood before it had been plucked from its own dimension to do the bidding of its new master. In the Brotherhoods favour for the task ahead – at least the beast was still hungry. Delanichi had retreated back behind the battlements of the wall to catch his breath and could not at first see what was coming for him. He had been marked for destruction by the demon and Telimus smiled within his black hood at the though of his new pet feasting upon the enemy magicians flesh. The demon stormed forward wading waist high through the sea of men in its way. Most of the soldiers were facing their front and had no idea of the ten foot demon passing through them until a taloned claw raked them out of its way. The smooth black skin of the vaguely humanoid figure flexed its defined muscles as it cuffed Aristrian soldiers away from its path. It only took one backward glance from the scattering men at the creatures grotesquely humanoid face and its protruding fangs before the screams of terror preceded its arrival at the wall. The men scrambled over each other like a parting wave in an effort to distance themselves from the thing. One Aristrian soldier who was too slow to move was scooped up in the demons long claws and flung into the ranks of Tanarian soldiers that had steadily been refilling the centre wall. He flew through the air screaming like a ragdoll and several soldiers were bowled from the wall as they were struck with his impact. In one giant leap the demon flew onto the battlements and hurled itself up onto the wall, several petrified defenders conquered their fears and found the courage to strike out at the demon, their blows hardly drew blood against its tough rubber like skin. With one strike it impaled the nearest man onto its taloned hand, showering the others around him in warm flesh as the demon ripped its sharp claws free from the dying man. The scene was horrific and men jumped backwards from the wall to escape the demons path. Delanichi's attention was instantly grasped by the huge demon towering above the troops on the wall; it scanned through the masses of men looking for the magician amongst their movement. There was only one man that stood out from the crowds of steel ants that scurried away and it locked eyes with the brown robed Magician. Delanichi attempted to shrink into his surroundings as the oversized head fixed its scanning gaze upon him. The huge drooling jaws promised only a painful death. The demon leapt forwards covering the ground to Delanichi in three bounds, it wanted to be rid of this foul world. He hardly had time to react and bring up his defences before it was upon him. He had been forced into using one of the slightly weaker spells for protection; it was faster to cast than the others and with the speed of the creature, this decision had already saved his life …for now. He was a man of considerable experience and had known the instant he had spotted the demon just how fast these creatures moved. The creature smashed into his invisible shield of magic and crashed into the ground dangerously close to where he stood. He felt the shock of its collision against the spell and wondered for a split second if his magic would hold as the soil where the barrier met with the ground was sheared away and flung into the air with the force of its impact. A brave pike man from the wall turned and stabbed the creature through its back; instead of the expected deep penetration from the long weapon it cut into the creatures tough hide little further than half the spears head, yet this was enough to bring a sickening cry from the creature and sent it whirling about in one giant leap back into the man. The pike-man was sheared apart in seconds under the frenzied clawing of the demon; a cloud of red mist hid the grizzly details of the man's slaughter before it returned to slam back into the invisible barrier that protected Delanichi once again. The brief seconds of the man's death had given the Magician a chance to prepare a more potent spell, this time for offence rather than defence. The demon was a predator and although it lacked any true intelligence it quickly adapted its approach with a hunter's instinct. It's great claws dug down into the compacted soil, like a dog digging for a bone – if it could not get through the shield, it would go under. Delanichi was now committed to his attack and realised that it would take vital seconds to switch spells back to extending his shield through the soil, he pressed on with finalising the magic. A hooked claw smashed through the surface of the ground before him and the demon pushed hard with its hind legs to squeeze its head and torso through the small gap it had created, its powerful limbs driving it forward as it lusted to taste the mans soft flesh. This thought and its hunger to feed drove it on to a new level of frenzy as it struggled to get at its prey. Delanichi suddenly realised that his back was pressed tightly against the rear of the magical shield that protected him like a dome, he had nowhere to go as the black monster emerged from the ground bypassing his protection. His offensive spell was ready and delivered just in time; two thick jets of white fire flowed from his open hands down onto the emerging terror. A hellish scream pierced the clatter of the battlefield as white hot magma spewed from Delanichi's hands and melted the creature like a corrosive acid, in the demons final dying act it crawled forward the last foot, hauling itself forwards and struck out as its carcass melted under the falling white fire. With his protective dome still in place Delanichi had no place to go and directed the fire down onto the demons head in a final effort to stop its advance. A large claw struck out and came down lacerating the magician's leg as the creature finally died. Delanichi breathed out a sigh of relief as the last of the creature melted away leaving just its extended arm behind, he quickly dispelled his magic and looked down at his wounded leg. His head swam with an unnatural dizziness as he beheld the open gash; with the rush of his initial adrenaline the wound had felt no worse than a punch to his leg. His brown robes turned red where they had been opened up with a neat cut that revealed his flesh exposed to the bone. The flesh of his leg was peeled back and his thigh had been opened up like a kipper with a long deep cut from hip to knee. He fell back into a puddle of his own blood and desperately struggled to remain conscious as he went into shock. Fortunately he was amongst friends who knew how to deal with the trauma of the battlefield; a nearby soldier quickly applied a tourniquet at the top of his leg and cut a section of Delanichi's robe into a bandage as he called for stretcher bearers. Delanichi's face turned as white as snow as he watched the people tend to his wounds; after collapsing he felt strangely detached as he was tugged onto a canvas stretcher; a weathered face loomed over him as the fellow worked to stabilize him before moving him. The field medic knew that this magician was one of their greatest assets to their survival and immediately used one of the few red crystals that he carried for real emergencies' on the open leg wound. The crystals were normally reserved for the most severe of wounds and this certainly came into that category for the potential threat of death from the huge loss of blood. Delanichi's delirious eyes were still fixed on the ongoing battle of the stone wall as the men worked on him. Where the demon had crossed the wall stood a new problem, as the men had scattered from the demon, one of the Su-Katii warriors had seized the advantage and tailgated it to the top, gaining access to the wall. He now worked his way along the narrow walkway slaughtering all in his path, some men simply jumped out of his way rather than meet with the death freely delivered by his blade. The pike-men on the wall did not have enough room to bring their long weapons to bear on the agile man; instead they discarded their pikes and reached for their swords, only to find a short silver blade already protruding from their chests. The wake that the lone Su-Katii was clearing provided unhindered access over the wall and the first Aristrian soldiers started to populate the gaps behind him. Delanichi realised the threat and felt his fool-hardy dreams of victory slip away. The devastating Su-Katii was now moving at a running pace along the wall, ducking or evading any strike against him whilst returning a deadly strike with every blow. At one point he leapt onto the very top of the battlements to avoid two large men that attempted to block his way and force him from the small gangway; the Su-Katii struck down at the nearest man piercing his armour through the collarbone and a thrust kick sent the second man flying from the wall. Aristrians soldiers continued to crest the walls behind him and a triumphant shout went up as they achieved their objective of taking the wall, only the barricades across the town's pathways stood in their way now and the Tanarians began to stream backwards towards their final stand. As Delanichi was lifted on the stretcher and jostled away he viewed the enemy beginning to jump down from the wall and advance toward the town, the Su-Katii warrior was at their lead.

'No, No – *Stop!*' shouted Delanichi as the men carried him away, he doubted that the bearers could outrun the advancing storm as they puffed to get away. Delanichi reached out and grabbed one of the running mans legs and caught his foot. The man fell over and the whole stretcher including the second man crashed into the ground. Delanichi shouted at the men, commanding them to leave him and get back to the town without him; he then hauled himself up, using the second gawping man as a human rope; through willpower alone he pulled himself up on to his unstable feet. After some words of enchantment his bad leg stopped its shaking and held firm. A temporary fix was all he needed. Turning about to face the horde of Aristrians that spilled over the wall, Delanichi spread his arms high in the air and shouted at the men following the advancing Su-Katii with great shouts of rage,

'*You will pay with your lives for invading this land*; damn you Tamar, where are you …I could do with a little help here.' He paused for a second as if expecting his cry to be answered; then began to chant a new spell as he painfully hobbled back towards the wall to meet with the advancing Su-Katii. The Aristrians and their leading knight vectored towards the tramp like figure that dragged his wounded leg and he was soon dwarfed by their approaching ranks, each side gaining momentum as they hurried to meet. They could not believe their luck, only one man faced them as the other Tanarians ran for the cover of the town. Delanichi's chanted words grew louder into the final bellowed words of magic as his resolve grew with his new enchantment. He approached their ranks and spread his arms horizontally like a bird. The line of men and Su-Katii were almost within striking distance when Delanichi's magic activated. In the seconds before the magician had cast his final spell he allowed himself a short chuckle at his predicament; he had never thought that he had it in him to be a hero, the fleeting thought quickly evaporated as nothing but the flash of Aristrian steel filled his view and his spell was finished. As Delanichi hobbled forward he combusted into a great ball of fire that extended out from his outstretched arms in a long line like wings and swept into the lead Su-Katii and the following Aristrian ranks like a great phoenix of fire. The army fled backwards from the approaching inferno, many unable to avoid the great wings of fire. Delanichi's magic did indeed take on the form of a great fiery bird and the molten eagle of death flapped its way back up to the town's wall incinerating hundreds before it – men caught in its path quickly disintegrated into falling ash. Only a handful of blackened and charred figures managed to slump back over the burning wall to the Aristrian side as the fires of hell continued to burn their comrade's bodies. Lord Banok looked up at the fireball that defused into the sky with shock; he had ceased his advance at the first wall and waited with the Brotherhood for their pet to do its work. As he observed the charred men regaining their feet on their side of the Tanarian wall he took away a strange thought from the day,

'How strange, he had never seen stone burn before?' The advancing Aristrians of the second wave halted in their tracks as they sensed their commander's apprehension and several of their burning comrades crawled back towards them for help. In the Tanarian ranks, General Larks seized the opportunity and rallied his men from their retreat away from the wall; fresh men were coming up from the town and helped to settle the earlier fear that had gripped his men. With the deadly

Su-Katii that had crossed the wall incinerated by Delanichi's magic the men had regained their fighting spirit and Larks knew the importance of holding the wall.

'Come on men; turn about and retake your positions on the wall – do this and the day will be ours.'

The men skirted the large burning segment of the wall avoiding the masses of charred corpses and took to the battlements to find the Aristrians retiring from the field. A great victorious roar went up and the Tanarians spirits were lifted.

'Fantastic,' though Larks, he must congratulate the wizard on such an amazing feat; he had killed hundreds and seized the day. Under the fog of the battle he had failed to see Delanichi's last stand.

'Where did that wizard go? Somebody, find me the wizard.'

Hundreds of leagues away, over on the western coast of Tanaria in the besieged sea port of Tagel the last of the Tanarian survivors prepared for their own challenges. The first challenge that faced them was actually far from being the defence of the strongly fortified town, the ancient keep's walls had seen off many such challenges in its long history. Instead the real issue emerged from the inside and the overflowing population – there were simply too many heads to house and mouths to feed. The civilian refugee population outnumbered the regular soldiers six to one. Those that were capable of fighting had been organised into different defence forces based on their age and ability, with the weakest groups being mostly made up from the old and women. These less capable units trained daily in the areas where their lack of combat effectiveness could be maximised, concentrating on such disciplines' as mastering the graceful art of the bow. The defenders had several months in which to train and prepare for the inevitable assault, besides there was little else to do as they waited, hemmed in by the great wooden counter wall that had been constructed by the enemy around the exposed land surrounding the town. Many attempts had been made to disturb the walls assembly, but with the slave labour of their captured kinsmen forced to work by their Su-Katii overlords there was no stopping its construction. Some in Tagel wondered if any attack would indeed even come; or if the enemy would just starve them out, but some amongst them knew the Su-Katii better than that.

Lord Candis, the only Su-Katii lord to side with the Tanarians in Tagel stood discussing his ideas and plans with Lord Mallet, the protector of Tagel; a position not only given to him as his given birthright – but earned with his own blood. Mallet felt the irritation from his old wound to his shoulder-blade as he stooped to look at the battle map that Candis was referencing. He was lopsided at the best of times, but leaning too much only brought pain to the old war wound.

'And what makes you so adamant that they will attack Lord Candis?' he enquired still not believing that the enemy would bother them after all this time. He was strongly of the opinion they would be starved out and eventually be forced to attack rather than defend. An attacking force would normally require a three to one number advantage to stand a chance of victory. It would be logical for the enemy to force them to attack, with their five to one advantage in trained soldiers as well as a defending position; an Aristrian victory would be assured.

'Why, do you ask when their tactic is obvious? Mallet questioned. Lord Candis shook his head as he responded,

'You obviously do not know the Su-Katii as I do my lord. You see, they will only starve you a little to bring a taste of fear and despair to your ranks. I agree, it would be the logical choice to just starve you into submission, but I know these Su-Katii and I can assure you, they have a very different agenda – they want to relive their old ways and boast of epic victories and glory.' Lord Mallet digested his words, but still did not believe them,

'How do you know these things Lord Candis? They are efficient in battle and will select the correct tactic to win.' Mallet gave a short emotionless laugh at Candis; the man was obviously out of touch with his order.

'How? I'll tell you how, because I feel what they feel, I tasted what they taste and with every passing day I want to do nothing more than free my swords and touch flesh with steel.'

Lord Mallet's eyebrows raised at his words, he knew a bad sign when he saw one. Lord Candis continued,

'So, I can assure you sir, staving you lot out will not bring them the relief or the satisfaction to the itch that we feel,' Candis paused and cleared his throat, '...Rather, should I say the itch that they have. *They will fight* ...and it will be soon.' Lord Candis studied Mallets reaction, this man had the full support of the army behind him and he needed to correctly access the measure of the man. Candis was one of the longer standing members of their ancient Order and over his numerous lifetimes of experience he had found many kinds of men in similar positions of power. He had learned to categorise them into three types of men, he named them the Whiner, the Diner and the Vagina. The Whiner always made a lot of noise, great speeches in good times and averted blame in the bad. Men would always followed a whiner but soon wish they hadn't when it came to the crunch, as on the whole he had found the whiner to be poor planners, full of self belief but no substance to back it up. The whiner normally came from noble blood; but although of noble blood, Lord Mallet did not fit this category. The Diner, in contrast would absorb every ounce of information you could feed it, they would swill the facts in their mouths like a master wine taster, gargle the flavours and then spit them out with total disregard. A Diner just used whatever was available to him with scant regard. They could consume an army with ill decisions in no time at all, throwing men's lives away for their own pig-headed appetite and they rarely achieved their goal. He was unsure yet if Lord Mallet fell into this category. If not, it only left him as a Vagina. They were just plain old fashioned twats but, like all genitalia, people were drawn to them and you knew what they were right from the start. But that was good for they were useful, you could fill them to the brim with facts and they would retain what you gave them. The problem with this archetype was you had to put up with the personality that went with it, upset it once and it would often do the opposite to what it should, just to spite you and left alone it could develop a bad smell. However nurture and treat it right and everyone would be pleased. Lord Candis decided not to push his point that Mallet was wrong, time would prove him right and reveal exactly what kind of leader this Lord would be.

That night in the harbour of Tagel the only ship at the moorings was made ready to attempt to run the blockade with the morning tide. Rizil the Captain of the vessel loomed over his men as they went about their preparations – to the men on deck he seemed to be everywhere on that vessel at once; nothing would be left to chance in the early morning departure. A dark cloaked figure strolled down the dockside and spoke briefly to the Marine that stood guard before the gangplank that led to the vessel. The visitor brought a welcome but brief distraction from the annoying seagulls that had repeatedly pestered him for food. After a short exchange the man was permitted onto the vessel and Captain Rizil joined the man in his cabin.

'Ah Lord Candis, good to see you again, I trust you are not here to join us on our return journey? Perhaps you came just to wish us luck?' The stocky Captains neck wrinkled as he looked up to the taller man with a broad smile.

Lord Candis raised an eyebrow in return,

'Or perhaps I came for another reason?' The Captain gave a broad smile, masking his true thoughts of where this conversation was heading.

'Where you are involved, there is little "perhaps" in the matter. Would you care for a glass of wine whist you discuss why you need my ship - or maybe something stronger?' asked the Rizil.

'Ah, Rizil there is no fooling you, is there?' Lord Candis realised that this man was definitely a Vagina, but he was lucky, for Lord Candis appreciated and recognised his own kind.

Chapter 6 – Reunited

It was yet another day beneath the blood red sky of the magical Rift that imprisoned both brother and sister in its eternal confines of time. In the world of men outside, only days had passed since Tamar the magician had crossed into the timeless Rift. The confinement of the sphere now held them both captive. Inside the Rift where time passed at an accelerated pace, the reunited pair had spent several months together and it seemed to them even longer. During this time forced together, they had already explored the full range of human emotions, actions and reactions against each other, from at first attempting to destroy one another, which they had soon found to be impossible, to eventually even sharing tears of laughter. Now they had both settled for a truce as the reality of their situation had struck home and they instead claimed their own space within Soredamor's halls, yet the chance to snipe at one another was often seized upon when the opportunity arose. They were indeed truly brother and sister, although Tamar could hardly believe it. He had used some of their time together as an opportunity to try and glean a little more information about his forgotten past. He had always looked upon the tales of the old gods a bit sceptically, but now, the probability that they were in fact his parents brought a whole new dimension to his interest.

'Tell me sister …tell me of our parents? You say they loved us dearly but I cannot remember them, if that statement is true, why then did our father imprison us?' he asked again, she always seemed to avoid or gloss over his recurring questions of the long past events.

'It was all so long ago Ambrose,' she replied shaking her head. Even without the effects of her persistent charm he could appreciate her natural beauty, but regarded her only as a sister.

'Please, we agreed to respect each others' ways, I don't go by that name any more.' He tried to keep things civil between them as they had agreed on a code of conduct between them as terms of their truce. Obviously those were just words and neither paid their agreement much heed. She just rolled her eyes at him and continued.

'Ok …Tamar, is that better? Those last days before our imprisonment were just crazy, I don't know how it all came about really and there are some memories that I struggle to recall, but the more that I think about it, the more I am drawn to think that father was just trying to protect us from the effects of time in these domes of magic. I sensed his spell switch from tracking his bloodline to our mother's, but I was too far away to hear all of his words and to finish a spell of that kind would take considerable time. I just sensed a panic in all of them, perhaps he intended to undo the spell after the danger had passed. We will never know. And you – how did you really escape the dome? Tell me? If you have done it once we can do it again. I can assure you after several more months stuck in here with me you will do anything to be free. Then just wait until the Brotherhood comes to visit this Rift, at first you will despise them but as the months turn into years and the years into millennia, you will start to crave new company. Do you really expect me to believe your story that you can't remember any of it? You are very forgetful for your age. Were you really just found wandering in the Uphrian forests as a feral child? Just open up your mind to me, I can help you to remember'. Tamar wanted to just yell at her, she had driven him mad this last week, but he was trying to turn over a new leaf in their relationship. It was becoming all too apparent that they could well be in for a very long stay together and she was probably right in her statements. He replied to her incessant comments seeking some peace.

'As I have told you a hundred times before, I really don't know how I escaped, whatever happened must have erased everything up here,' he tapped his head and felt her searching his mind once again. Her powers were so great that she did not require the spoken words of power of lesser magicians. He inwardly smiled as he prepared a thought that would repulse her. He anticipated her predictable and regular probing of his mind, she was constantly searching for the truth of his release in some hidden or unprotected memory and she quickly recoiled from the image that he created of them lying naked together. He burst out laughing, don't worry Sis, I don't care for this thought much myself; it withers my staff for sure but it also certainly works at keeping you out of my head.' She sighed back at him with disgust as he lectured her.

'In any case, I don't know why you want to escape the tranquillity you have here; things aren't exactly rosy on the outside, and did you know that all the destruction going on is declared in your name. What do you think of that? Would father have approved of the Tanarian children being slaughtered in your name?'

'You think I don't know? She snapped back, 'You think everything is just describable in terms of black and white; you know nothing. Get me out of this bloody place and I will show them right from wrong. I will tear their souls from their bodies if they so much as look at me the wrong way.'

It was Tamar's turn to roll his eyes; she just didn't get it – but then she had endured endless visits from the Brotherhood reassuring her that she was their god. Their constant whisperings in her ears had surely inflated her ego to the levels of an immortal soul. She noticed his disapproving look and turned her back on him in a sulk as she continued to mutter on to herself.

'You haven't got the faintest clue, you have only had the realisation that you are a god for five minutes …what do you know of it? You have already seen first hand how incompetent those magicians are, they can't free me, they can't manage to kill you. What does that tell you of their Order? If you tell the Brotherhood to go left, they will end up going right. Oh, they will head off in the right direction at first, but after a while they will just veer off and do their own thing. What do you expect? They are men. You will learn this eventually, dear brother …mark my words, you will learn.' As her anger mounted with her words he suddenly realised that it would make her easier to read and reached out into her mind, two could play at that game, he looked away as he whispered the needed incantation. For a moment he glimpsed into the depths of her mind. She hoped for nothing more than to be free and return to her love, but he also sensed that she was also hiding something from him. The portcullis of her mind came crashing down and he clutched his head with the sudden pain of her ejection.

'Naughty naughty Tamar, keep your nose out of where it doesn't belong.' He took heed of her words, but it would not be the last time he would attempt to penetrate her mental defences. Now that he had found a trace of a secret locked away inside her he was like a bloodhound on its trail …as was she. He questioned her directly on what he had seen.

'How do you ever hope to rejoin with Gorran? He is long since dead and necromancy will never bring him back as he was, if at all. You would need to find his body; that far back – no chance …and then you have the worlds to traverse, impossible.' He had decided to lay his cards on the table and see how they played; there was nothing else to do today, besides he wanted to find out what exactly he had been trying to stop all these years, he hoped she would reveal more.

'Ok Tamar, you have seen a glimpse of my mind and I will play along with you out of boredom alone – after all, we have nothing to hide …we are all family here, now if you can find the time,' she broke into a short burst of laughter, 'Then prepare to hear my confessions. Yes I loved Gorran, nothing will ever change that and I still do. Yes, I will do anything in my power to meet with him once again. Anything – do you understand that, that's what true love is, maybe you will find out for yourself one day? But I want the man – not the corpse, do not suggest such foul things of me, not even I would stoop to such lows. Yes, I sleep with the Brotherhood Masters to search their minds and learn of further magic, magic that may help me escape or join with my Gorran once again. I'll tell you, it is a small price to pay for hope, for once you have looked into the twisted minds of men such as Anak you would understand the true depths of my despair and that these people really deserve nothing from me.' She was at last being honest with him which oddly made him feel a little inferior to her in that moment.

'But, you cannot turn back time,' he replied in a more sympathetic tone.

'Can I not? My magic has developed well beyond that of father's and yet I am sure it would require his magic to do so. If I can get out of this place perhaps we shall see.' She sighed at the depressing thought of never regaining her freedom.

'The swords, of course you would need the swords – they hold the power of the old world and father worked his own magic into their blades,' his analytical mind had spoken out loud, betraying his train of deduction at her comments. He shook his head at her,

'Who knows what dangers such a path would release upon this world?' He reassured himself that he had been right to attempt to thwart her efforts.

'What would it matter if this time never existed, brother? I can already sense your anguish at this course of action, you are weak brother - but think of this, Perhaps this future would be far less cruel without me and the Brotherhood fuelling the anger of the nations? Have you considered what could happen in this world if our history had the chance to be re-run? Perhaps we need to be brutal and destructive to rebuild the paths of our fate in a different way. Besides should it be possible it would not be down to me to mould this world, for I would not be hanging around in this land for a second longer than needed, should I be able to return my life would be rebuilt through the Rift, with Gorran in his world.'

In the lands outside the magical Rift that held both brother and sister captive, several leagues lower in the valley beyond, stood the sparsely populated village of Hickhem. Three new guests now stayed in the only tavern in the village; they clearly stood out from the inbred generations of the locals. Outlanders were easy to spot in the region – two women, mother and daughter, shared the large family room with a younger man. The locals' tongues had already started to wag for it was not long before, that the very same lady had visited with a different man on her arm. The gossip of this visit would surely keep the village talking for several weeks. Athene gave her mother yet another hug. Each morning, seeing her mother again brought her a joy that could not be measured. Her frail mother returned her warm embrace,
'My little chicken, I thank the heavens, every day that I can be with you, I truly thought I would never see you again.' Her words brought a tear to Athene's eye; the use of her mother's pet name for her tugged a forgotten cord inside her heart and her mother's words had been spoken with the despair that only over a hundred years captivity in the Rift could bring.
'Thank Tamar mother, not the heavens – if you are going to pray, pray for his safe return, which to be honest I had expected long before now.' Barrad cut into their conversation,

'I'm sorry, but you know my thoughts on this …if he has not returned by now, he will be her slave. I can tell you, once you have locked eyes with her charms you can think of nothing else, the rest of the world seems so grey and colourless in comparison to her beauty. Her eyes can look so deep into your soul that you…' His voice petered out half way through his sentence as he became lost in his memories. Both women took a small measure of offence at his words as if they were directed at them, although neither showed their true displeasure at his delusional comments. The poor man had spent years under her all-consuming charms and it would take some time before he once again become himself. Athene felt somehow inadequate when Barrad talked about Soredamor in such a way and underneath her initial resentment she just pitied the poor wretch. Barrad had at first been inconsolable at his separation from Soredamor, but with each passing day he drew upon his vast inner strength and took one step closer to becoming the man that he had once been. The past few days spent languishing in the Tavern had been serenely peaceful, away from the troubles of wizards and warring nations. They had waited briefly outside the Rift's entrance for Tamar's return, but then fearing that the Brotherhood may arrive they made their way out through the cave and down into valley to the village of Hickhem below. Luckily Athene had found a discarded pack from her previous visit to the rancid cave, which contained some clean clothes that fitted both mother and daughter and, more importantly, enough coin to pay for their stay. There was even a spare dagger that Titus had always insisted she carry with her and now it was their only weapon between them. On its discovery in the pack Barrad had quickly taken ownership of the blade.

They had tried to keep a low profile in the village over the last couple of days, expecting Tamar's quick return and a rapid departure, but that was proving to be extremely difficult with the locals' flapping gums in these back waters of Aristria. They knew that they were running the risk of discovery by staying, and their action was all too predictable, but both Barrad and Sasha - Athene's mother, were in no way ready to travel any distance and with no horses at their disposal they were forced to remain in the village. It came as no real surprise to them when the dark-robed magician eventually came knocking at their door. Athene had thought it strange that the man should politely knock first before announcing himself, for he was defiantly not one of Tamar's men, and for a moment everyone in the room just froze.

'*Listen up*, everyone within this room hold fast and open this door, I only wish to speak with you …please, do not do anything rash or attempt to flee, it will only waste our time.' commanded the hooded figure by the door. Reluctantly and with little choice Barrad drew the dagger and stood by the door, pulling Athene close in to him to allow her unique ability to dampen any magic to also fully protect him. He then opened the door, just a little bit ajar to peak out at the waiting hooded figure,

'It's the Brotherhood, they have found us,' cursed the Su-Katii. Before he had time to consider opening the door further and running the man through, the waiting figure called out,

'Easy Barrad, I present you no harm, you are only partially correct in your statement …I was once part of the Brotherhood, but like your Tamar I no longer serve their master.' Barrad clenched his dagger as he weighed up the Magician's words and suspecting deceit around the corner,

'Why should I believe you Wizard?' Zerch pulled back his hooded face to be seen through the small gap and replied,

'*Why*, ha – because of the very fact that I am talking to you now of course,' Barrad could not argue with the magician's logic, a true Brotherhood disciple would not have wasted any time to negotiate with him or even knock, they would have used a surprise attack to attempt to destroy them. However their order was devious enough to attempt some kind of deception? Zerch continued under Barrads watchful eye,

'Besides I would not linger too long in your indecision to kill me; that is if you ever want to get back to your command before your men are annihilated, I can assure you – I am your only hope of a swift return to them.' Barrad fully opened the door, seeing no point in lingering like a doorman; Zerch's words had struck the right chord, yet his dagger was still raised in threat or promise. The point of a long-sword extended from behind the door frame as Garth, Zerch's Sword-master and bodyguard, wisely placed his blade between Barrad's temptation and his master's life. Barrad's eyes narrowed as he regarded the newcomer, who looked strangely familiar.

'I have seen you before, haven't I, in the Temple I think?' Barrad asked the newcomer blocking his way. Garth nodded,

'That could well be a possibility. I spent a considerable amount of time with the order along time ago, but never attained the final seal to join their ranks.' Both men regarded each other, straining for a better view of the others exposed neck line where the distinctive Su-Katii tattoos would have been visible, should they of existed on either man.

'No Tattoos,' both men said in unison and with some relief.

'Good, now that you are reunited, perhaps you two love-birds should get your own room whilst I talk to the woman,' Zerch commented with a sarcastic tone but a straight face. Barrad should have been offended at the magician's comment, but the man's words only reinforced that fact that he was not of the same school of thought as the rest of the Brotherhood. The magician walked into the room before he was invited, as if he owned the place, stopping briefly only to give a quick nod at the two women.

'Ladies,' he moved directly to a seat moaning that he had been on his feet all day, then once seated he raised his finger in the air and pointed towards the younger of the pair.

'Athene, the dispeller of magic I presume. Please allow me to present myself. I am Zerch.' Athene's nose wrinkled as she regarded this man of whom she had heard Tamar talk several times about in the past. She recalled that he had always held his ability in high regard, but Tamar's opinion of the man had always been somewhat tainted. He had been Tress's master once. Athene's mouth started before her brain could stop it; her mood was wearing thin with the man's over-familiar manner.

'Well let's not mess about, get to your point you wretched man.' She felt her temper starting to rise. Zerch shock his head as if he had just tasted a corked wine,

'With manners like that young lady, I can see why the Aristrians are trying to stamp out your country.' Athene's mother grasped her daughter's hand soothingly, before it could rise to lash-out in anger.

'Our guest is probably correct; we have lived like animals for too long, would you care for a drink Master Zerch?' Sasha reached for a bottle of red and the clay cups that they had in their room. He nodded,

'Ah it would seem that the daughter has still much to learn from the mother.' He took a sip from the offered drink and then continued.

'Allow me to tell you a short story as we sit here pleasantly chatting. You could call it a little bit of light entertainment to pass away the day. There was once a simple boy who wanted nothing more in life than to feel the love of his mother and father. Quite a simple and common dream really, but very few people in this world actually manage to achieve it. Anyway, one day the dark shadows of magic fell across their family; you know? The kind of shadows cast by magicians and gods. The little boy was not simple or stupid; he knew that such powerful shadows were far too mighty to stand against, so he instead learnt to become patient giving him the time he needed to understand and play their game, he was very patient indeed. One day like his father he eventually joined the order of Keth with big smiles imposed across his face as his family were torn apart and devoured by the shadow that further stretched across the lands. I joined their order with the sole intention of destroying it from the inside and I have become very good at my work. The shadow grew dominating many in its shade and it did not take long before I found others who had also been wronged by its spread. Athene, it was I who freed your lover, Titus from his imprisonment in the Su-Katii Rift.' Garth cleared his throat loudly,

'*Ok,*' Zerch conceded, 'Ok …technically it was Garth that carried out the deed, but it was my idea and plan. The task cost poor old Garth his place among their *glorious* order, but it was a lucky escape if you ask me.' Garth quickly added a resounding,

'Thank god.'

Athene's wandering attention was grasped as Titus's name was mentioned. She was starting to understand that magicians just couldn't hold a normal conversation and perhaps even liked to add a little drama a bit more than they should.

'If your tale is true, why not just side with Tamar and fight the threat that that faces you both?' Zerch's eyes narrowed at Athene's comment,

'Things are not that clear cut and the moment you cease to work alone, your communications would be traced by the Brotherhood, they are bad at many things but seeking out traitors within their own ranks is not one of them. Besides, you would be foolish to think that Magician is the answer to all of your problems. He does nothing more than plant small acorns and call them trees.' Athene's face reddened and she snapped back at Zerch's comments,

'At least he is out there actively trying to do something and his acorns will grow. You claim to be a patient man - you just have to wait.' Zerch sipped his wine, enjoying her snappy reaction,

'But he's not out there, is he? He is in the Rift, which brings me to the main point of my visit. The *mighty* magician has not returned to you and yet you have no idea why. Let me enlighten you. It is because he is a part of the very thing you seek to stop. He is also what you simple minded folk would call a god, he is one of them - Soredamor's little brother and the magic that holds her captive now also holds him.' Athene shook her head at his words,

'No...'

Garth spoke up, backing his master's words; they were simple but reassuring of the facts,

'He is right you know, why else has he not returned?' Everyone standing in the room sat down as they digested Zerch's revelation. Athene's head spun as she churned over their words again and again,

'Why should we believe your words, magicians and deceit go hand in hand?' she contested. Zerch gave a brief smile back,

'You are not totally blind then ...I am not in the habit of seeking any praise or a pat on the back for the things I do. I just do them because they must be done. But if you must know, apart from freeing Titus who went on to kill the one who hunted you, I have also saved your life once,' his finger extended to point at Barrad. 'Did you really think your speed in drawing your sword from its scabbard so superior to your peers? Ha, even from a distance I was able to expand the metal of Thulsa's blades making them impossible to draw in time to strike you down.'

Barrad went white, casting his mind back to the moment when he had faced his commander and made the first steps of rebellion against his Order,

'What?' Zerch took another sip of his wine, the corners of his mouth extended into a smug smile.

'Well I couldn't have the great saviour of the Tanarian nation falling at the first hurdle. You took action and that was enough for me to back your cause. Now what else could I brag about to inflate my status in your eyes? Perhaps you may even agree that I plant my trees fully formed? Would the fact that I have destroyed Bellack and have Kerric feeding from my hand align you to my cause?' Athene snorted, 'Bellack was banished, not killed – I know I was there.'

Zerch allowed his inclined mouth to break into a broad smile,

'Correct. He was banished but then I brought him back again and now he is no more.'

'Oh? Really? ...*Good*,' replied Athene. Zerch turned to Garth,

'Good she says, I have brought about the end of the founding powers that corrupted the Su-Katii, I suspect his death will eventually weaken their magic sufficiently to free the warriors from their slavery and all she can say is '*Good*,' Why thank you ...it makes it all worth while,' he said sarcastically.

'With their masters destroyed, their magic will fade; it will just be their own greed and bloodlust that drives them on. Anyway people, I have talked more today of my deeds than at any time in my life, I think they are worthy credentials to assure you that I seek to destroy Soredamor and her Brotherhood. I will not beat about the bush any longer with my own intentions. I will see Soredamor dead for what she did to my family. Barrad we must transport you to your army at once, I can provide you with a Portal. The Brotherhood moves against them with the full might of the Aristrian army. They are divided and will lose without you. Hell they may lose with you, but I know you will try your best. Sasha, I propose we will take you to a place of safety, you are a treasure that needs to be preserved and I'm sure this will be a prerequisite to your daughter's aid. I have listened to old Garth here and he reminds me that a young boy's dreams can become a reality. Athene, we must first travel to the Rift of Hadrak's imprisonment and have a dry run of your ability to neutralise magic. He has no skill in magic and will present the world little threat if he is released and we find that he cannot be destroyed. If we can free him from the Rift and then slay him it will guarantee that we will be able to free your Tamar and destroy Soredamor without risking her presence on our world. You were right about one thing girl – The population of your homeland will be slaughtered without my aid. If my theory is correct and Hadrak can be defeated, there is hope, if not we must forever turn our back on them and fight for our lives.'

Barrad pondered his words,

'Slay Hadrak; that is one sword fight I would not relish, he may well be the source of the Su-Katii, but he is certainly not the source of the problem – besides I am no assassin to kill my former mentors.'

Zerch sighed,

'I am beginning to dislike being correct all of the time, and you are also correct Barrad – you are a general not an assassin, besides you have your own war to fight. Only a killer with a grudge would be suitable for such work. Titus, you may come in now,' he shouted out loudly. Footsteps approached the door and Titus filled the doorway. Athene's heart pounded in her chest. She didn't know if it was anger, fury or desire that made it beat so wildly? She sat rooted to her seat, a cold sweat came over her as she gripped tightly to its arm-rests, frightened that her impulse to run into his arms would betray her, the conjured and replayed image of Tress embracing him in her mind halted her impulses.

'He is right you know. Bellack is dead, I have seen his severed head with my own eyes and I will have my revenge on Hadrak,' he nodded at Athene casually, 'Once this task is done there is still a chance for us my dear,' Titus quickly added as he glanced over at her for the first time, worryingly he almost sounded serious. Zerch relaxed back in his seat and took another gulp of his wine,

'You see I already have my killer,' he commented looking rather smug. 'But do I have your agreement to assist me?' Barrad stood, regarding the ancient Su-Katii warrior with a hint of curiosity. He had heard of this man in legend alone and judging by the way Titus had regarded him when he had entered he could spot a fellow Su-Katii a league away, even without his distinctive swords.

'Ah, the legendary Titus stands before us. They say you have never been bested with the blade, is this true?' asked Barrad.

'I don't know who says these things about me, for I have never left anyone alive to tell such tails,' Titus replied. Barrad gave a slight smirk at his arrogance rather than his comment,

'Oh I don't know, Hadrak makes a point of telling everyone in the Temple that he remained long after your encounter and that you may have been outstanding with a blade but not so good when faced with fruit ... a peach was it?' Barrad's tone held a hint of mockery in his final words.

'Over the years my blades have sliced many skulls and they go through them as easy as cutting fruit. Perhaps you would like to see how well they cut? They say that a man is the sum of his achievements, mine stretch so far back that history has now forgotten them.' Barrad instantly responded to his boasts,

'Man has probably forgotten your deeds because they were worthless. I do not brag of yesterday's achievements, my deeds are made in the present and the future – forget the past.' Titus shook his head, his hands patted both of this sword grips and his voice lowered to a more chilling tone.

'Not everyone has a future before them Barrad, yes I have heard of your lucky little victory at Monaki and your brief escapades, but I should remind you young pup, that I do not follow the Su-Katii code and will not hesitate like the others in the Order. I have slain more Su-Katii than I have had meals - one more would make no difference.'

'As have I, but in far fewer years,' replied Barrad in their macho standoff. The meeting of Su-Katii often involved a heated exchange, it was their way – but like two cats meeting in confrontation, after much hissing and spitting it was rare that claws would draw blood. Barrad attempted to make the picking of his fingernails with the small dagger in his hands look as provocative and menacing as possible, but only to mock his opponent's actions,

'Now, now children – calm yourselves down, we are all on the same side here. Save your aggression for the gods.' Zerch suggested, both men deflated their chests and made light of the other's comments as Athene screwed her face up at Zerch and changed the subject,

'If you are telling me that Tamar is a god, then what kind of a man are you Zerch?'

'Oh me, I am nothing more than just a bitter old man who has decided it is the right time to step out from the shadows,' replied the magician.

Chapter 7 – A Devine Leader

Corvus, King of Nordheim and champion of the Uphrians was unusually nervous at attending the gathering of the clans. The last such event involving the gathering of the Uphrian clans had been a bloody affair, mostly through his doing. At least the days of hanging about and waiting for their decision to unite under his war-banner would at last be over. During the last few days of waiting for the clans' leaders to assemble, Ievia had spent much time with him explaining their customs and running through the clans' histories and the main players that would be involved in the meeting, although one of the clan leaders' names consistently cropped up more than any in their conversations; Kildraken; the leader of the Arrow-head and largest of all the Uphrian clans. Corvus understood the complexities involved when holding a position of power and knew that once a man reaches the peak of his reign he would not relinquish it without a fight. After absorbing every sentence that Ievia was willing to teach him of their ways, it seemed to him that their culture held a complex web of power in which the Shamans appeared to hold all of the strings; a leader held a sword whilst the Shamans held the divine blessing of their gods. He had spent the evenings alone with Ievia either talking further of the clans or recounting stories of his own homeland. She was an attentive listener and would hang off his every word. He had only needed to reject her vehement advances the once for her to meet with the understanding that she should keep her space on the other nights. Ievia had heard talk of lands where only the men were permitted to make advances towards their women; backward lands in her eyes – it was obvious to her that Corvus must come from one such place and she would respect his odd custom for now. Instead they shared laughter on several occasions as he recounted several stories of his youth. He had been surprised when she seemed to enjoy the ones about his brawls and battles the most. He had recounted them several times at her request and she had seemed content during their telling, staring up with starry eyes from the animal furs of the tent's floor as she lay back watching him jump about recounting the action. She could play the waiting game for now; she was seen by her people to be sharing his tent and as his wife it was expected by her people – they did not need to know that he not truly claimed her yet. Corvus had only just allowed her into his tent, and a married woman sleeping anywhere other than her husband's tent was seen as shameful in Uphrian culture. A woman would be seen as deficient in her duty and in some cases they had even been ejected from the clan. Ievia was pleased with the progress that she had made with her stubborn husband. She was yet to 'make baby' with him but had at least made some contact with him - he had certainly enjoyed the back massage she had given him the night before the meeting of the clans, but him falling asleep with relaxation was not quite her plan.

Shaman Artio had arranged the gathering of the clans' leaders and their Shamans the next morning, the event was to mark the recovery of the dagger of Taric, a task that no one had ever previously returned alive from, and as Uphrian legend would have it, apparently made Corvus the beacon of light to lead their people into a new age of unity and prosperity, if you believe that kind of stuff. Artio arrived and announced to Corvus,

'They are gathered and ready for you Lord of Lords,' Corvus had noticed that the Shaman had started adding extra titles to his name since his return from the allegedly impossible trial to retrieve the dagger. He didn't like it one bit.

'Just call me Corvus if you please,' commented the Nordheimer as he followed the old man over to a large tent that had been constructed out of animal hide; it had been erected solely for the meeting and could easily hold a hundred men. Every villager in the settlement had seemed visibly on edge as the various bands of warriors and Shamans had arrived, it was not surprising, as with their bodyguards they almost outnumbered the village's population. A young lad came running up to Corvus as he paced nervously outside the great hide tent, Artio had entered alone to warm up the audience leaving him under the inquisitive gaze of the groups of bodyguards that surrounded the structure. The men who had been present at the Shalk-tor quickly averted their eyes from him. The lad bowed and passed on his message before scampering off.

'War-lord, they are ready for you.'

The stuffy air inside the tent hung in Corvus's throat as he met the gazes of close to sixty men, their eyes intently fixed on his defiant stance as he stood in the entrance way deliberating on which way this meeting was going to go. The clansmen that had attended the Shalk-tor instantly recognised the figure with a dread that did not normally flood into such proud men. One Shaman amongst the crowds; the master of ceremonies from the Shalk-tor slid backwards into the crowd, without his wolf-skin mask he would be more difficult to be recognised. Artio started the meeting by running over the events that had led to this day, describing the completion and success with the 'Trial of the Ring' by Corvus and he finished his speech by quoting the words of an ancient Uphrian scroll.

'We wait respectful to our ancient laws; the lost blade will mark our true beginning and reveal the Son of the Gods.' Artio paused, 'Lord Corvus, show them the blade and accept your destiny. I give you the Son of the Gods.' A clan chieftain close to the back muttered several words to his accompanying Shaman,

'Son of a bitch foreigner, more like.' The tent was filled with several other similar comments being made as Corvus held aloft the recovered weapon. He had to admit to himself the sword of Taric was obviously not designed to overwhelm an audience with its impressive stature. Displaying the dagger as he had been instructed to do so by Artio only seemed to deflate the moment. Kildraken Frostbane, chieftain of the Arrow-head clan and probably the most powerful man in Uphrian lands didn't waste a second and seized upon the moment; he stepped forwards and challenged Artio's words.

'What is this you are trying to foist upon us, a foreigner? As long as I have eyes in my head, he is no son to the gods. If he were he would be Uphrian. I think your mounting years turns your mind to mush, old man.' He directed his last comment at Artio as he defiantly spat on the floor. Several men in the crowds gave a cheer of encouragement to Kildraken before he waved their noisy tones down far enough to continue.

'It should be I who leads the clans. After all, the Arrow-head is the greatest of all and has been for centuries.' Artio displayed the first signs of anger that Corvus had seen in the old man since his arrival in the forest, but being accustomed to the quick-witted negotiations in Nordheim he immediately responded to the comment himself.

'Well now, it seems to me that your clan have squandered their time in power, for you have achieved nothing of worth over these last centuries.' Kildraken was outraged and rushed forwards in anger, Corvus stood his ground and the chieftain stopped inches from his face delivering his words with a hateful glare,

'My people will never follow a foreigner, how do we know this is even the real blade of the gods? You outlanders can do little other than attempt to deceive us.' The shouting and the threats inside the tent only served to relax Corvus. This place wasn't so different after all, in

Nordheim it was not uncommon for negotiations to result in bloodshed and he began to feel at home.

'You would dare challenge the judgment of the Shamans?' questioned Artio. 'We all bore witness to the trial, do you question our judgment?' He glared at each of the other Shamans present,

'Perhaps you were so used to our brave men dying in the trial that you were not paying attention to the task. You must follow our law.' Kildraken's Shaman stood up by his side, his age almost matched that of Artio.

'You wrongly interpret the scrolls Artio - the lost blade will mark our true beginning and reveal the Son of the Gods. All this is merely telling us is that now is the time of our salvation. This ox that you present to us is not the chosen one; he will just unveil the true Son of the Gods who is standing here already. He is over there,' he pointed at Kildraken.' The tent broke into a full scale argument as sixty voices struggled to be heard at once. It was obvious from what Ievia had told him of the clans that they considered this nothing more than a ploy from a lesser clan to steal the established power of the mighty Arrow-head clan. Corvus had at first thought to strike down Kildraken to dispel the growing myth that he could possibly be the chosen one, for Kildraken's Shaman had already started to preach that he was some kind of divine being. He had halted his temptations before it went too far; a tingling sensation had started to flood into his hands from the crystals embedded into his skin at the mere thought of killing the man. Corvus cleared his mind of such things; perhaps the other Shamans were right? He did not understand these people and suddenly he wanted no part of it or them. How had he come to be so embroiled in their affairs? For some reason the name Morben entered his mind. He was a damned fool for taking on the old Shaman's request. He should have ignored the man and just gone home. As the noise of argument flooded the tent he realised it was indeed time to go home and leave these people to sort out their own problems. He had seen enough, with a swipe of his hand he cast the sword of Taric into the ground and stormed out of the tent. He paused in thought for a moment as the fresh air hit his face. The way to his left took him back into the village and Ievia, he had few possessions back there and he liked the girl in her own abrupt way, but he had his own issues to resolve. To the right was the forest. He turned right and begun his journey home.

Much further down on the west coast of Tanaria, a small group of riders fled for their lives. Brin, the lead rider, guided his men across the open terrain; he whipped his horse into a full gallop with the need to escape the full Aristrian cavalry regiment that pursued them. Earlier that day Brin and his small band of marauders had struck at a seemingly soft target, as they had done many times during this last week. They operated like a well oiled machine when they had struck and run at the enemy lines this month; every individual knew exactly what was needed of them in the grim task ahead. Each man was silently resolute as they continued with their self-appointed task to harass the rear echelons of the Aristrian war machine. The small convoy of six wagons had appeared an ideal target, only twelve teamsters and six armed outriders driving their cargo of iron and bronze rods towards the lines at Tagel. Unknown to them they had been shadowed by a larger force of cavalry who had been waiting for the men to take the bait. The small convoy was quickly stamped out, but before they had time to place their cargo beyond use by leading the wagons the further league east to the sea cliffs, their rear scouts had soon appeared, galloping up to them screaming warnings and raising the alarm like mad men.

'Aristrian cavalry ...and lots of them, get your arses out of here now.' The men had continued past them and bolted down the road ahead, hoping to get as much distance between them and the pursuing unit as possible. They had played this game of cat and mouse several times before this week, they all knew that the stakes were high, but their well-placed scouts had always alerted them to any danger well in advance and their numerous escape routes had saved the day.

The first realisation that today was not going to end well came to Brin as he noticed the quickly climbing hillside to the left of the track while to the right there was a league of land which eventually met with the sea. He suddenly realised that with such a large force blocking their rear they would be in serious shit if another force was placed to cut off their only avenue of flight – the road ahead. The open expanse of land between them and the sea had lured them into a false sense of security, had there been fewer men in pursuit, they may have stood a chance at doubling back past them. But when Brin spotted the shield-wall and surrounding riders to his front, he realised that they had been driven down this road into a well-laid trap. He reined his horse in, bringing their group to a halt, its nostrils flared as it took the opportunity to suck in fresh breath. The leather padding of his helmet stuck to his forehead with sweat as Brin raised himself in the saddle attempting to gain a better view of the ground ahead as the true panic of the situation hit home. Nearly sixty riders swung about as Brin wheeled the men around, the hundreds of men pursing them now blocked their retreat in an extended line. Lord Mako cantered forwards on his fine white warhorse to speak to one of his officers in the front rank,

'I want some prisoners today, I don't care how many, but don't disappoint me. Make sure that one is amongst them,' he indicated at the lead rider of the marauders.

The man nodded, filled with a mixture of responsibility and dread at the task – it was not easy to keep someone alive during a battle, especially when they were on the opposing side. He then rode off to spread the word along the ranks of his advancing men. Brin quickly formulated his battle plan, he would steer his group of riders towards the cliffs and the sea in the hope of finding a track down onto the beach. If not, he hoped this action would stretch their lines as they rushed after him, then they would turn about and try to smash through their weakened lines. Seeing Mako on the field ensured that surrender was not an option to Brin. There was little cover on the open grassland as they closed the distance to the cliff edge and several arrows from their pursuers began to fall amongst their ranks. One man tumbled from the saddle towards the rear of their group, a barbed arrow through his back. Brin and his men cursed as they were met with an eighty-foot drop as their panting beasts stammered to a halt near the edge of the great drop to the sea. There were no paths of escape down the sheer drop that met them, nor even a visible beach – just rocks and white surf met their desperate gazes holding the promise of a watery grave. It was make or break time for them, they wheeled about and spurred their mounts into the net of horseman closing in on them. There were at least three ranks of Aristrian horsemen to smash their way through, before they would see another chance to run for their lives for a few moments more. With a defiant war cry, the last of the Tanarian marauders broke into a charge before crashing into the enemy lines. They were swamped by men on every side and each man fought for his own life as they hacked through the wall of men and horses to the slim brightness of daylight beyond. Several men were knocked from their saddles as they were crushed from all sides. For a moment in the frenzy it seemed that Mako's words had been forgotten. Brin smashed his sword into the face of the man blocking his way, his horse bit and kicked at the press of men surrounding him. A large mace flashed towards his face, but he leaned back in the saddle, avoiding the blow but its swing continued past his body to smash into his mount's head. The beast keeled over taking Brin with it and the darkness of the crush consumed him.

Brin stirred to the warmth of an open camp fire, its huge raging flames devoured a pile of tree trunks that had been felled to last the night and their burning illuminated the surrounding Aristrian camp. He looked down with a dizzy head and a swollen eye at his bound arms and legs. Thick ropes held him tight, unable to move his body to check the function of his aching limbs. Eight of his comrades were similarly trussed up by his side and all were attached together with one common strand of rope. A man at the opposite end of the rope groaned with pain, he had sustained a crushing blow to his hip and was in a bad way. Brin couldn't see the man from his position - only hear his agonising groans. The whimpering Tanarian was rewarded for his noise with a kick to his face to encourage his silence from a passing Aristrian soldier.

'Shut your face you Tanarian scum,' he followed the kick with a short and vicious laugh before moving on.

'Did anyone escape?' whispered Brin to the nearest man, unable to move his strained neck far enough around to see the man.

'I don't know, I think so …but there is little hope for them. There were so many,' replied the voice.

'Morde, is that you?' asked Brin, pleased that he had survived. The nickname of his companion's altered ego had stuck with the men.

'You forgot to say 'Sir' you insubordinate wretch.' Ruby whispered back in his best Captain Morde voice. It was all he could do to fight the fear of their predicament and in better times such a comment would have been preceded by laughter, but not today. Their future promised to be short and bleak. During this war neither side had built up any reputation for their treatment of prisoners and with Brin's marauders partisan activities, they had more reason to be hated by their enemies than most. Judging by the noise, the Aristrians seemed to be enjoying their celebrations with the successful completion of their mission to remove the thorn that had been stuck in their great imperial arse for so long. The men were allowed a full ration of wine, not enough to get stinking drunk, but Brin knew it would be enough to make the evening very dangerous for them. As the night went on the soldiers' shouts grew louder as their bragging of the day's battle and victory grew. The moment of their capture was being relived by the excited men with vivid accounts of the action being relayed to the listening men who had avoided the action. The mention of several fallen comrades eventually turned the mood of the group to one of anger. As if suddenly sensing the changing atmosphere in the camp, Lord Mako appeared and filled their view, stepping from the shadows into the firelight as he judged his men's mood changing. The Aristrian ranks went silent as the Su-Katii regarded his prisoners, walking slowly past the bound men, his cold and calculating eyes regarded each man in turn. Eight sets of Tanarian eyes returned his gaze with utter contempt. They had all ridden with Mako days before and had seen what the man could do with a pair of blades in his hands. The pure hatred directed towards this man from Brin was plain to see, for the death of his long term friend Hugh at this man's hands replayed in his mind. Brin regretted some of his own command decisions leading up to the death of his friend, but was in no doubt who had struck the killing blow. Brin regretted some of his command decisions leading up to the death of his friend but was in no doubt who had struck the killing blow. Mako smiled to himself as he regarded Brin's upturned face and remarked to an accompanying soldier,

'That one there, he really hates me – you can see it in his eyes. Yes, you were the company sergeant, I remember you now. We will be having words in the morning,' Mako smiled at the thought and walked on to stop at the end of the line of bound men.

'Cut free that end man …I am tired of his noise - let the men have their fun, you may beat him to death. That should quell their appetite for revenge tonight.' The Su-Katii turned and left, as the badly wounded man on the end was eagerly cut free and the soldiers quickly gathered and jostled to get a good slot in dishing out some punishment. Little Marc had joined Brin's marauders with the Trail-blazers and had proved himself as a capable scout. He died in less than a minute as the crowd pummelled him to death with their fists and sticks. It was not a pretty sight to behold, but Brin forced himself to watch the event, letting his anger flood into every fibre of his being. He may need to call upon it later and he swore to himself that one day he would see Mako dead.

Chapter 8 – A Time to Run

The blue and cloudless sky over the town of Ubecka marked the perfect weather for the second assault. The Aristrian troops stood ready, today there would be no magicians to turn back their advancing army in a wall of flames. Algar stood hunched over his great iron hammer as he surveyed the formations of men assembling ready for today's battle. He was a tower of a man and was always visible over the others around him, even as now, when he was slumped over. As Algar surveyed the scorched and charred wall that blocked their advance, he questioned himself as to why they needed this war? There was no political gain in destroying their neighbours, other than claiming their land and riches. He wondered at how he could ever have been such a fool to be taken in by Thulsa and buy into his great plan of unifying the two nations? The original plan had somehow warped along the way; the reality was that there was no merging of the nations, just the total destruction of the Tanarian nation. Thulsa was no visionary of the new age. The man was now as dead as his grand dreams. Many of his fellow Su-Katii knights had also fallen to the consuming hunger of his plan and mostly to one man's blades in particular. Fortunately for some unknown reason the rogue Su-Katii had not stood with the defenders, yet they had still lost two of their Order to the Wizard on the last assault, leaving only Lord Banok and himself as the remaining Su-Katii in this army group. They had also lost many men from the army in the first assault and the devastation of this war played heavily on his mind today. He had once stood on the Tanarian side of the peace treaty during those older and better times, one of the six Su-Katii warriors assigned to bring peace between the two warring nations all those years ago. The treaty had worked and they had enjoyed twenty years of peace and prosperity. What a fool he had been to break the nation's trust, yet here he stood about to deliver the final blow against them. How had it come to this? This blow would be used more to erase his shameful act of treachery rather than to finish off an old adversary. Still, he would wipe the slate clean today; a bitter taste could always be washed from one's mouth. The order was given and the men advanced once more towards the battered and burnt wall of Ubecka. A detachment of the Brotherhood magicians were assigned near the front of the army and they began the hostilities with a ranged bombardment of the defenders, raining a variety of unpleasant surprises down upon the cowering men before the main arm of the army struck. The more established of the spell masters had been reassigned and moved on to assist with the assault of Tagel at Lord Aden's request leaving only the less skilled of their order remaining to assist in this battle, not that any watching Aristrian could tell the difference from their destructive display. To the untrained eye it was an impressive display of magic; the Brotherhood made up in numbers what they lacked in skill. A dark and menacing cloud drifted over the well defended wall and the ranks of men behind began to cough and collapse as the poisonous vapours took effect. Men collapsed, falling backwards from the ramparts, others frothed and vomited as they took to their knees attempting to escape the fumes from the dark clouds. The Aristrian army continued to march forward to meet with the wall and although they had been assured the cloud would disperse before their arrival, not all had faith in the Brotherhood's statement. Their worries were put to rest as their assault ladders touched the wall, the dark cloud quickly dissipated and the Brotherhood members ceased their chanting. Today the Aristrian soldiers took the wall easily and with little fight. Once again the Tanarians fled backwards, this time to the barricades of the town; volleys of arrows covered their retreat, cutting down the over-eager men who pursued them as the Aristrian war-machine reformed their organised ranks about the wall. Tress cursed as she watched the stone wall fall into the hands of the enemy. This signalled the beginning of the end in her eyes as the enemy was reforming into an armoured tortoise-like formation to advance into the town. She realised that with them facing the combined force of magicians and Su-Katii the town would not hold out long, it was time to do what she did best, run and hide. She had enjoyed the peace and quiet of the governor's residence over the past few days after Titus's unannounced departure. She had been trying to decide what her next move should be, She had already found it hard enough to adjust to the reality of this world from her prolonged stay in the Su-Katii Rift, the years inside it just didn't seem real. The clash of steel sounded through the town as the two armies clashed, but before she left there was one thing that she needed to do. Tress rushed through the corridors to Delanichi's room, without stopping she opened the door and rushed in. She was instantly pushed backwards from the doorway by an unseen force, falling backwards onto her arse. She had been in such a hurry that she had not detected the invisible barrier that protected the room. She should have known that a magician would never leave his room unprotected, especially with such valuable items inside. Fortunately she was not without skill in the art of breaking and entering, be it physical or mystical, she had mastered them both, although it seemed a lifetime since she had needed to employ such methods. She used a spell that Zerch had taught her to indicate the weaker points in the protective magic. Her old master had repeated to her on many occasions that magic was not a solid mass but was perhaps best described as being more liquid in consistency. As such, there were areas in a spell of protection that were slightly thinner or weaker than others. Once the first spell that she used had identified these weaker points, the second would focus its resonance on these points and shatter the spell. She had yet to find a protection spell that she could not break, the only element that was needed in these cases was time. The sounds of battle reminded her of the struggle outside and she realised that it had definitely got closer and louder.

'Come on Tress, think,' she said to herself after her first attempt to breach the magic failed. The crackle of a transportation Portal broke her concentration; could it be Tamar returning or perhaps the Brotherhood striking behind enemy lines? She abandoned her spell and hurriedly pulled her enchanted cloak about her to conceal her presence. It would be no coincidence that the Portal opened here, Delanichi's room held two magic swords and the book of Magnus, a prize for the taking but most of all she wanted to recover her old Sabre, Sum from the booty. A small figure clad in furs appeared through the Portal. His blond hair and well-kept beard was neatly trimmed and worn in the traditional Nordheim style, this clearly marked him as a man of that region and, as with many magicians, his age was difficult to judge. Tress was aware of many of Tamar's agents, although she had met with very few and this man fitted the description of Ragnor, a very private man from the Nordheim region. In the light of the battle being fought on their doorstep and her pressing need to get out of here she decided to take the chance that she was right. She came about behind the man as he stopped and regarded the invisible sphere protecting the room. Tress felt a little embarrassed with herself when he did not bash into the invisible barrier as she had done. She came out of the shadows behind him, holding a dagger to his throat.

'What do you seek here stranger?' she demanded. The Magician hid his shock at the sudden threat well, by going limp in her grip.

'Easy now friend, my name is Ragnor ...I have

answered Delanichi's call for aid, but I see I am already too late.' Tress lowered the dagger,

'Well I wouldn't say that, you are just in time to help me dispel this shield.' She extended her hand politely,

'Tress, pleased to meet you.' He looked down at her extended hand with a wrinkled nose and gave a limp handshake just to get rid of the extended hand. She quickly highlighted the weak points that she had already discovered and explained what she had already tried against the protective barrier.

'Hmm, how strange - that should have worked, lets try it again.' Ragnor agreed. His skills in magic far surpassed her own, yet were less specialised to this purpose. He was the last of Tamar's agents skilled in magic. She attempted the dispelling of the barrier once again, chanting the magical words as he observed. Annoyingly, when she was done the barrier still remained; Ragnor scratched his head.

'What is wrong? As I said before, it should have worked? Delanichi always was a tricky one – how could he have devised such an unbreakable barrier?' The screams of the dying outside reminded Tress of the time-critical situation, she moved to the window and could see a group of soldiers had broken through one of the barriers drawn across the road into the town. General Onus led the reserve detachment to meet the men, pushing the Aristrians backwards during the fray.

'Come on Ragnor, think – its getting messy out there.' Her pitch was raised adding to their stress. He spoke to himself working out the possibilities,

'How do you make the impossible, possible? You can't.'

'You just make it seem impossible,' added Tress, then they both jumped, breaking their concentration as a sudden thunderbolt exploded into the barricade outside, the Brotherhood was closing in.

'Exactly,' Ragnor responded after a moment of

thought,

'Ah, I think I understand it now. If we could say one thing of our departed friend, it would be that he was always full of tricks. Would you not agree? You see the barrier is not real at all – it is an illusion. We are wasting our efforts trying to dispel the shield when none is actually there. All we needed to do was this.' He chanted three words several times then walked into the room. Tress smiled, she was beginning to understand why Tamar had always referred to him as 'The Trickster'. Ragnor recovered the book as Tress replaced her sword with an old friend, she held the Sabre of Sum up to the light beholding its impressive blade,

'I think you should take the other sword Ragnor, you may be able to use its powers to your advantage?' He shook his head,

'I doubt that, but I will attempt to find a place for it – swords are for using,' he frowned back.

'Now what?' she asked as another clap of thunder rattled the windows, followed by the screams of the dying outside.

'I guess we fight,' stated Ragnor.

'I think that is folly, we may need to spill some blood to get out of this place, but I can tell you now, we should run and find a better time to fight, the odds are against us here.'

Algar stood well back from his men and watched his troops push into the town; he had no stomach for the hand to hand fighting today and the army was doing well enough with out the use of his skill. Lord Banok did not share his same reserve; he was in the thick of the fighting leaving a trail of bodies as he led his men deeper through the streets. The Tanarian army had ceased their fruitless attempts to staunch the flood of men pouring in between the town houses; instead they carried out a fighting retreat backwards towards the river, all other routes were cut off to them, as an Aristrian semi-circle surrounded the town. Once they reached the fast flowing river that backed onto the town they would be trapped and the real slaughter would begin. They all knew that the Aristrians would not accept any terms of surrender today. Two members of the Brotherhood rounded the corner of a large town house, a position where they would have a clear line of sight on the riverbank, a position where they could rain death down upon the defenders for some time. A squad of Aristrian infantry ran past the two men to chase down some stragglers. The swirl of a cloak and the flash of a sabre left one of the Brotherhood magicians headless, in less than a breath Tress had skewered the second man to the door behind; with her face pressed close to the man's dark hood she whispered,

'You have cast your last spell you motherless scum, now release your last breath.' She twisted her blade upwards and cut deep into his diaphragm as she withdrew the steel. Several more Aristrian soldiers rounded the corner almost running into her in their eagerness to pursue the Tanarians. She sidestepped the first man, slamming the hilt of her sabre into the second man's face; he went down as if pole-axed and she swung about in the space she had just created to deal with the others. The three following men attempted to engage her making the mistake of thinking the woman easy prey, but she read their body movements with an ease that only years with the Su-Katii could bring. She parried the leading strike to her head, swinging her body around with her arcing blade to slam her elbow into the man's throat, the soldier clutched at his throat as he dropped to his knees fighting for breath through his broken neck. The soldiers were shocked at her competence but quick to react. She intercepted the second strikes from the other two men; then with a sword kata technique she swept her blade about her body in a figure of eight motion, delivering death to both men. She shook the blood from her blade as the first man, who had already passed her in his hurry, turned about in shock to see his companions slain. It was the first time she had needed to fight since leaving the Rift, but Tress had used the skills taught by Renademus to good effect. She thrust forward with a double stab at the final soldier and the man fell backwards onto the floor in an attempt to avoid her blade. She kept on coming and he raised his sword in defence attempting to block, with a sweep of her sword Sum cut through the man's defending blade, shearing it in two and continuing on to embed itself deep in the man's head. He went limp and she pulled free her sabre, then with the patter of fresh feet approaching she turned tail and ran back towards the massed Tanarians who had reformed a shield wall along the banks of the river for their final stand. Masses of enemy solders funnelled in and crammed the streets leading to the river as far as the eye could see. Lord Banok caught his breath long enough to smile after he dispatched a boy of no more than fourteen who had taken a wrong turn towards him as he fled through the town. He had been unsure if the brat had been in the army or just a civilian, what did it matter – it was one less piece of vermin to roam the streets. He looked on at their reformed ranks along the river; realising that he had the enemy exactly where he wanted them. Oh well, at least the Tanarians had the pride to continue the fight, rather than beg for their lives.

'Now Ragnor, now.' Ragnor stood on the far bank of the river chanting a powerful spell as Tress gave him the signal. The magician knelt down and placed his hands into the icy cold water,

'I call upon the icy wastes of Nordheim to freeze over this water,' he bellowed out his words with an unnatural voice that carried over the clatter of battle. Ice formed about his hand and accelerated by his magic it rapidly spread out across the expanse of water. Even with the strong current surging through the water the ice creaked and groaned as it expanded across to the far bank reaching the Tanarian defenders. Tress did not stop her returning sprint at the Tanarian shield wall and continued to rush right past the men and skidded onto the ice.

'Come on, this way, follow me - the ice will hold …escape now or you will fall.' She did not look back to see the thousands of men follow her. With the leading Brotherhood Magicians slain, and the others stuck in the crush of men filling the streets of the town, the best part of the Tanarian army was across the river and away before they were in a position to do anything. After several acolytes arrived through the press of the army they shouted out, stopping the Aristrian soldiers from following.

'Hold fast men! If you follow, your bloated bodies will be pulled from the shores, the spell can be reversed quick enough to see you all drowned. *Hold fast I say.*' Only a handful of men were stupid enough to disregard their words. They were quickly pulled under the surface, deep into the icy cold waters when Ragnor dispelled his magic with the passing of the last Tanarians. He turned to Tress with a victorious grin across his face,

'You were right Tress, there is some measure in running after all, but we must be quick. To stand any chance, we must head north to the nearest forests and mountain ranges, we will stand a better chance in a harsher terrain, than out on the open steps, perhaps I can then better use the elements to protect us.' She nodded,

'I think the fact that we have found a magician will halt their advance alone, or at least make them think twice about following.' Ragnor turned back around to face the town, chanted several more words of power, then he followed the departing army. At first nothing appeared to happen, but then as the breeze picked up it blew into a violent gale that swept across the town and a great thunder clap shuddered through the sky. The wind grew stronger and colder and soon turned to hailstones. The conquerors of Ubecka took to the houses for cover as the great storm broke about them. Ragnor's magic had the desired effect, forcing the army to seek shelter. They would ride out the storm; then destroy the remaining Tanarians at their leisure for there certainly was no escape for them now; the only direction in which they could flee was into Aristria.

After several hours of forced march, the weary and fleeing army came to a halt. They needed to reorganise in better order – lick their wounds and deploy their scouts rather than just running away in a disorganised rabble, they needed to put as much ground between them and the town as possible but if they were hit as they moved like this it would be devastating. The Brotherhood would be less eager to use their magic to travel ahead of the Tanarians to set an ambush, now that they knew a magician was once again amongst them. What Ragnor found difficult to explain to the remaining Generals as they reorganised was, that his magic was not particularly tailored for offensive means. He had explained his abilities well to the group of men, his training in magic could only harness the powers of nature, but the Generals were very bad listeners. However, Ragnor was inventive and if his life hung in the balance he would find a way to focus his energy to some more practical means. General Larks stood impatiently waiting for the others; General Onus was helped to their brief meeting by a procession of soldiers. He was a large round man and was not easy to assist; he had been wounded in the battle and he needed three men to help him.

'Damn buggers seem to have got lucky today,' grumbled Onus as he pressed a bandage to his left eye, he also had secondary wounds to his shoulder and leg where he had barged himself through a group of Aristrians like a raging bull. Blood was still trickling down from his damaged shoulder-guard but none of the wounds were fatal.

'But I'm still standing,' the soldier supporting him rolled his eyes as his strong arms strained to hold his weight. Onus bellowed out his words with bravado,

'How typical of the Aristrians; failing to do a job properly,' General Larks nodded in way of a greeting and approval of his words,

'Where is Dellneck? Someone get him,' said Larks. Tress shook her head,

'That won't be necessary; he fell, back in the town. He was fighting with the rearguard action when the Brotherhood singled him out. I was trying to get to him …but I was too late.' She paused for a moment before finishing her words,

'I made them pay for it.' She said in little more than a whisper.

'He was a good man,' said Larks, more because it sounded the right thing to say rather then his true opinion of the man, it was one less rival for his command of the army. Onus staggered and lost his footing, but the men with him caught him.

'Take care of him,' commented General Larks. Tress touched his shoulder lightly,

'Well General; it looks like you have your wish at last, you now have the command of the army. At least, what's left of it,' she added. He took offence at her words,

'I never wanted it like this,' he said with a sigh. Ragnor who had remained silent during their initial exchange abruptly stated,

'Well, you are now and that's that. You have a big task before you and every leader needs to be more than just a man, you will need a symbol, something to give the men hope in these dark moments. I think you will need the sword. He produced the sword from a wrapped bundle that he carried and offered the unveiled great sword Thulnir, hilt first to the General.

'Please, take it. It should be in a warrior's hands.' Larks eyes almost popped out of their sockets as its steel glistened with an unnatural blue flicker.

'It is no ordinary blade,' stated Ragnor, 'It is magic.'

'No shit,' Larks snapped back, 'Sorry, forgive my manners, I am just a little taken back by today's events and such an impressive gift.' he said as he inspected the blade. It was as light as a dagger and its craftsmanship promised that it carried an edge to match. 'I ...I would be honoured to accept your gift,' said the General, for once struggling for words. As Tress watched the scene she thought to herself how it was often the undeserving ones that made it in life and holding to that thought she turned to the General and cleared both her throat and her thoughts,

'Well, go on then man. Show off the sword to the troops and announce your leadership, they need to know that they still have a leader alive, go inspire them. Then when you are done we need to get moving again.'

Chapter 9 – Back Into the Red

Cardus was completely still and quiet, as was normal in the middle of the night on the island. The moon reflected its light gaze from the surrounding sea and lapping shores whilst the inhabitants of the small town lay asleep in their beds. Zerch's Portal broke the peaceful serenity of the island, illuminating the sky well away from the town. In the ground around the grand amber pillars of the God-King's Rift, the new Portal threw fresh flickers of light from the sheer cliff-face behind. The night sky suddenly returned to the duller light emitted by the constant glow of the Vortex that had marked the path into the Su-Katii temple of war for untold generations. Several figures emerged, having spanned many leagues in fleeting seconds - Titus, Garth, Zerch and finally Athene, stepped through the transport Portal and into a swarm of moths that had gathered during the night and constantly swarmed about the ambient light of the Vortex. They quickly batted aside the little pests and the transport Portal shut abruptly after Athene passed through. They were met with the occasional fizz as the humming creatures ventured too close to the Vortex's dispersing energies. The air surrounding the entrance had the distinct whiff of a crispy critter as its magic destroyed anything smaller than a man's fist. Myridin's magic had indeed been constructed with the most intricate design. Before the group had departed for Hadrak they had created a Portal for Barrad to pass on to his army, well as close to it as Zerch's magic would allow. He was a fit fellow and should catch up with them soon enough. They had then moved on, stopping off en-route at a small Aristrian farmstead. It was a remote lot, far from the gaze of the military and the war, and was deemed a safe place to leave Athene's mother. Zerch had several safe-houses that he used and had reassured them that the family that owned this lot were amongst the most pleasant he knew. They left Sasha here to regain her strength with a simple farming family who were for some untold reason in his service, the elderly couple who owned the place were hardly menacing, the grey haired man had a stump of a right hand and his wife a friendly smile and kind eyes. Athene had been hostile to the idea of leaving her mother again, but she knew deep down, given where they were heading next, that Sasha would be better off kept well away from the danger they were about to face. During their brief meeting Athene thought that the couple seemed honest enough folk and more importantly, impartial to the ongoing war. It was not to say that she didn't have any concerns about leaving her mother in the lands of the enemy, but in this mixed-up world it had actually seemed like the best choice. Besides there was no way that she wanted her mother to witness the devastation that may follow their venture into the Rift. All this time Titus had been like an over-eager child who kept on pushing them to get going or hurry up. It was obvious that he wanted to get on with it and as soon as they had arrived in Cardus he had started herding everyone towards the amber pillars. Since his freedom from being imprisoned in this very Rift, he had dreamt of little else other than destroying the god within. Hadrak had stolen everything from him, from his position in the Order to his life with his wife, absolutely everything. Athene had considered before that he just needed to let the past go, but now with Zerch's plan it had brought it all bobbing back to the surface. Until he met Athene and witnessed first hand her effect on magic he had thought the dream of Hadrak's destruction impossible, but now he would find out. Titus had initially saved her from the clutches of the Brotherhood to fulfil his lust for revenge, yet she had quenched his desires in other ways. With every day that she stayed with him she reminded him a little more of his long past wife and the sensations of what it was like to live.

A more cautious Zerch attempted to slow down the rushed events and double-check that everything was ready. The Su-Katii had waited several years since his freedom from the Rift, a little longer would not hurt.

'Hold on a moment Titus, slow down, let's just check that everything is ready,' Zerch insisted.

Titus continued up to the Rift's entrance regardless of the magician's words, almost frog-marching Athene up to the entrance,

'What is there to check Wizard? We go in, grab his Lordship and drag him out to his long-awaited freedom then give him a grand send off. I have my swords, nets, rope and a bucket full of hatred to deliver.' Zerch rolled his eyes at the impatience of the man.

'I was thinking more about going over our course of action in the event that Hadrak cannot be killed. Perhaps we will need to coordinate how we should force him back into the Rift?' Titus ignored the magician and leapt into the Vortex dragging Athene in behind him. Zerch rolled his eyes once again,

'Who's the fool Garth, him for rushing in, or me for freeing him? Come on, let's be after him,' Zerch and his Swordmaster rushed in after them for they knew that any delay could present a significant difference to their arrival time inside the Rift.

The unusual vibration that filled the air in the proximity of the Rift's entrance soon disappeared on Athene's arrival and the air almost seemed to thin to breath around her presence. Titus knew this place well and wondered if it had been undisturbed since his last visit weeks before? On that visit he had been unable to kill Hadrak in his own domain, yet he had done the next best thing. Today with Athene at his side he was sure he would have his revenge. He ran forward with burning anticipation of what may await him at the large structure that lurked before them, leaving Athene lagging behind. Running through the gate's arch and into the training court like an excited child he ignored the great pools of dry blood and drag marks that stretched across its paving slabs, he knew exactly how each one of those blood stains had marked the floor and smiled to himself contently as he remembered that battle. He halted in the centre of the courtyard accessing the architecture of the grand building before him.

Athene took her time wandering in, taking in the sights of the Temple in awe but surprised that Titus should stop to view such sites; he had never been one to appreciate such things. Catching up with Titus she beheld the ghastly scenes of dried gore about them and almost bumped into him as she took in the gruesome marks. Her hand held tightly to his shoulder as she steadied herself, the simple action would have seemed so right a few weeks ago, but now it felt so wrong – it could have been the shoulder of a stranger, she retracted her hand and then instantly regretted it. She realised that it was not the buildings that he stood admiring. Her gaze followed Titus's amused stare up to the building before them.

He broke into a fit of laughter before he called out to the golden haired figure that hung from the open window by his feet. He dangled at the end of around ten yards of rope, attached by his ankles and trussed up with a degree of expertise like a pig bound for market. To top it all off, the man had a rather uncomfortable looking gag lodged in his mouth. His eyes bulged and he twitched and struggled against his tight bindings. Titus had been unable to slay Hadrak on his last visit into the Rift, the mystical powers that held the god had rendered the feat impossible - so he had done the next best thing he could to torment him, he had tied him up and left him in the most awkward position possible. He had hung there upside down suspended from the window for over two weeks by the time of the outside world; inside the Rift however, that time had translated into a lingering punishment to the god. Was it months or years that he had hung like a lump of ageing meat? He could not tell, he only knew that as the time had passed his body had all but numbed to the initial agony of his suspended position and he was none to pleased to see Titus of all people smirking back up at him again. Titus continued to enjoy mocking the dangling god,

'Ah Hadrak, it is so good to see you hanging around these parts. It would seem that even the folk of Cardus can not be bothered with you any more. What does it feel like to be so insignificant these days? Although I must admit that I had expected some fool to have wandered by and set you free by now, but it cheers me up all the more to see you are still exactly where I left you. But fear not my lord, I will have you cut down from there in a jiffy,' he said with a tone of mock concern. Athene could not help but feel pity for the hanging man. She knew that this so-called god had caused Titus to miss out on the better years of his life with his wife and children whilst he lingered inside the Rift, suspended in the limbo of his death as Hadrak's prisoner. Athene listened to his cold mocking tones and wondered if Titus's wife had actually just had a lucky escape, or if these were actually deserving words from the harsh mouthed warrior. She watched his confident stance and posture and for a moment her imagination placed her as his wife and with empathy she tried to picture what she may have thought of this event, in a fleeting second her thoughts drifted off to other wifely duties and she began to imagine herself beneath him once again; she had found him to be most attentive and a skilled lover - it was not a thought that she wanted to push quickly from her mind although she knew she should. It was as if he was two men in the same body, one tender and gentle when in her arms, the other nothing more than a maverick predator. She began to wonder if it was just her, perhaps she wanted too much from the man? Had he really had a thing for Tress or was it her over-paranoid imagination, the lines had become blurred but she had to believe her eyes. She had seen them kiss, but perhaps it was just a kiss and nothing more? He certainly was not with her now. She ran out of time to contemplate her feelings as the rest of their party arrived through the Rift. Titus darted into the building and moments later reappeared at the window that held Hadrak, slicing at the supporting rope, he cut the god free, allowing his body to unceremoniously drop two floors onto the stone slabs below. With a muffled and gagged cry he bounced from the floor, but on later inspection appeared unhurt from the drop that would have killed any normal man. When Titus returned they discussed what needed to be done as Hadrak looked up at them with large apprehensive eyes, like a baby seal pup awaiting its slaughter.

'Lets just drag him out as he is, then if he passes the Rift we can just slit his throat,' suggested Zerch. The two warriors nodded slowly in agreement, but Zerch could tell in their eyes that the taste of a simple slaughter had not been their initial intent.

'Come on then, move it – When we get close to the Rift, move nice and close in to us Athene.' Zerch started to organise the men to drag Hadrak through the Rift, but he did not include himself in any part of the physical work. Many hands made light work and Hadrak was soon approaching the swirling mass of the Rift. He had expected the familiar crash as he struck the magical barrier of the entranceway; he had felt the sensation of being repulsed from it a thousand times before. But this time as he was dragged forwards through it, the red colouration of the surrounding dome faded and became almost translucent as Athene neared its edge. A flash of light struck his eyes as he passed through the Rift, back into the long-forgotten world beyond. For a second he could not believe his eyes, for the first time in millennia, the old stars of the night's sky sparkled down at him. It was a wondrous sight, one that he would have liked to enjoy longer. Zerch stood above him triumphantly; his plans could not have gone better if he tried. There was but one task left to complete this night.

'Right then, here we are at last ...which one of you lucky boys wants to have the pleasure of the kill?' Zerch asked knowing full well that Titus was his man. From their earlier attitude he was only mildly surprised when they failed to jump to volunteer, although he had hoped that Titus might surprise him. These warriors were all the same, they would battle each other all day until the cows came home, but set them a simple task of plunging a dagger into a helpless man's throat and they cowered away like milkmaids. He had learnt this lesson before with Garth and like that day he was prepared to get his own hands dirty. His previous words had been nothing more than a courtesy. Zerch withdrew his long belt knife,

'No takers?' Titus stopped him, raising his finger,

'Hold fast a moment Wizard, this is not right. It is true that I came here to slay this god or man or whatever he may be now. But I came here for the fight of my life, not to slaughter him like a beast. I owe Hadrak nothing but my hatred for wasting the best years of my life; he removed my family from me and destroyed old friendships.' Hadrak began to make a noise in protest against his tight gage, Titus cuffed him one across the back of his head restoring his silence before continuing his rant. 'Worst of all, it pains me to admit it but there is still a fragment of the old code in me, I may have to admittedly dig deep to find it – but I know it is there.' Titus paused for a moment wondering if he would regret his next words.

'There is no honour in slitting his throat; I'm afraid it

simply would not quench my thirst for revenge.' Zerch shook his head as if in pain,

'No, you are right, there is no honour – but it must be done all the same. I thought you had abandoned the concept of honour Titus? I will never understand your kind. But your revenge – now that's a motive I can understand.' Zerch stepped forwards raising his dagger as if they had not just had their conversation. Titus's swords were unleashed and at the magicians throat before he could blink. Zerch was impressed with the man's speed, he thought to himself that with such an impressive display of agility honed over the years in the Rift merely to draw a weapon from its sheath, perhaps Barrad had been a fool to believe the story he had fed him about using his magic to expand his opponent's blades causing them to get stuck in their scabbards. He was easily misled to aid his belief in Zerch, he should have had more faith in his own ability, he had to face it – the kid was just too damned quick for his opponent, yet he had seen the doubt in his mind from this encounter with Thulsa and used it to bring him onboard and, more importantly, Athene. He had then been all to eager to believe his words and Zerch had sent him packing on his merry way well away from his affairs, back to an impossible war in which he would probably die.

'Do not think about casting any spells wizard. Remember, Athene stands so close, your breath would be wasted.' Zerch lowered the knife with disappointment, he could wait, besides it was unimportant to him if Hadrak died tied up or fighting – just as long as he died. He had noticed that Garth, his supposed Swordmaster and bodyguard, had made no reaction to counter Titus's move. Perhaps he should have stayed in the Temple a little longer? Zerch knew better than to make any rash move alone. The simple fact was that each warrior knew that should the other make any sudden movements it could be taken as an indication to fight and would start a bloodbath. Titus had just made the wise choice to free his weapons first.

'Well Titus, what do you propose we do now then?' Zerch asked through the mounting tension. Titus looked the Magician in the eye, allowing Garth to stay in his peripheral vision; he had judged in a split second that he would not make a move against Athene, it was not in the warrior's temperament and besides they needed her to deal with Soredamor, any move to slay her would clearly be a bluff.

Athene felt the tension between the men and didn't know which way too turn. Titus spoke up first,

'Well it would appear that we are all of split purpose here, I will lay my cards on the table before this goes too far. I seek only revenge here, but I will not kill him in cold blood, release him and we will fight and one of us will have the death that a Su-Katii deserves.' Garth spoke for the first time, until now he had only listened. He knew well that he was a more than competent swordsman, but in such company he needed to tread carefully.

'Now that would be a fight that I would like to see and a suitable end for any warrior. I say fight; if Hadrak wins he will also win his freedom. He knew that his master would only see the god dead if not now, later – but he had not been lying when he said that he would like to watch the fight. Garth and Zerch also realised that if Hadrak could slay Titus it would be likely that Garth would fall to his blade as well, but in agreeing to his freedom it would stop Hadrak immediately turning on them should he win. They would pick the right time to break their deal and use magic to slay him. Zerch announced to them all,

'It is agreed then, you have my word – Kill Titus and you will be set free,' he almost wanted Hadrak to win; Titus had been nothing but annoying from the start and had got under Zerch's skin. Athene moved forwards to

Hadrak, she was the only one who could move freely without threat. She reached down and tugged free Hadrak's gag and reached for her water skin, pouring a little into his mouth.

'Lets see what he has to say on the matter' Hadrak moved his mouth with no sound coming from his parched lips, he swallowed again, building up the moisture in his dry throat before he spoke with a harsh and croaking tone,

'Oh I'll fight you, I'm not afraid of you Titus. I am after all an honourable man myself …after I have killed this upstart and am released - I can assure you …my Su-Katii will get what's coming to them also.' Titus quickly replied wanting the last word,

'As will you. Now listen, this is what will happen, I will cut you free Hadrak,' Zerch's eyes narrowed with anger. Titus continued,

'You will then have until sunrise to stretch your limbs and prepare for our combat; you see I am already turning over a new leaf and have developed some compassion, I will grant you this final kindness to see your last sunrise. Garth you will retrieve Hadrak's blade from the Rift, I would hate to kill him without his own blade to hand, I want no excuses as to your defeat.' Hadrak went to speak, but Titus shouted over his words as well,

'These are my terms, if I hear your voice again before sunrise I will just slaughter you where you stand, just nod if you agree to this …*good*,' he spat out the last word. Hadrak nodded, as did Garth. Zerch carefully considered Titus's words, was he just getting rid of Garth to strike at him? No, this Su-Katii could not think one step ahead as he could, he just acted, but perhaps things would not work out as badly as he had initially thought.

He sheathed his knife and backed off. Athene proceeded to cut free Hadrak's bonds. Silently and for a change, she had been pleased with Titus's insistence to fight, rather than just kill. To her it seemed right and fitting. Perhaps there were more dimensions to this Su-Katii than she had earlier thought.

Chapter 10 – Just another Wall

A thick mist floated out from behind the Aristrian wall that hemmed in the ancient Keep of Tagel and covered the surrounding grounds. The pale mist moved unnaturally against the sea breeze and all who stood on the wall watching it knew that it marked only one thing; the battle for Tagel had begun. Telimus and his two fellow Brotherhood Masters stood with linked hands, chanting their magic inside the confines of their tent which boarded the northern Aristrian wall. They had travelled down country at the request of Lord Aden, the acting commander of the Su-Katii. He had demanded the finest magical support to complement his assault on Tagel and once the magicians had arrived, the battle had begun. Telimus did not like splitting his forces one bit; although he considered the bulk of the men that he had left behind at Ubecka both weak and incompetent. Yes they thought themselves mighty and able to confront anyone or anything with their magic, but he knew better – still they would be more than enough to deal with mere soldiers. He had accessed each man many times over their careers and had decided to keep the strongest closest to him. Even worse, that fool Kerric was roaming around the countryside doing his own thing as usual, he worried that with the separation from his men, Kerric may attempt to gain their favour and further cement a claim to leading the Brotherhood; it was another reason to keep the strongest of his order close. The struggle for the leadership of the Brotherhood of Keth was a complex issue, but from their long history in meddling with the affairs of men one fact had always remained, gaining a grand victory had always counted for a lot; power was always linked to victory and no one had ever taken the leadership with out some kind of grand achievement. Telimus was aiming for the largest prize of all - Tagel. Of all the Masters, the Su-Katii commander Lord Aden had come only to Telimus himself and asked for support, not approach that weed Kerric, if the Su-Katii leader saw him as the head of their Order then so would the others. The move only cemented his claim. Aden had demanded a magical mist be summoned to conceal the advance of his men across the long killing fields that the defenders had cut back to better facilitate their archers. He had sent in his arrow fodder first, to probe the grounds for any nasty surprises, but then followed them up with a regiment of his heavy infantry, experienced men that could capitalise on an opportunity should they breach the first wall or men that could withdraw with discipline should their first attack fail. Aden was an accomplished General and he did not underestimate how well the Tanarians were prepared for them. They had had months to prepare for this day, so today his goal was a realistic one, just one wall was his hope and expectation. Besides there was another wall after this one before they could even reach the old stone wall of the town and if they breached that there were the reputed impregnable walls and causeway of the unconquered Keep to deal with. They would take small steps and peel them back each day like an onion except hopefully without the tears, well at least not for them. Aden knew the reality of a siege and that with each wall he seized the defenders would be compressed inwards in an ever-decreasing circle, meaning that each wall would be harder to take than the last. But for today he would settle very happily for just the one wall. He also knew that these statistics were based upon conventional warfare where one side did not command the might of three Brotherhood spell masters. The defending Tanarians had no magicians amongst their number, just the holy men from the chapel. Their small order knew nothing more than several prayers for good winds and returning fishermen rather than the kind of true magic that the Brotherhood possessed. However commander Mallet recognised the prelude to an assault when he saw one and deployed the army to a full state of readiness as the unusual mist began to form. Men, women and even children of the town strained to listen for sounds of approaching men across the three hundred yard flatland that surrounded their first wall. The civilians had been formed into squads of militia five hundred strong and after several months of hardship and practice they were now quite proficient with the bow. They had been trained to fire volleys as one, rather than being individually accurate. Mixed with the combat troops of the first wall were several units of regulars from the Tagel garrison. These men carried the traditional longbows that could bring down a man at over two hundred yards and each man carried a long-sword for the close-in work. Everyone strained, staring into the thick white cloud that enveloped them, listening for any sound that would betray the enemy advance as the mist thickened about their walls. They were not to know that the magical mist also dampened sound as well as sight, the Brotherhood hoped that their ignorance would be their undoing. A group of nervous women huddled to the rear of the massed archers behind the wall had drawn back their arrows in preparation; they had been gossiping and had missed the order to relax their drawn bows. Their fingers strained as they held back the taut strings. One of the ladies' hands shook with the strain and the arrow was released early, the others around her misinterpreted the action and followed her lead and soon the first slightly premature release of over five hundred arrows took flight. The front rank of the Aristrian skirmishers had only a hundred yards left to go before they reached the first wall and then the arrows fell, they had been advancing cautiously avoiding several spike pits as they advanced; but now as the arrows fell they threw caution to the wind and ran for the wall. The ground in front of the Tanarian wall echoed with the unexpected sound of dying men. The magical mist muffled the sounds and clatter of their approach, but the gut-wrenching screams of an arrow thudding into a man's groin was enough to penetrate any mist. The officer commanding the archers was about to issue a bollocking for wasting ammunition and firing before ordered, but on hearing the scream beyond the wall his words quickly changed into the shouted commands for rapid fire; those screams were far to near to the wall for comfort. The first wall was no more than five foot tall, yet it sat on top of a rampart giving it extra height. It could have been constructed higher, but this height was planned, it placed the attackers' heads level with their sword swings and also tempted more of the attackers to expose themselves by attempting the climb over the wall, rather than waiting to scale it with ladders from which they could strike or parry as they advanced. The longbow men lining the wall followed suit and let loose into the whiteness that surrounded them, seconds later the wave of Aristrian skirmishers reached the wall, they emerged from the white with murder in their eyes. They were lightly armed with spears and hand axes that were better suited for striking upwards at an opponent. They wore only light armour, reinforced cloth and few carried shields. They were the people of the border regions, an auxiliary to the main force and Lord Aden had decided them best suited for the first wave. Had they reached the wall concealed in the mist their numbers would have been much greater, however the unexpected volley had taken its toll on the lightly armoured troops. Yet they were proud men who had gladly accepted the honour of leading the battle and their fallen comrades would soon be avenged. The rhythmic patter of feet followed their rabble as the heavy infantry followed at double time, with their large shields raised against the threat of falling arrows they dashed for the wall. Men scrambled up the rampart through the hail of arrows that rained down upon them, many did not make the climb and tumbled backwards as the deadly longbow arrows ripped through them. Alwin and his brothers had volunteered for the auxiliary in the early days of the war; they had grown up in the farming regions that bordered the great Uphrian forests. They had seen the war as an opportunity to get away from the generations of boredom working the fields and joined on mass. A chance to earn some serious coin, and besides nearly every man of eligible age (and some younger) had signed up. They all had dreams of joining the Aristrian heavy infantry together. Who didn't? They were the cream of the army and he had heard that they got better rations and more coin – but in their attempts to enlist the reality was that only proven veterans were permitted into their ranks and the rabble of country bumpkins were sent away from the garrison to the sound of laughter. His next hope had been to join the cavalry, as, after growing up on a farm, he could ride well, but they had also been somewhat selective to a man's breeding. Apparently you needed a letter of recommendation or be of good standing in credit to make their ranks. Being little more than a peasant in the eyes of the state, this door was also closed to him. It had seemed a lot more difficult to pledge his service to the state than he had first thought. But thankfully after much searching, the open arms of the Aristrian auxiliary were always open to him and his brothers. They were actually open to anyone else for that matter and he had met with a variety of colourful characters during his brief training and subsequent deployment to Tanaria. Why, there was Umber the desecrator of women, he was a true pleasure to engage in conversation, Rinc, the street brawler – better not to annoy him, and Tolan, the tax dodger and general fraudster – never play this man at dice or lend him money. Yet he had saved the best to last. Of all the characters he had met in the auxiliary, Garr the bully and sodomiser of young recruits was held with the deepest of disregard. He should be too, for it was he who had smashed his face repetitively against a tree trunk when he had refused his demands to share his tent. Better to carry a scar on his face than a shameful memory for the rest of his life. Unfortunately as an unofficial punishment for the accusations made against his fellow recruits his vocal brothers had been moved away to other units and once Alwin realised that he was on his own he soon began to understand how the army really worked and quickly learned to stay quiet. Alwin slipped on the muddy bank as an arrow whistled past him where his head had been seconds before, a scream came from his left as the arrow impacted into another man's thigh. Alwin was discovering that a massed battle was a totally confusing and random entity, it moved like a raging fire blowing past some and scorching others. Several men ran past him and leapt at the wall, trying to scale it with one leap, their split heads and broken bodies quickly fell back to its base. He caught sign of movement as a head peeked up over the wall, with a knee-jerk reaction to the sight he threw his spear up at the small target, he heard the clang of metal as the spear flew true and impacted with the helmeted figure and a space appeared on the wall. He pulled out his hand axe and threw it into the wall at leg height, then grabbing two similar axes from the fallen men about him. Alwin chopped the second axe into the wood higher up than the first. He had made his own ladder to climb as he noticed several proper ladders being shoved to the wall on either side of his own improvised one. He gave a quick prayer to his god and climbed the ladder of axes, quickly shimmying up and over the top to gain the wall. He found his section relatively empty, the bulk of the defenders had moved further down to push back the ladders to his sides, only one archer stood nearby, unfortunately for him he had just fired off his drawn arrow, the mans eyes budged with sudden fear at

Alwin's unexpected appearance. Alwin was surprised with the encounter; he had never thought his scrawny appearance could ever evoke such terror in another man's eyes. He was of a small frame, spindly but strong and he dashed forwards and struck the man about the head with his axe as his opponent fumbled to drop his bow and went for his sword. He grabbed a nearby torch that still burned from one of the defenders' night watch positions and advanced on the remaining Tanarians protecting the ramparts, driving the enemy away from the nearest ladders. A Tanarian soldier turned from beating back the men on the wall noticing Alwin at the last moment, he shoved the burning flame into a Tanarian soldier's helmeted face then struck another behind him with his axe. Garr climbed up the ladder and patted his shoulder,

'Thanks, Little Elm, I've got your back,' said Garr with a wink. Garr had named him in jest after the tree that he had repetitively smashed his face against following their disagreement, a name that had soon stuck around the camp. Rinc and Umber followed them up as they fought off the counter attack that attempted to halt the breach of the wall. The fighting became brutal and bloody as Rinc gutted a man who approached them from the opposite side. He had no room to move as several more men pressed down on him, he smashed his axe handle several times into the first man's face until it left just a bloody mess, then grabbing him in a headlock, he used the man's body as a human shield to fend off the multiple attackers. Alwin was soon at his side as the others did indeed guard their backs, then back to back they fended off another wave of attackers that came at them from along the boardwalks. Alwin saw nothing but red as he tasted the blood lust of battle, without regard for his own safety, he advanced into the enemy unleashing death and pushing the fearful men back. They were nevertheless relieved to see the sparkle of plate armour and the blue crests from the first wave of the heavy infantry to reach the wall and ascend the ladders. Alwin jumped backwards exhausted, and rested behind the forming shield-wall of the infantry that rushed on to the rampart, his cloth armour was now soaked red with the mingled blood of his enemies and his own. The Tanarians had clearly lost the wall and were now fleeing backwards to their second wall,

'We've done it, lads …we've taken the bloody wall,' Rinc cheered. Even with the clearing mist the sky suddenly darkened as the fleeing Tanarians let loose their final volley to cover their retreat. Arrows impacted all around them as they scrambled for the close cover of the heavy infantry who had moved with a well-trained motion into a protective formation of shields. As they waited for the hissing of the arrows to stop, Alwin noticed the body of Umber on the floor, the several arrows which jutted from his neck and torso confirmed that he was far beyond help. Alwin thought it strange that back in the camp he would not have given this man a second thought, yet now as he looked at his broken body he shed a small tear for the man. The first wall had been won, but at a price.

'Consolidate and hold? What are you thinking sir? Forgive my opinion my Lord, but surely we should be pushing forward and seizing the opportunity,' protested General Tolace of the Aristrian regular army. Lord Aden disliked his attitude, but let his comments go – he was in a particularly good mood. Day one and his objective had been met. The losses to the auxiliary skirmishers had been high, but acceptable, and at one stage it looked as though his plan had almost failed, but one tenacious group had managed to successfully take a section of the wall and hold it long enough for the big boys to get there. He did not want to fully commit his forces yet, for he suspected that the enemy may have a magician up their sleeves; how else had they known to fire into his hidden troops crossing the mist? Telimus had assured him that they had no such resources but the Su-Katii General knew that surprise was often the best weapon; he would wait and consolidate his position on the wall whist the Brotherhood searched for their Wizard. Besides, by delaying the second assault it gave them more time to fortify their position on the first wall and move up their equipment for the next push. As a side effect, it also gave him more time to enjoy and savour this war. Such events did not come along often. They started immediately with his plans and moved their battle camp up to the first Tanarian wall. It was so kind of the enemy to provide them with a new wall to tighten the noose and protect them from the harsh sea breezes that could suddenly blow so hard that the camp fires were almost extinguished or fend of the hazard of flying hot ashes scattered through the camp. Out on the open ground of their old camp, the sudden high winds had presented a considerable fire hazard. He was about to dismiss the General, but before he did he commanded him to present the men that had held the wall today. He would set an example to his army that bravery is expected but will also be rewarded. He would present them each with a finely crafted sword and some coin. Yes, that was it he thought, he would present a sword to the victors of each wall. The next ones would be harder to earn, but the 'Champion of the Wall,' would become a sought after title.

Chapter 11 – Senseless

Corvus had moved through the Uphrian forest at speed for days, well, with as much speed as he could muster. It was not endurance that he lacked, just a poor path selection and an unnatural attraction for every kind of sticky or spiky plant in the forest. He rolled his eyes and tutted out loud as his foot caught on yet another vine-like plant. As usual he just ploughed on through the entanglement of the great forest; the vine unravelled and snared itself on other branches as he carried on, unwilling to stop, and soon it was caught on several smaller trees until the long trail eventually jarred and tripped him. He sat there huffing; perhaps he should have taken a guide instead of storming off as he did. He was used to moving through forests with a little more grace back in his homeland of Nordheim, but there the shadows of the pines and heavy snow would deal more effectively with the masses of weeds and annoying smaller bushes that harried him so. After undertaking the trial and discovering that his newfound powers were not limitless, he had decided not to call upon the power of the crystals in his skin to solve any minor issues and he considered this to be one of them. Had he however been able to get a clear field of sight through this dense nightmare, he may have been tempted to use their powers to cross the distance in the blink of an eye, but the forest was so thick this was out of the question. He sat there fed up and annoyed as the forest bugs began to investigate the alien mass that had just planted itself in their small domain. Back there in the great tent he had thought for a moment that he could pull the various Uphrian clans together into one unstoppable force, but to what end? He didn't really have any plan or true passion for their well being? He would have only marched their warriors back to Nordheim as his own private army to reclaim his son or destroy the Brotherhood for his own satisfaction and revenge. This was not really what was right for the clans and in his heart he had felt his selfish needs calling out to his actions. He had come to his senses in time – normally it took a conversation with Amiria telling him what a fool he had been before he saw the sense in his actions and corrected his course. Perhaps even now his dead wife had brought him to his senses from the spirit world? Perhaps Kildraken was better for them after all? Although as he considered the thoughts of leading the clans he did allow himself a quick chuckle at the conjured image of King Saya standing on his castle wall looking out towards Nordheim with the desire of conquest, as twenty thousand clansmen crested the horizon. That would certainly quell his thirst for the conquest of his lands.

'Ah dream on Corvus,' he said out loud.

'You dream of me husband?' A voice to his front made his eyes instantly shoot upwards. It was Ievia, his new wife. Much to her displeasure he knew she would soon be bringing up the subject of their unconsummated marriage, though he could not fault the girl – it was not through want of her trying. He chuckled at his luck as she stood there with her hands on her hips looking both cross and confused; she was the last person he had expected to see this far from the village.

'Why you walk around in circles for three days?' She asked genuinely puzzled, thinking that perhaps this was the way foreigners found enough peace to make a big decision.

'I'm going home,' declared Corvus deciding that from now on the truth was always going to be the best option. He got up and started walking on.

'You heading back to my home, not yours that way,' stated Ievia. She started to walk off in the opposite direction,

'This way Aristria ...*My husband*, this way...' Corus

stopped and swallowed his pride and fell in behind her, although he had not liked the way she had said her last words. Oh well perhaps someone was looking over him, it would seem that he had found his guide.

She had taken the discovery of his impromptu leaving very well and had seemed totally unfazed by it all. As he followed along behind her it suddenly occurred to him that she had assumed that she was coming with him. Maybe he had just been circling the camp waiting for her arrival in her eyes? He churned over this concept in his head as he followed along behind, the feeling of both disgust and envy grew in him as he watched her move with natural grace, passing effortlessly through the tangle of the forest. Corvus suddenly pulled his gaze away from her, embarrassed as he realised his lecherous eyes had just been soaking her up over the past few minutes. He conceded to himself that he had deliberately followed the pleasing curve of her back downwards, admiring her athletic build and hips that were pumping those sleek legs effortlessly over logs and branches.

'It will almost be a shame to let her go,' he thought, 'I had better wait until I'm free of this damn forest first before I tell her I'm going home alone.' He resolutely decided to stick with his new policy of honesty. They carried on moving through the forest and Corvus's mind began to wander to thoughts of home. He was filled with doubt at his absence and he wondered how many of his people had actually survived Bellack's curse and whether, perhaps, a new leader had risen to fill his place. How long should his people wait without a King? It could prove to be an awkward return coming back to a people who no longer needed or wanted him or he could be faced with the threat of a new ruler? His people were steeped in tradition and blood had always ruled his land; his blood. He was sure his people would honour the old ways …If the old ways still survived? But of course the way of the sword would always settle any dispute and with this he was supremely confident of his return to power. Ievia broke his train of thought as she loudly called out, but the words were not aimed at him.

'Hey, get out of here, go away …leave us.'

'Who are you shouting at?' asked Corvus, he couldn't see anything in the claustrophobic darkness of the forest, she pointed at some bushes to their rear and a group of people moved out from the cover. It was a small group of warriors from the Longtooth clan. The men filed out from the forest, there were a lot more than Corvus had first seen, the string of men kept on coming to form a semi-circle around him. As the last man finally came out Corvus estimated around eighty men in total.

'And what the hell do you lot think you are doing? Eh?' Corvus grumbled at the group. The group mumbled amongst itself for a moment then one of the warriors was reluctantly pushed forward to speak for the group.

'We're coming with you,' he stated with a blank expression as if it was a stupid question. A grumble grew in Corvus's throat,

'Go home the lot of you and leave me be, you have your village and families to look after,' he barked. 'With all of those other clans visiting you should be watching over your people, not chasing after me. Come on Ievia. Let's get going,' and with that he sprinted off in the direction she had been heading. She followed moving as graceful as a gazelle through the undergrowth and for once she struggled to keep up with the lumbering giant that just cleared a space in the forest as he moved through it.

Later as they approached the edge of the forest Ievia was glad to feel the fresh breeze of the flat lands whisking through the trees, she was dripping with sweat to match the frantic pace of her husband who was hardly out of breath. He had been desperate to lose the following warriors and he didn't have a clue whether they had even attempted to follow them. Corvus stopped before the edge of the trees and for the first time looked back; there was no sign of the men following. He chuckled to himself and strolled out into the open fields commenting back at Ievia,

'Nothing moves as fast through the forest as a Uphrian. *Really?* Ha, they obviously have not met with many Nordheimers,' he faced forwards and viewed the entire clan of the Longtooth stood there waiting for him in the clearing, this number also included the eighty warriors he had bumped into before, Shaman Artio stood there expectantly and even the accompanying families and children of the Clan showed an amused look at his arrival. Corvus's jaw dropped.

'What the…' he mouthed as he cleared his eyes to be sure; how could they have outpaced him?

Ievia walked to his side and gave him a small hug,

'We your people now Corvus, the other clans foolish and not follow you …but Longtooth clan knows you the one. You master the trial and you owe me baby still,' she whispered in his ear proudly.

Shaman Artio came forward to Corvus,

'What she is trying to tell you is that we are your clan now and the clan moves as one whole mass, women and warriors, everyone goes together, it has always been that way and always will. If you are returning to the east then we are coming with you. Your home is our home. The moment you returned with the sword our ancient law decrees that we follow you …you can't escape your fate Corvus, you completed the trial – you are chosen. And if you are thinking of using your powers to blink away, forget it, for we will still follow you for it is now our duty, we have no choice. It would be much safer for the little ones if you stay with us; you are a strong leader and these are no longer our own lands that we are standing on. Corvus was clearly unhappy with the arrangement.   But the old Shaman's words were beginning to sink in.   He approached the watching crowds, there was a train of several forest horses behind them packed with provisions and their tents; they really had just upped and moved on-mass. He raised his hands and addressed the crowd as Shaman Artio flashed him a look that could kill,

'Remember my words, we are pledged to you, there is no going back for us. Our power of choice is removed in this matter.'

Corvus screwed up his face and after a rumble of disapproval against his better judgement he changed his original tack.

'Listen up people of the Longtooth …my new family. Today you have joined an even bigger family, today you have also become Nordheimers as I have become Uphrian and you will indeed be the first clan to meet with your distant brothers. We travel to Nordheim to join with my family and we'll smash the skulls of any who try to stop us.' Finishing his words he began to stomp off through the field ahead as several of the younger warriors gave out some loud approving whoops of appreciation. Ievia let him go several yards before calling out to him,

'Corvus, you go wrong way again, this way is south.' Corvus ignored her words and continued walking forwards and picked the large lone daisy that he had spotted in the grassy field.   Plucking the flower he returned to her and continued in her direction.

'In my country it is customary to give a pretty lady a flower, now what was it you were calling about?' He had never thought a flower could save him from looking a fool, but was pleased to be surprised. Ievia took the flower with her face beaming at her first gift; it was always nice to see her normally stern expression washed away. She gave Corvus an appreciative hug, then bit the head off the flower and chewed it, enjoying the fragrant flavour. She quickly finished munching down the plant and Artio tapped Corvus on his shoulder,

'In our culture the best gift is the kind you can eat and the edible daisy is delicious, I think you know more about our ways than you let on.' Corvus's frown quickly changed to a more light-hearted expression and he muttered under his breath,

'I would say a strong drink is a better gift, and I could do with one now.' The couple led the clan south, taking them down through the open fields of the Aristrian lowlands. Their number was close to seven hundred, the clan must have had many people spread across their territories that Corvus had not seen, yet less than half were fighting men; still this was nothing compared to the thousands under Kildraken in the Arrowhead clan.

The Aristrian farmer watched the procession of the Uphrian clan moving across his fields from a comfortable distance and he gawped in wonder for a moment. No one had witnessed a clan on the move outside of the forest in many lifetimes; it could only mean one thing – trouble. He called for his son, who had been busy with the field labourers,

'Son, get the horses,' there was no response from the boy.

'*Devon, get the bloody horses right now*,' he screamed and ran for their secured mounts. The farmers of the region were far from poor as the governor handed out an extra grant to encourage landholders to work the lands that bordered the once volatile area. Although the Uphrians had remained relatively passive in this region for as far back as anyone could now remember, historically it was an unpopular area in which to settle. With the vast open lands of the farming expanses the horse was a dominant factor for the Aristrians in this region and had always been necessary for their work or survival. Devon came running over dragging their horses behind him; their stock was well bred and nimble.

'What is it father?' he began to enquire but needed no reply when he spotted the long column of Uphrians dominating the horizon. In contrast to the Aristrian settlers in this region, few Uphrians could ride with any skill and the horses were mostly used as pack animals. The generations of wild forest horses wondering through the thickets and branches had rendered their breed little use for any other purpose.

'Go and ride to the garrison son, go tell them the Uphrians are coming …on second thoughts you go back home and tell your mother to leave for the stockade, I'll go.' The farmer slapped the horse's hindquarters and quickly departed.

Corvus had felt good about himself for the last two days; it must have been the thoughts of returning home that filled him with a sense of euphoria. They had made good progress over the open ground; the clan had moved quicker than he had anticipated, seemingly unburdened by the young or the old. He had passed away the time of the journey chatting further to Ievia. A conversation with her was always interesting as she never sat on the line of indecision; he found her directness refreshing, too much so sometimes. As they all travelled on he became uneasy during the late morning when two lone Aristrian knights approached from their flank. He thought it strange that there were only two riders. In his experience only lightly armoured scouts went out in so few numbers, heavy cavalry normally moved in greater numbers. They were perhaps a league away to their right flank but even at that distance he could make out their holstered lances and heavy armour, even their mounts sparkled with the shine of polished steel as the sun crossed their path. They rode around the ambling clan in a complete circle and then disappeared. Chieftain Ion, who, until Corvus had appeared back from the trial had been the clan leader, had strongly advised that no action be taken against the riders; after all they were still in a state of peace. The clan's original chieftain had accepted Corvus's leadership with surprising grace; he had expected a more hostile attitude from the man. Shaman Artio seemed to have done a good job of ensuring that everyone respected the old ways. He had reinforced this view with Corvus shortly after setting off,

'It is important to remember the lessons of our past; for they set the standards for the future. We are a people steeped in tradition. Morben knew this and with his false accusation a large shadow was cast upon our people.

We like to stay in the shade Corvus, so we will follow you.' Corvus had grunted and walked away at the time, figuring that perhaps the sun had got to Artio's head as he was sounding more and more like Morben each day with his strange rambling prophesies.

The Aristrian riders had appeared to be counting their numbers and completing a reconnaissance on the group before departing. They had not been apprehensive in the least of the group, nor tried to communicate or parlay. Come the evening the clan set up their night camp as they had several times before. The clan had needed to adapt their ways to their new unfamiliar surroundings, vast open ground instead of their beloved forest; but they were a bright bunch and adjusted as best they could. Instead of building vine walls to control access into the overnight camp they took to digging a surrounding ditch for their night's rest. With the appearance of the riders during the day Corvus had the night watch doubled, there was little else that could be done in this barren landscape. The night was spent around the small campfires but there was little to burn in these lands so the fires were extinguished shortly after cooking for the nights were mild enough. Corvus had retired to his tent with Ievia for the night as he had done so on each night of their journey, he was not troubled with the day-to-day running of the camp and he had no desire to put Chieftain Ion's nose out of joint by countermanding his orders, the man knew his own people best. Ievia shared the pile of furs with Corvus although he kept his undergarments on as his final line of defence against her repeated advances. He had allowed her to stay the nights with him after slowly becoming aware of their culture; the shame of sleeping in a different tent would have been unbearable to a Uphrian woman and would suggest that Corvus was less of a man. Besides, their time together gave him a chance to taunt her further after their day's conversations, although he rarely got the better of her and in truth he had enjoyed the odd flirt. At the end of each night on their journey she had finished their conversation and undressed before him. He was unsure if she was deliberately trying to raise his blood pressure as she slipped from her clothes so naturally but he had found an appropriate spot on the tent wall to fix his gaze or on another night he had quickly extinguish the yellow crystal that illuminated the tent, with a leather cup. Yet tonight he had allowed his eyes to linger a little longer than he should as she unashamedly undressed before him then hopped under the furs to assume her usual snuggle. He had nicknamed her his second blanket the night before, for she would wrap herself about him each night holding onto him tight. She had quickly responded by naming him her snoring donkey.

'Snoring Donkey? What are you thinking woman, I am a King I'll have you know,' 'Ok, you king of donkeys then,' she grinned back at him, 'Never mind Corvus, I like donkey rides,' she snuggled in closer. Corvus decided quickly that he would not use pet names again.

With his new found blanket he discovered that Ievia was athletically pert to the touch and brought a stirring of desire as he sought sleep. Something long and hard poked its way between them as she ground against his body, he could feel himself blushing with her proximity; it was the horned handle of her thigh dagger. She giggled and sat up. She had rushed to seize the moment to take advantage of his intimacy, forgetting to fully remove her usual attire. Bending over from their bed of furs she removed the bindings that held the thigh dagger in place. They were a popular accessory amongst the clanswomen, worn under a skirt and close to hand. If you had listened to the camp gossip, several men were reputed to have lost their manhood to such well-concealed blades and they were certainly not conducive to creating the seductive mood that she had intended. She was a persistent creature of habit and at the end of each night of their journey she had adopted the same routine with her repeated words stating her desires before rolling over with an angry pout across her face at his response.

'Corvus, Corvus …you ready to make baby with me now?' she would ask. Each night his same reply would whisper back,

'I'm sorry Ievia, I'm not ready …I just need more time.' Tonight however, when she asked the question there was no reply. In truth he was still mulling over her comment about the donkey in his head, in some places this could be perceived as a complement, they were rather well endowed after all, yet in another land a donkey was no more than an insult, an ass. Which was he?

She lay still for a moment considering the meaning of the silence; if she were to roll into him now perhaps she would be his this night. However if she were to roll away and rejected him - giving him a taste of his own medicine, then perhaps he could be hers? Her body and desires urged her to grab the first opportunity she had to take; as her husband had proven temperamental too say the least, but her head won the day. As they both lay there in deliberation she rolled over turning her back on him as she had done on the other nights, but without his prompt. She had judged his crumbling willpower well. Corvus's mind was split in half, two voices argued inside his head as he felt his urges grow at the signs of her rejection,

'Just roll over and rub her back for a while, she'll come around to your expert hands and before you know it she will be yours to enjoy as you please,' argued one voice, his body liked this thought. The other voice just repeated one word,

'Amiria, Amiria …Amiria.' The second voice just repeated his dead wife's name and threatened to effectively calm his desire. The first voice argued back,

'It is not a crime to sleep with her Corvus, there is nothing wrong with it; after all she is your wife – just take her now and move on with your life.'

'Remember Amiria, how can you move on? You killed your love with your own hands; who knows what your hands may do to Ievia?'

'I know, these hands will bring pleasure to us both,' said the other voice. His body rolled about in torment as his head swam in indecision, he glanced over to see the smooth curve of her exposed back facing him; she was motionless, perhaps she was already asleep? Ievia lay there perfectly still willing his rough hands to reach out and touch her. 'Touch me, kiss me …take me,' said her inner voice repeatedly. No action is sometimes the best action, thought Corvus, his hand moved to steady himself and rested on her silky smooth skin, her softness was calming to his inner turmoil and he instinctively began to stroke her, the action was more to comfort himself than her – but she felt nice to the touch all the same. She wriggled into him and a smile spread across her face. Shaman Artio suddenly burst into the tent in a flustered panic and the smile disappeared as fast as it had grown.

'*Corvus. Danger rapidly approaches, I have just had a*

vision and we must prepare for battle at once ...the Aristrians are coming!'

Corvus growled with mixed emotion and muttered angrily to himself as he hurriedly dressed,

'Bloody hell, will people not leave me be? I was just...' he stopped and turned to Ievia and with one bark from his mouth he commanded her to stay in the tent. She looked offended at his command so he grabbed her in his arms and gave her a vigorous kiss, the type that sucked the air from a lover's body. She slid back down into the pile of furs; her legs had gone unusually weak as he followed the Shaman out from the tent. Ion had already started to make preparations; the warriors were awake and had formed the first ranks in a defensive circle. The women and young ones stood in the ranks behind them and had already begun to apply war paint to the warriors of the first ranks. The Uphrians had a tradition of being tenacious hand-to-hand fighters, taking down their enemies as quickly as possible with the largest weapon available. On the battlefield they were without archers in their order of battle; the only ranged weapons that they carried, consisted of spears and long throwing darts with which they hunted each day. They were more than proficient with their complete arsenal; but they relied heavily on their infamous Uphrian charge to quickly smash their opponents. One of the roaming sentries came sprinting back into the camp, leaping the surrounding ditch in his hurry to report. He scrabbled up the bank to speak with chieftain Ion; Artio and Corvus were also stood in a group discussing their defensive plans.

'Aristrian cavalry approaches, there are many,' he had listened with his ear to the ground as they closed on them through the veil of the night; he knew there were many, long before he could make out their silhouettes against the faint moonlight. Artio commanded some men to go forwards and place yellow lighting crystals at one hundred yards around their position. The light would illuminate their attackers as they approached and also serve as a range marker for their fearsome charge. With the Shaman's visionary warning and the fact that they had arrived in such large numbers, it could only mean one thing. They were here to fight.

The Aristrian force consisted entirely of cavalry; the six hundred heavily armoured knights providing the muscle, accompanied by nearly four hundred lightly armoured cavalry archers, the bane of many a good man on the open fields. After hearing the disturbing news that the Uphrians had invaded their lands the regional governor had decided to put all of his eggs in one basket and muster the entire region's forces together and crush this war-band as an example to the other clans. This show of force was more an elaborate bluff than a showing of their true might, for their strength in this region should have easily numbered ten times as many, but with the war effort against Tanaria there had been some inevitable changes. This was precisely why the governor had authorised the use of everything he could muster; the people of the region must not know how weak their border forces had become. The first riders to reach the yellow crystal light were the mounted archers; they came to a halt on the far side of the light, keeping the crystals between them and the camp, then without the faintest hint of a parlay or warning, they fired a volley into the Uphrian encampment. At one hundred yards this was easy pickings for the archers. There was little cover in the camp and with few shields between the Uphrian ranks many were indiscriminately hit by the first volley. Women, children and warriors alike fell to the hiss of their falling arrows. Ion did not hesitate to react as the enemy let loose their first volley, he called the charge and with a loud war-cry, hundreds of men surged forwards towards the mounted archers. The Aristrians quickly wheeled about their mounts, sending another volley into the running men as they rode off into the darkness of the night. The arrows peppered the ranks of charging men as the Uphrians reached the light, several men charged onwards with their comrades with arrows horribly jutting from their bodies, such was the adrenalin of their charge. A new sound echoed through the fields above the screams of the dying and wounded. It was the rhythmic pounding and clatter of six hundred heavily armoured knights galloping past the retreating archers with the front rank of the Uphrian line in the sights of their levelled lances. Everyone saw the incoming danger but with the knights charging out of the darkness there was little time to react. The Uphrian warriors would be decimated, not even their ferocious charge could stand up to a headlong clash with the heavy cavalry. A large crystal axe formed itself into Corvus's hands as he saw the danger before him. He had not even noticed the weapon forming into his grip as he watched until the sharp edge of the forming blade cut into his leg drawing blood. He had not advanced with the warriors and felt detached from the events unfolding around him. Suddenly a giant brown bear brushed past the warriors into the light, it dwarfed the men as it passed. The charging cavalry entered the area of light at full pelt and the great war-bear rose up onto its hind legs and let rip a bone-curdling roar. The semi-circle of approaching Aristrian riders fought to maintain control of their panicked mounts. Even the most experienced war-horses shied away in fear from the scent of the imposing creature in their path. Horses halted abruptly in their tracks, others attempted to alter their course in a panic to get away, they smashed into their terrified companions as utter chaos halted their charge. Armoured men were flung from their saddles and trampled under hoof as the giant war-bear ripped into the halted riders, intent on slaughter. The Uphrian warriors did not hesitate for a second and ploughed forward into the confused riders with devastating effect. Their two-handed axes and great-swords felled both man and beast alike as they reeled about in their panic. Ion himself cleft the first man he encountered almost in two. After several moments of screaming, death and confusion the Aristrians disengaged, dragging their battered ranks back into the safety of the night. The twang of bow strings drew the panting warriors' gaze to their right, nervously seeking the unseen shafts as they fought for breath from their excursions. The great bear sniffed the air then shot off into the night as the new wave of arrows fell dropping several more Uphrians. A series of new screams tore through the darkness to the men's right, as the bear's teeth and claws ripped through the flesh of both horse and man. Corvus concentrated on the sounds of battle across the fields and the small green crystal shards embedded deep into his skin pulsed with their invoked power. In the blink of an eye he was teleported amongst the Aristrian archers and his crystal axe swung with precision, singing its deadly song. The first soldier's shocked face was quickly sliced open with the sharp crystal axe. Corvus continued to wade amongst them with lethal efficiency and a great economy of movement – for every step forward left a fresh body behind him, as with each swing he felled another rider. As he went about his grim work the mixed crystals imbedded in his flesh gave off a magical glow, almost like a warning light to the men in his way. The retreating men were stuck between the giant bear or the crystal king who worked their way towards each other through waves of blood. The battle was brief and only a lucky few Aristrians were sensible enough to turn tail and ride off into the black of night. Commander Hermana, of the Aristrian nobility, was one of the first to turn and lead his men far away from the devastation behind him; he could not comprehend in his mind how things had gone so wrong.

It had seemed a simple task, one which he would now need to answer for.

After the fighting was done Corvus faced the great bear, he saw pain in its almost human eyes and it was then that he noticed the host of arrows jutting from its thick fury side. Corvus patted its head as the weakened rear legs of the creature gave way,

'You did well,' he whispered to the wheezing beast, the animal growled back at him in a low tone. The uncaring growl from the animal kind of reminded him of himself in some way. As the creature relaxed, resting its huge jaws on the ground it shut its eyes and passed away. Corvus turned away, saddened by the night's events and the stupid actions of these men, why had they attacked them? For what? Was all this death purely a penalty for merely crossing their lands? When he turned about Shaman Artio's cold body lay in place of the giant bear's, several arrows were jutting from his side. He walked slowly back to his remaining family, the senseless struggle and loss was beyond him. Little did he know at the time that come the first light over six hundred Aristrians were found to have perished in the night's failed attack, the Aristrian military machine in this region was effectively demolished in one swipe and its knights disgraced in their failure. The Uphrian losses were also grim; they totalled one hundred and seventy two warriors, thirty seven women and nineteen children. On returning back to the camp one of the elder women came running out to Corvus and called out to him as he assessed the numerous bodies scattered about the camp, it was an unpleasant scene to return to.

'Corvus, come quickly. It's Ievia, she's been hit,'

Chapter 12 - The Slayer of Gods

Outside the Su-Katii Rift on the distant Isle of Cardus, a very human-feeling Hadrak sat stretching his limbs as he sat waiting for the sun to rise. Garth had returned into the Rift to recover Hadrak's weapon of choice for his upcoming duel with Titus, his huge two-handed Great-sword. It had been years since Garth had studied in the training yard of the Temple but he still knew his way around the place well enough, he had retrieved weapons from the armoury thousands of times during his previous stay. Garth's hand lingered as he held onto the armoury door's handle; the memories of this place flooded back though him as it were only yesterday. His master had secured his place in the Temple at an early age; Master Zerch was a meticulous planner and had hardly aged a day since he placed him as a young lad in the temple. Garth's only communications and orders were received and acted upon on the few stays of leave enforced in the Su-Katii training regime. Zerch had sponsored his parents and as long as he followed his orders he would continue to support his large family with ample coin, their agreement had worked out well for Garth's family. His three brothers and four sisters had enjoyed a fine upbringing thanks to his labours in the Temple. His father had lost his hand in a milling accident and struggled to support his family; they had been hard times in those days long past. The memories of his youth reached to the far extent of his memory and now he could only remember the endless hunger he had felt as a child. Zerch had offered his generous support at a price and although he carried out the magicians tasks as a child, Garth had never expected that some day he would work full time for his original sponsor. He had known from the start of his training that he would not be blessed to walk amongst the Su-Katii ranks and when outside of the Su-Katii Rift the little voice in his head from Zerch's communication had confirmed this belief. When the time was right he had done as he always had, he followed his orders and then ran before he could be discovered. He opened the door and advanced into the armoury, his eyes widening at the view before him. Scattered across the floor were a string of bodies, some headless, some armless, others just hacked beyond recognition. They were a mess and all of the corpses were either children or the very old. Garth surveyed the grisly scene of dried blood and body parts before him; Titus had indeed visited the Temple weeks before, his handiwork was plain to see. Garth sighed to himself, it was an ugly scene but still it was not any of his business, he picked his way through the corpses to the weapon racks and retrieved Hadrak's great sword that stood out from the smaller blades; he also picked up the golden breast-plate that he had seen him wear on occasion, then turned about and headed back out of the Rift. There was no doubt in his mind that Titus was responsible for their slaughter, he was not a betting man, but from seeing the carnage his money would definitely be on Titus when he got out.

Hadrak smiled as Garth returned with gifts, after his request being fulfilled for his weapons and armour, he realised that he would actually get the chance to fight. He had kept his word to Titus and remained silent as he had little choice. Hadrak had genuinely been surprised with the killer and had never expected Titus to behave with the slightest shred of decency, allowing him to fight rather than being simply stuck with the magician's dagger. What a display he intended to give them today, could he really be killed outside of the Rift? He had been kept from the real world for so long that such worries had never even entered his mind before. Hadrak buckled on the breast-plate and limbered up with the great sword, swinging it about himself in a series of large circular motions, using a well-practiced sword Kata to get his circulation pumping. The first rays of sun crested the horizon illuminating the vast sea surrounding the island. It promised to be a fine day, displaying nothing but a pure blue sky above. Titus stood up withdrawing his swords, it was time.

'Right then, let's be having you. You may speak your last words now and then we fight; any final words from the condemned?' He smirked at Hadrak.

'Yes, indeed - I'm waiting to hear them from you, for it is you who is condemned,' replied the god. Titus laughed,

'All that time in the Rift waiting for your moment of freedom, unlimited time and yet you come back at me with such poor wit. It is just as well that I will soon remove your dull head from your shoulders before you infect us with laughter. Come now, you have savoured your freedom for too long already ...*On Guard*.' The two men circled each other reading every movement of their opponent, when one man took a step forward the other took a step back, always keeping the same distance between them. Each man attempted to manoeuvre the other into facing the rising sun, the oldest trick in the book – but still effective. It was Hadrak that broke the stand off and attacked first. He stepped backwards and as Titus advanced to match his pace he switched direction and drove into the man, double-thrusting high to fill Titus's view with his sword's point and then low to the groin. Titus knew his best chance would be to turn the long blade aside and then close from the side where his shorter blades could stab or strike with better effect. He followed his instinct and parried each thrust with a different sword, noticing that the strikes had not been over-extended, leaving little room for a potential counter-attack and the sword was quickly pulled back to be re-used again. Titus had closed in on his opponent but suspected the thrusts to be more of a feint rather than an all out attack and maintained his tight guard. Instead of opening his defences, he delivered a sweeping kick to Hadrak's legs sending him to the floor. Hadrak had already started to swing around making the most of his compromised position and struck out with a sweeping blow to Titus's legs, the nimble Su-Katii jumped backwards, bringing his knees up into his chest and evaded the leg-chopping swing. Hadrak quickly regained his feet in the space he had created and looked for a new opening. Titus had noticed that in this encounter the god was fighting with a lot better judgment and poise than in his last two bouts when they had crossed swords inside the Rift. Then, he had fought without care or fear of death, but with the certainty of a true death at stake, neither man put a foot wrong and pushed their skills on to the limit. Half an hour or more must have passed and both men continued to quickly engage each other then disengage, catching their breath and then unleashing another six-move combination. Garth watched the awesome display of their art, with a growing doubt that he would still be standing after such a fight, but then his master would have just slit Hadrak's throat long before cutting his bonds. Zerch watched on in utter boredom, but his interest would suddenly spark up when either man came close to harm. Titus caught his breath and Hadrak jeered at him.

'What's the matter, do you need a rest? Did you bite off too much for your big mouth to chew Titus? Yes you could beat me inside my Rift, but in there after thousands of years of swordplay I had lost the heart for fighting. Here outside, it is a different matter …I have tasted life again and you will not take it from me.' Titus shook his head,

'Save your breath, you will need it …but not for long,' he leapt forward and renewed his attack, raining down a relentless assault of blows at the god's head and torso but each blow was either parried or dodged by

Hadrak, there were no counter-attacks or disengagements this time, it was all he could do to stop the reckless assault. Titus's new strategy of only attack would soon bring death to one of them and they both knew it. A rare smile spread across Zerch's face as he sensed the end was nearing for one of these men, it crossed his mind that they may even kill each other; they were both too dangerous for their own good but he doubted that he would ever be so lucky. Suddenly one of Titus's swords snapped just before the hand guard, it was the one of lower craftsmanship that he had replaced from his encounter with Tress, Hadrak instantly seized the chance to attack and he thrust forwards at his opponent's torso. Titus turned his body and his hand swept over the god's guard and hacked deeply into his hand with the snapped blade. Titus smiled in satisfaction as the god's face drained white, wracked with pain. It had been a risky move, deliberately angling the weaker sword to break. He had already attempted every other trick in the book to force the opening that he had needed. As with many sword fights, reacting to an opportunity would often bring victory ...or sometimes defeat. Hadrak had taken the bait instantly seizing the opening when he saw it. It had all appeared so natural to him. He had been a far better swordsman than Titus had first judged, but lacked the predator-like cunning to win this encounter. It took less than a minute to work around his ineffective guard with his wounded hand – next he took off Hadrak's good sword-hand as the heavy blade failed to keep pace with his own. Titus turned his back on the man as if to walk away as blood flowed from the two wounds inflicted on Hadrak's hands; the great sword fell to the floor. A life with the lack of use from his hands would enter a new chapter of living hell for Hadrak.

'Titus, do it,' hissed the god through a face contorted with pain. Titus had been wrong about his long-lived thoughts for revenge. It had not been completely satisfying and the fight had been the toughest of his life, he had been a worthy opponent and perhaps Hadrak deserved better, Titus swung about and plunged his sword through the expectant man's breast-plate, it grated through his diaphragm and his body slumped forward. Hadrak's eyes looked almost thankful as he slid from his sword to the ground, his mouth moved slowly but no words were formed. He lay still and Titus slumped to the floor with exhaustion and relief.

'And that is that then... they become mortal,' commented Zerch. 'I do believe that our business here is concluded gentlemen, I will prepare a portal. I am a man of my word. Where do you wish to go Titus? Do you wish to join the fight against the empire? I could transport you to Ubecka or even Tagel; they could use a man such as yourself there.' Titus shook his head slowly, raising his hand to Athene to indicate that she should help pull him up. She had watched the fight with interest, it had been an amazing spectacle and her heart had been in her mouth several times when Titus had narrowly escaped a fatal strike. She had known as she watched that she still cared for the man, there was nothing like a close shave with death to make you realise such things; but he would need to change his ways before she accepted him back. She knew that he was a swordsman and there was little hope of changing this, it was in his breeding. It was his commitment to her that would need to change, if he wanted her he would need to prove it, no more of this brooding that he had taken to. She decided to sit on these thoughts, no need to seem too eager and pre-warn him. She would take things slowly and let him work hard at lighting her interest, that way he would have a chance to show his genuine commitment. She accepted his outstretched hand and helped him up.

'Where are you going then Titus?' Zerch asked.

'I think for now you'll be pleased to know that I'm

coming with you – where Athene goes, I follow …well it's her fault for looking so good. I only follow because I can't take my eyes of your arse,' she protested with a roll of her eyes as he winked back at her with his boyish grin. . He would also need to work on his words of flattery she considered; perhaps she would need to invest a lot of time in this man.

'My days of revenge are at last fulfilled and done,' Titus stated as if that was the end of the matter. Zerch shook his head,

'Don't worry Titus, we won't need your swords to deal with Soredamor, you can hang them up if you like and retire? Go start a new life away from the war, I hear Menchata is nice, I have the power to take you wherever you like,' he patted a small bag that he had strapped to his belt. Zerch looked across at Athene,

'I assure you that I will get her back to you safe and sound after we release and deal with Soredamor.' Titus wasn't having any of it, he knew when he wasn't wanted but he could tell in Athene's eyes that she wanted him to stay.

'I see, but that won't be necessary, I mean no disrespect, but your man there may not be up to the task, where as I on the other hand have an exceptional record in that department. When it comes to slaying gods no man is better qualified, for I have a one hundred percent success rate. I have no direct quarrel with Soredamor, but if her Brotherhood poses a threat to my Athene, I will see an end to her.' Athene did not like the way he referred to her as belonging to him.

'Very well Titus, have it your way. With this, we should be able to travel directly to Soredamor's cave, even from this distance, it is called a Dimesia and it is a very rare relic.' He reached into the small bag that he carried and withdrew a gold and crystal-like globe. He placed it on the ground twisting some unknown mechanism that enclosed the stone and the relic sprung into life, projecting a new Portal of transport above it. Zerch suggested that he and Garth went through first, then Athene and Titus last,

'It is imperative that I go first, should we meet with the Brotherhood then...' Titus stopped the magician's planning,

No, what does order really matter? My swords can deal with anyone,' he pushed them to one side and raised a finger as Zerch went to make comment.

'I think that I will go first, I am tired of following.' Zerch sighed and replied,

'Be my guest Titus,'

'Ok, I will,' he responded and walked with a purpose through the instantly formed portal that appeared from the Relic.

Titus felt the familiar surge of power as he was transported across the nation. He looked about him on arrival, it was a bright day and the sunlight shone down upon him. There was no cave, only a courtyard, which surrounded him. This was not Soredamor's cave entrance. The Portal closed behind him before he had time to react.

'Oh Shit,' remarked Titus.

Chapter 13 – Trust

Kerric the Magician sat mulling over his earlier meeting with Zerch as he appreciated the Governor of Ubecka's fine wine. Zerch had turned up out of the blue and warned him that the time had arrived when he needed to make a choice and take a side as the other Masters were jostling for power and saw him as a joke. This was nothing that he didn't already know, but before Zerch had departed, he also made the bold statement that Soredamor would soon be free from the Rift within the week. He hounded Zerch with questions, but the tight-lipped magician would answer none; he just reiterated his words,

'Trust in my powers Kerric, now is the time for action, stand with me against the other Masters and together we can defeat them. Meet with me on the fields to the rear of Tagel in two days' time and I promise you by the end of this week she will be free.' He had annoyingly refused all further attempts for conversation repeating only

'Make your choice,' and left Kerric to his thoughts. Would he still be in the Goddesses' favour once she was free? After his failure to apprehend the rogue Magician Tamar, he thought perhaps not - but as far as he knew none of the other Masters had found the time to report back to their queen and his illusion of having a firm grip on the rein on the Brotherhood could still remain. All of his failures had of course been Telimus's fault for his early departure and lack of preparation of his disciples, how could anyone work with a man so set in his ways? Now that Telimus had cleared off to Tagel on his personal escapade for fame and recognition Kerric had arrived at Ubecka deciding that he needed to show his face and campaign to the remaining Acolytes who were assisting the army. They needed to be reminded who exactly had been assigned the leadership of the Brotherhood; there was still a chance that he could increase his powerbase here. He knew exactly why old Telimus had seized the opportunity to assist the army and had rushed off early without him attempting to destroy Tamar weeks before. It was all in an effort to cement his own leadership; by leading their strike force against the Tanarians he had cleverly reinforced his claim for the command of the Brotherhood. Only the Spell masters could convey the words of their god and they all seemed to be in Telimus's pocket. He considered the situation, Telimus had taken the most skilled Masters with him to Tagel to surround himself with his strongest and most loyal. Only the dross of the Brotherhood and the lesser-skilled Masters remained here in Ubecka. Unfortunately the reality of Kerric's position was that he was amongst this number. It did not matter that their God had given him her blessing for the leadership. The fact remained, if she had not conveyed this to the other Masters, or they all denied this claim, he was scuttled either way. Was it still really worth attempting to lead the Brotherhood or should he implement Zerch's plan? He would invite them all for dinner, to celebrate their victory and find out where their alliances truly lay. Only then after could he return to his Queen and reinforce his position.

Dinner began as expected with the nine brotherhood disciples at the long table, a tasty plate filled with roast chicken lightly flavoured with paprika was placed before each man. A fine red wine was selected to wash it all down and soon a dinner conversation sharper than the knife used to carve up the flavoursome feast was struck up.

'Kerric, this is delicious, at last you have found your true vocation in life, a serving hand,' suggested one of the two Masters present, the long line of pasty white faces lining the table broke into a low laugh at the comment. It was rare that the men exposed their faces from their long hoods. The other Master present snorted with outrage and seemingly jumped to his defence,

'How dare you say this of Kerric, have you not eyes in your head man? Look I have two knives set at my place on the table. Can't you even get the laying of the table right? Perhaps you have set this table as well as you run your campaign.' The laughter grew louder at Kerric, even the acolytes who had unusually been permitted to eat with their masters joined in with the laughter. Kerric stifled his growing anger.

'Master Gylos, I merely provided the biggest backstabber in the room with a spare tool. Now enough of these snipes, they are beneath me; I am here to celebrate with you in our victory over the Tanarians, I am also here to discuss how we will finally complete our true mission and free Soredamor.'

Master Gylos could not let the insults stop there, he was just warming up and the strong wine had fuelled his disgust of the man. This upstart had risen above his station, why from the very first time he had met with Bellack's risen acolyte, he had been an embarrassment.

'Remind me once again Kerric, just how did you help win this victory here? If my memory serves me correctly you were distinctly absent in the taking of the town? But perhaps your absence was the best help that you could provide?' Kerric shook his head at the Master's comment,

'Gylos, Gylos …Gylos when a sword swings as it chops at your head do you watch the blade or the arm that wields it?' Gylos drained his goblet, then replied,

'You watched neither, because you weren't bloody well there, you will lead nothing Kerric. If you think you can win us over with a good meal and some wine, you are madder than I thought. As for releasing our god, many a great man has tried before you and you do not fall into that category. Why the only 'freeing' that you could provide was freeing yourself of your clothes on your arrival to our Order. I will save you the further embarrassment of this evening; your dulcet tones will only annoy me further. I speak for all of us. We are all pledged to Telimus, he will be the one to free our Queen, not a pathetic little sub-human like you Kerric.' Kerric rose from the table, his face was flushed red; he pushed aside his chair and stomped off without a word, to the sound of their following laughter. His suspicions were all confirmed and he would allow them this last laugh, after all what did their opinion matter, they would all be dead from his slow working poison before sunrise. They had never suspected such a bold plan in the heart of the army's camp from a sub-human such as himself. He had decided to go with Zerch's plan to eliminate the rest of the competition in the Brotherhood long before the men had arrived. It had just made sense; it was looking likely that Soredamor would soon be free if Zerch's words were true and he had no desire to share her with those soon to be dead fools; the poison would sit dormant for several hours then its effects would be felt fast. The Brotherhood needed to be eliminated if they would not follow him; they were nothing more than a threat to his claim on Soredamor. He would just need to tread very cautiously, for there were still some extremely sharp and powerful men that he faced and he knew that Zerch was especially astute. Any man that could just turn his enemy into a friend to achieve a goal was to be watched very closely indeed. He realised that Zerch was just playing him in some way, it was to be expected and he would think less of the man if he was not being manipulated. In his eyes, it was simply what every good magician did; he was most probably using him to bring a war to the Brotherhood he considered. If the Brotherhood were split into smaller fragments it would be far easier to destroy. There was an obvious hatred of the Order in

Zerch but Kerric simply didn't care if his hidden agenda involved the deaths of the rival Masters', this just aligned with his own plans, as long as his own death was not included in that number. If he could make it through to see Soredamor's release, his powers would grow more formidable but until that time he would need to rely on his sharp wit to survive. With his action of coming here today Kerric had firmly chosen his side of the conflict and with the sighting of Zerch in his quarters by the house servants, he would use this new information to implicate him in the disciples' deaths, accelerating the conflict to come and sending a clear message to the more powerful Masters that he did not stand alone. He suspected the servants that had been assigned to him on his arrival had been placed to spy on him so after they had spotted Master Zerch's arrival he had used his magic to put them into a temporary slumber. When they awoke they would reinforce his account of the men's death and Zerch's involvement. Zerch had already taken care of the arrangements and details of the poisoning; he had reassured Kerric that he had a man in place to carry out the task. Kerric had nervously taken the antidote on leaving the room. It was a giant leap of faith, the poison was uncommon and very specialised it would be unlikely that the other men would have the time to workout the variant and seek its cure.

'You had better be a man of your word Zerch,' he had said with shaking hands as he filled his mouth with the odd tasting powder. As he saw it there was little choice in his action. If he did not act against the Brotherhood Zerch would likely destroy him, if not today another time. He had seen the man in action, and to say his skills in magic were impressive would be an understatement, his action today would align him with a powerful ally. He would leave this place immediately and visit his Queen, reassuring her of her release. It was also part of his backup plan; he would make sure that he was inside Soredamor's Rift when the poison was due to strike. Should he be double-crossed by Zerch he would be protected from the true death inside the Rift; no poison was going to finish him off when he could protect himself with his cunning. Should he fall to the poison within the Rift he would have several hours to rectify the problem after his body was returned back to life in the real world. Whilst he was back in the presence of his Queen, he could also make events appear as though he were slightly more pivotal in her upcoming release, hopefully ensuring that he gained her favour. He would even tolerate her pet Su-Katii for now, her fun with her favourite slave would not last – he would see to that. He placed a diamond on the floor in preparation of his transport but his mind was still in overdrive, thinking through every thread of the unfolding events. Zerch would not reveal to him how he was to free the Queen, but it was obvious, there was only one way - he must have the girl. It would be expected that Zerch would turn against him after the destruction of the other Masters. He stopped in thought. 'The crafty bastard,' that was it, Zerch was engineering a situation of chaos, hoping Kerric would keep the Brotherhood busy with a war whilst he sneaked in and took the glory for freeing their Queen. 'Yes, yes that's it,' Zerch would not double-cross him today; he was needed to further his master-plan. He decided that he would play along for now it would help cover his disloyal intentions. He would prove himself reliable for now to cement their alliance and ensure that he carries out the second more important task of stirring up trouble in the Brotherhood. Zerch had told him that if he was man enough to side with him and slaughter the remaining Brotherhood at Ubecka he would stand with him in two days' time for the final battle against Telimus and the other Masters at Tagel. Zerch's unwitting mistake had been in the telling of this sentence. He had not needed Kerric to kill the remaining

Brotherhood in Ubecka, yes he had gathered them conveniently together in one group but Zerch had already provisioned for their deaths. He was frighteningly good at planning and had people infiltrated into the Aristrian army, Zerch could have easily of just killed him along with the other Brotherhood in one sitting. 'No,' he had spared him to gain his trust for the next task and perhaps a greater drop. He knew now that if he turned up to fight that battle with Telimus he would likely be standing alone. That would be the moment when Zerch would free their Queen, not after the battle for the leadership at Tagel, not at the end of the week. He was sure that the battle would ensure that Zerch could go about his business with Soredamor undisturbed by any surprise visits and perhaps lose a few more Masters in the process.

'Well you won't have her, she's mine. I may not be your equal in magic Zerch, but I make up for what I lack in cunning,' he said to himself in way of self-congratulation to his thought process. He spoke the words of power and the transport Portal began to form.

The sun crested the horizon on the western coast of Tanaria, rising above the sea that stretched out from its shores and bringing warmth to the surviving members of Brin's Marauders who had been lucky enough to make it through the night. As the previous night's festivities had grown with the drunken mood in the Aristrian camp the men had soon forgotten Mako's single offering of the beating to death of Little Marc. Fuelled by alcohol, their anger had turned back towards the prisoners. They danced about the cowering men singing their drunken songs planting the occasional swift kick to a man's head or body until one man found the urge to display his skill with a knife to the other revellers. The soldier pulled out his blade and before any of his companions could stop him he gutted the nearest Tanarian like a fish. The man's entrails spilled onto his knees as the Aristrian soldier went about his grim work on the bound man's torso, carving away at him like a butcher enjoying his work. The agonising screams of the dying man quickly brought Mako from his tent before the butcher had selected his next victim. The singing men immediately stopped their noise when a less than impressed looking Mako appeared in his under-garments and all eyes fell upon his glistening drawn swords. The screaming Tanarian whose guts hung like a blanket in his lap was bound several men further down from Brin. The man continued to scream almost to sunrise before eventually dying, a sound that Mako had insisted be left to play out its unwelcome sound to reinforce the event of his next actions.

'Are you men totally without a brain in your head or was there never one to start with?' Mako shouted above the dying man's screams. He then marched up to the Aristrian butcher and his blade licked out; the butcher's hand went instantly to the side of his head, cradling the pain that wracked his head as Mako sliced his ear cleanly off. As the man cowered in pain the Su-Katii stabbed the severed ear from the ground with the tip of his sword and lifted it his mouth, and shouted into it,

'Can you hear my words a little clearer now? I said you could have one of the prisoners, not two or anymore.' The cowering butcher nodded in agreement to his words as blood trickled in between his clamped fingers pressed to his head,

'Yes Sir, Sorry Sir ...I, ' The mans words froze as Mako's blade quickly thrust forwards into his throat, it's tip shattering the man's spine and protruding from the back. Mako pulled the blade free as the body dropped and cleaned it on the dead man, addressing his soldiers as he did so.

'My words are never to be disobeyed or taken as idle suggestions. You are soldiers and you take orders from me, if you don't you will end up the same as this fool whilst I command,' he kicked the dead Aristrian at his feet.

'If you fail to follow my orders again I will apply decimation to your ranks and then we will find out who can count amongst you. Are we clear now?' The men all responded correctly and Mako added before marching back to his tent,

'Now leave that injured man to cry us all off to sleep, his noise will remind you to listen to my orders.'

The night had not been good and the morning was no worse, every man in the camp hated the prisoners all the more if that was indeed possible. The death of one of their own, by their own had turned their burning eyes of hatred firmly on the small group of bound men. But at least none of the soldiers dared to do anything about it now; Mako was not a man to be trifled with. As the troops broke camp preparing to head back to Tagel, Mako began his interviews with the six remaining Tanarians. Only a handful of men had broken out of their well-laid trap the day before, Mako hated to admit it but the Brotherhood's visions had been most helpful in eliminating these parasites. Mako would make a grand show of personally thanking Telimus for his aid on his return. Personally he despised the man, but he was useful and had proven that he could deliver results; it would be the correct protocol to maintain a working relationship with such a valuable resource. He would leave four squads of riders to hunt down the escaped men that smashed through their ranks to their short-lived freedom. He would not need the Magician's help again for such a small threat; the scattered men presented no real threat in such small numbers, all scattered and alone they would not last long against his men. He had greater problems now that the assault on the stronghold had finally begun and with the threat to their rear echelons neutralised he realised that he was already missing out on the main battle.

Brin waited his turn to be untied from the post and was the last man from the chain to meet with the Lord. Everyone who had been untied and taken before him had not returned. He had only the dead man for company as he waited his turn, he reflected sadly on how his wife Peta would take the sad news of his passing. There had been much screaming coming from within the tent that was obscured from his view and the events within, it was a chilling noise - not the sort of sound that a man makes when meeting with his maker, more the type of screams made when undergoing one of the many forms of torture or interrogation. A group of soldiers came over to regard his dishevelled form; then with his hands still bound together he was dragged by two burly men the short distance into Lord Mako's tent and forced onto his knees before him. There was a second man with a sadistic look about him rearranging an array of metal tools which sat on top of a large box that seemed to vibrate with movement. He hated Mako more than anyone he had ever met, but from the look written across the other man's face he instantly reached the same status as his Nemisis.

'Ah and finally, the one with the hatred burning in his eyes like the fires of hell,' Mako said in way of greeting, quickly looking up as he continued to finish off his bowl of porridge.

'...well, perhaps you should just say "A little more so than the others sir," added the second man as he regarded Brin.

'You are the real leader of the group, are you not? Don't deny it. We have already forced it out of your so called commander Morde, or should I say Mr Ruby before you. Don't despair Brin, I know your name and mission, but I had to use the flesh worms before I got what I wanted from him, the lucky little creatures got through a half pound of flesh before he finally started to tell us the truth,' Mako smiled and gently tapped the nearby box that seemed to vibrate with movement from within, the movement from the box intensified. 'I did think Commander Morde a rather queer fellow, in our last encounter, but I guess like all armies it is usually the company sergeant that is truly running the show.'

Brin sneered back at the pompous warrior,

'Where are the rest of my men, what have you done with them?'

Mako smiled back and tapped the box again, just to annoy the creatures within.

'Well, I would say at least six pounds of them are inside the worms, I have got to hand it to the Brotherhood they do find the most interesting creatures, I had never even heard of such things until Telimus brought them to my attention.'

'My men?' demand Brin staring into the Mako's well groomed face.

'Ah …at last, a good old fashioned commander, how refreshing, even now you put their lives above your own. Ok, if you really want to know I'll tell you. One did not have the strength to live and three did not have the right to live after giving up their information so freely to me. Your commander Morde is currently being healed by the crystal, I want him fit as a fiddle for you and he will be having a little spar to entertain the Magicians on our arrival back at Tagel.' Brin struggled against the strong hands that held him. Mako grasped Brin by the chin so his upturned face could look directly into his own,

'I remember you also from the docks, when we crossed swords. Yes, that was it – when all were going backwards you came forwards. It would appear that you are a brave and resourceful man, from both your daring strikes against us and our own little exchange. Such a shame you were born on the wrong side of the border,' he released his grasp and finished the last few spoonfuls of his meal in silent deliberation before speaking again.

'You have done well in your campaign Brin and if the truth be known I would not have found you had it not been for the Brotherhood's magic.' He looked upset for the first time and he was, well at least in the fact that had needed their magic to bring this great campaigner to his knees. He had a dash of respect for the man who had shown more flare than any man in his own ranks.

'You will not be harmed any further; I need no intelligence from you that the others have not already given up. In tribute to providing me with some decent competition these last weeks you will remain bound but void of any ill treatment until it is time for your little sideshow. I believe the winner will go free,' he lied. Well it was not entirely a lie; he would go free in a certain way. Mako knew full well that the men were not to fight, instead the Brotherhood had requested that the commander of the force be used for some kind of transformation spell that would bring terror to the defenders of Tagel and Commander Morde's body already lay in the shallow grave with the others. In his moment of kindness he thought it less stressful to the man if he thought at least one of his men also lived. Mako had been correct in one thing that he had said, he did have respect for his opponent, he was of course a lesser man than himself, but even the 'One-lifers' could earn some respect from their bravery and that was his reason for causing him no further pain. He decided that he deserved this small sliver of homage, good opponents were rare.

'Put him in the wagon, the worms have eaten enough today,' commanded Lord Mako; his assistant's expression showed its deflated disapproval at his playtime being cut short.

Chapter 14 – Impulse

Tamar stirred from his sleep. He felt the presence of something disturbing the normal equilibrium of the Rift. He had only felt a similar disturbance weeks before, when a person from the outside world had passed through the Rift and sought an audience with his Queen, that time he had sensed the mortal form that had entered their domain, he had instantly recognised the being, it had been Kerric seeking out Soredamor. He could not resist a chance to display his amplified powers as he moved away from the dampening field that hampered his magic near the edge of the Rift. He destroyed the mortal in a moment as he conversed with his sister in the grounds just beyond the residence. He could effectively wield his magic when well away from the unseen force that held them both captive. It seemed to him that the use of his powers was greatly enhanced and had an intoxicating effect when used inside. He remembered with distinct enjoyment the shocked look of surprise on the man's face as the bolt of energy had burnt through his body when he emerged from Soredamor's balcony as they spoke. She immediately reacted, summoning up a great wind that blew her disciple's corpse through the Rift's entrance and back to the real world and on to a new resurrection. It was a shame that death was not permanent within. In the days following the incident he had apologised for his little outbreak to his sister, he had been taken away with his reactions and had forgotten that he was attempting to be more civil. It was however undeniable that it had felt good to slay Kerric even if the result was not final, but he had contemplated on that moment many times and realised that his blatant abuse of power had taken him one step closer to behaving like the divine being that he denied he would become. It was inevitable that with time he would become no better than his sister, for time was the one guaranteed resource in this place.

There had been no other visitors in the years before Kerric, but today's visitor was different from the last – Tamar could not read the thoughts of the new intruder, or even sense them for that matter; he had only felt the disturbance to the Rift and this shocked him to the core. It could mean only one thing; Athene had just entered the Rift.

Tamar bolted for the door grabbing a robe from the end of his bed and sliding his feet into his sandals as he rapidly made his way outside. If he could sense the arrival of the intruder his sister was also sure to be aware of the disturbance. Soredamor's eyes flicked wide open from her pleasant dreams of Gorran, a smile spread across her face with disbelief she could hardly believe the moment had come, the several words that Kerric had managed to utter into her ear before his destruction were correct. Who would have thought it that out of all the great Masters that had passed through her bed chambers it would be the fool that brought about her freedom. She could already sense the effect of Athene's passing inside the Rift. The endless years inside this prison had developed her senses to a heightened level; they were tuned to the consistent pattern of the Rift at a far greater level than her brother's. Her Brotherhood would be greatly rewarded for this moment. Kerric had hardly the time to speak his garbled message before Tamar had struck him down and she had dismissed his claims, as she had heard them a thousand times before. Brother and sister came rushing out of their separate sides of the building to meet at the entrance, each wary of the other and instantly giving the other a wide birth. Athene walked down the path from the Rift's entrance, she craned her head in every direction like an excited child taking in the new sights around her. She spotted Tamar and ran to him,

'*Tamar, it is true you are alive.*' As she closed to the Magician he felt agitated, not, for once, at the potential of her close contact, but more of his sister's watching eyes. She removed any choice of reaction from him as she flung herself around him in a big encircling hug. The years already passed inside the Rift and the on set of loneliness must have truly been taking their toll on him, for he quite enjoyed it.

'You should not have come for me Athene, but I must admit I am glad to see you,' Tamar said quietly to her.

'As am I,' added Soredamor overriding their voices as her mouth pursed attempting to contain a growing smile. An arc of raw power shot from her hands towards Athene as she stood close to Tamar, the magician's jaw dropped, was his sister so petty that she would risk their freedom for her revenge of Kerric? Her arc of white power dissipated into thin air inches from Athene as she stood there unbothered.

'Sorry,' Soredamor smirked as she shrugged her shoulders, 'But I just had to be sure that it was true?'

'Are you satisfied?' questioned Athene.

'Oh yes, without a doubt. Now I guess this is the part when your Tamar uses his physical strength to restrain me and stop me from leaving this place with you. After all I am just a defenceless woman trying to return to her lover.' Soredamor had just realised the truth of the situation, standing next to Athene she appeared little more than a normal woman, displaying a new array of powerless inefficiencies which she had never before realised that she possessed.

'You are not as dainty as you make out bitch, you held my mother here for years of your time and that's exactly why I'm going to give you your freedom – so you can die of old age like the rest of us outside.

'Careful, you don't know what you are doing Athene,' Tamar protested.

'Trust me,' she whispered into his ear. After a brief moment of disbelief, Soredamor approached them with a new sparkle in her eyes and cut in on their private conversation of whispers; she spoke down at Athene as though she were supreme.

'I would normally make anyone pay for insulting me so, but today when you offer me so much, your petty words just pale into insignificance …as for your mother - had you come sooner she would have suffered less. Call me a bitch, a whore, whatever takes your fancy or makes you feel better – you are probably right, but let's not stand around here all day; let us all walk together from this place once and for all? Here let us join hands to ensure none are left behind,' she suggested extending her hands to them both. Tamar nodded; he had only been inside this Rift for a miniscule fraction of the time that his sister had spent here but he had already been bored stiff by the stay,

'Yes Athene let's go, but you must know, crazy as it may sound, that she is my sister.

'Really,' she said with a convincing shocked tone.

'*Yes*, I still find it hard to believe myself. Now let us depart this place once and forever,' he said and they joined hands and walked back towards the Rift's entrance. Soredamor took one last backward glance and then rubbed the forming tear from her eyes; she could not believe the moment had come. They entered the crackling vortex of the Rift together.

It had taken Athene some persuasion from Zerch to enter the Rift after their arrival at the cave that led into the Goddesses' Rift. After they had found Titus absent at their destination she had begun to get a bad feeling about this whole affair. She suddenly realised the depth of her situation, she was in a cave with two powerful and dangerous men whom she hardly knew, her immunity to magic would not stop her falling foul of their physical demands should they choose to get nasty with her. She had realised their words were nothing more than a role play, but dared not to challenge them whilst they were remaining civil enough. She needed an ally; she needed Tamar at her side so their paths were after all aligned in some twisted way. Zerch had scratched his head looking confused,

'I don't know what happened, where is he? There must have been a disturbance coming to this place, perhaps the transport was split and your Su-Katii has emerged somewhere else? From the short time that she had spent with Zerch she had found it difficult to believe that he could be confused about the application of magic, but with only the three of them in this cave and the Rift before them she began to feel a little intimidated as Garth shuffled forwards and blocked the one path out. If she was to find Tamar inside, this would be the best place for her to go, so she just needed to get on with it. She had not enjoyed witnessing the death of Hadrak and the thought of her actions assisting in another death was one she would rather forget, although she knew that she would be sure to revisit these moments later in her thoughts on the nights when sleep would not come so fast. She knew that Tamar would be vital in protecting her country folk in the days to come, but really she knew that it came down to the fact that she just could not abandon a friend. She had paused taking in a deep breath before entering the vibrating vortex before her. Was Zerch really intent on slaying his god? He was of the Brotherhood after all and she wondered for just a split second in doubt if this was just an elaborate cover story to gain freedom for Soredamor. No, she had already witnessed Hadrak's death at his command but then again what a perfect way to mislead her. She pushed the silly thoughts quickly from her head. It was time for action and not thinking. She entered the vortex.

Titus looked about the courtyard of the extensive villa before him, slowly surveying the ground where he had just arrived; he didn't recognise the place at all. Large surrounding trees tightly hemmed in the perimeter wall and cast their swaying shadows over the complex. Something struck him as being wrong about the place and his eyes went back to the surrounding trees, as he concentrated on their distant texture they seemed to be slightly distorted and the shadows cast did not match the size of the trees. The place was obviously enchanted and apparently deserted,

'Hello? Is anyone about?' Titus called out as he moved through the quarters, opening doors and peeking into each room as he moved through the grounds. The place was well maintained, not showing any signs of being neglected. He stopped on entering a bedroom and drew his swords; a red cloak lay draped over a chair - the type issued to the Order of the Su-Katii. He peeked out of the window and up at the sky for sanity's sake – yes, there was a grey cloud filling the hazy sky, he breathed a sigh of relief, this was no Rift. He moved on, now with a little more caution but still calling out. It was not until he reached the rear of the structure, passing by several doors that he could not manage to force open with either his hands or sword before he found signs of life.

'Hello,' called out a tall man from the rear gardens. The slender figure approached Titus, he wore a simple robe but his eyes were drawn to the long scar that travelled down the length of the man's left cheek. He would have been by no means a handsome man without the mark and Titus actually thought it enhanced his middle aged looks, for it gave him an edge of character. Perhaps when his fine looks eventually started to fade he may also scar himself in such a way for the very same purpose, as it would be unlikely that anyone else he crossed swords with would be up to the task, he thought briefly with a smile.

'Where am I?' Titus demanded.

'Why, if you don't know where you are sir, then you don't belong here,' replied the older man. Titus sighed and shook his head in disgust,

'*Oh no*, I must be in the company of fucking Wizards to get a response like that to such a simple question. Now here, let's try another easy one – what happens to your heart when I stick this sword through it?' The older man looked down at the swords and Titus's menacing stance.

'It stops?' he said apprehensively, almost forming the words as a question but failing to fully comprehend the threat in Titus's words.

'Yes, correct it stops. Exceptional, you are capable of giving a straight answer, so perhaps you only know a little magic. But if you'd like your heart to carry on beating the way it does at the moment you will tell me where the hell I am?' the anger and frustration now clearly showed through in Titus's voice.

The elder man raised his hands in a peaceful gesture and replied,

'Take it easy my rude friend. You are in Tanaria; this place is hidden from the eyes of men so I was surprised at your confusion, you are standing in the residence of Tamar the Magician. Do you know him? I am Cedar, his caretaker.' Titus nodded,

'Oh yes, I know Tamar alright – that explains a lot in the way you answer my questions.' Cedar lowered his hands slowly so as not to agitate the swordsman.

'Would you care to join me in some refreshments and we can discuss your business here?' The scared man was at last making sense and with the surprise of his visit and the sharing of a bottle there was little chance of something more malicious from Cedar. Titus introduced himself and explained his unexpected arrival to Cedar; he figured that he had little to lose by telling the man the truth and began to recount his story. Cedar stopped him when he talked about Zerch opening the portal. Something didn't sound right in Titus's description of the event.

'What do you mean he twisted the device? Did he not just place a diamond on the floor or was there something else? I only ask because to open a Transport Portal from Cardus to here would be impossible with a standard diamond, even if enhanced by the power of the crystals. No, this is not right; there are also magical defences in place here that would stop such a thing. Please think back and describe every detail.' Titus could clearly remember seeing the unusual device in Zerch's hands and described it, being clueless to its importance.

'Ah, there is only one such relic that could transport you so far or change its path so rapidly - they must have used a Dimesia, but I thought them all destroyed,' stated Cedar.

'A what?' Titus asked dumbly.

'You know – a Dimesia.' Cedar took one quick glance at Titus darkening frown, 'Oh, - I guess you don't. They were ancient relics made by the old Masters, in the days when men devoted their art and time to crafting, rather than killing. They were said to hold the ability to remember several pre-set positions anywhere in the world and open a route of transport back to it when the correct sequence was replayed into the device. Each device could hold many locations in its memory. Zerch must have selected one of the unknown preselects on the device, for I have little doubt from what you have described to me that he would have desired to send you back in the direction of any allies.' Titus didn't necessarily agree with the man's opinions, for Zerch had already proved his worth in some ways to him, after all he had been instrumental in his own personal revenge and his face betrayed his doubt as he considered the man's motives. Cedar hammered home his disgust at Zerch although he had never actually met the man and most of his opinion was based on hearsay from the spoken words about the villa.

'What ever he has told you will be a lie, that one is a snake – even the Brotherhood distrust him. If he has removed you from his company it must be for a reason, I expect Athene has outlived her usefulness, no that's it, you outlived your usefulness.' Titus went to speak but Cedar in his slightly enraged state cut him short,

'People tend to turn up dead after Zerch visits, or sometimes not turn up at all.' Titus's eyes widened at his last comment wary that Athene was in their dubious company, his anguished thought showed across his face.

'Did you love her?' Cedar asked knowingly and as if she was already no more. Titus nodded back like a child after a reprimand as he absorbed Cedar's words. The old man seized upon the moment,

'Well then I guess I may be able to help, if only to spite that old toad Zerch. I have never actually met the man; few have - I have just seen the trail of destruction left in his wake. It would appear that he is playing a deadly game, he seems to have had a hand in eliminating an unhealthy amount of the land's Spell masters, be they Brotherhood or those pledged to Tamar.' Titus took a second before his brain caught up with the man's words,

'Help, you said – how can you help?'

'Well, I know little of magic – but Master Tamar did instruct me how to create a Portal, for emergencies …I guess this situation counts as one. I guess there is still enough power left inside the roadside shrine to boost our range and create the second Portal that will be needed to take us to Soredamor's Rift. I believe that Master Tamar is captive inside her domain, I would be obliged if you can find a way to free him.' Titus laughed out loud, the though actually appealed to him; not so much for the rescue or having to tolerate the man, but more for the thought of seeing him squirm, knowing that he would be indebted to a thickhead Su-Katii warrior. Of course the heroic rescue that he pictured would have nothing to do with impressing Athene? Oh no. But the more he dwelt on these thoughts, the more he began to appreciate the danger that she could be facing.

While Cedar stalked off to find the required diamonds Titus contemplated old scarface's words. *Ha*, free Tamar; that would be a turnaround that he would not forget in a hurry. Tamar would hate it and he could enjoy ridiculing the man for years. With the undercurrents of his relentless thoughts for vengeance finally quelled Titus found the fuel that had steered his path and motivated him each and every day now deficient. He now felt drained by the day's events and the aching in his arms still reminding him of the fact that he had been far from idle. His thoughts returned to Tamar and with his fires of revenge nothing more than just hot cinders, perhaps there needed to be other ways in his life to seek thrills than just the blade. Perhaps a knight in shining armour may help to convince Athene of his undying affections for her and if this didn't work – to hell with her, he might as well quell his inquisitive itch and go sleep with Tress, after all if he was accused of it and his relationship was truly finished with Athene, he may as well do the deed? His angered thoughts began to build, dragging the particles of his frustration and desire into the conjured image of Tress. Her body was certainly a more attractive offering than her soul, but it was in a man's nature to want the most flavoursome samples of meat that he was yet to try. He pictured her hourglass figure in the most salacious of poses and he began to undress her in his mind. Unfortunately he felt his own disappointment at their physical involvement together; he had only ever slept with Athene – in the flesh at least, even if it was contrary to Athene's belief, he had only beheld Tress's covered beauty and not the temptation of her naked flesh. Shame, he recalled her curvy figure and she certainly filled her leather leggings far better than anyone else he had seen. He had enjoyed hunting her; perhaps a time would come for a new kind of hunt between them? A smile grew across his face as he wondered what could have happened if the two women had swapped bodies the other way around.

'Devil get out of my head,' he said with a chuckle, 'The woman is a viper.'

Back outside Soredamor's cave Zerch stood waiting anxiously for Athene's return with their prize. He knew that he would have only moments to wait, even if she languished away her time inside. Most of his life he had been planning with baited anticipation for this very moment; it had been a full-time job thinking through the endless continuity plans and gathering the necessary relics to complete his grand schemes, he could not afford anything to be left to chance. His whole life had been a giant game of chess against an opponent that only stood in his mind. There was only ever one motivation to all of this, he did not seek Soredamor's affections like the others, and he had learnt how to unleash her shackles a long time ago. It had been his father's misguided desires to have nothing else but Soredamor in his life that had destroyed his childhood and driven his mother to her eventual suicide – she could not compete with the power of a god in his life, he knew that when he joined the Brotherhood he would also need to taste the same addictive fruit as his father. He had to understand the nature of the beast in order to destroy it. His hand trembled as he thought of her, she had been intoxicating and his body had been flung into the pit of her will and his soul would have also been claimed as hers like the others, if it had been in his body at the time. Before he followed in the footstep of his father and became a Master in the Brotherhood of Keth he had carried out his first step in the long path of retribution and revenge. In those early days he did his own dirty work and after much research he had located an ancient relic that would make his first steps to his plans of revenge possible. He was talented and had rapidly risen through the lower ranks of the Brotherhood but then that was to be expected, magic was in his blood. His initial rise to power had actually been too steep and he had needed to ease back his climb to the position of Master. He could not hold that rank until he had recovered the relic that he sought - the 'Heart of Ellacker, for with the rank would come his introduction to Soredamor.' The ancient relic was reputed to have the power to hold a person's soul trapped within the impressive cut diamond that had somehow found itself in the royal treasury. Its theft had been easy for Zerch; very few physical restraints could stop his developing skills in magic and after the use of two portals he found himself a rich man. At the time the Brotherhood had been requested to investigate the robbery after no signs of force were found. He remembered with a rare chuckle how he had been assigned to investigate his own crime, such a menial task was below a Master but a potential Master would jump at such an appointment. Even more amusing to him was the confession from the poor wretch that he had framed, he had not even needed to charm the unfortunate man before he screamed out his confessions of stealing the wealth from the vault during the very first round of torture. Unfortunately the wealth was never recovered before the poor wretches frail hart gave out. He had used the relic trapping his own soul inside the diamond before destroying his father and taking the step up into the ranks of the Masters. It had been all too easy at the time to complete the callous acts that were required from him to achieve the results that he desired, with his soul separated from his body he lived beyond the normal codes of men. After his fathers quarters mysteriously exploded whilst he was busy conducting experiments into new paths of magic, Zerch had been perfectly placed to fill the immediate opening. After the tragic accident there had been many questions, but here had not been enough left of the man to discover his smashed skull after Zerch had first clubbed him to his death before arranging the explosion. With the first step of his vengeance completed and his father slain, his soul had been protected from the eternal grasp of Soredamor inside the relic; her tender hooks could only extend to the pleasures of his flesh. The theory was simple - there was no chance of her contaminating his soul when it would not be present in his body. This initial part of his plan had gone well; he had soon become a Master like his father, but unlike him his soul was still his own. Everything was falling into place, apart from the unexpected theft of the Heart of Ellacker and the loss of his soul within. It had taken hundreds of years to find the relic once again and he had used his new fledgling slave to retrieve it. Tress had not known the importance of her first mission at the time, which was just as well for her. With his soul eventually returned to his body, he could no longer return into the Rift for in doing so he could lose everything that he had worked towards, it would only take one slip to fall under her charms and his extensive plans and years of work would be finished. He had used the centuries well, preparing for the other mountains that he knew he would need to overcome. It had been at the time of his father's death that he had realised just how dangerous the entity of magic was to this world. It held power far beyond that which any man or god should control or wield and it was then he had vowed to himself that he would remove the problem once and for all. The mission before him was simple, they all had to go.

Seconds later the three figures emerged from the Rift. Hand in hand they marched into the dimly illuminated light of the cave, where Athene moved forwards the yellow glow from the crystals imbedded into the rock-face closest to her extinguished.

'Kill them,' Zerch immediately commanded his Sword master into action. With Athene placed in such close proximity to brother and sister their powers were neutralised in the narrow passageway and their only way out was now blocked by the advancing swordsman, his trap was perfectly placed.

Two blades were drawn from their scabbards in the blink of an eye and Garth advanced quickly to make his kill, it was a shame in his eyes to slay such an exquisite creature, but this was the moment his master had been waiting for, years of hate released in seconds. The enchanted chain necklace that his master insisted he wore to protect him from her charms suddenly grew extremely hot with the energy it had just absorbed, but once he moved close to Athene its protection wouldn't matter. There was only the slightest hesitation as he closed in on his prey, Zerch had said "them". Did he mean all of them or just Soredamor as he had previously rehearsed? Fear showed in Soredamor's beautiful eyes as her first view of the outside world was filled with the sudden danger and she instinctively edged backwards towards the Rift as Garth lined himself up to strike. She was powerless to act so close to Athene and Garth knew that he could cover the killing ground before she would reach the Rift. He had practiced the lessons of covering the ground rapidly and making the kill a thousand times inside the regime of the Su-Katii training grounds. Step, leap, thrust, extend and kill was the simple manoeuvre that he lined himself up to complete.

'Do it now Garth, quickly - I command you,' Zerch screamed hysterically sensing his hesitation, pulling out his own dagger as his tension grew. Garth lunged forwards to stab at Soredamor, foolishly Tamar jumped out in front of her with his arms raised,

'No,' he shouted as the blade plunged into his chest,

Athene joined him in his scream of terror.

'Good, good now finish them all off,' called out Zerch from the shadows behind.

'Kill Soredamor.' Garth pulled backwards freeing his leading blade and raised his other to strike. A thrown dagger whistled past Zerch from behind and thudded into Garth's back. The warrior's expression changed to that of pain and his eyes widened with surprise. He felt a second thud pierce through the top of his spine as another thrown dagger hit home and shattered his upper vertebrae, suddenly Garth felt no more. The swordsman fell forward paralysed and dying, revealing the two protruding dagger handles jutting from his back as Garth collapsed forwards onto his face. Titus came running down the cave towards them, with both his daggers thrown he withdrew his blades; it was now Zerch that was the caged animal trapped between Titus and the Rift. Zerch was still in a state of shock at seeing his Swordmaster die, it was apparent to him now that not every calculation could be accounted for. How had Titus found his way back so quick? He had transported him far away and only magic could have brought him back so rapidly. He had personally seen to it that all those with the power had been accounted for or slain; all perhaps bar Ragnor, who was the final member of Tamar's little band of rebels who had so far escaped his shadow with the Nordheimer going into hiding, but he had recently reappeared and Zerch knew him to be well occupied with the Tanarian army. He doubted that Ragnor would have been able to assist Titus in this matter. There must be someone else involved, someone he had missed. Luckily Zerch was still outside Athene's anti-magic aura and he quickly pulled out the Dimesia relic fumbling with its mechanism as Titus closed the distance towards him and prepared to throw his sword. A Portal instantaneously appeared from the relic and Zerch disappeared; he had set it to the same destination as he had first sent Titus, he would route out this missed entity and destroy them. Titus's sword clattered from the cave wall scoring out chunks of crystal and rock as it hit the empty space where Zerch had been as the Portal closed as quickly as it had opened.

Tamar lay on the floor as white as a sheet as Athene pressed her blood-covered hands over his chest,

'Why?' she cried, 'Why save her...' she wept as she lay over the dying magician.

Titus retrieved his blade, he had replaced his broken sword from a small selection found in Tamar's villa; Cedar had found him something suitable before transporting him to the Cave. He pulled out the two daggers from Garth's back as he passed the corpse and replaced them about himself,

'Sorry Garth, but had you finished your time in the temple you would not have left your back so unguarded, especially with a Magician like Zerch to your rear.' He tutted loudly at the corpse before peering over at Tamar and the ever-growing pool of bright frothy blood escaping between Athene's fingers as she pushed down on his chest desperately attempting to halt its flow.

'Is he done for?' Titus asked casually, not enjoying the sight as much as he had first expected. The man's life and deeds were like pulling a splinter from your arse; you were initially relieved to be rid of the invading wood, but once gone, the resulting wound would linger and pain you all the more each time you sat down. He knew with regret that his passing would affect Athene in ways he could not even begin to comprehend, he had left his mark on her and his passing may even hinder his plans of repairing their relationship.

'Get away from my brother you abomination,' hissed Soredamor at Athene.

'Get away from him now, or he will die,' she added with a more concerned tone. Athene blinked incomprehensibly at him, still in shock before Titus grabbed her and dragged her away to where Zerch had been stood.

'Did I hear that correctly ...Brother?' Titus asked Athene as his eyes began to roll upwards in disbelief. She nodded slowly as she stared down at her blood-stained hands. Soredamor began to chant, holding her hands above Tamar's chest; she waved them in circles above his pale body for some time as her chants changed tempo. Titus attempted to reassure Athene as best he could,

'Don't worry I think the wound has just missed his heart but there are still some large arteries that exist there, if it has missed them he may still live, if not he will probably be dead in a minute.' She was most reassured by his clinical outlook.

A red light glowed from Soredamor's hands as she finished her incantations, the crystal lighting of the cave flickered as her hands touched Tamar's wound. Tamar's hand reached out and grabbed her arm. Through teeth gritted with pain he looked up into her tear-filled eyes,

'I have seen your secret sister ...I know you are pregnant.' With her emotions so exposed her body and mind had been easy to read and even racked with the pain of his wounds he could not resist reaching out with his magic. Some colour returned to his face, 'It was not until you left the Rift that the tiny foetus in your belly tasted life once more, I sensed it's heart begin to beat again.' In between his pain he puffed out his words, 'The innocent must not die.' She stroked his head in her hands before they fell to rest on her stomach, they gently caressed it as if seeking signs of the life within, she replied distantly,

'It must be Gorran's child. Honestly, I did not know, I had a suspicion all those years ago but I thought I had lost it when I was placed inside the Rift,'

'Titus approached, looming over the two of them.

'Is he going to make it?' he enquired,

'Of course, it takes more than just cold steel to finish our bloodline, that fool Zerch forgets he is dealing with a god. I will remind him of that soon.' She replied looking him up and down, her first impression of the man was that he looked like a magnificent specimen but she resisted the temptation to charm him to her control, besides he stood too close to Athene for now and from their familiar interaction and her glances at him when he was paying her no attention she assumed that they had a connection. Perhaps she should refrain from radiating her powers until at least she had acclimatised to this world and seen what was waiting for her in this very different land from which she left? Titus replied with a sceptical grunt,

'Go tell the corpse of Hadrak that, he lies slain outside his Rift,' he said with a smirk.

'Hadrak is dead?' She paused for a moment letting the words sink in, 'He is no loss. He was not from my father's line, good riddance to the little bastard, he was...' her words faded. Titus quickly changed the subject before she asked the details of his death,

'If Tamar is going to live with your ...*oh so powerful magic*, lets not waste any time. I'll give him a shove back into the Rift so he can fully recover quicker and then we can be away from this place once and for all.' Titus suggested, thinking that Athene could always go back in and retrieve him again.

'No, it will be pointless and you would need *her*,' she pointed at Athene, 'To set him free again.' Titus frowned disliking her tone,

'But I have done so in the past, it worked well enough for me,' he replied.

'That is because you are not a god, for you mortals inside the Rift, time does not stay entirely still, it still creeps forwards but at a minute pace; for a god it stands totally still, he will not heal inside just linger in the same state.' She had begun to lose interest half-way through her explanation, having to explain the ways of gods was quiet tedious to her over the centuries. 'I want to see daylight, let us move him to more comfortable surrounds, he just needs some time to rest. You look like a strong lad,' Soredamor ran her soft hand along his arm to touch his face, as Athene stood with jaw agape feeling her temper rise.

'Carry him outside and I'll see where this can take us.' Soredamor commanded the Su-Katii as if he were already under the powers of her charm then moved her hand up to a crystal jutting from the rocky wall; it fell into her hand as if the stone had never been held by the cave's ancient grasp. They followed her commands resentfully, not because of her beguiling aura, but because they made sense, Athene's presence saw to that. Although even without it, a stunningly attractive woman had a certain way of getting men to help her needs that did not require magic. It was an experience that Soredamor had totally forgotten, surrounded with her Brotherhood in her exile and every new reaction in the world beyond was like tasting life again. She concentrated her magic for a second when away from Athene and she could feel the living presence of the child in her womb. She smiled a beaming smile and felt the true joy of her release. They walked through the cave with Titus carrying Tamar like a child in his arms and Soredamor leading the way out like a young girl excited at the prospect of the blue sky, Athene thought deeply about the strange situation. Tamar was her brother and after seeking to stop her for years he had put himself before her in harm's way, was the bond of family stronger than his own concerns? If so where did it leave them? She was a god to the Brotherhood, but would they all heel to her commands or was some new kind of terror about to be unleashed upon the world? To be honest she didn't think it could get much worse than the current state of affairs and up till now Soredamor had not seemed as bad as everyone had made out, actually she seemed quiet normal. Well bossy, but normal ...well, that was normal for a woman of power. Of course Athene absolutely hated her guts for her mind-numbing beauty, 'But that was only natural as well – right?' she reassured herself. As the bombardment of questions filtered through her mind one concern kept on riding to the top. She seemed to be the only thing that could quell her powers. In Soredamor's eyes this made her a threat to her power and most expendable.

One outside, Soredamor revelled under the grey clouds, even displaying a brief solo waltz to some imaginary music; it was not quiet the blue she had hoped for but today grey would do very nicely. In any case it would only take several words of magic to blow away the lingering grey and reveal the beauty of the blue sky beyond. She appeared quiet understandably to be in the best of moods and unreserved about showing her joy, a far cry from the stuffy attitude of her wounded brother. Titus had pointed out the village of Hickhem in the distance far below in the valley, the only shelter for leagues around. Soredamor quickly took a trip back into the cave collecting a variety of crystals exposed in the walls and then returned and summoned a Portal to take them all to the village. Titus noticed the speed in which the Portal had formed, if speed was an indication at the power of the spell's caster. It was obvious to him that she should be feared.

The Portal opened up inside the small village tavern leaving the locals cowering in shock; eventually the innkeeper poked his head above the counter where he had attempted to hide himself from the magical force that had suddenly invaded his space. He gazed up at the group's arrival.

The blinding light disbursed and the innkeeper was surprised to see the familiar outlanders who had visited before, he knew they were not to be trusted; the dark haired lady had a different man on her arm each time she stayed. He decided that he would not make any comment; the new man looked just as handy as the last. He was suddenly taken back by the perfection of the accompanying lady and stood their gawping before he found his words,

'Will it be... err ...the usual room?' he enquired nervously.

Kerric arrived back in the cave outside Soredamor's Rift later that day. He had naturally been pleased with his prediction that Zerch's poisoning had not been extended to him; especially after the nasty and unexpected surprise that he found waiting for him the day before. On his initial return to Soredamor he was genuinely shocked, who would have thought it? Tamar the magician was also sharing his beloved god's Rift. He had found out the hard way as well – with a lightning bolt burning through his heart as he strolled towards the main building. It was definitely not an experience that he would like to repeat in a hurry. He had been forced to retreat and wait out the long cold night in a nearby cave – so much for his backup plan. He had spent that night wide awake wondering if his calculations had been correct and stressing about the poison. If he fell asleep, would he wakeup or would it be his last night in this world? It had been a most draining experience. One that had disturbed his sleep to the point where he had unexpectedly nodded off for a moment as he counted down the many hours before he timed his return and became the saviour of his Queen. He was going to place a series of well prepared spells about the area of the Rift and set his trap; he would steal Athene and use her to free his queen, claiming the glory as his own. However after suddenly waking up and finding out that he had slept late into the morning he cursed his own failings and on finding Garth's body leaking its mess about the floor he realised that his play was now all too late. He entered the empty Rift in a fit of fury and confirmed his disbelief, he was too late.

Chapter 15 – The Glory of War

In Tagel, the defence of the second wall had indeed seen off the first wave of the Aristrian assault, but as their beaten men were repelled and returned, disheartened, to their lines Telimus and his brethren had used their powers and called fire from the sky, concentrating their efforts over a twenty yard segment of the wall. It had burned the wooden palisade and men to little more than ash and the Aristrian cavalry had seized upon the opportunity and turned their mounts about to thunder through the extinguished embers bringing havoc to their lines. The power of the Brotherhood was well-demonstrated, forcing yet another retreat to the Tanarian lines. Later that day the Aristrian battle camp advanced another step closer to the Keep. Lord Aden planned his next move over the model he had constructed of the ground ahead; he was keen to keep their momentum and victories moving. He had spent a considerable amount of time matching little twigs and stones to represent the various walls; he even made a little pond depicting the sea. He was a stickler for details and was proud of his creation, so when the group of commanders arrived from the auxiliary for their orders briefing and accidentally planted a foot into the side of his model he was less than pleased. The man badly attempted to fix the broken wall that he had destroyed as Lord Aden dished out a tongue-lashing to the man. It was only when the heavy infantry commander arrived that Aden's mood brightened, as the new commander observed with his suggestions,

'Ah it would appear that the Auxiliaries have pre-empted our next action against the enemy and have altered your model to match the destruction we shall unleash, for mark my word sir, once we deploy the siege engines that wall will soon be smashed down.' The confident words of the ordinary soldiers brought a smile of satisfaction to his face; he went easy on his model wrecker and continued with his briefing. Only the old town wall now stood between them and the soft underbelly of the town and then the real prize - the Keep. Yes, there was a causeway to traverse and yes, the Keep's walls were nearly fifty yards high, but this problem would be addressed on another day and his wizards would be sure to find a way in. So far, things were going well for them, far better than he had expected. They had lost no more than ten percent of their troops in the two assaults, he had expected that number to be closer to twenty percent by now and the fallen men had mostly been his shock troops and fodder. His heavy infantry were still fresh and ready to prove themselves. He knew well that the next two hurdles would be the biggest issue; a stone wall was a different kind of problem to the wooden structures which they had faced so far. Still those wizards were really making a difference for them; he had only needed to commit one of his four remaining Su-Katii to the walls during the fighting. His Su-Katii were keen to get stuck in to the combat, yet he did not like to commit them on the walls – they were at their most vulnerable on a ladder and unstoppable on their feet. Yet fighting was what they were bred for and if one should fall, so what; Lord Mako would return soon to bolster their numbers and the Su-Katii alone could probably take this keep, but the men needed to gain the feeling of being useful and the Aristrians needed to be seen as the victors in this war. Telimus had informed him that Mako's hunting trip had been most successful and he would soon return. Lord Aden had decided to add some extra surprises to today's events, feeling confident with his victories - besides he needed a test run of the machines before they reached the Keep. He had prepared for war today in the old way, the way that wars were conducted before the resources of magicians were employed. Yes, today's assault of the town promised to be a most glorious slaughter.

Lord Mallet looked down from the ramparts of the Keep at the advancing shield wall approaching the town. The Aristrians had looked as if they were marching in a parade the way they proudly positioned themselves on the field. They stopped just outside of bow range, which was determined by several skirmishers firing arrows towards the wall before them. Several trains of oxen appeared at the rear, near the distant Aristrian tree line, they slowly dragged out a series of siege engines. A procession of twelve devices was slowly pulled forwards.

'My, my. We have been busy; haven't we my Aristrian friends,' Mallet murmured to himself as he realised that they had only constructed two Trebuchets in the same period, but most of their wood resources had been used on the walls. As he watched he could see that there were two main variants of device, the Ballista; a huge crossbow type of mechanism that was capable of firing large bolts over twice the distance of any bow, they also carried several modified bolts shaped into a grappling hook that could be attached to large coils of rope which could then be used to scale high walls or even possibly pull down segments of it. The second type was the Trebuchet, a larger wagon-like device with a throwing arm and counterweight used to propel large rocks high over the walls, more commonly known to the troops as 'death from above,' if you are unlucky enough to be within three hundred yards of it. No, wait, Lord Mallet strained his eyes; further down on the distant tree line there was another machine, one he had not seen the like of before. It looked almost like a child's slide yet with a much more pronounced lip that could be angled up as well as down. Lining its surrounds were a large array of chopped tree trunks, cut to approximately the size of a grown man. Lord Mallet especially didn't like the prospect of contraptions that he had never seen before and for the first time spoke a little prayer before raising the order to evacuate the town. He knew it would be perceived that they were going to lose the wall if he gave the command, but so far the Aristrians had carved them up like butter, if they did breach the thick stone walls they would soon flood the town.

'I want everyone who is beyond fighting age or ability to move back to the Keep right now,' he yelled at Tarqin, the Keep's house steward. Tarqin moved slowly with his usual grace, even when shouted at. He was a result of generations of the same family holding a noble position in court for centuries and little seemed to faze him, in fact Mallet could never recall seeing the man run. To Tarqin, it was the little things that bothered him the most and he had a good eye for detail. After digesting Lord Mallet's orders he replied,

'My Lord, I take it that you do know that there is no room for the civilians in the Keep?'

'Of course I know, but we cannot leave them to be pulverised by that lot. Move as many as you can into the Keep, then fill up the land to the cliffs on the north shore, as the Aristrians will need to pass our walls to get around to them, after that fill the causeway and I see three small vessels in the harbour, I would suggest you also fill them and cast off. Find any place you can, just get them out of the town.' Mallet directed.

Tarqin cringed and protested at the suggestion,

'The north face blows a gale like no other, they would be lucky to cling to that small rocky outcrop.' Mallet placed a hand over his eyes at the reality of Tarqin's words.

'Oh, then place the larger specimens of the population there, I don't bloody know? What do you think; it's got to be better than being squashed by a falling rock.'

Tarqin rolled his eyes,

'Sir, I can assure you that everyone is quite skinny

during our siege, with low supplies you will find it difficult to find 'larger specimens' anywhere. Well that is perhaps all apart from Commander Thorsten. I can see my ribs poking through when I undress whereas he on the other hand is lucky if he can see his dick.' Tarqin displayed an unusual streak of bitchiness in his voice as his hunger overtook his constraint. Mallet's patience was beginning to wear thin, his original order had not yet been relayed and his subordinate was becoming stroppy, this simply would not do.

'Get those people back from the wall and into safety immediately and enough of the back-chat Tarqin; just get it done.' Lord Mallet stormed off; he needed to get to the wall as his people would look to him for inspiration.

On his arrival he was surprised to see that a welcoming party was awaiting him,

Commander Thorsten was already there, with his standard bearer standing proudly behind him flying the predatory fish of Tagel's banner. Next to him stood Lord Candis and a handful of officers; very few of them had made it through the early days of the war, the surprise attacks from Aristria combined with the betrayal of the Su-Katii had been devastating. Candis stepped forwards and whispered in Mallet's ear,

'I decided that it was time that the 'dinner' came out and led by example. He was none to happy with my suggestion but he didn't dare to refuse.' Lord Candis turned to the others gathered around and bellowed out,

'What are you lot all doing stood together like that? Spread out along the wall or one falling rock will take the lot of you out.' The officers grumbled at being shouted at but jumped to his command, spread out this way they could also reinforce the men's morale all along the wall. As the men watched on, it seemed to take an age before the enemy siege engines were eventually dragged up into place; their position gave them an improved range and put them beyond the return fire of mere arrows or bolts from the wall.

'Bring forwards our Trebuchets, they are of no use two streets back, get them as close to the walls as possible,' commanded Lord Candis. 'Now I want all of the massed archers to move six streets back but wait for the command to come forwards,' he added. There was no point in lining the areas behind the wall with falling rock-fodder, the archers were quick and agile, with only light armour. They could remain out of harm's way and dash backwards and forwards when needed. With this move only the enemy cavalry would have any chance of crossing the ground swiftly enough to avoid their archers repositioning themselves and with their ranks being made up mostly of the upper class' and nobles it was a fair bet that they would never lower themselves to dismounting and scaling a wall. If a breach looked likely he would recall the archers in force, Candis was sure that there would be no assault until they were sufficiently tenderised. Shortly after, the first rock thudded into the muddy clearing twenty yards forwards of their position. The Aristrians began to make their adjustments, the first single shots should be easy to avoid, but once the relentless storm of several war machines working together began, they knew it would be a different matter. Lord Candis looked above the battlements, the siege engines were formed in a long line with light infantry to their flanks and archers on the wall behind. Beyond the gate and wooden wall that yesterday had been in Tanarian hands, the crests and banners of the massed heavy infantry and the tips of cavalry lances could be seen. Lord Aden had kept these tight formations well back from the return fire of their two measly siege engines. Candis ran his eyes over the positions of the enemy units surrounding the wall.

'Yes,' he muttered too himself, 'Yes, I think the risk is worth it. Lord Mallet, form up your cavalry. Get every flammable liquid that you can lay your hands on; I believe there will be time to assault their war machines. If we strike quickly with cavalry, by the time they see us coming they will never be able to squeeze enough men through that gate entrance to engage us with any force. There should be enough time to do some damage to those engines and get your men back again. Get your riders ready. Strike, light, and then ride for your life.' A great whoosh raced past their heads as a giant boulder hurtled its way out towards the enemy from their redeployed Trebuchet, everyone instinctively ducked at the sound. It took some time for the cavalry to muster and for the Aristrians to find their aim, just as the runner returned bring news of the cavalry being formed up and ready did the first rock smash into a segment of the wall. Two men were instantly flattened and a load of flint and brick shrapnel scattered the otherwise lucky nearby men in the area. A cheer went up across the field as the Aristrians found their aim.

'I'll give them something to bloody cheer about, send in the cavalry,' Lord Candis commanded. 'Archers stand by to take up the wall,' he wanted the archers ready to protect the returning horsemen with a blanket of arrows. The runner ran back to relay the command as a volley of giant spear-like bolts flew over the walls from the Aristrian Ballista. Few were hit, but when they did strike they were messy, Candis knew they were better used for intimidation rather than mass casualties, this knowledge would do the men on the wall little good. The riders came pelting through the cobbled streets filling the air with their crescendo of hooves. The gatemen waited until the last minute before opening the heavy town gates. For a moment Candis thought it too late and cringed, expecting a pileup of riders into the door, but he drew relief when he saw the men emerging in the ground outside.

'Charge,' yelled their young commander, a man by the name of Ryce who spurred his men on. The riders streamed out of the two entrances from the town to stamp across the mud-stricken field that met with the second wall. The Aristrian infantry on the edges of the siege engines broke ranks and ran forwards in an unorganised mob, spurred on by their shouting commanders to block the path to the war-machines. They were no match for the charging cavalry who rode easily through them to arrive at the siege engines first. The infantry were churned into the mud as several companies of riders stopped and engaged them, leaving the bulk of the riders to move on and put fire to the war machines.

Lord Aden had been genuinely surprised at the boldness of the Tanarian move; he thought such a move almost beyond these cowardly degenerates - it had Candis's name written all over it. But luckily he always prepared for every eventuality; well really there was no luck in it, just several lifetimes of practice in the Su-Katii Temple; it was training and repetition that made good commanders. He raised his left arm to signal the Brotherhood. Fyren of the Brotherhood was a promising up-and-coming Spell-master who had taken up with Telimus and was standing on duty as the others of his kind rested from their earlier endeavours. He crested the wooden wall behind the war machines where he had been instructed to wait out of sight. It was now his time to shine. He had already prepared his first spell behind the palisade and unleashed it as he rose. A storm of ice and freezing water erupted from the magic formed about his hands spreading out in a cone around the burning engines which had already been put to flame. Several of the nearest riders were almost frozen solid to the ground with their steeds as they were enveloped in the forming ice storm. Capitan Ryce was caught on the edge of the white cloud that was now beginning to dissipate and spotted the Brotherhood Magician as the storm's source, he peaked over the rim of his frozen shield that he had raised to protection him from the icy cloud, the coldness against the wood penetrated through to his arm. He raised his arm high and circled his sword in the air, giving his men the signal to retreat back to the town. A random gust of wind blew across from the sea, helping to disperse the icy cloud. The Spell-master's hood was blown back in the gale revealing the Albino's deathly pale glare; he had already begun a new spell. Ryce knew little of magic but he instinctively knew that he needed to act quickly. The hooded Brotherhood had proven deadly so far and the rumours amongst the common troops almost overstretched their actual deeds. His troops were returning to the safety of their lines, hopefully before the Aristrian cavalry could emerge from their gate, but the Wizard's chanting gave the promise that not all of his men would make it back. Ryce turned about and spurred his warhorse through the intensifying volleys of arrows that had harassed their ranks and continued on towards the Wizard. A pike man ran out at him attempting to unhorse him, he beat the point away with his shield and leaned over to drive his sword back into the man's torso, riding on with the Wizard in his sights. Two arrows crossed his path, one bouncing harmlessly from his shield the other whistling past his face. Two more men rushed out in front of the Magician, his personal bodyguard - an axe man and a swordsman; the pale albino's eyes were bulging with the frustration of his unstopped advance, a choice loomed before him, he could waste the powerful spell on one single man to protect himself or unleash it on the masses of escaping riders, perhaps even wiping out the force. He needed to impress Telimus and gaining rank and respect within the Order was everything, so in a split second he decided on mass destruction, the Servain guard and the archers had better do their job. The power gathered in the air about his hands as the prepared lightning intensified and grew in power. Ryce's warhorse reared on its hind legs as the swordsman struck out beating the steed about its armoured neck. The warhorse's hooves struck out at the man and the enraged animal bit and stomped back at the man until he was soon bowled over by the mighty animal. A large war axe swung at Ryce from the other man and he managed to catch Ryce on his raised shield. The blow shattered a large segment from his frozen shield, numbed his arm with its impact and the guard's follow-up blow knocked him from the saddle. He spat the blood from his mouth feeling the cold steel of the inside of his close-faced helm pressing against his face and just managed to raise his sword in time to meet the decapitating blow that sought his neck. The vibration of clashing steel jarred his arm and he clambered forwards on all fours attempting to reach the magician. Ryce looked around at the pursuing man, smashing the rim of his damaged shield into his opponent's chin in the moment when he raised back his axe to strike at him again. His head snapped backwards with the impact and a stream of lightning forked past them into the retreating Tanarians as their private little fight to reach the Brotherhood magician continued. Ryce heard the screaming of both horse and men from the ground behind him and he scrambled forward to the source of the arcing lightning that swept over his men. A hand grabbed his ankle from the dropped man, he swung his sword behind him and suddenly he was free to strike at the Albino. Fyren had almost forgotten about the advancing soldier as he revelled in the destruction of the fleeing men. The power of his magic was both exhilarating and intoxicating to him at the same time. The armoured knight removed the anchoring arm that held him and jumped onto the jutting structure of the palisade; his sword thrust aimed upwards and Ryce sank his sword into the wizard's lower belly. Fyren looked down at the wound in disbelief; his spell of destruction was halted as the air need for his magical chants was robbed from his lungs, then he toppled forward from the palisade. Ryce jumped down from the wall hacking down at the pile of black robes at his feet. A distant shout of approval came from the Tanarian walls as Ryce stumbled through the thick mud back towards his lines. He killed the wounded Servain guardsman on the ground as he passed. Several arrows whistled passed his face reminding Ryce of the threat behind. The lead Aristrian cavalry-men had already advanced through the gate onto the field in response to their attack; they spotted the stumbling knight and lining him up in their sights they broke into a charge, levelling their lances with the anticipation of the strike.

Lord Candis pointed out the struggling knight to Mallet as they watched from the wall,

'Your commander has inspired the men, it's a shame he will soon be dead. Divert your archers' fire to the left, I find the best heroes are ones that are still drawing breath.'

An arrow hammered into the running knight's broken shield, another bounced from his helmet, he shook his head and continued, a third arrow impacted into his arse, its point jutting out near his right hip. Every man on the wall stood with baited breath watching the drama unfold and willing the lone soldier to make it back to the wall alive.

'Damn it,' cursed Candis and he vaulted over the wall, landing like a cat crouching in the mud below. He ran forward towards the injured knight limping back to his lines, he should have reacted earlier as the group of riders were now on their final charge. The horseman loomed above the muddy knight as he fell once more into the cold sludge of the field. A large rock suddenly impacted into the group of men bearing down on Ryce, scattering them, the Tanarian trebuchet was still in action. Broken horses neighed in agony as their shattered bodies joined with the mud. The impact splattered dirt and crud over those not directly affected by the blunt trauma in a blinding mess. Lord Candis leapt over the broken bodies, his swords quickly slicing through all in his path to the fallen knight. He helped Ryce to his feet then briefly stopped his assistance to run through an approaching soldier.

'Stop gawping men! Covering fire,' yelled Lord Mallet and the archers opened up on the following cavalry. Their weight of fire was sufficient to prevent a sustained action against the returning men and none were too keen to face the deadly Su-Katii as he dragged the injured man back to safety. The beating of shields and the sound of cheers echoed along the wall as the men returned, but their noise was quickly quelled as an operational Trebuchet dropped a boulder through a town house behind them. Several of the Aristrian war machines were still operational, saved by the Brotherhood magician and the majority of the others would just needed some minor repairs to bring them back in to service.

Telimus who had not been resting with the others had been admiring Fyren's work from the distance of the left flank; his chain lighting spell took down at least thirty riders on its first blast. He was pleased he had brought the man with him, although he had estimated that he could have taken down a few more. The three Brotherhood Masters had been spread out along the wall as their acolytes rested. Teon had taken the right flank, where the Su-Katii stood surveying the battlefield due to its slightly raised ground. Teon did not take Fyren's death well; it had been rumoured that the two were a little more than just friends but such an accusation would never be levelled against a Master and the acolytes knew better than to talk of such things. Teon was enraged at the sight of the unmoving black robes of Fyren lying on the field, without regard he jumped down from the palisade and ran towards the Tanarian wall, his feet did not sink deep into the mud like the others had, his magic held his feet above the surface of the partially flooded field allowing his dark robe to flutter menacingly behind him; it was not often that the Brotherhood had a need to run and the unusual sight drew many eyes. Lord Aden could ill afford to lose another Spell-master through the stupidity of his vengeance, especially not on the same day as his fellow, it would be bad for morale; he also knew well that Candis was still on the Tanarian wall, ever ready to strike at an opportune target. Aden immediately dispatched two of his Su-Katii to protect the magician, with his stern words echoing in their ears,

'Keep him alive. Do not fail me.' Both men grabbed large shields from the troops behind them and ran off after Teon who was not stopping for anyone. Fortunately the magician was unfit and easy to catch. He burbled a mixture of spells, chants and curses as he neared the Tanarian wall. A number of arrows were directed against him, yet he simply extended his hand and they bounced from an invisible shield before him.

'You will pay in blood for slaying Fyren.' he bellowed at the wall before casting his magic. The ground about the wall before him begun to shake, it vibrated as if struck by an earthquake. Soldiers were flung from their footings and fell from the wall and the repercussion of their screams spread a wave of fear along the wall. Teon clenched his fists, the look of true loathing filled his dark eyes. Unusually for the Brotherhood his skin was deeply tanned, but not from his time spent in the sun, it was from his breeding, generations of his family had been raised in the warmer climates of the north coast. His short-cropped black hair revealed a well-defined bald spot which dripped with sweat at his magical exertions. The wall gave a large shudder as if giving in to the Master's will and a large segment collapsed. The Aristrians knew a gift horse when they saw one and the order was quickly given to advance.

Telimus who had joined with Lord Aden turned to

him and commented without a trace of humour,

'Had I known that his magic would have been enhanced so much by Fyren's death and anger I would have killed him myself.'

Chapter 16 – Forgotten Love

Tress left the temporary hilltop camp that the beaten army had erected to make her own solo reconnaissance of the surrounding lands. They had followed the river north for the last two days in an effort to flee the pursuing army; they had been driven further into the heartland of Aristria and were closing on Monumentium, its capital. They realised that the army was being driven north by the pursuing forces and had diverted away from the main roads that led towards the capital; these well-maintained tracks would only aid their pursuers' cavalry in catching them. Instead they crossed the rougher terrain through the broken tree lines and steeper hills to hinder pursuit. They suspected that a second force had been sent down from the capital to capture them in a pincer movement and they had looked to Ragnor for guidance, hoping that he could conduct some kind of mystical recognisance, but to their dismay he explained to the gathered commanders that he was just not that kind of magician.

'I am an Elementalist,' he had explained as if everyone should understand the schools of magic.

'I study the ways of nature in order to complement this world, not to harm it.' As a result of his meeting Tress was now going out on her own reconnaissance. The last fighting from the rear guard had occurred two exhausting days ago and the lack of contact with the enemy actually made everyone more nervous than during the bouts of fighting. She started her patrol by doing a complete circle about the surrounding lands of the hill. She chose to take her time as her feet were throbbing sore from their days of marching. She was in no danger of being discovered with her enchanted cloak to hide her safely away, although she was always aware that the Aristrians had Magicians on their side. Apart from these dark agents she was more than confident in her own abilities. What with her time spent in the Temple she was sure that she could handle anything she ran into. Her plan was to sweep the immediate area and then push forward towards the capital for a few leagues to get the lie of the land or perhaps find a better defensive position than the temporary hill camp that the army had adopted. Moving down the incline with the first taste of being away from the army and on her own again, she realised that she had not had the usual urge that overcame her to run, this was normally her very first instinct. This revelation scared her, for she knew it meant that she had changed and had not even questioned her inevitable return to the doomed force. As she moved stealthily through the trees she passed a small group of Aristrian rangers, cavalrymen who had clung to the darkness of the surrounding trees to conceal their presence. They were the eyes and ears of the pursuing army; but as she investigated their position further, there was no sign of their main force. These men were trained to live in the harshest of environments without the warmth of fire or hot rations for months on end. They were known as the 'horse-wives' amongst their own, for they often would sleep against their horses to maintain body heat and were always attentive at their sides. To lose your mount as a scout would often follow with your life. She thought to pass the group of four men by, avoiding their concealed camp as this had been her habit over the years, it was always better to avoid a situation as a thief, people who look for trouble often find too much. That was now the problem, for she was no longer a thief and these men could well be the only ones that had found the army for all she knew? She couldn't take that chance of letting them report back the army's position. They had to die. She circled back around, picking her way through the dense undergrowth and trees that they had selected for a reconnaissance point. She first cleared the area for signs of any other soldiers but they appeared to be alone in these parts, apart from one returning soldier, a fifth man who slowly worked his way back to the others from his group. Even with her enchanted cloak she had to be careful as she followed him back towards the others, her feet could still disturb the plant life as she moved. The fifth figure entered their camp, crouching low through the branches he approached silently with his drab cloak wrapped around him concealing his figure against the dark surrounds. A struggle occurred as the lone figure covered the sentry's mouth with his hand and stabbed the unfortunate man in the back of the skull with a dagger; the lifeless body fell and his sword was quickly recovered from his lifeless body. Tress recognised with growing admiration the distinct way in which the warrior moved into the next encounter, the movements of the Temple trained instantly drew her attention. Barrad moved forward and slew the other three men in no more than the duration of a heart-beat, only one of the dead men actually managed to free his sword and put up any kind of defence. Tress closed the distance to the camp to gain a better view of the panther-like man that had stalked into their camp with deadly effect.

'Barrad,' she called out, just loud enough to hear. He shot around and stared into the area where she stood, his eyes moved past her and sought the source of the voice he had just heard, it sounded familiar he thought.

'Barrad,' she repeated, forgetting in her excitement at seeing him that her enchanted cloak still concealed her. Tutting at her own stupidity she threw back its hood and dispelled its power rushing forward to meet with him. Barrad's eyes opened wide with disbelief as Tress suddenly appeared from thin air before him, she was the last person he had expected to see in this wilderness.

'Tress, can it be?' he said as he lowered his sword and she rushed to embrace him. 'Tamar must have been right; he had said it was our destiny.' Coincidence had a way of filling a willing mind full of romantic notions.

'Of course it is, now kiss me you foolish man.' His lips enveloped hers in a passionate embrace and he unashamedly enjoyed the energy of her ravaging mouth. She pursed her soft lips against his then gently released him from her embrace allowing him air before reapplying him with a coating of quick kisses on his lips and cheeks. Instinctively he had returned her pleasing embrace and began kissing her gently on her neck, his focus moved entirely to Tress. He halted immediately as he realised what he was doing. Soredamor had always insisted that he kiss her neck in that exact way before they made love. He shuddered at the thought of the years he had spent as her slave inside the Rift; his reactions had been like that of a trained pet attending to its masters needs. His eyes had feasted many times on Soredamor's enticing body as his mind battled the desires being forced upon him – each and every time he had fought against her will he had lost his battle. For all those years he had helplessly watched on, as if he were a stranger watching his own body commanded by her will fulfilling her every need. This encounter with Tress actually felt alien to him in having a choice. Tress also struggled in that moment; his wandering kisses to her neck took her mood in a direction very different from her initial overfriendly embrace. She was suddenly acutely aware of their surroundings. Trying desperately to draw her attention away from anything but him, they were in a hidden camp in the heart of Aristria, with possibly thousands of men surrounding them in the lands beyond them. In their indecision and thoughts they were like two broken toys that played together, each broken in their own unique way yet mending the other. She was also acutely aware that if she did follow her body's willingness to run away with its desires it was likely that the memory of Barrad would be erased within weeks or even less. It was also likely that if she dared to walk that path of temptation she should act with haste, for once they returned to the Tanarian camp together all future possibilities of intimacy were unlikely; there was just too much to keep a general occupied in a battle camp, it was also likely that they may not live to see the war concluded. Was it better to love and forget than never to love at all? It was a bitter sweet pill to swallow; a moment of happiness together could lose every precious memory of him. She was acutely aware of the odds at stake and Barrad's decision on the matter. His bulge pressed into her tight leather leggings as his arousal grew, grinding against her as his kisses continued to work their way down to the top of her exposed cleavage. Tamar had said that he was the one she would never forget? She had suspected that to be a lie, it was the way of magicians to make people have hope or use them to their own means. He kissed her neck again and she moaned gently in his ear; her sounds of pleasure doubled his efforts to ravage her. There was certainly a part of her that was willing to test Tamar's statement. The promise of Barrad being removed from her mind was too much for her; she had genuine feelings for him and could not bear the thought that this would be cleansed from her heart by Zerch's curse. With a deep breath of resolve, she pulled herself free of his encircling arms and warm breath, trying to establish her own space and distance herself from her own temptations.

'It's so good to see you Barrad, you are so special to me,' she touched his face with the palm of her hand; his cheeks were flushed and hot. 'Now, we should be getting you back to your men, they need your leadership, you will give them hope.' She panted her words out between deep breaths regaining her composure. He drew in a long deep breath, then nodded with agreement,

'Yes, you are right …a woman like you and a Su-Katii …it wouldn't work? I don't know what came over me.' She looked offended,

'What do you mean, a woman like me? What's wrong with me?' Barrad flushed even redder with embarrassment, he had only let those mindless words fall aimlessly from his mouth to deflate their mixed up passions; he didn't want to believe them.

'Err, no *Tress*, hang on a minute, that's not what I meant. It's me, I'm damaged goods. You have tortured my dreams by being in them each night for a hundred years, but with each such thought, forbidden to my touch as Soredamor held me close each night as her slave,' he looked distant as he spoke.

'By my words I meant that you are unique and perhaps far too good for me. You once told me to remind you of our first kiss, well there has not been a day gone by that I have forgotten it.' His words hit a note in her mind, she too had endured a lifetime in the Su-Katii Rift but under a different regime, one in which the God-king enjoyed more than she could remember. Now only the written words of her diary replayed the experience with Hadrak and recounted her service to him. Fate had made them slaves to another and they both had a level of empathy with the other's feelings.

'You are perfect in every conceivable way Tress and it would probably be best if you did not return to the army with me, with your skills and that cloak you have a chance at life.' He turned unable to look at her without his lustful thoughts distracting him and he recovered a second blade from one of the bodies on the chance that he might need it on his return to the army,

'I had better get going,' he said to her lurking shadow behind him. She absorbed his words, then responded,

'Perfect in every way huh? I would be less than perfect if I allowed you to walk away from me now, there may not be a tomorrow for the likes of us.' Her arm snaked out and grabbed him, drawing him back into the warmth of her body. 'You're not going any where yet soldier,' she said and kissed him firmly. 'Did I tell you that I know some magic? I can read your future. There is a new mission of conquest ahead of you.' Tress's eyes widened with pleasure as he drew her in tightly against him,

'Well it maybe more of an invasion force that a conquest,' she said suggestively with an excited giggle as she felt the firmness of his manhood stretching his thin robe. Her hand reached down and caressed him, 'Oh my, it would appear that you have a rather sizable invasion force stood ready.' What followed was not the passion-filled fantasy that she had envisioned many times since their separation, it was in its own feral way far better than those sugar-coated thoughts. She cast her eyes to the sky to avoid those of the corpses on the ground behind him as he trapped her back against the trunk of a large tree. Their passion and kissing was frenzied as they desperately fumbled at their own clothing and then each other's. Tress almost fell as she struggled to wriggle out of her long boots and the leather leggings that hugged her figure so well. Luckily strong arms caught her and assisted her to rip them from her limbs. His rough hand slid between her thighs and against her palpitating body as his fire-filled lips locked once more with her own. She needed no climb to find her arousal and sensed his pressing need for her. She guided him into her private sanctum and her deep guttural moan left him with no doubt that she wanted more. There was nothing gentle in their encounter as a hundred years of dreams were unleashed, he grasped her hair pulling back her head - it was as if he needed to rid his years of submissiveness to Soredamor with his domination. Like a man possessed he took her against the tree trunk, there was no passion in the act just the delicious pleasure of his deep thrusts; each one developed a new sound from her panting chest. All of the small animals and birds had rapidly abandoned the furiously shaking branches above them and fled the increasing sounds of the two interlocked and seemingly fighting beasts below.   A final scream penetrated the trees sending birds further away flying up in panic. Then both slid down the tree trunk exhausted, each mentally and physically reflecting and feeding from the sensations that still shuddered through them.

'Oh my god Barrad, your an animal,' Tress said, then took in a deep breath as she collapsed on top of him. She just clung tightly to him frightened that she may lose him and this memory forever; without even the energy to wipe at the trickle that ran down her leg. She kissed him again.

'You are something else,' Barrad whispered sweetly in her ear. He returned her kiss and their energy began to return.

'Well of course I am,' Tress said with a wink and smiled down at her lover's flushed cheeks and content face, he looked so innocent in that moment. Tress kissed him again,

'Let's do it again,' she suggested.

'I am yours to command, although you may have to compete with Dellneck to book a slot between my briefings, I may have other lands to invade,' he replied jokingly.

'I meant now,' she met his mouth to silence him; she did not wish to mention that Dellneck did not survive the battle of Ubecka; she knew it would kill the mood. He pulled his lips from hers,

'I may have lost myself in the moment, but with all that noise that we just created the Aristrians would have heard us back in Ubecka.' Tress just knew that the clock could be ticking until he was forgotten and wanted to make the best of their time together and put the legendary Su-Katii stamina to the test.

'Forget this war for a moment, there is nothing here

apart from a sexy lady in your lap; tell me, what are you going to do about that Barrad?' She loosened the straps of her leather breastplate, the armour hung awkwardly from their early frenzied attempts to remove the cumbersome item in a hurry. She slowly revealed enough of herself to stir his response. The twang of four bowstrings brought the same evasive reaction from both of the lovers. They both dived from their position, with only microseconds between two of the arrows impact. Barrad slapped one shaft from its path with the flat of his hand and nudged the second arrow from its deadly path with his angled forearm; the arrowhead drew a line of blood from its sharp head as its course was diverted. The other two arrows thudded into the tree trunk where they had just been.

It would appear there was more than one set of horse-wives concealed in the area. Tress snatched for her cloak pulling it about herself covering up her half-naked form and as she grabbed the Sabre of Sum she disappeared from sight. Barrad just grabbed his swords and, naked as he was, charged at the men that had sneaked forwards on them as they embraced. Tress could not help but let out a short laugh at the strange scene of Barrad running forward with his bits jangling about as he charged the men with a long war cry. She thought back to her time in the Rift.

'Inside this place we will teach you how to counter any and every kind of attack,' Frenson her instructor had promised. It had been a lie; this kind of naked attack tactic had never been covered in the Temple. There was little real danger for them facing the four men, for they were both predators of the Rift, these 'One-lifers' were doomed from the moment they fired upon then. She wondered with a hint of shame at how long they had been observing them. One man from the group of four had read the situation a little better than the rest and the moment his arrow had been released he recognised the dual sword-wielding style of the man that had slain their second squad, he turned tail and took flight back to the horses left to their rear. The clash of steel and following screams of his companions reassured Miltak that he had made the correct decision. A sudden fear grew in each of the Aristrian soldier's bellies at their targets' reaction to their shots which should have left two fresh corpses. The fourth man slipping away from their ranks was missed as they gawped at the naked madman that charged towards them. To the waiting men the Su-Katii's stampede across the ground looked random and misjudged, but in reality each and every bound of his legs had already been judged to place him in the optimal attack angle to slay the three men. The lead Aristrian swung wildly and missed, Barrad had bounded high before coming into their range setting a pattern that the men had subconsciously followed, with his last bound he changed his pace and ducked low, forcing them to misjudge his attack and opened up a wide gash through the first Aristrian's body as he passed, his second blade thrust forward impaling the second man's diaphragm as he raised his sword to strike and the third man found a muddy foot thrust kicked high into his face, the raised leg revealing more than the man had wanted to see. His view was soon obstructed by that of white noise and stars as Barrad's heel smashed the man's nose guard into his face. A second later the trees seemed to opened up as two folds of Tress's cloak parted and the tip of the silver Sabre of Sum burst through the man's front. There was no catching the runner as he took to the saddle and scattered the horses as he escaped. Tress turned to Barrad with a face straining to contain her amusement at the scene before her.

'Do you realise how ridiculous you look killing people in the buff,' she smirked allowing her gaze to drop.

'Hey,' he tutted, 'I'm not just a piece of meat you

know – my face is up here. Perhaps it is you who is over dressed?' he snorted out, giving her a cheeky grin. His smile dropped as her words replayed in his mind.

'Ridiculous? *Really*? You didn't think that ten minutes ago, I think it was more "Oh my god, you were ridiculously good.' I don't need clothes on to be good at anything I turn my hand to.' Tress rolled her eyes at his comment,

'Oh no. My curse must be returning and taking effect, I forget again ...Perhaps you should prove it,' Tress said with a lust-filled smile and marched over and clung to him in an embrace that was sure to end with the wildlife fleeing the area again as their new journey of discovery begun.

Miltak rode hard, putting as much distance between the Su-Katii and himself as possible, he only began to relax when he spotted the muddy tracks that would lead him to the Aristrian forces that had tracked down and surrounded the resting place of the Tanarian army. He could see as he rode into their battle camp that they had begun to surround the hill above. With his breaking news Miltak was taken directly to the command post where Lord Banok was barking commands about at his officers, he wanted to contain their escape. The other scouts that had been deployed had located the hill camp and seen better luck than his own unit; still thanks to his quick thinking, at least he was still alive.

'What news do you have for me scout?' enquired the Battle Lord as he noticed the man loitering, waiting to be addressed.

'Lord Barrad sir, he has returned ...it must have been him, he was deadly.' Banok did not like the man's words; it implied that he himself was not as deadly as his counterpart.

'How do you know it was him man, what did he look like?' Miltak went silent for a moment as he tried to construct his words better in his head before delivering them, but Lord Banok's anger brought them flowing quickly out.

'He was with a woman and well sir, he ... he, was err ...naked sir, but he fought with two swords,' he quickly blurted out after. 'We thought we could kill him whilst he was otherwise distracted. We found him three leagues to the south-east of here sir.'

It was a simple task for Lord Banok to decide that this was indeed the General returned. Only a Su-Katii could slay a squad of men naked whilst on the job. This Barrad was turning into quite a man and Banok was pleased that he had turned against his own; a hunt was always at its best when you have a dangerous prey to chase. He dismissed the relieved man who appeared surprised that his commander had believed his words so quickly. What was even better news to Banok was that Barrad was still away from his army and he now had a force in place to keep them both separated, although he was so close it would be better to act against them quickly whilst they were still without solid leadership. The thought amused him that Barrad had been so blasé as to be caught rutting with a woman, was he really that unconcerned at the Aristrians presence. No, once the amusement passed his appraisal of his opponent begun to concern him, this was a schoolboy error; perhaps he had overestimated him?' He churned over his thoughts again, 'And who was this woman?' If only he had still had the Brotherhood at his disposal. The discovery of their poisoned bodies had left them with many questions.

Chapter 17 – Freedom

In the quiet tavern deep in the Hinter Mountains, little more noise than the wind making the shutters creak, disturbed brother and sister. Soredamor tended to Tamar's wound once again; he lay there unconscious, induced by her magic so that she could properly concentrate on finishing her task. The first magic she had used without doubt had saved his life and the magic that she now repeatedly used on him would accelerate his recovery and rid him of any deformity of movement. There was no point in spending an eternity imprisoned with nothing but the pursuit of magic to keep you sane, if you couldn't then pull a few impressive healing spells out of the bag. In all honesty, she had never seen the value in such things being an immortal, and had only turned to learning this path of magic because she had already learnt every other conceivable path. Boredom has a lot to answer for one's sanity. Athene and Titus had taken up residence in the adjoining room and judging from the sound of their voices carrying through the wall, they appeared to have plenty to talk about to occupy their time as she went about the business of healing her brother. A concern passed through Soredamor's mind, it was more a feeling that she seemed to be taking on the same feeble emotions as the infestation of this world. She actually felt obliged to heal him in return for his life saving deed, rather than being driven to the action through an affinity with the man or from the ties of family love. It was a simple equation to her, he had saved her life, now she would save his and then they would see how they both stood and go their separate ways before she absorbed further bad habits from the man. Inside the Rift they had turned on each other in a continuous game of cat and mouse, it had certainly livened the place up for a while and little

Ambrose had managed to hold his own rather well against her. She now had the whole world before her and was exulted in the knowledge that Gorran's baby was alive inside her. She genuinely had not known until Tamar had revealed this revelation to her outside the Rift. Her hand instinctively went to her stomach. She had not truly known about her state before entering the Rift and after a millennium inside she had no real indication other than a gut instinct from the time of her first imprisonment that Gorran may have a legacy, but with nothing happening inside the Rift, showing no signs of a baby or even pregnancy she had disregarded the instinct until Tamar's comment. The child must have been in a state of stasis or perhaps even died shortly after she had been imprisoned in the Rift, only to be resurrected once more on return to the real world. Who knows? She didn't care for she was overjoyed at the fact, which made her next dilemma even harder. If she gathered the swords and combined their powers to return back to her beloved Gorran as had been her original plan on her freedom, every event in this future would be erased and potentially his child along with it. She thought through the possibilities, returning to her lover would require her to pluck a moment in time from the past in which to return. Her calculations suggested that her return would erase the old Soredamor and her lover would have to make do with a slightly more mature lady, a little taller but with a fuller breast – she was sure he would not object. She had only actually aged around eight or so years when the Portal of Worlds collapsed and would still be considered an exquisite and very desirable lady by any stranger that should happen to cast eyes upon her and view her without the aid of her magic. Going back would return her to his arms as she now was and boy could she teach him a thing or two. If he did not love her in her prime he would quickly appreciate the pleasures that her experience could bring.

The new dilemma was that her spell could only carry *her* back across the span of time; she had not made any calculations for transporting another within her? Or would the new life in her stomach be carried back along with her through the decades? This was an unknown territory, the child was a part of her and was already swaying her course of action; the burgeoning instinct of motherhood was now straining her decision on a path that had before been clear to her. She strained to remember Gorran's face and to her horror drew a blank. No, she had to return to him.

'The future can be rebuilt,' she said resolutely out loud, a tear from the suppressed mother within trickled down her check. Tamar stirred from his slumber.

'What did you say?' he mumbled as he began to come around. Soredamor waved her hand above him using a new spell,

'Sleep little brother, sleep. Forgive me, but I will give you a better future - for I will see you again at the Portal of Worlds.' Soredamor dropped a crystal and a Transport portal instantly formed as it hit the ground. Soredamor stepped through into the vision beyond and the air instantly collapsed in the room shaking the doors and windows as it refilled the void of the Portal.

A flock of birds took to flight, startled by the sudden appearance of the transport Portal amongst the densely populated pines of the Uphrian lands. Soredamor gracefully weaved through the trees towards the vast clearing beyond; the camp of the Arrow-head clan filled her loathing gaze. She had come for the sword, she would have them all to achieve her aim and she felt its presence nearby. Her father's magic stood out clear as day above the other paths of magic that could be seen in this place. She whispered a spell thinking of her wounded brother as she walked into the savage's camp, no degenerate barbarians would get lucky today.

Soredamor walked calmly past the gawping sentries who stood immobile, their jaws openly gawping at the exquisite creature that had walked in from the forest. Soredamor walked past the racks of stretched animal skins left to dry in the sun with an upturned nose, such unpleasant smells had been alien to her in the confines of the Rift. Her gaze was fixed on the high-roofed tent that stood out from the centre of the other sprawling timber lodges and canvas tents that constituted the home of this clan. Hundreds of people stopped as she passed, they were frozen in their tracks, looking on at the slender female that walked as if she owned the place towards their chieftain's tent. A wave of silence followed in her wake in what had previously been a bustling street.

Kildraken Frostbane sat cross-legged in his tent surrounded by his usual group of toadying underlings, they discussed his plans to expand their lands and make a name for himself and the clan once again – after all he was the chosen one and his acquiescent followers nodded with every word departing his mouth. Kildraken's Shaman listened approvingly to this bold plan of dominating the surrounding clans. The two guards stationed outside the tent collapsed to the floor, one falling inside the tent with a clatter that suddenly drew everyone's attention to the entrance. Soredamor stooped low, avoiding the array of preserved animal heads that lined the entrance and marked the owner's status; she slid through the open tent flap standing in the light. Her gaze ran over everyone in the room one by one. Each person felt incredibly uncomfortable almost as if she had stared into their very souls as her gaze passed, finally her eyes fixed on the sitting outline of Kildraken. The bare-chested chieftain raised his head looking up at the lascivious outline of the woman standing in his tent, his heavily muscular chest panted with delight. What a gift his Shaman must have found for him to mark the creation of his plan? She spoke with an air of authority,

'How dare you look up at me you worthless dog! Avert your eyes from your betters or I shall burn them out.' She was angered by the lust that she could feel emanating from this barbarian towards her; these simple creatures were so easy to read. She had spent so many submissive years effectively a slave to the Brotherhood Master's desires that even the smallest lustful thought radiating from this worm's empty head had managed to anger her. The Shaman cringed with embarrassment for his master as Kildraken looked away, it was her magic – did he not know? He could sense the intense power radiating from this foreign woman. His duty was always to his master who had to be protected at all costs. He was their people's hope for a better future, so he reacted swiftly to her presence. Whoever she was, she needed to be stopped and she would soon find out that he commanded considerable power himself. The Shaman called upon the power of the air to expel this intruder from his lord's tent and the power of the wind gushed out from his outstretched hands towards her. The spell blew with an extreme force surrounding Soredamor's fine figure and ruffling her hair; a large segment of the tent wall ripped away from its frame and blew away into the distance, yet she remained as if stuck to the floor.

Soredamor turned towards the surprised Shaman who had expected to be earning the praise of his lord by now, his eyes were fearful of this strange woman, his magic had never failed him before.

'You poor, poor thing, is that what you call magic? It actually explains a lot. Here, let me put an end to your suffering.' Soredamor waved her hand as if dismissing a fly and the Shaman went cart-wheeling into one of the tent's thick timber struts, he was shaken and dazed as he looked up to see the lady approach and she place her foot on his head. The other men in the tent still stood captivated with an uncomprehending grin spread across their faces as they stood immobile in their charmed state.

'Kiss my feet mortal and know your betters, for the time of men and your futile excuse for magic has ended,' she tapped his groggy head with her foot.

'Do you hear me worm? Your time is ended. It is time for you to return back into the ground where you belong.' Soredamor raised her arms about her ready to destroy the man but then suddenly froze in contemplation.

'Tell your people that Soredamor has returned.' Fear was often spread better if there was someone alive to actually spread the word of her return. She was a queen without a people, for she did not seek to rule these people or any others for that matter, she just wanted to make sure they knew of her power and stayed well out of her way. She waved her hand again and the Shaman was propelled out through the ripped tent, he flew off as if catapulted into the sky and was quickly forgotten. She commanded the powers of destruction, life and death and these savages would be the first to bow to a display of her limitless powers – great waves of white fire spewed forth from her waved hands, her magic enveloping the remains of the tent and several others beyond it. The combustible tent went up in a fireball and all except Soredamor burnt to a crisp. As suddenly as the fire began the inferno ceased. Like a phoenix in the flames Soredamor stood unscathed amongst the blackened debris of ash, then with a single magical word from her lips a new gust of wind rippled across the ground cleansing it of the cremated corpses and incinerated litter. When the wind had passed only the silver short sword of Taric remained on the scorched earth. Soredamor smiled as she spotted the sword and advanced to recover the blade. As she bent over to pick up the weapon from the scorched ground a long throwing dart arched through the sky from the sprawl of the tents beyond, it flew through the air and bounced from the invisible shield that protected her back from such Neanderthal attacks. The thrower quickly ducked back into the seething crowd of angry warriors that had begun to gather, the effects of her initial spell were wearing off.

Soredamor picked up the sword, pleased with its easy recovery, ignoring the angered crowds she stared into the depths of the blade for a moment rekindling an ancient memory, but the memory was quickly replaced with an all-consuming wave of anger as another hunting dart bounced from her protective spell, returning her thoughts to the enraged crowd.

'You must learn to respect your betters,' she muttered and came about on the crowds in a wave of white fire. The screams of the dying could be heard for leagues.

Shaman Tilttolan of the Arrowhead tribe came around amongst a pile of soft forest branches where he had been flung by the magical force. The smell of crushed pine trees hung in his nostrils. He had never before seen such power and her presence in this world truly frightened him. Was that... could that really be Soredamor returned? She had been more beautiful than the legends had described her? Tilttolan felt the pain rip through him as he first tried to move, his leg appeared to be cleanly snapped and as he moved his arm he noticed the blood pouring from a broken branch that had impaled his bicep. It was painful but nothing that his magic couldn't repair. He looked across the trees as he smelt the distinct smell of burning wood and flesh. Thick plumes of black smoke rose through the trees in the area where the Arrow-head clan were camped. This new and deep wound appeared to be something that would not be so easy to fix. One word fell from his mouth

'Soredamor.'

In the darkness of the night, across the open flatlands that stretched beyond the great Uphrian forests

Corvus ran back to his tent after the surprise attack from the Aristrian riders. The pounding of his feet matched the pace of his pounding heart that rang in his ears as the unusual sensation of fear worked its way over him and covered him with a thin layer of cold sweat. He had to find Ievia, where was Ievia? She was not in his tent where he left her and had told her to stay. He grabbed one of the elder women rushing past,

'Ievia, where is Ievia?' he questioned, she raised an arm and pointed into the darkness from where she had just ran from. He moved off into the night, he knew that the largest tent had been pitched in this direction. Corvus could hear the sounds from within the tent before he could see it. Groans and cries of pain were coming from within, the injured had been centralised under its large canvas roof where they could be tended to better. The elder woman who he had earlier stopped returned with arms full of bandages and barged passed Corvus in a hurry as he stood gawping, at the tent's entrance, he was hesitant about entering – he dreaded what he might find inside. He sucked in a long gulp of air that filled his lungs and this seemed to give him the resolve that he needed, eventually he entered. His eyes adjusted to the dim yellow light of the crystal lit glow and he began to scan the rows of injured that lined the floor. His mind raced with the possibilities of what he may find, some of the injured were barely recognisable with terrible cuts to their faces. It could take a while to identify her. He felt a tap on the back of his shoulder,

'Who you looking for?' Ievia asked him casually.

'Ievia, I though you were...' Corvus sucked in another breath quickly and got a grip of himself. 'I thought you were injured?'

'I am, but just a little, it nothing,' she looked down at her side and a large blood soaked bandage was wrapped about her hip.

'Wooden arrow hit my hip, I faint at first ...but I ok

now. These others here worse than me, I help mend them,' she explained and then ignoring her own wound limped off to help the elder lady go about the business of tending the other wounded. She stopped and shouted back to Corvus,

'You get out now, this no place for fit warriors.' The tent of the wounded was seen as an embarrassing place to be for an Uphrian warrior, it was woman's work to tend to the injured and to a warrior being injured implied defeat.

'I see you in the morning,' Ievia said to him with a wink. He stood there speechless for a moment trying to make sense of why the Aristrians had attacked them in the first place; his conclusion was simple – you can't even begin to make sense of the senseless. This angered him all the more as he looked at the broken bodies scattering the floor; the crystals in his skin flickered with activity and Corvus felt their power rise, he needed to right the wrong that had taken place here, he needed to cleanse the guilt that he had felt for leading these people into this harm and make some sense of this pointless waste. He felt responsible. Back in Nordheim he had led many warriors to their deaths in the numerous battles and skirmishes that he had fought in to defend their lands – he had never felt such guilt then? Why should he be so affected by this worthless emotion now? These new feelings had troubled him all the more since the discovery that he had slain his own wife, a memory which he regretted beyond words, but he realised that with it he was a changed man over these past months; but the need to put things right plagued him beyond reason. He felt the power of the crystals rise with his emotions and he reached out and grabbed Ievia, placing his hands to her wound, she recoiled with pain as his hands almost burnt as she squirmed in his hold, but his grasp held her firm. The red crystals in his skin glowed and he sensed her wound's torn flesh move and knit together as the blood cells accelerated their recovery. She groaned in his hands and steadied herself, grabbing onto his broad shoulders as she began to feel better once more; the corner of his mouth curled upwards into a smile. He released Ievia and moved on to the next of the wounded repeating the process and continued to work his way around the tent until all had been tended to. The elder lady dropped the bandages that she held as she watched in amazement at the miracle taking place before her. She waved the shape of the protective horn in the air before her, but continued to watch the giant Nordheimer move from person to person healing all that he touched; she had never witnessed true magic before.

Corvus departed the tent feeling drained, he decided not to ponder on the things that had just happened for too long and took himself off to bed, alone. With the morning came the discovery of the true aftermath of the battle, both sides had taken a real pounding during the nights encounter, but only the Aristrian bodies remained. The fallen Uphrians had been gathered together and prepared for their final journey to a shallow grave. It was their way. The first order of the new day was to hold a council on the night's events. This meeting even came before breakfast, which displeased Corvus's grumbling stomach immensely. Chieftain Ion sat awaiting his presence, to his left sat an old lady – Glinda; she represented the families and had been newly appointed in her duties in the absence of a clan Shaman. It seemed strange to be having a meeting without the 'Bear' present to offer his opinion, although the whispers around the camp fires suggested that Glinda knew a little of the art. She had acted mostly as the village midwife over the generations and had delivered half the clan in her time, it was said that she had never failed to deliver a baby; but how these kind of powers would be useful to Corvus remained to be seen. Ievia, who normally attended these meetings at his side remained asleep in the tent of the wounded, he had checked on her first thing and had been hit by a wall of snoring; everyone inside remained soundly asleep. He had decided not to disturb them, they obviously needed the rest. Chieftain Ion looked at him for direction,

'What are your orders Corvus? Do we turn about and sack their villages or continue on your journey to your lands?' Glinda spoke up,

'Yes, I heard what happened last night in the tent and the people are calling you a god, they will follow you anywhere Corvus – I say attack and kill these bastards, put their heads on spikes and drag their entrails across the fields for dogs to feast upon. Blood for blood Corvus; that is our way.' She drew her belt knife and made some simulated thrusts. Corvus was taken back by her over enthusiastic reaction; he had expected them all to be filled with defeat and perhaps want to turn back to the protection of their great forests. He was pleased with their fighting spirit.

'Put the knife away Glinda, draw it next when you have an Aristrian throat exposed. I think that any nation that attacks people for merely crossing their lands, killing women and children alike deserves to be punished. I say we go and teach these buggers a lesson in manners and throw off the Aristrian leash from your people forever.' Ion nodded in agreement,

'The other clans were wrong not to follow you Corvus, I don't care if it were only you and I facing those prairie dogs, I would follow you into their den. Shaman Artio was right when he said you were the one to lead us into this new age. Let us have our vengeance and if necessary die like men.' Glinda clapped both men about their shoulders,

'Let us slaughter this vermin and wear their intestines as belts,' she concluded. Corvus flinched at her words,

'Well …let us just agree that they will pay for their

deeds, Ion prepare to break camp I want the clan lined up in battle formation, fighting wedge as we move. We will follow their fleeing hoof-tracks back to their villages and destroy them.

Chapter 18 - True Despair

The battle for Tagel had moved on, Lord Candis had held back the initial breach with the men of the wall late into the night; the battle had been relentless with neither side willing to give up any ground. Lord Aden had known better than to withdraw his troops for the day as had been his usual custom earlier in the war, he had the taste of victory between his teeth and was not prepared to let it go. The advantage of the breach that Teon had given him was not to be missed and he would throw his troops at it all night if he needed to, he was committed to make it work. Lord Candis was certainly making a big difference in beating back their assaults; the Tanarians had held their shield wall with impressive discipline with Candis at its centre he had made the Aristrians pay for their assault with many lives. The defenders had held fast for some time and even the Temple trained Candis was feeling severely fatigued. Lord Aden pondered the option of sending in his own Su-Katii, if he committed the three men from his order now he may take down the last big threat to their victory, but fighting Su-Katii against Su-Katii worried him, it was a dangerous move and although he despised the man, he actually rated Lord Candis amongst the more experienced of their number. He swayed to the thought that it would be better to keep his wolves to face lambs. The Brotherhood magicians were also out of the question, they needed more time to recuperate from their excursions and so their use could not be employed until perhaps the morning. It was going to be a long night for everyone. Candis was edging away from the strength of his youth and moving into the realms of middle-age and certainly fought with the cunning that such age brings. As he reconsidered his plans unable to wait for the victory he sought he estimated that he may lose at least one of his

Su-Katii at worse with their use, apart from Mako his men were not long from the Temple. As he neared a final decision two factors changed his initial decision to commit his Su-Katii knights. Firstly a runner brought him news that the caberisors were back in business after the Tanarians bold attack. The caberisor was the next generation of siege engine, its development had moved away from the standard rock and bolt slingers and its operators had ensured him that their use was guaranteed to bring a breach to any eight foot wall. A boast with which he would almost be equally delighted with if it did not match up to, for he had threatened the obnoxious and boastful Capitan of the unit with his life should he fail to deliver on his confident words. The old and simple threats were often just as effective as the new trend amongst his colleges to only remove limbs or other body parts. The man had instantly regretted his words, for a moment forgetting who he was addressing. The second bit of news that halted his Su-Katii from making their assault was that Lord Mako had arrived back at the rear echelon, successful from his rebel hunting trip. In light of this news he decided to send in the caberisors a hundred yards further down the wall. He would play the waiting game and keep Candis and the men protecting the Tanarian wall awake through the night, wear them down totally and prolong their fear, especially if the caberisors actually delivered on their promise. The plan was actually very simple, all of the best ones were, all they needed to do was make a second breach for Lord Candis was only one man and could not be in all places at once. The wall would have already fallen into their hands if it had not been for this rouge Su-Katii; they just needed to stretch them at multiple points. If the siege machines actually worked, they could make the extra openings that they needed and then wear them down until all the rest of his resources came back into play. He would do this whilst he rotated his men through rest periods; his army was large enough to ensure he had fresh troops for the morning assault. Aden himself would stay up only long enough to decide if the Captain should live to see another sun rise before he went off to enjoy another good night's sleep.

The right flank archers fired volley after volley into, and over, the daunting wall before them, as a number of men pushed three caberisors forwards, the thin wagon wheels of the contraptions sunk deeply into the difficult mud slowing their initial pace. The siege engines needed to get a little too close for comfort to the wall and the oxen that had been pulling the devices had long since been shot down by the wall's defenders bringing the devices to a stop. The dead oxen had been difficult to unhitch and manoeuvre around under the heavy fire from the wall. Thirty yards more was the Capitan's requirement to activate the device with success, he watched from the rear of one of the devices as the men unhitched the caberisors under fire. The heavy infantry that covered the workers now had their large shields peppered with arrow strikes and several were bleeding, but protected by their efforts the rest of the men slowly dragged and pushed the caberisors forwards by hand. The Capitan egged them on with encouraging words as each man slipped into the mud or fell to the storm of arrows that intensified around them; he called for more replacements to come forward and fill the gaps. Only ten more yards and then his life would be spared, by this point he didn't care how many men it took to push these things forwards, or fell in the arrow storm, he would have his ten yards. Only several shield men from the original fifty dotted the ground ahead, trying to protect the human beasts of burden as best they could with their long tower shields. They heard the Tanarian shouts from the wall before the others and understood their shouts of 'Bring Fire,' all too well. A man in front of one of the wagons was shot through the neck and went down fast, the movement of the engine carried forwards crushing onto the mans back with a sickening crack of his vertebra. The wooden wheel stuck on the fallen man like a wedge and the fire from the wall intensified, this time one of the protecting shield-men next to the engine fell.

'Come on men; pull - Five more yards, that's all. For God's sake, shift that bloody thing.' An arrow punched right through the man next to him, pinning the man's forearm to the wood and further slowing their progress, the Capitan rolled his eyes with frustration and stormed forwards cursing to himself as he filled a fallen man's place. He gave the crushed corpse stuck under the wheel a swift kick of disgust as he passed, it was Ali - he had always been a useless loafer and even in death he was causing him trouble. He began to pull at the caberisor with all his might. The glow of fire could easily be seen against the dark of night as they moved along the wall getting into a position where the large buckets of burning coal could be thrown down onto the machines effectively. A good shovel man could just about reach the floundering Aristrians with the hot coal and a good shot from the Tanarian wall. Men carrying animal bladders full of combustible oil followed the coal bearers closely. With a final feat of backbreaking effort, the caberisors were moved into position and the Capitan and his men clambered over the large timber structures making the final preparation for their firing, another man fell with an arrow in his back as he prepped the machine for firing, 'It didn't matter,' thought the Capitan, he had just completed his task and they were almost ready to fire and the scream of arrows arching through the sky from their own ranks resulted in some satisfying and agonizing cries echoing back from the wall in revenge. If the caberisors worked, there would be many more joining them soon. The covering fire permitted him to finish his work. The Captain yelled for the torch bearer to fire the weapons. From the ranks of archers behind the siege engines, three men with lit torches came dashing forward to light the launcher kindling. The large wad of hemp at the machine's rear ignited the fuse and activated the caberisor. Two of the men made it to their marks and lit the fuses, shouting out for everyone to stand clear; the third man was cut down by the return fire. The Capitan could not risk only two of the caberisors firing, so with an impulse he ran back through the mud for the dropped torch. It smouldered in the waterlogged mud with indecision, the animal fat in its tip barely keeping the flame alive. Picking it up, he waved it back into life as the rest of his men ran back past him, clearing the area away from the weapons. Nobody had actually conducted a live firing test of the caberisors before; all calculations were based upon the engineers and Brotherhood's designs and a series of scaled models. A concerning hissing sound began to erupt from the two siege engines that had been ignited, the reaction was invoked as the burning flames heated the carefully measured mixture of crushed crystals at the base of the bronze tipped lines of connected tree trunks. The Capitan only stopped for a second to regard the possibility of the dangerous reaction about to occur; he clambered onto the large wood frame of the last caberisor and he pushed the smouldering torch onto the wick fuse. After what seemed like an age the reassuring spark and burn of its ignition took place and the Captain jumped down into the mud to return to his men. The other two caberisors rocked the ground with large explosions that fired off a string of logs joined with chains in a high arc over the Tanarian wall. Each log was bound to another in a string that dragged the following log behind it over the wall. As Lord Aden watched the event from a distance, it reminded him of a long string of sausages being fired over the wall by each device, each sausage being hollowed out and filled with a devastating concoction of explosive powders and crushed crystals.

The secondary fuses ignited and Lord Aden was forced to avert his eyes from the three following explosions. The force was so large that the men in the surrounding area were knocked from their feet and great chunks of wall and house fell on both Tanarian and Aristrian alike. Lord Aden strained against the plumes of dust that filled his view waiting with anticipation to see the results of the caberisors. He did not need to wait long before the fresh sea breeze blew the thick clouds of destruction inland. The clouds moved away revealing the serious devastation to the wall, a large crater just existed where there had only been wall before. Looking through the rubble a fire had taken hold in the town houses behind the Tanarian wall and the area where the caberisors had stood was now just a charred black circle. One of the wooden siege engines had been flung high into the air with the explosion and strangely the Capitan of the caberisors was never seen again, he was quickly forgotten.

A large smile spread across Aden's face, against his better judgment the Capitan had been right. I want the archers to keep those gaps open until the morning with harassing fire. Rotate the men and wear them down, we will attack in earnest with the light; he turned and retired back to his tent. Aden knew instinctively that he should push the opening with a night assault and tactically it would have been a sound decision, yet for some dark unknowing reason it pleased him immensely that the anxiety of the impending attack hanging over the defenders would drive great wedges of fear into their ranks. It was almost as if their lingering fear was the catalyst for his enjoyment in this war, this was a feeling that he had never before experienced in any other campaign. He would sleep tightly enjoying the sensation.

The Aristrian commander rose an hour before first light, the several hours of deep sleep had refreshed him sufficiently for the day ahead. He went directly to the Brotherhood's tent and picked his way through the four acolytes who slept scattered about on the floor like dogs around their master's feet. He held his position above them regarding them with disgusted. He resisted the small temptation that came over him to slay them, as the wheezing sound of their breathing irritated him more than their ripe smell; he still needed them. He decided to have some fun with them instead by irritating them with his joyful shouts as he woke both of the masters and their dogs; everyone in the tent got the same treatment, they all had no choice but to wake with his loud and joyous shouts,

'Good morning my black clad friends, let's be having those sleepy heads up now; rise and shine, up and at em.' The entire room grumbled with displeasure and Aden enjoyed the sleepy and disoriented looks on their faces as he shouted his words out loudly as if he were addressing a room of raw recruits. He had really wanted to shake the pasty white figures that had been snoring loudly, awake, but had thought better of it at the last moment; you never know what reaction you may get from a flustered magician. Besides Telimus had looked so frail in his bed that he may snap if rustled about harshly and he couldn't have that. He informed the grumbling men of Mako's arrival in the early hours of the morning and was questioned immediately if his man had captured the target which they had set for him. He nodded and their mood seemed to change for the better; he left the tent to check on the status of the night's events and important matters of war. During the night the archers had followed orders and rotated though four groups, each maintaining a steady rate of fire onto the wall. The fires that had initially taken hold in the town from the siege engines had disappointedly been extinguished, but on the plus side it was reported that two more of their trebuchet had been repaired and were now back in

service; they had already been raining large rocks onto the enemy since first light. All in all, things were looking as good as the morning weather and after the Brotherhood had finished their breakfast the main event of the day would begin. Telimus had promised a display of magic like no other should the appropriate vessel for his enchantments be delivered, and Mako's captured prize had apparently seen to that requirement. This prospect excited Lord Aden, as up to now the Brotherhood had proved most effective and their words carried a certainty that only the insane would doubt. Lord Mako who had approached during Aden's wakeup calls now stood present, he clearly did not share his enthusiasm for their dark arts.

'We can easily take the breach in the walls without those lot; you should have attacked last night whilst you had the initiative,' Mako commented.

'Relax Mako, let them have their show,' Aden replied. His comment seemed to irritate the other Su-Katii and Mako quickly remarked back,

'Why? I could take either of those breaches myself, they are nothing special. I guarantee you Candis would fall to my blade, he would be nothing more than another corpse to step over, just say the word.' Aden shook his head dismissively and Mako did not linger to make his point, instead he simply stormed off. Mako thought it stupid to play up to these Wizards, they loved to bathe in power and he knew having the Su-Katii suck up to them would not look good in front of the men. It was also time to give up his prisoner to the black robed vermin, which grated him a little; the man was his captive and he disliked their commanding tone, as if he were just another one of their underlings. Brin had proved most taxing to capture and should have deserved a swift blow to the back of the skull, a warrior's death, rather than the warped and deranged side show that these wizards had in store for him. Still, he gave the command to his men to deliver his prisoner all the same. Mako wandered off into the deserted grounds to the rear of the army for some fresh air, he had no wish to witness their magic; he would return later when there was some proper killing to be done again.

The acolytes had begun the spell's preparations long before Brin was dragged forwards by his bindings and hoisted up onto the captured Tanarian wall. The two Masters stood close together on its rampart facing out towards the dark muddy plain that stained the ground before the opposing stone wall of Tagel. They were aligned directly with the breaches caused by the siege engines.

'*Where are my men*? What have you done with them?' Brin shouted as he was forced towards a large cart wheel that had been secured and prepared to take his bindings. With a cuff about his face the four men that had dragged him forwards secured his arms and legs against the ropes that were waiting for him, with a final tug to test that he could not go anywhere one of the men came in close to his face.

'Shut your mouth you Tanarian scum, you'll be seeing the rest of your men soon enough.' The men withdrew, taunting Brin as they left. Telimus turned to Aden and called out, addressing the commander who stood watching before the ranks of soldiers waiting to assault the wall,

'If I were you, I would suggest that you move a little further back, we don't want to tempt fate now do we?' Aden didn't have any idea about what the magician was getting at, but he listened to his advice. With a deep breath he bellowed out,

'The army will retire twenty paces, on my mark. *Backwards march!*' and the massed ranks of several thousand men marched backwards as one. After the clatter of their movement, silence once again blew through their tight ranks, each man in the army stood watching and wondering what the Brotherhood would do next. The two Masters scattered a circle of stones around the base of the wagon wheel that secured Brin, he struggled to kick the stones away, but his feet were held too tight to reach. The two masters began to join in with the chants of their acolytes who had continued to build the spell.

'*What are you doing*?' shouted Brin, 'Stop it, stop it.' His screams became more desperate as he began to feel the discomfort of the changes developing in his body. The Masters' chants became louder and an inhuman cry of '*No*' left Brin's lips; he could not resist or halt the changes that their magic forced into him. The green crystals glowed with power and they moved inwards across the floor to touch with Brin's feet, like a magnet to metal. A crystalline liquid leaked out from the vibrating stones and slowly the green fluid spread its way up his body enveloping and distorting his skin as it passed. The Masters gave a nod at their chanting acolytes and the men reached behind them and emptied several bags of red and blue crystals onto the ground surrounding the wagon wheel; they instantly moved towards the contorted body of Brin like a swarm of hungry bees. The man's body now vibrated without the sound of his pain, he slumped as if unconscious hanging by his bonds with only the movements of the crystals inside him swaying his body savagely against his bindings. Brin suddenly gave a gasp as his lungs filled with air and his body began to mutate; his skin further distorted to a craggy texture and his body grew larger and larger. The bonds that held the creature to the wheel snapped with the strain of its rapid growth, sending splinters of the wheel and fragments of hemp in all directions. Teon looked on through the shaded peak of his hooded cloak, impressed with the results of their combined powers and new creation, yet drained by the magical process involved.

He had seen several Rock-beast mutations created with the crystals before, but this one was truly impressive and beyond compare. It rose from its crouch at their verbal command and towered above them at close to twenty feet tall, the red pulses of the crystals were clear to see across its dull stone-like flesh.

'It is time for you to return home Commander,' Telimus said in little more than a whisper and the giant creature lumbered off in the direction of the town, the ground shuddered with the dull thump of every footstep from the creature. The Magician had been correct in his statement and Lord Aden was suitably impressed with today's display, although it had obviously taken a lot out of the wizards, for they slumped to their knees with exhaustion as the beast moved ever closer to the Tanarian lines. Through their combined powers and a shared consciousness they still maintained control of the giant creature. He decided that he would give the monstrosity a few minutes to crush their defence of the wall and then send in his troops for the mop up operation.

The men of the Tanarian shield wall watched the glistening Rock-beast approach, no one had actually realised the true size of the thing until its looming figure was halfway across the muddy field that separated the two forces. Many sets of eyes were fixed wide with terror as they beheld the huge jagged fists that were clenched and raised, ready to strike. The promise of a quick death at the enlarged hands was almost guaranteed. Even Lord Candis who stood with the other men in the shield wall was transfixed and beginning to contemplate how he might survive this day against such a foe.

'Steady men, hold fast,' commanded one of the officers from behind, as the creature's shadow dwarfed them. With its approach Candis realised the answer to his earlier question.

'Men, if you want to live past today you need to turn and

run. *Break ranks and run for your lives,'* he bellowed as he moved from his position, leading by example. This had not been his expected response and the men hesitated not wanting to be the first to break and show their true fear. The huge fists of the beast came hammering down as it was suddenly upon them. A crater was instantly formed where Lord Candis had been stood a second before, two men of the shield wall who had remained in place were squashed like flies. A large rocky foot swept forwards sending another section of the wall of men flying into the air behind, they landed broken and still; one unlucky man out of the flying group landed impaled on a nearby fence. Several Tanarian solders halted their retreat and turned to hack at the creature's legs, but it was futile, their strikes and blows could reach no higher than the creature's thighs. Only the men on the sides of the wall could thrust their spears at the beast's chest as it passed. With each futile blow it was like hitting stone and apart from a few chipped shavings of rock and broken blades, little real damage was inflicted on the giant. It didn't take long for the men on the wall to realise the helpless situation and follow Lord Candis's example. The defenders quickly turned and ran for their lives through the rat runs and deserted streets of Tagel.

Back in the Aristrian lines Lord Aden raised his hand and bellowed out the order to advance to his massed troops, the battle standards were raised and the distinct jingle of armour, weapons and steel filled the air with their movement. Each army created its own unique sound as it moved forwards and Lord Aden considered this army to play a melody to his ears. Telimus turned his hooded face towards Teon and reminded him of their next priority,

'The Su-Katii, we must find the Tanarian Su-Katii. Find him and kill him.' The dark vale of Teon's hood nodded back in agreement and the giant burst into the streets of Tagel in pursuit.

Lord Candis glanced quickly over his shoulder as he sprinted down the streets at the following Rock-beast; the tremors of its gaining footsteps disturbed him. The beast had acquired its target and hunted it with a single minded purpose; it stepped on a soldier that got in its way, crushing the man underfoot with a short scream and Candis dodged from the main street into a side alley. The long causeway that led to the towering walls of the keep were but a few streets away, almost tempting him to make the long exposed dash for their refuge. The Keep's tall walls would provide sufficient protection from the colossal creature ...he hoped. They were easily three times its height, but the potential pounding it could dish out may still remain a threat. His mind was racing, already calculating the next steps of their defence before his more immediate problem of escape was resolved. The creature quickly rounded the street corner, slipping and putting its leg through a deserted cottage wall, wattle and plaster showered the alley way as it withdrew its foot and continued its hunt. Candis knew that there was little hope in outrunning the Rock-beast, he would never make it across the causeway and if he did it would just run him down on the final path. It was obviously controlled and hunting him alone. He looked about in desperation and ducked into an open doorway to his left for cover. The deserted building had once been a grain store for the docks. Its long sectioned rooms had once housed tonnes of grain and the place still stunk of the stuff, even though its contents had long since been moved to the Keep or consumed. He backed off, resting against the wall panting, regaining his breath for his next sprint as heavy footsteps thundered through the alley outside damaging the surrounding buildings as the alleyway narrowed. The sound outside suddenly stopped and Candis instinctively knew that the creature must have spotted his path of retreat. Guided by the control of the Brotherhood it was acting with their cunning and intelligence, it had been the only open doorway available. He dodged to his left as a large fist smashed through the wall as if it were nothing more than parchment, he was showered in debris but unhurt; his sword slashed and stabbed with little effect at the hand that fumbled blindly through the building to grab him. He skilfully evaded it until a second hand smashed through the wall to his rear, he realised that he was now trapped between them and as the beast's hands clapped together he leaped forwards at the creature, out through a broken rip in the buildings wall. The creature had moved down onto its knees to get into the building and Candis suddenly came face to face with the large amorphous head that regarded him callously. Every element of what had once been Brin was locked away and buried deep in its mutated bulk. The beast rocked forward and head-butted the Su-Katii back into the hole in the wall. A loud animal-like scream came from Candis's lips as the shadow of the creature's fist filled the air in the damaged building above him. The giant fist punched into the building and a temporary silence settled with the dust in the back alley.

Chapter 19 - Hide and Seek

Tamar came around from his deep and dreamless sleep; the past twenty-four hours were little more than a blur to him as he rubbed away the tiredness from his eyes. His hand instinctively moved to check his wounded chest as his memories returned, the fatal gaping hole was now replaced with just a hard mound of tender white scar tissue. He sat up and drew in a deep breath of air, his chest felt fine apart from nothing more than a dull ache in the region of the wound; he deliberately coughed loudly to test his lungs, again everything seemed fine. The stupidity of his thoughtless action came flooding back to him, it had been a split second impulse to jump in front of his sister, a futile knee-jerk reaction after sensing the heart-beat of her innocent unborn child stir into life moments after she had escaped the Rift. He was not usually this heroic or sentimental, but forgetting the problems with his sister, the unborn infant was still of his family and needed to be protected. He could not remember his father in any way, yet he knew that his impulsive actions were justified and that his long dead father would be smiling in his grave at his brave move. He clung to this thought, enjoying it for a moment.

'Tamar the saviour,' he said aloud and chuckled to himself. The door to his quarters opened and Athene and Titus entered together; Athene's face lit up with a large smile on seeing Tamar recovered, he had looked on deaths door last time she had seen him. She jumped about excitedly but stopped her first reaction to run over and give him a hug before she reached the man; Titus followed her in and stopped to look disinterestedly out of the room's window, then later gave the Magician the slightest nod of recognition.

'You're up then. Where's your sister?' Titus asked.

Tamar sat for a moment recalling his delirious memories.

'I don't really know, but I'm sure I can guess,' he sprang into life realising that he was fully healed from his ordeal and covered himself quickly with his robes.

'Please leave the room for a moment, I need to use my magic to find her at once,' Titus rolled his eyes at the request, but left with Athene. Tamar began his spell, seeking out his sister. His spirit soared through the sky following the trailing particles of magic that led far across Aristria all the way to the great Uphrian forests. He arrived at a great clearing in the forest that was deserted and the ground was nothing more than ash and cinders, as he neared he could see the many charred corpses amongst the debris that had only recently burnt itself out. He was drawn towards one corpse in particular; his spirit hands reached down and touched the grotesquely burnt husk.

'Kildraken,' he murmured. He felt the presence of a more powerful magic from the ground close to his side and recognised the aura of where the blade 'Taric' had rested. The ground was left with a dagger-shaped mark where the ground had not been burnt around the blade.

'Oh no,' the thought crossed his mind; she was going after all of the swords. He desperately sought her path again, but realised that it was not necessary to follow her, she would be going for the other swords; he would only have to do the same to find her. She was actually serious about attempting to undo time. It was a crazy ambition and he doubted that what she desired was even possible, yet she could do untold damage to this world in any attempt. This madness had to be stopped, but how to stop Soredamor without injuring the child that she carried? This feat would be a challenge, but a worthy one to save the bloodline of his family. Tamar pondered these thoughts as he returned to his physical body, he realised that he would require Athene at his side to challenge her, which also meant that he would need to convince the thick-skulled Su-Katii of the true danger that they all faced and then there was also the problem of Zerch to contend with. Zerch had actually been right to attempt to destroy her, for with such stakes at hand Soredamor just had to be stopped, but who knows what bitter and twisted means that wretch would resort to in order to exact his vengeance. He had already agreed to deal with Zerch once and for all on the outstanding debt to Tress, but impeding his sister's recovery of the swords was now his number one priority. If she could not be stopped in time they may all be done for, although he considered momentarily that Zerch had already proved himself to be highly resourceful and not without skill, he may yet need such a man to stop Soredamor and she was certainly on his hit list. His deal with Tress may need to wait. He sucked in a great gasp of air as his soul returned to his body.

Soon after, the door opened and Titus and Athene returned. The question remained in Tamar's head, how would they take his request for their aid? There was only one way to find out, so he came straight out with it.

'I need to leave this place at once and stop Soredamor, I have seen the desires inside her mind and she wishes to return back to her lover.' Tamar stated.

'Well let the bitch go and scratch at her itch, it will be one less problem for us to worry about,' said Titus, uncaringly. The man's attitude immediately infuriated Tamar; Titus had a knack of pushing all the wrong buttons with the Magician.

'Well, my astute scholar of life, if that bitch scratches her itch, as you so elegantly put it; then you may well find that you never get to scratch your own itches ever again; for if she gets her way you would never even get to exist …tempting as that thought might seem, I cannot allow this.' Tamar locked eyes with Titus as his words grabbed his attention although he did not fully comprehend them. Titus rolled his eyes as he digested his words then smiled back,

'Sounds bad, imagine a world without me? How is this possible?' Tamar instantly thought that perhaps the prospect of a world without the arrogant warrior would not be so bad after all and struggled hard not to abuse him further, he reluctantly held his tongue for he really would need his aid.

'Soredamor seeks the three swords, she already has one of them and she will be after the others as we speak. If she gets all three, she may well have the power to attempt a very dangerous spell, one in which she could go back in time and perhaps change our present time line or damage the past.'

'What do you mean, *perhaps*? You don't really know do you?' insisted Titus, pressuring the magician for an answer. Tamar's face reddened noticeably at his persistent tact.

'No. You are correct Titus, I don't know, it is beyond my skill in magic to attempt such a thing and that on its own makes it a very dangerous spell indeed. It may work; it may not, who knows? Do you? Are you willing to throw away your's and Athene's life on the vague possibility that she may not destroy our world? All that I can tell you is that even though she is my sister she must be stopped and in the face of such danger, I for one can swallow my pride and ask for your help. Now, you can either help me to stop her or perhaps just stay the hell out of my way, either way we must act fast.' Titus stared back at Tamar sizing up his words, the perspiration on his brow and flushed cheeks all reinforced the genuine distress that he had detected in his voice, but these Magicians were a tricky bunch and it was prudent to always suspect a deception, it was the Su-Katii way. Athene jarred him sharply in the ribs, halting his dissection of Tamar's words.

'*Titus*, you promised me earlier in my room that you had turned to a new chapter of your life, well now seems like a good time to prove it. Well, I'm going to help you Tamar in whichever way I can.' Titus looked like a schoolboy being told off, but his first instinct and appraisal of Tamar's body-language told him that the Magician believed his own words and if Athene went with him, he knew that he could not leave her with him. Who knows what danger he would put her in to meet with his own needs.

'What about you Tamar? I don't get it. One minute you want to kill your sister, the next you throw yourself in front of her killer. Do you really know what you are doing? Do you have the guts to see this through?' Titus demanded.

'I do, have you?' he replied. Titus had already killed one so-called god; why not make it two or even three? He nodded slowly at the magician.

'OK, I'm in.' he stated with a frown. 'You will need someone who has some experience in the department of slaying gods, I'm your man.' Tamar actually betrayed his shocked expression, he felt robbed at the shortness of their argument but gladly accepted his decision and moved swiftly on to business,

'Right then, the other swords are in Ubecka, so that's where she will be heading next. I must contact Delanichi's first to warn him and then together we will stop her.' Titus raised his hand,

'I'll stop you right there, things have moved on somewhat since your stay in the Rift, the Aristrians now hold the town and I think that there is more that you should know. It's about Delanichi and the army.' Titus began to talk and Tamar listened.

In a not too distant forest that surrounded the encamped Tanarian army, Tress had just finished adjusting the straps on her armour when she suddenly turned to Barrad with a shocked look across her face,

'Did you hear that? What the hell was that?' A

slight tremor rippled through the ground and the surrounding trees seemed to groan in protest as the disturbance shuddered through their precious soil. A plume of dark smoke rose above the hill that overlooked the area and marked the site where the Tanarian army was camped; Tress knew that only magic or a natural disaster could invoke such a violent reaction. Barrad was just as surprised as Tress at the disturbance and for some unknown reason he instantly thought of Soredamor. They were preparing to pick their way through the last leg of the numerous roaming patrols that were out hunting for them, they were returning after reaching the decision to try and get Barrad back to his surrounded army. The patrols had not stood a chance against them; they were no prey to be hunted. So far those that they chose to avoid had been spotted easily by Tress as she used her cloak to conceal her passing, scouting out the ground ahead before Barrad moved forward. When they had needed to fight it had been quick and bloody, they had both walked away unscathed in every encounter. A second thunderclap sounded from the hill and the distant sound of screaming carried to them with the southerly wind. Tress came running back to Barrad as the sky darkened with the expanding smoke and returned to his view to discuss the unnatural occurrence on the hill.

'I must get back to my army and quick, they need me,' Barrad stated.

'I would not do that if I were you,' came a stern voice from behind them. Barrad swung around, swords at the ready as he wondered at how anyone had gotten so close behind him without his knowledge. Tamar steeped forwards from the shadows of the trees, a rare drip of sweat hung from his brow with the exertion of his uphill climb through the forest; he had used a short spell of transport to carry him the last leg of the trip once he had spotted Barrad ahead. A wide smile instantly spread across Tress's face,

'Tamar, what in Kraken's sake are you doing here? How did you find us?' The Magician only showed the briefest of smiles in return.

'Oh for better times, you are in mortal danger Tress - Soredamor is released and she has just taken the second sword 'Thulnir' from your General Larks up there, the smoke you see is where she has laid waste to those that tried to stop her. She now seeks the final blade, Sum, I see that you still have it safe for now, but I can assure you she will come for it.' Barrad shook his head, 'Can she not stay out of our matters? With Soredamor's rampage of destruction up there, I guarantee you that the Aristrian army will storm the hill whilst we are at our weakest, the Su-Katii will cease upon any advantage and her magic is not one to be missed. My men will perish without strong leadership, I need to get up there.'

Titus and Athene came running in from their right; they had split up into two groups to find them. Tress felt a shiver go down the length of her spine as she saw Titus approaching, she noticed that her heart rate had increased with a great thumping sound from her chest; she thought it so loud that the others may even hear it. She had not yet had an encounter with that particular Su-Katii in which she had avoided feeling either pain or pleasure and his sight sent her blood racing as she realised that she could still remember every nerve tingling inch of him. He had instantly clocked her long blonde hair and enticing figure hidden partially in her cloak and recognised her the moment he had stepped from the trees. He felt almost embarrassed at seeing her and oddly jealous of Barrad at her side as her hand extended to run lightly along the Generals under-arm as he spoke of departing to his army. The simple action instantly told Titus that they were lovers. You cannot simply forget the towering years of training inside the Temple so easily, with her arm and body slightly pressing in to him and partly concealed beneath his field of vision it was one of the few positions that would be nearly impossible to counter, should she wish to strike. She could have easily eased a dagger from her belt to strike him before he could even stop the blow. Every Su-Katii was trained to instinctively move away from any encounter which could not be countered. The simple gesture would have been missed by any normal being, but her proximity and position summed up their whole situation in a single glance to Titus. Only a person that had shared a bed with a Su-Katii would be trusted too such an extent and often if the warrior was wise, not even then.

'Ah, I see Tamar has found you,' said Titus, hiding his thoughts on Tress by acting overly disappointed that they had just wasted their time searching for the pair in the denser part of the forest. The two Su-Katii warriors gave each other the briefest of nods in recognition, followed by a long sideways glance. Titus's eyes fell unwittingly back upon Tress's ample cleavage pressed upwards by her tight leather armour, she looked at him inquisitively and tilted her head slightly as she suddenly realised what had fixed his gaze; he knew that he was busted but was certainly not embarrassed. He glanced quickly back over at Athene; her attentions were elsewhere, but for all the sights in the forest surrounding him that one just kept on drawing his eyes back no matter where he looked. Tress cocked her head to one side and returned his glazed stare, she now realised why her heart was pumping so fast; the memories of their time together came flooding into her mind. She could still remember every single jaded moment with Titus, a sensation that she had never encountered or recalled from any man before. She remembered when his sudden presence had stifled her wish to escape; it was the single exciting memory of that nature inside the prison of her mind. She treasured his pleasuring touch and recalling it even now brought her face to a flush with its recall. She could remember it all too well, every exquisite inch of him, and that was exactly the problem, he had filled her dreams with both fantasies and nightmares. Her only other memories to draw upon of that most private nature were far from private, the scared memory of the gang of Su-Katii pinning her to the table and painfully pleasuring themselves, was not one she would ever relish. She had not been in her own body during that encounter, but it had hurt all the same. She felt Athene's cold stare on her as she pondered her thoughts, did she know what had occurred between them on that day? How should she react to her? She suddenly realised that she was clinging tightly to Barrad's arm and was filled with dread as she stared at him blankly attempting to recall his name.

'No,' she gasped. His name sprang out from the closing mist into her mind and she repeated his name several times, reassuring herself of his memory, but she knew deep within that his memory was fading faster than anyone before him. Zerch's magic was indeed brutal; the magician had designed his curse with his usual efficiency. Once she had crossed over the line of physical contact, the deeper that Tress's emotions ran for someone, the quicker their memory would fade. She took a deep breath to wash away her mounting panic.

'So nice to see you both *together*,' Tress sniped at the couple. 'No,' she thought to herself, she just could not go on with this and came over in a cold sweat; she was already starting to forget Barrad and could do nothing to stop it. She felt so helpless; she could not allow this to happen. Earlier today it had been one of the most memorable moments of her life, one that she had no desire to lose. She turned to Tamar with panic in her eyes her hand fingered the ornate handle of her sabre,

'Please Tamar you are still in debt to me, I need you to repay it now,' he dismissed the question with a wave of his hand as if it were nothing more than just a trivial request, he wrongly assumed that she meant his debt in dealing with Zerch. He had more worrying thoughts on his mind with Soredamor on the loose.

'Help me Tamar - you promised,' she demanded.

'And I will but let us get away from here first, Soredamor may yet come for you, if I found you I'm sure she can,' he replied and patted her shoulder, which had the effect of momentarily calming her. She paused in thought regaining control of her volatile emotions, the silence of the forest settling her thoughts.

'Why did she not just come for Sum after finishing them off up there,' she nodded up at the hill top that could just about be seen through the canopy of the trees. Tamar scratched the bristles of his chin,

'Both you and the sword are still hidden from her, the Dragon's tooth amulet that you have about your neck conceals your presence here. Soredamor is following the paths of magic from the old world to lead her back to the swords; but when that fails she will also try and track you through the magic of this world. We will have the time that we need to prepare, as I predict that it may take some time for her to locate you. What she does not know is the fact that you are being guarded by the magic from another, totally different world than our own. The dragons of the old tales were short lived in our world and did not originate in either this or the world of the swords; they came from their own place or dimension. Who knows where? None can really remember, and as far as I know the amulet's masking signature was only know to Sorus and myself; but I have seen enough of my sister's intellect to know that she will eventually work this out, as, unfortunately she surpasses me in her ability.'

'That's reassuring to know,' Titus commented out of habit, hardly even realising that he had said the words. Athene threw him a dark look in return.

'The sword of Sum must be placed inside the Rift, it is the only option as I see it; if she goes back in to the Rift after it, she will not come back out.' Tamar suggested. Titus shook his head with disagreement.

'You are a good Wizard Tamar, you know I hate to admit that, but you are a terrible strategist. She would only send her Brotherhood or another of her charmed folk back into the Rift to recover it. I think she could probably control anyone of us by all accounts, eh Barrad? No, what you must do is set a trap where the situation favours you and deal with her once and for all. You have all the bait you need, you can take the sword to her Rift to entice her out in to the open, but from what you say she is smart and would be one step ahead of you, she would have prepared her own ambush and I doubt it if you will make it in. It would be you who is at the disadvantage.'

'What do you suggest then, oh master tactician?' Tamar enquired, admittedly seeing the wisdom in Titus's words yet still lacing his own with a trace of sarcasm. Titus frowned at the tone but was pleased that Tamar had finally admitted his superior ability before lecturing the group.

'I have hunted men for several years now and I can tell you; the ones that run never make it. If your hunter is stronger or better prepared than the prey it will always ends the same way. You die. If Soredamor is as powerful as you say Tamar then we have only one cause of action available to us, we find as many allies as we can, then chose our ground and fight. I hope an injured beast is more dangerous than a cornered one,' he patted Tamar on his shoulder as he passed making the magician flinch away from his personal contact and all watched his following speech with an interest in its final suggestion.

'Your rush to find the sword has also brought its own risks Tamar; I know little about magic Tamar but a lot about hunting. From what you have been saying I would wager that your sister has also been following you. I'm sure that you also have a unique signature, I know little about your magic ways, but I'm sure a sister could easily track her brother? I wonder how long we have before she is drawn to you.' Tress shuddered at Titus's suggestion, she had already been churning over Barrad's words that the army on the hill would fall and the thought of Soredamor returning for her drove her over the edge.

'Damn it, you really have done this before,' Tamar thought but hid his anguish well at potentially leading his sister to the sword. Titus continued his speech as if he were directing a set of battle orders; during his speech Tress pulled her cloak about her shoulders and disappeared. All eyes were turned away from her and she slipped off unnoticed, her old instincts had at last caught up with her - it was now time to run. Titus continued to talk drawing in their attention.

'We must unite and fight her as one, put aside your troubles with Zerch and fight her together, oh and next time try to let the sword-strike hit her, Tamar, we cannot show sudden acts of compassion in this coming battle. We also have another advantage; we have Athene and her power to render Soredamor's magic useless. I suggest we use the Rift as a lure, but not her Rift where she will be prepared and expecting you, I say we use Hadrak's Rift to spring our trap and I for one will pledge my swords to defend it.' Athene was genuinely surprised at Titus in that moment, she never thought he had it in him to draw a line and choose a side. She liked this new trait in Titus; it was amazing what a little 'End of the world' threat could do to inject her admiration for the warrior again, he looked supremely confident and entrancing to her as he laid out his plan.

'Em, one question,' Barrad raised his hand, all eyes turned on Barrad and he suddenly wished he had stayed quiet.

'Where has Tress gone?' he said with an unknowing shrug. Titus could not help but see the pointlessness of his speech if they would not follow its actions, he quickly added,

'And like all plans we will always need a continuity plan when the first one goes to crap.' Tamar started to walk away from the group to distance himself from Athene,

'I will use my powers to try and find her,' he stated. Barrad called over to the Magician as he drew his swords,

'That won't be necessary, I know exactly where she will be headed,' he raised a sword and pointed at the hill, the sound of battle carried down from its crest.

'I don't think she would desert us,' Barrad said. Before anyone had any chance to speak Barrad shot off up the hill at a sprint. The others looked at each other for a second before Titus reluctantly drew his two swords with a sigh and they all rapidly followed on.

Chapter 20 - Commander Hermana

Corvus and his clan had followed the trail of retreating horses for several days, not even the rapid pace of the Uphrians could gain any ground on the mounted riders that had tried to evade them. They had come across two of the Aristrians' number who had been badly wounded during their battle, the men had been unable to ride any further and had fallen from their saddles and been left on the ground to die. They had been beaten to death by their scouts before Corvus had a chance to interrogate them, but from the look of their original wounds they would not have lasted much longer, or provided much information. It was yet another indication that the Aristrians knew they were being pursued and were desperate to get away. With a single-minded determination that seemed to run deep in his family or as his mother used to say 'Simple bone headed stubbornness,' he continued after the remaining Aristrian knights regardless. It did not matter to him that they had little hope of catching up with the horsemen, they would need to eventually rest or take refuge somewhere and he would catch up and deal with the murdering scum if it was the last thing he did. During their last few days of pursuit he had found himself filling his time with an endless list of things to completely fill his time, checking on their supplies, rotating their scouts, the list went on and on as they covered the ground. He had also worked his way around his new found people, getting to know as many as the time permitted as they jogged along, maintaining their enhanced pace. At first he had not realised his subconscious intentions, but with the endless list of chores and excuses that he filled his days and nights with, he at last began to realise that his subconscious actions were starting to become more apparent to his conscious mind. He began to realise that he was actually trying to distance himself away from Ievia at every chance. He didn't know why, but ever since her injury he could not bear to think of her, it was as if his mind was attempting to place her out of his reach and away from harm. He had been stung once by allowing himself to care for a woman and then destroying her and his subconscious mind was not allowing him to walk this path again; if she was out of sight she would be out of mind. It would be best for them both. Besides this, he only gave his clan three hours of sleep each night to recuperate from the day's forced march. There had always been another task that needed attending before his own sleep and had found her already asleep when he returned for his own; although the power of the crystal shards in his skin could maintain his stamina to levels far beyond that of any other man. His curse was also a hidden gift. Their routine over the past few days was the only way to attempt to gain ground on the riders who he hoped were resting for longer. Had it been just the warriors with him, he would have pushed them on through the night without stopping, but the old and the young needed the extra break; although with three days of relentless pursuit with little sleep, people were getting a little short with one another. He needed to move as one unit, as, if he dared to split his force, the quicker cavalry may turn about and outflank him or perhaps ride past to attack the weaker force that would be left behind. Fortunately his new-found people were a tough bunch and even the elders in their numbers seemed quite capable. Ievia had noticed his obvious lack of attention directed towards her, she had known her husband was busy but judging from her cold reaction to him when they passed she had seen his actions for exactly what they were and it had signalled the undoing of her advances to the Nordheim King. As the clan jogged along at a steady pace through the late afternoon Corvus pondered his own feelings towards his new wife. Did he not crave her continued touch or seek the warmth that she offered to share with him each night? No, this was not the case, each time he looked at her he could think of little else, well at least until she displayed her unpleasant frown or the angel of Amiria would fill his thoughts with a bucket of ice water to calm his fires. Perhaps he was just afraid of loving again, 'Afraid,' now there was a word he had always ejected from his mind as soon as he thought it? He stopped the pointless line of thought and emptied the topic from his mind. The terrain had changed from the flat fields to a more varied and diverse tundra. Corvus welcomed this change for it would slow his prey and the broken land would only help to hinder the cavalry, especially when it came to the fighting. He wondered where this pursuit was taking them? Unfortunately few in his clan had ever ventured outside of their forest and knew little of the lands beyond. On the positive side they had been heading south and this only served to lead him closer back to his beloved Nordheim. One of the lead scouts suddenly came running back to Corvus; he had noticed the man's excited body language as he returned from one of the higher outcrops that dotted the area.

'I see them, many riders directly to our front,' the excitement spread through the clan like a wave, even though these very same riders had inflicted many casualties against them days before. However, unlike the battered riders that they pursued, thanks to Corvus's strange new ability the clan's injured were now fully recovered and ready to fight again. The recovered folk of the clan did not cower away from the possible injury and death that could meet them once again, they had already had a taste of what they faced; but they were bred from generations of warriors and would not let their clan down. In comparison after the crush of the Uphrian charge, many of the riders had sustained some form of minor injury to aggravate their escape and bring discomfort to their retreat. Corvus picked up the pace and they moved forward following his lead, without the usual jubilant war cries, moving low and hugging the ground between the rises in the horizon to close on the riders as much as possible with stealth. Corvus could feel the excitement spreading through his people as their feet trampled the long grass on their approach. Not a single word was uttered amongst his people, it was almost as if they all shared the same linked empathy of movement as the whole clan moved like one large creature to their line of attack. Men and women alike silently applied lime powder and war paint for the imminent attack. The line of the clan warriors snaked its way forwards through the long grass moving like panthers preparing to strike. Corvus was leading the advance, selecting the best route through the undulating ground before him. He stopped and crawled up on his belly to one of the higher points of ground. He smiled to himself as he calculated the distance to the riders, who now just trundled slowly forwards, blasé to the clan's presence close behind them. The riders must have assumed that they had evaded their pursuers for they were most relaxed in the way they moved.

Chieftain Ion crawled up next to him to take a look.

'What do you think Ion, are they within reach of your charge or will we risk losing them again?' Ion grunted with approval.

'I think we can get them, even if they manage to evade us we will take down many with our darts, but we need to act fast, before they make it to the rock snake in the distance.' Corus looked at the man perplexed.

'You what? *Rock snake?*' he questioned.

'Yes, the large serpent in the distance,' Ion raised his hand and pointed. Corvus quickly slapped his hand down; he didn't want a stray waving hand to give away their position and looked through the haze of the sun in their eyes to the distant skyline. What appeared to be a long wall travelled the line of the horizon, it was so long that Corvus had initially thought it the horizon on his first glance.

'Kraken's balls, what is that thing,' he whispered under his breath. Ion brought his attention back to the swift decision that was need,

'Shall we strike now Corvus?' The large king nodded his agreement and a long crystal axe began to form into his hands.

The mass of figures, with painted flesh and weapons held aloft suddenly burst out from the low grounds; their first twenty yards was covered in silence trampling through the knee high grass then busting into the open like stampeding cattle. A shout of alarm went up from the rear guard of the Aristrian cavalry, their raised alarm had the tone of panic deeply ingrained in its pitch. A moment of bustling confusion enveloped the rear of the cavalry column as some of the riders jostled and bumped their way to the clearest path of escape whilst others instinctively swung about to deal with the threat. The lack of direct orders from the front allowed the charging Uphrians to gain the ground they needed to release their hail of darts at the startled riders. Several of the clan's men were taken down in their charge by the quick reactions of several cavalry archers before the mass of thrown darts fell into their ranks. Horses and men wheeled about into each other with bone-chilling whinnies from their mounts as the darts punched into their exposed flesh, only a small number of the heavy cavalry were spared injury thanks to their superior heavily-plated armour repelling the steel rain. The lightly armoured cavalry archers were intermingled in the ranks of the heavy cavalry depriving them of the mobility that they usually relished. Unable to evade they truly felt the brunt of the Uphrian revenge. A bugle sounded to the front of the column of riders; it gave the first true indication of their orders, it sounded the

Aristrians' retreat. The men had relaxed on seeing the Aristrian city stretching out before them, they were almost home free. Each of the riders now had instructions on their course of action and spurs were dug deep into the flanks of their war horses, directing them to follow the riders ahead. The Uphrians struck the rear of the column with force; their flanks quickly spread about the riders who peered down at them in shock as they pivoted around the giant axe-man in their centre. The images of the creatures proudly painted on the bare chests of the clansmen were the last view many of the rear riders saw before being impaled by the frenzy of swinging blades that desperately sought their flesh. The front riders broke free of the sprawl to their rear and headed west for the great snake on the horizon. Corvus swung his axe in rapid succession finishing off the last man that had been isolated from the fleeing group; the rest of the clan were also making good their bloody revenge. Focusing on the now distant group of riders Corvus sought to continue his blood lust, he knew the power of the crystals in his skin could carry him to them in an instant. He focused on the group and in an instance was amongst them, his crystal axe struck home through the nearest rider's lap, felling both man and horse in one gore splattered strike. The group did not stop, suddenly seeing Corvus amongst them prompted them to split, riding desperately for the wall, they had all seen the giant axe-man in action nights before and knew the results of his work. Corvus breathed heavily with the exhaustion of the battle and halted his chase of the riders, it was their leader that he was after but in their panic and dust each man looked alike to him. Perhaps he had been felled already? His axe relaxed and rested on the ground and he stood there silent with his jaw aghast as he began to comprehend the size structure that stood before him. The clan finished their slaughter of the remaining riders that had been isolated and left behind. With their grim work finished they begun to advance up to their king who now stood in awe at the structure before him; the fleeing cavalry men were now forgotten. Eventually they reached Corvus side and joined him in wonder at the giant structure before them.

'What is it?' Ion asked bemused and slightly puzzled, having only ever seen the confines of the great Uphrian forest thought his lifetime.

'That my friend, that is a city, not just any old city either I wager, it the biggest thing I have ever seen in my life.' Corvus's native capital, Croweheim could easily have fitted twenty times into its great walls and he was amazed at its vastness. He had only ever seen walls bigger on the Great Gate that guarded the entrance from his own lands into Tanaria and was truly impressed with the structure before him. He wanted to see more and focused on the highest point of the wall and with the power of the crystals still strong within him he was instantly transported and perched on its tall wall. He felt the surge of a strong wind blowing through his hair and looked down upon the city beyond. He studied the true vastness of the sprawled city before him as he clung to a flagpole and even watched the exhausted cavalry men ride through the gates that had been opened before them. Any ideas of pursuit were quickly dismissed as they soon vanished from sight in the tangle of streets. Their commander had taken the unpopular decision at the time to ride on for days and head for Monumentium, the Aristrian capital, rather than lead any pursuit back to the smaller and nearer border fort where they had initially formed up. He watched until a blowing squall brought with it the putrid stench of the poorer quarters and the nearby sewage facility. With one pulse from the crystals in his skin he reappeared back on the ground before chieftain Ion and cleared his throat of the foul stench. His first instinct was to turn his clan around and run as far from this place as possible; there must be over fifty thousand people in such a vast city. Corvus surveyed the nervous faces of the warriors who quickly put on a show of false bravado as they felt Corvus's gaze full upon them. The women stood defiant like the warriors, whilst the young ones and the elders made no such show, but stood there, displaying their willingness to blindly jump at his command. It was apparent he had won the respect of his people, but to continue would be suicidal. He felt the weight of their responsibility on his broad shoulders again, a burden that he was unwillingly familiar with as a King. How many of them would survive if they ran, there were no large forests or mountains to take cover from their cavalry out here. The only peaks on the horizon crested from the ground on the far side of the city, they would have to pass the numerous gates to the little safety that it offered. No wonder the riders had been in such a hurry to get here. Corvus felt very alone in that moment; until a smooth warm hand slipped into his palm, he turned with eyes wide it was Ievia, she hesitantly moved forward and encircled him in a hug. It was as if the burden of his command was taken from him in an instant. Now that is true magic he though briefly to himself.

'We all going to die?' Ievia asked tentatively, but her voice lacked any real concern, she was preoccupied with her happiness to be accepted in his arms once again. She had learned to appreciate the few short moments when her husband for once showed some recognition of her. A broad and sinister grin slowly spread across Corvus's face as the smell of the city wafted passed his nostrils again; he suddenly realised that he knew that smell, he had recognised it from his many campaigns. It was the smell of a settlement in disarray. Famine, war and disease were all factors that could make a place smell as sweet as that wafting fragrance. He was determined that he would not die running; it was simply not his style.

'We have all got to go some time, the trick as my

father used to say is to take some unwelcome friends with you. In our case we may even get a group discount at the doors of hell.' He planted a kiss on her lips and instantly a happy-faced Ievia felt a warm glow of uncaring joy on her cheeks. She looked up at him lovingly,

'If we going to die we make baby now?' It sounded more like an order than a request. Corvus glanced down at her big puppy dog eyes; he had not even realised he had kissed her in his elated state of things racing around his mind and now he felt embarrassed at leading her to the wrong conclusion.

'No Ievia, we make war now. *Prepare for a siege. We'll bring this city to its knees,*' he suddenly bellowed out to the clan, the crowd cheered; but instead of the hustle of people preparing for action, the entire clan stood still gazing back at him.

'What, what's up?' Corvus asked Ion who had a blank expression across his face like the others.

'Err, em, what is a siege Corvus?' Ion questioned inquisitively, asking almost as if he did not want to be the one asking the same question that sat in everyone's minds.

'Oh,' Corvus muttered, this was going to be interesting, he had not considered that in the Uphrian forests the concept of siege warfare was an alien topic. These people only knew how to strike and run.

'OK people, listen up. We can make this work. We are going to make our camp here and surround that nearest gate over there. We are too few to set a force on every gate that leads into that place. It looks to me as if the city has four ways in; but that won't matter, they'll take one look at our small force and just come out of that nearest gate to meet us. We will have more than our pound of flesh by the time we are done here, but I assure you all, we will not leave until we have our justice,' he said defiantly to the clan. This time when he had finished his speech they moved about their business of preparing for battle with some urgency.

Inside the law courts of the Aristrian capital the commander of the flatlands cavalry regiment was summoned in front of the city council. He was in ill temper, he had barely the time to pat the dust of the trail from his cloak or wash the blood from his hands before he had been summoned. Commander Hermana was already irritated by their request; he was exhausted and as he walked to the hall he could taste nothing but grit and dust as he licked his lips preparing to speak. He viewed the delegates filtering into the hall with equal distaste and thought it strange that the only man wearing any insignia was the head of the city watch; it was otherwise a procession of greybeards, merchants led by a tall lean woman with a hooked nose like a hawk who pushed past the commander to take centre stage. She held his eye for but a second looking down her long nose at him, he felt insulted as he realised that she pulled the strings and now he would have to communicate military matters to the uneducated and even worse, a woman. Emella Grey, mistress of the council addressed him without even turning to face the force commander. Commander Hermana, of the flatlands cavalry ground his teeth restraining his anger as he was addressed by the woman.

'And what made you think coming here with your little tail tucked between your legs was a good idea commander?' She swung about and the contempt for the military man seemed to ooze from every pore in her body and she instantly put him on the back foot. He looked her up and down slowly with equal contempt, he made no attempt to hide the sneer written across his face; he had just been defending their frontier to protect people like her from these savages. He had sacrificed years of his life in service and lost a lot of good men to protect what? People like this?

'I see no insignia of rank on your shoulders madam; do you even belong in this meeting? I was expecting to report matters to a proper general, I have military matters to discuss.' Commander Hermana stood there rocking on the balls of his feet looking up at the tall roof of the hall dismissively, signalling the end of his conversation with the woman and carried on as if waiting for his General. Emella Gray was no spring chicken to be dismissed so easily and the Commander had further provoked her wrath.

'Listen to me you insolent retard. Do you have any capacity for thoughts other than breeding with your horses floating about in that poor excuse of a brain? Did you see any of your beloved soldiers waving you into our city with great throws of glory and paving your path with hand picked ferns? *No.* I thought not, because you will struggle to find a single soldier in our city.' Hermana blinked as he strained to recall the finer details of his entrance, there had been none. Emella continued,

'So let me start again and introduce myself, I am Emella Gray head woman and chief negotiator in the council of merchants. We are the only people in the city who have coin enough to pay the city guards' wages and keep this place in any state of order. You as I understand it are Commander Hermana, from the flatland garrisons, the cretin who had the brainless lack of foresight to attack the only hostile force in the region and then gather them up and lead them back to us. I truly am in awe of your military prowess, your stupidity is beyond compare Commander; the streets are already in riot at the mere mention of the force outside.' Emella had no qualms in unleashing her tongue at the man, but the four guards of the town watch who were permanently assigned to guard the string of merchants grew uneasy, expecting the Commander to lash out at such insults. His hand strained in his glove wanting to strike out and slap her down to the ground where she belonged, but every ounce of his officer's code prevented him, a man of fine breeding knew how to hold back this urges, even if they were warranted. Remembering this, his frustrated face changed, he forced it to became a charade of smiles and over politeness in return.

'I would hardly call that rabble a hostile force they are but a handful,' he said. Emella instantly replied,

'Then why did you flee them so?' Hermana sucked in his red cheeks as if a sour taste were in his mouth.

'Forgive me *Lady* Gray,' he over-emphasised the title, 'But what exactly happened to our army garrisoned here?' She glared at him, taken back for a second at his change of tact; perhaps he was not as much of a fool as she had first taken him for. Those bred into high society knew well how to play the games of court and Hermana had managed to control his rage and turn it into feigned politeness. She had failed in her plan. She had hoped to lure the Commander into striking her; she would have been within her rights to have him removed from his command and as the only man of rank in the city his removal would have meant that she could commandeer his men, removing another threat to her growing power and influence in the city. These last few days in the city had been desperate as the place fell about their ankles in disarray, it had been dog eat dog and she aimed to be the biggest dog in town. Had he second-guessed her plan?

'The army? They have left us to sort out our own affairs when we need them most. They have been called out to the South to finish off the last of the Tanarians. They will be crushed between our two forces.' Commander Hermana raised an eyebrow,

'Oh, really? And how many men does the town watch consist off?' She ignored his probing question,

'Ah, I thought so; I have nearly five hundred warriors still under my command, we may be a little battered and bruised; but I think perhaps your tone should hold a little more respect; I wager it is I who holds the reins of the strongest force in the city.' The colour drained from her cheeks and she turned with an arrogant look,

'Then Commander, the problem outside our gates is yours to deal with, isn't it? You brought it to us you deal with it.' she turned and left the room, the procession of greybeards followed her as if on a leash; grumbling their agreement as they left.

Chapter 21 – Bravery

Across the continent in the ruins of the deserted warehouse in Tagel, Lord Candis was struck squarely on the chest by the large pummelling blow from the giant Rock-beast that sought to destroy him. He fell to the floor from the unavoidable impact. His ribs had been crushed into the cavity of his chest and bright red blood frothed from his mouth as he fought for his last gulps of air. The creature that had once been Brin had felt its blow strike home, the fragile little man had at last been squashed like a fly; it now cocked its head through the large hole that it had created in the wall of the warehouse for a better view of the dying creature. Lord Candis slumped to his knees; his swords lay on the floor before him where they had been knocked from his hands by the creature's deadly blow. The man's head rolled to one side and his body remained lifeless; the creature's giant hand reached into the building to prod the body, its finger extended and his head followed to look along its extended hand. A flicker of life blinked into Candis's eyes and his hand reached upwards and clutched at his throat, with a final jerk he ripped his wedding ring free that he wore on the chain about his neck and threw it into the crevice of the creature's open mouth that loomed before him.

'Choke on that you son of a bitch,' he spluttered as the ring went down with a slight cough from the monstrosity and the light faded from the fallen Su-Katii's eyes, Lord Candis slumped backwards to the smashed floor, never to move again. The giant Rock-beast's eyes suddenly widened as a burning sensation flared up in its throat. The creature's eyes bulged as the magicians in the Aristrian lines struggled to maintain control of their prized pet and the Rock-beast thrashed wildly at the side of the tightly packed streets, smashing at the buildings in its frustration. The ring that the creature had involuntary swallowed was no ordinary ring; it was given to Lord Candis by his late wife as their wedding gift. He had always kept this gift close to his heart as a reminder of his once great love and unknown to him it had protected him well against the scourge of the Brotherhood's magic. Its steel was forged by monks and then blessed by the Temple priests at Allbathron; an ancient and now forgotten sect. The enchantments in the ring held considerable power and had been the only thing stopping the Brotherhood of Keth from controlling Lord Candis like the other Su-Katii puppets; the ancient and malevolent magic in their tattoos enslaved all bar Lord Candis, who unknowingly was protected by his wife's ring; although he always suspected its more than just a wedding ring. He could have sworn that he heard her voice driving his impulses in those final moments before he joined her with her in the afterlife. The creature now gripped at its throat and rolled through the streets in a frenzy of movement as the swallowed ring began to neutralize the magic of the Brotherhood. It was not by mere chance alone that the priests at Allbathron mysteriously disappeared and their Temple burnt down; years before the Brotherhood had discovered their powers to be a potential threat to their dominance and had taken steps to halt their advances in magic and erase their memory from this world. The beast screamed and bellowed, an eerie sound that no man who heard it would ever wish to hear again as slowly its huge bulk began to decrease in size; Seagulls diverted their flight in panic eager to distance themselves from the unsavoury place and the creature clenched its fist and struck out, smashing through another building's wall.

Teon turned to Telimus bewildered at how they had lost control of the beast? He suddenly felt the exhaustion of the spell being broken wash over him and he staggered, steadying himself on the rampart. He had no visibility of the beast and could not control what he could not see. Had the creature been killed? It was as if it did not exist; his disappointment followed his sudden exhaustion; he had hoped to be controlling the beast pummelling through the Keep's high walls by now.

'Don't worry Teon our work for this day is done, look the army has moved into the town, we have done enough.' Terminus was correct as always, the creature had served its purpose and cleared the way into Tagel, the army would halt at the causeway hemming in the Tanarians in one tight little nest and soon they would be destroyed. Teon threw back his dark hood to better inhale the sea air and froze for a split second as a dark shape caught his eye from the peripherals of his vision.

'What?' An orange flash streaked through the sky and burnt through the left side of his body, instantly setting his robes alight and incinerating the remaining cloth before he could bring his defences to bear. The burning robes made little difference to the young Master's wounds as the massive trauma from the initial spell that struck him killed Teon outright.

Kerric smiled with satisfaction as he repeated the spell that Tamar had used against him in the Rift, as always a death in the Rift proving its effectiveness in learning something new.

'Let's see, who the Master is now,' he goaded at the fallen man ever aware that now the real fight was about to begin. Kerric had been unable to tell the two Masters apart from the rear, both men wore the same robes, black with gold inlayed hoods. It had not been until he had fully committed to his spell that Teon revealed himself. It would have been better for him if it had been Telimus that he struck, but Kerric understood his lot in life, things never went as he foresaw or hoped, but he figured that in the long run this only served to make him more flexible than his opponents. With the most powerful man in his order turning to do battle with him, he would not complain if Zerch were to show up as they had arranged. Kerric had fully expected this fight to end one way or another without Zerch's arrival. It was his hour to define himself as a man; if he wanted Soredamor to himself Telimus was the last hurdle of the Brotherhood to stand in his way. The acolytes were lying exhausted at their masters' feet and would not put up much of a fight in this battle, they were already spent from the efforts of the Rock-beast and the army had advanced away into the town giving them space to resolve their conflict undisturbed. Kerric had waited concealed from their view at the now deserted outer wall, watching their exertions to control the Rock-beast. He had picked his time well and knew instinctively that now was his best chance to strike, when his opponents were at their weakest, even alone he believed he could be victorious and with Soredamor as his prize he was prepared to try. Telimus recovered from the shock of Teon's death quickly and reacted like a shocked cat, not knowing at first what had hit his fellow Master he reacted by instinct alone; smashing a powder vile that he always kept close to hand on the ground, after a chemical reaction the vile instantly bellowed out plumes of black smoke about the surprised men giving their master time to hide and prepare. The nearby acolytes spluttered and coughed as the acrid smoke hit the back of their throats; they were already weak with exhaustion and the best they could manage was to crawl forwards through the mud on their hands and knees to escape the enveloping cloud. Kerric rained flames of burning lightning into the group, destroying the acolytes one by one as they crawled out through the sludge and appeared, his arcing bolts of orange lighting burning through everyone he struck. He threw several more bolts of energy into the dark cloud hoping to strike lucky as his confidence grew with each acolyte's death. Kerric's eyes desperately sought Telimus amongst their numbers and just as he was considering using his magic to disperse the cloud the strong sea breeze picked up and did the work for him. Only the charred and contorted bodies of the acolytes and Teon remained. A surge of panic shuddered through him as he realised that he had lost the initiative in this encounter, a wise man would simply disengage now and wait to pick his moment again, but the thoughts of having sole claim on Soredamor drove him to uncaring heights of stupidly. He must have her to himself. He cast a spell of protection against any possible attack and pivoted nervously on the balls of his feet as he sought any traces of magic that may lead him to his prey. A blast of white light struck Kerric from behind; even with his magical protection in place the force of the blast knocked him from his feet. Muddy and sodden he quickly glanced over his body; everything was still intact, his magic shield had held. He glanced behind him, Telimus stood with his hood drawn back to reveal the hateful sneer written across his wrinkled face, his hands motioned movements that would draw further magic from the surrounding air.

'You have missed your chance you worthless maggot,' Telimus cursed, his every word oozed with contempt and a second blast of white fire surrounded Kerric in a long and continuous streak. Kerric had just about managed to reinforce his protective spell, but could feel the raw power of Telimus start to burn through his defences. Sweat poured from his brow with the raising temperature and exertions of maintaining his magic as he stood firm in the eye of the storm that Telimus directed against him. Even in his weakened state Telimus was more than a match for Kerric and this realisation was beginning to dawn on Kerric as the temperature rose. He reached out with his left hand in desperation, throwing a returning arc of orange lighting back at the gloating Telimus; Kerric's heart sunk as his fiery bolt was waved aside with little effort from the Brotherhood Master; it had been his best shot. Kerric's dwindling dreams flashed before his eyes as his protective shield began to collapse; he had no continuity plan for this encounter.

'How very foolish of you Kerric; did you really think yourself a match for my powers, I will burn you just enough to ensure that you endure a slow and painful death.' Telimus broke into a smile as he intensified his powers. Suddenly a green light blinded both men as a cyclone of power erupted against Telimus throwing him from his feet and breaking more than one bone with its impact.

'That wretch may not be your match, but I am up to the challenge,' Zerch's words were a welcome sound as Kerric fought for breath through the dissipating field of heat that surrounded him, Telimus spell against him had ceased but his magic still hung in the air like a foul stench. Both Telimus and Zerch unleashed everything they had in their armoury at each other, in one great storm of clashing magic, the air thundered and the ground shuddered as their powers locked horns. Bolts of lightning flew off into the sky as their attacks were skilfully countered or deflected. One stray bolt of power was deflected into Tagel, bringing down a town house in a pile of rubble from a single strike and the men of the Army instinctively took to cover from the unknown threat that had exploded close by. Kerric watched in awe at the display of the two Masters at the peak of their ability. At one point he thought Zerch incinerated by a flaming wall of fire that Telimus summoned about him, but the canny magician simply walked forth like a phoenix from the flames as their heat was neutralised and blasted Telimus back with a burst of green fire in return. It was soon apparent which man had the better of the other as Zerch advanced towards the Brotherhood magician who scrabbled backwards through the mud. Zerch threw several more bolts of intense light at the wounded man; Telimus's shaking hand extended to meet the pulses of light, his fingers black and burnt yet still deflecting them up into the clouds. The Brotherhood magician suddenly clenched his hand in pain with the passing of the final bolt; it felt as if the flesh had been stripped from his fingers. Telimus uttered two words of magic and raised himself to his feet in a ridged pendulum motion. His magic assisting to pull himself upright from the mud back onto his shaky legs and slowly his arm moved with a mind of its own as the broken bones began to reset themselves. Kerric had recovered himself from his near fatal ordeal and spotted his opportunity to strike, now that Telimus's focus was away from him. A line of stockpiled weapons sat spread out along the outer Tanarian wall; Kerric now used his powers to project them at Telimus. The Brotherhood Master sensed the use of magic behind him and swung around to be struck in the chest by a flying axe, he staggered backwards a pace, hardly showing the pain, a following spear thrust through the centre of his torso as he staggered backwards to remain impaled on its long shaft. Telimus coughed up a shower of blood and his head hinged forwards to hang limply from his neck.

'Ha, how do you like that? Who's the Master now Telimus?' Kerric shouted in victory as the dying Master's blood dripped slowly from his mouth. Telimus's dilated pupils pulsed with a red light and his deathly white face looked up at Kerric with a emotionless gaze. Kerric shivered as Telimus fixed him with his piercing stare and his dead hand reached forwards to drag his body from the impaled spear. The dying Master knew many paths of magic and had begun to invoke the curse of death magic in his final moments on this earth. He was without doubt powerful enough to have mastered the most guarded of arts. The corpse's shadow began to elongate and move across the ground towards Kerric who had no counter against this unknown spell, even in death Telimus threatened his vengeance. Kerric scrambled backwards through the mud on his hands and knees in an attempt to avoid the growing shadow. A single blast of green fire from Zerch's extended hands incinerated Telimus's body. The creeping shadow dispersed with the inferno bringing a wave of relief to Kerric. Both Zerch and Kerric locked eyes apprehensively in an uneasy stand-off, each man expecting the other to act. Zerch broke the tension first.

'Did you doubt my word back there Master Kerric, I told you I would be here to stand together with you against the last of the Keth. I do believe that you are the last of their order now, let us leave this place together and discuss your claim on Soredamor. *Relax brother*, she is all yours, but there is more that you should know, come let us leave this place and I will explain along the way.' Kerric was relieved that his words were not followed with a lightning bolt to finish him off as he felt his own fatigue from the battle, had their roles been reversed he would have finished him whilst he had the chance. There was thankfully more to Zerch than he had first assumed. With a breath of relief he nodded in agreement and followed the Master.

A strong sea breeze blew the debris of war through the deserted town of Tagel. The entire complement of the garrison stood ready, manning the battlements of the ancient Keep that looked out across the war scared settlement and smashed walls of the town. With the town now firmly in the hands of the enemy it would not be long before the Aristrians would be making their advance across the causeway and attempt to breach the Keep. Silky, one of Brin's remaining marauders leaned on his long spear as he watched the invaders' massed ranks squeeze through the two breaches on the town wall from his lofty position, his eyes burnt with anger and resentment. He was one of the few soldiers who had fought the invaders from behind their own lines and also met with them on the walls in this conflict. His wife, Greta was also lucky enough to have found a place inside the safety of the Keep rather than on the far side of the outer wall like the other poor wretches. The folk stuck beyond the Keep's protection were managing as best they could on the grassy outcrop that faced the sea. A pulley system had been arranged to lower what supplies could be spared to fend off the blowing gales that swept around the harbour Keep. The majority of the defenders from the walls and town had recovered safely back to the Keep and Silky awaited the familiar glint of Aristrian steel to fully fill his field of vision; a view that would signal the day was about to become a little more hectic. Instead a loan figure came staggering out from the deserted streets, the man staggered back and forth as he wandered towards the Keep as if in a daze. Every head on the wall turned and regarded the figure with fascination as several archers notched and drew their arrows with the anticipation of an easy kill. Something about the figure looked familiar to Silky and he pushed forward on the battlements to gain a better view of the man, his identity quickly dawned upon him.

'*Brin*, Brin is that you? Lower your bows you bunch of pricks he's one of us. Open the gates and let him in,' Silky shouted to the men about him. An officer on a higher platform above him screwed his face up at the commotion below, he considered that the gates should remain firmly shut and shouted out to stop any foolish reaction to the man's requests,

'Hold fast men; the gate must remain shut, who knows what we could be letting into our Keep. It could be another deception from their Wizards?' Another voice shouted louder than all others from along the line, it was Lord Mallet.

'Belay that order. I know that man well, Brin is on one of my marauders, let him in, he is one of ours.' The men did not react, confused by the different orders being shouted about them.

'Well *hurry up*, before we let the whole bloody Aristrian army in.' Mallet bellowed angrily, he expected his men to jump at his words when an order was given and after his following shouts, they quickly complied. Moments later, the large reinforced doors to the Keep opened up - just wide enough for a single man to pass through. The loan figure brushed through the doors, moving by instinct alone and collapsing into the arms of the men at the door. Brin had at last returned home.

With the discovered bodies of the slain Brotherhood magicians, the Aristrians held back their first assault; it had been the first bad omen of their campaign. Lord Aden had observed the light show going on behind their ranks as his army had been preparing to move forwards on the Keep, but by the time he had returned back to the rear wall the only thing that he found was a liberal scattering of black-robed bodies. This was a massive blow to the combat effectiveness of his force and his men knew it too; nearly all of his rapid gains had been made from the impressive power of the Brotherhood magicians. In hand to hand combat his Su-Katii were as good as gods, but when faced with a problem such as a wall or dealing with hundreds of men in a single blow he had come to understand just what a difference a wizard could make to a battle. The men had feared their magic more than the sword. With Lord Mako's eventual return came their long and heated discussion of their next assault. Aden had been relying on the Brotherhood to smash open the doors to the Keep, he had become complacent with their mounting victories and had neglected to contemplate any other plans should their main assets be destroyed; how human he had become in his ways. Aden was both furious and disgusted with himself, but not as much as Mako clearly showed. Now attempting to put this blunder behind him they had resolved to work together on their new plan of attack. It would not be easy, with nearly eighty foot high walls to breach and a narrow causeway to cross - that was only accessible at low tide, it was formidably defended. The long thin pathway had been designed hundreds of years ago to prevent any opposing siege machines being brought to bear against its walls and the heavily reinforced doors were locked tight. Each individual design in the Keep's defence was well implemented and when put together they ensured that the taking of the Keep would prove a real challenge. Both men knew well that the most sound tactic would be to just sit back and starve them out, but that could take months and with the impressive glories of the battles over the last few days both men had a taste to continue with a direct assault. This was all going to boil down to 'bragging rights,' and with another Battlegroup engaging the Tanarians to the north, each man wanted the bloodiest battle possible to belittle the stories of their comrades'. The other problem as Lord Mako so kindly pointed out was that whoever or whatever had destroyed the Brotherhood magicians was still out there. Defeating Telimus would have been no easy feat, he had watched the man in action several times and the Brotherhood magician was as good at his craft as his plentiful boasts, the prospect of his killer on the loose behind their lines was not one to be relished. Still war stopped for no-man and come the morning they made their first assault on the castle.

The line of Aristrian heavy infantry marched forwards against the brisk wind that opposed them from the sea. It was late morning and the army had needed to wait until the water had fully withdrawn from the causeway before mounting their attack. It felt strange to the men stood around; they were not accustomed to waiting for mother-nature before they could make war. The routine of mounting a full-blown attack at first light was not practical for they may lose a number of men if they were forced to wade up to their chests in heavy armour through the strong tides. The only way to the Keep was over the sunken causeway that regularly smothered the stone paving at high tide and led across to the peninsular. The plan for today was that the heavy infantry would move forwards against the weight of fire and projectiles that rained down on their advancing line of men. Then protected in their tight formation with shields raised and interlocked they would hold fast whilst the lighter troops came through their protected rat-run of shields and attempt to scale the walls or split into groups and work at the door. With this tactic they could afford the men the protection of heavy armour to get close and have the greater mobility needed to attempt to scale the challenging walls. It was as if the heavens had opened up with arrows as the studded sandaled feet thudded their way just past the halfway point of the draining causeway. The long pathway had been marked by the defenders to indicate the best range for their bows and they knew when to hit them the hardest. The heavily armoured men put every last ounce of their confidence in their armour and shields as they marched forwards in their thin tortoise like formation. Arrows hissed into their wooden and leather bindings of their outer shell; they even absorbed the larger javelins that hurtled down upon them although with their javelin's shafts jutting out from their outer shell their movement was further hindered. The majority of the lethal rain was soaked up by their well-rehearsed tactics and superior armour, but several men felt the sting of an arrow as it found soft flesh as a hand or foot was accidentally exposed. The heavy infantry now filled the length of the causeway; the tactic was working well so far. The few men that met with the more serious injuries were being taken back to the far end of the line, where the ground opened out to the wider docks and the Keep's entrance.

As the armoured column had advanced up to the main door heavier projectiles fell upon them; rocks, lumps of iron and even shit fell upon them from above. It had actually been Lord Candis's suggestion to save up the excrement and drop it amongst the attackers to ensure the outside of the wall was as unpleasant a place as possible for the enemy to gather. More than one Aristrian retched as a big bucket load of crap splattered through the gaps in their shields and decorated their armour.

Alwin looked across at Rinc with a smile; they had done well to make it this far to see the battle for the Keep and had gained a considerable stash of plunder along the way. They awaited the distinctive drumbeat to signal their advance and time to assault. Alwin had a bad feeling about today and hadn't seen the familiar dark-robed wizards that usually preceded the assault. So far they had proved a good omen and the men had almost become superstitious about their appearance. The rapid beating of the drums echoed from the narrow streets of the town and marked the signal for the light infantry to move forward and attempt the first assault. The men were split into two groups, those assigned to attempt to breach the doors and the remainder to scale the walls and fight their way back down to open the doors; neither job was to be relished. Everyone moving forwards wished that they had the privilege of being in the heavy infantry today, they always seemed to get the best deal. The heavy infantry were set to block any counter assault from the masses of Tanarian civilians that had huddled around to the back of the Keep. The Aristrian soldiers would not risk advancing around the length of the walls, with only a small gap from the wall to the sea. The Tanarians could easily rain death down upon them if any attempt were made to attack the civilians outside of the wall. Alwin decided to count himself lucky - he was in the third wave of men today. He watched the first wave of men rush off through the tunnel of shields and felt the dread of the task ahead, it began to fill his belly with butterflies as he tilted his neck back to look up at the daunting walls of the fortress. It was not long before the first grappling hooks flew upwards and waves of bodies fell screaming back down as they were cut or hacked back down from the walls battlements. This process of bloody slaughter went on for a short period before the drums sounded again and the second wave of men rushed forwards; many swore and cursed as they moved off. Alwin's anxiety grew as he watched the slaughter continue of the second wave of troops, very few of the men made the long climb up the knotted ropes and chains to make it to the top and those that did soon fell back down with a split skull. All the time throughout this futile assault the repeated clang of heavy axes reverberated from the reinforced steel and outer oak doors of the Keep. The stream of the advancing men from the second wave had all but dried up and Alwin fearfully awaited the inevitable call for the third wave to attack. The Aristrian drums echoed through the streets and Alwin stepped forward in his duty, but a neighbouring hand reached out to grab him by the collar halting his movement.

'Hold fast you fool, that was the retreat being sounded, not the advance.' Alwin felt as if a burden had been lifted from his soul.

Thankfully the Su-Katii leadership had quickly assessed that throwing an endless stream of men at the wall was not going to work today. In two waves only a handful of men had made it through the lethal barrage and none were able to climb over the well-defended battlements. They at least had the intelligence to halt the senseless loss of lives and had already begun to plot a new tactic to breach this seemingly impregnable fortress. Alwin slumped to the ground with relief, after watching the first wave of the assault he was beginning to think that he would not be around to enjoy his hard won wealth.

Chapter 22 - Sum

The branches of the trees and bushes whipped past Tress as she ran for the hill top, the thick bush eventually gave way to the rough scrub land that led to the top of the hill. Formations of Aristrian troops were already in place and advancing upwards to meet with the battered men on the summit with the glint of murder in their eyes. Tress almost ran into the back of one of the troops as she emerged from the thick cover; the momentum of her sprint carrying her out from the cover of the trees. She jumped to the side in an effort to stop and thankfully the Aristrian soldiers could not detect her close proximity protected by the magic of her cloak. High above the front ranks of the war machine clashed with the defenders on the peak and the sounds of agony and death filled the air above them as the battle was fully joined. Now that Tress had arrived she was unsure of exactly what her intentions should be? It was instinct that had drawn her back and the need to run away from Tamar, Soredamor was sure to follow his path to seek the sword. Now that she stood by the massed ranks of the two Aristrian battle groups she felt dwarfed and insignificant in their presence. She simply stood there in a state of indecision as another voice in her head whispered a new tune,

'Leave this place now; Soredamor will be seeking you, just turn and run. Lives can be remade anew elsewhere.' She shook the whispering voice from her head.

'*No*,' she had always been a stubborn one, even to herself. If she could kill the Su-Katii leaders of this army their attack would crumble? She had spent time in the Su-Katii temple and was more than a match for any 'one-lifer,' but against a full blown Su-Katii knight she was already doubting her chances, which meant as Renademus used to tell her, 'If doubt existed - she had already lost the battle.' She rallied somewhat with the thought that she also knew a little magic, which might give her an advantage over any swordsman? The screams of dying men forced a decision from her to react. If the battered Tanarian army fell today the war would be as good as finished. She was not about to let that happen. Best to start at the beginning and work her way up, she decided, her cloak would not keep her concealed in such a tight press, so it was time to show her hand. An attack from the rear of an army was also an effective means of spreading panic, although from a lone woman it was more likely that she may just get laughed off the battlefield. She would see who had the last laugh today. Suddenly the rear rank of the Aristrian war-machine broke into a blood-curdling scream as a silver sabre cut through bone and flesh alike and a frenzied female appeared out of thin air slaying several men of the rear rank in seconds. Men turned with apprehension at the sounds of battle so close to their backs, they could see no army advancing into their rear, just one lone woman bringing a circle of death to any who approached her; the bodies of the dead surrounded her in a semi-circle of blood as foolish men made an attempt to take her life. Renademus had taught her well. Lord Algar watched from a distance the slaughter of several more of his men who attempted to pass her iron guard. He had been standing back from the battle as he let his men march forwards, contemplating on his thoughts – during the events of this last week, things had just seemed wrong to him. Ever since the slaughter of his fellow Su-Katii in the farm house by that murderous pig Titus, his heart and resolve for this war had started to fade. He had questioned his involvement here several times during their pursuit of the Tanarians and had it not been for Lord Banok's resolve in finishing this war and forcing peace and order onto the lands, by delivering an Aristrian victory he would have walked away a long time ago. In reality it was only the shame from his personal involvement that forced him to stay; each night he would still hear the screams of the men under his former command, as they were put to the sword. Algar was once a Tanarian commander in the days before the Brotherhood twisted the Su-Katii to their will; his dreams were still filled with those days as were his nightmares. Lord Algar watched the woman fight for a moment noting the style and precision of her blows, it was obvious to him that she had spent time in the Temple yet her technique lacked some refinement, none the less it was effective against the men of his army. Of course, she would need to be stopped. He reluctantly huffed at the job in hand with a great exhale from his lungs and hefted his large war hammer up from the floor onto his shoulder,

'It is time to smash some skulls again my old friend,' he said to his hammer, he had often made comment to his weapon as if it were an old friend but the Iron lump was a poor conversationalist. He advanced towards Tress; it would be a shame to ruin such a pretty little face with his hammer and he consoled himself that he would take no pleasure in this necessary work. Half of his regiment turned and followed the giant Su-Katii, more in interest than the belief that he actually needed any assistance in this fight, besides there were more than enough men to deal with the Tanarians to their front. Tress spotted the new mass of men pealing around to face her, led by the huge bearded Su-Katii. She instinctively knew that even without the distinctive twin swords that would normally hang from a Su-Katii's belt, that this man was a warrior of the Temple; his movements alone betrayed his heritage and pedigree, the men around him seemed to fade away into her peripheral vision. Her stomach clenched as tight as a knot and the urge to flee grew with every step of his advance, this man was the biggest god-damned Su-Katii she had ever set eyes on. A spear thrust towards her from a man to her side, it instantly snapped her out of her feeling of growing dread. She side-stepped the blow, chopping away the tip of the weapon from its shaft and impaled her sabre into the man's groin. With a scream, the man slid from her blade, he followed the noise with the appropriate amount of flailing from such a messy wound and soon his dead weight toppled him to the blood-soaked ground with the other fallen warriors. Algar advanced ever closer and the panic inside her grew to an unprecedented level. The Sabre of Sum pulsed with an unnatural glow of pale blue and a white noise filled the air with an intensity that matched the glow of the sabre that flared up as bright as the sun in her hands. In an instant, the panic inside Tress was unbolted and the flood gates of her emotions were opened wide, intensified by Sum and the ancient magic of Merlin her emotions were turned into a terrible scream of terror that spread through every Aristrian man on the battlefield. Immediately, each man saw his own terrors replayed before his eyes and the men of the army scattered from their own apparitions in a moment of pure terror. Thousands of men scattered in every direction driven to the very peak of madness by their own hallucinations. Algar ran terrified with the rest of his men, but found his own bravery before any other, and he slowed his pace as he neared the edge of the battlefield, trembling and weak, he fought for his breath still haunted by the cancer-ridden face of the apparition of himself that was still fresh in his mind. Only the men fighting on the very peak of the hill led by Lord Banok had escaped the magical influences of the sword of Sum, they were far fewer in number than the Tanarian defenders and turned about to regard the unravelling commotion behind; they had expected to find several thousand men to their rear. The Tanarians of the front rank soon found out that when Lord Banok himself was cornered, he was a more dangerous prospect than any amount of his soldiers. Algar looked fearfully back across the carnage of the field; focusing his gaze back on the confident lady with the glowing sabre, he questioned himself as to whether he had the nerve to face her and his question was soon answered. Titus and the others emerged from the tree line; they wasted no time running across to Tress's side. Algar's eyes only needed to focus on Titus, before his forehead creased with a cross-hatch of displeasure at seeing that whore-son once more. Yet for all the hatred that filled his considerable volume, the sight of the ancient Su-Katii triggered an involuntary feeling of respect in the man's ability, judging on his own encounter with this man the legends of his deeds within the halls of the Su-Katii were, for once, not over-rated. He allowed the fear that still flowed through his veins to spread further through him and down to his feet. He allowed them to carry him off away from this place with the rest of the other men as quick as he could manage. He had no desire to face that man again; he was beyond caring any more and with the controlling power of the Brotherhood all but gone from him, he turned and ran for his life into the surrounding woodland.

The reverberations of a huge impact and the accompanying thunderclap of magic blasted into the lines of Aristrian soldiers dangerously close to Lord Banok's side. The Warlord swung about in shock to behold a new threat that had entered the battlefield. Banok had been so engrossed in the battle at the front line that he had no idea of the chaos that had just unfolded behind him. Where the hell were his men? The thin line of weary Tanarian soldiers who had been desperately holding out on the hill top were relieved when the lethal Su-Katii had ceased his onslaught. Many good men had fallen to his blades today; he had appeared to be unstoppable as he moved forward leaving bodies in his wake. The Tanarians had already been in a state of panic after the strangely besotting woman had appeared from nowhere in the centre of their camp destroying the Nordheim magician and eliminating their commander. The men of the army had taken on the look of adoring fools, helpless to act against the enchanting goddess as she went about her casual destruction of Ragnor and Larks in their command post. She had promptly retrieved their general's greatsword after the brief struggle and then departed in the blink of an eye. Lord Banok instantly made a combat assessment of his situation in a split second and reacted; his army was no longer behind him and a number of hostiles including a wizard were approaching from his rear. Although they had been beating back their opponents, after the recent show of force from the wizard Banok's men were quickly realising that the change of their fortunes was unravelling fast, many broke ranks and disengaged from the enemy as they also discovered with mounting panic that their troops behind were missing. They had been in the thick of the fighting and beyond the influence of the magic when the power of Sum had raged across the battlefield. Only now did they discover its effects against the men behind. It was a quick and easy decision; the remaining Aristrians broke into a Rout. Lord Banok realised that his best chance to slip away unnoticed was with the other men, he needed to use the mass confusion that swept across the field for his own escape; he knew he would be a prime target as he withdrew. His escape was not to happen, Titus had spotted him already and was cutting his way across the Aristrian lines to vector in on Banok and block his way. He slew any men who strayed to close to his blades as they pushed past him in the squeeze of their panic to escape. As he advanced Titus called out towards the fleeing commander, somehow his voice carried over the chaos of the field,

'Your chance to flee this field in shame has passed you by Su-Katii; come here and face me alone, I'll make your passing quick. Of course, you will gain your life, should you be able to get past me. Now, before I send you on your way to the underworld, what is your name? I like to know the names of those I slay.'

'Why, I am Lord Banok, second in command to the Su-Katii order - you will know my name better when I carve it into your chest. I presume you sir are Lord Barrad, the little upstart that has been making such a fuss, I will gladly face you in single combat and when I am done with you this day I will skewer your head on top of my sword and used it as a banner to gather my forces and crush the last of your men here. Lord Banok had never met with Barrad for he had held a field command during the years of his training inside the Rift. Algar had not disclosed the real details of what had actually happened back at the farmhouse in Ubecka to any other living soul on that fateful night, so without this insight it was reasonable for Banok to wrongly assume that the only Su-Katii to stand against them was Barrad. Banok had no inkling that the Su-Katii before him was the ancient killer unleashed from a time now forgotten to most men.

'Allow me to correct you, I think you will find that is Barrad over there,' Titus indicated with his sword as another Su-Katii warrior rejoined with his men to his right flank and their jubilant cries went up amongst the Tanarian lines at the return of their general. Banok looked puzzled for a moment as he digested the news. Only this single man stood in his way, it must be a bluff he thought for there was only Barrad and Candis that had rejected their plans of domination within the order. He attacked reassuring himself that he would quickly end this and be on his way.

Their swords sung out in a deadly song as each well-placed blow was parried and countered with another. Banok quickly learnt, after receiving a shallow slice to his face from a very near miss of a piercing jab at his eye, that his opponent was not bluffing.

'Allow my blades to do the talking and correctly introduce me; I am Titus from the real order of the Su-Katii. Perhaps you have heard of me in your bedtime stories?' he launched a blistering array of strikes at Banok who struggled to keep pace with the attack. Panting for breath Banok backed away attempting to disengage and struggled to find any space in his opponent's attack pattern to return a strike.

'No, It cannot be. You are long dead,' panted Banok managing to strike back at the man's head. Titus sidestepped and turned aside Banok's secondary blade that had already moved into the optimum space to parry such a counter attack. His blade stopped Titus's second strike but the shoulder lunge that followed barged into Banok, forcing him from his feet. Before the Su-Katii lord could hit the floor Titus's sword lashed out spraying the bright red blood of his opponent's jugular across the ground. Titus turned without a backward glance and calmly walked away from the dying man that futilely clutched at the unstoppable flow of blood that spurted from his body.

'I think it is you who is dead Lord Banok,' Titus commented as he returned to the Tanarian lines. Titus looked sheepishly at Athene who had stood with Tamar watching the combat unfold. She had watched the fight with an element of fascination rather than fear for Titus, she had come to realise that with the blade he was apparently unstoppable. Tress had also watched on, but with a more analytical appreciation of his skill. During the fight Zerch's magic had worked as regular as clockwork erasing the last traces of Barrad from her memories. Unknown to all but Zerch, his curse worked quicker against any man that she really harboured feelings for. With the last blows of her combat she had locked away the memories of the repeated rape in the farm house, she had placed these thoughts in the darkest cell of her mind so that her mind could only be filled with pleasing thoughts and watched her one and only lover gloriously finish off his opponent. She was looking though eyes that were not truly her own and it altered her perception of the world about her. The stirring memories of Titus ravishing her filled her mind, they had been experienced in a body unaffected by the magical erasure of her mind and, as he was her only memorable experience of what the pleasures of tender lovemaking could be like, he was about as close as she came to finding love. The memory of Barrad was now no more and she watched on feeding on her memories and wanting more. Titus noticed Tress's flushed cheeks and wanting eyes as the two women stood together with similar expressions across their faces as they followed his return. He could not help compare the two roses that may bear thorns against one another or even him. He had been stung by both in different ways. Tress was taller and leaner and without doubt the more physically attractive of the two, her ample bust held his eyes for longer than it should and stole his eyes away from the sculptured curve of her slim hips. He grumbled through his throat as he pulled his eyes away from her, he had taken her mind but desired her body. On the other hand Athene was altogether less curvaceous when stood next to Tress, with dark hair and a pleasing petite build ...she also had never stabbed him, which was a bonus - but she was difficult to please. They had enjoyed each other many times and he would do nothing to change that, for deep down she reminded him a little of his long dead wife. She nagged him just the same. He knew that both women desired him, he had lived enough years to realise that, and besides who could blame them. He walked passed Tress and hugged Athene in his arms as he felt the other woman's eyes burn into his back. His rejection would be his revenge for the dagger in his back. He decided that she must be like a dog on heat from the signals that he spotted between her and Barrad or perhaps she was trying to pick a fight between them? He didn't wish to kill the young general so all the better to steer clear, he considered – it would probably annoy her the more. Why did life have to be so complicated he pondered; why could he not just have both women like the Uphrians did?

Barrad had wasted little time with the celebrations of his return; it was back to business as usual and he had already called for a head count. The army was depleted and they would need to reorganise and change their order of battle to make them more effective; he began the task of reorganising his men into smaller fighting units. To his horror he was shocked at how little of his command structure remained. Most of his officers of status were fallen and of all his fellow generals that he had left behind, only the wounded Onus remained. Lady fate was a strange creature he thought, this man was the only one out of his original Generals that he had refused to keep on under his command, and yet at the end of the day he was the last man standing. Of the twenty thousand men that he had originally commanded before his capture by the Brotherhood and Soredamor he had barely more than three thousand left. Not all had perished at the hands of the enemy, when things had started to go wrong in Ubecka many had faded away into countryside in their individual efforts to get away. The main force of the Aristrians had focused upon the escaping army rather than the trickle of men evaporating away from them; many had actually made it away to a small measure of safety. Barrad walked through his men as they rested; making sure that every single man saw his face. He was pleased to see some familiar faces had made it. The natural selection of war had ensured that only the skilled or the lucky remained, ensuring that the remaining veterans were a tenacious bunch. Barrad accessed his remaining men, he could see in their eyes they would fight again for him if needed, they may be battered but they were certainly not defeated. Tamar had sat cross-legged on the floor in a state of meditation as Barrad went about his work with the reorganisation of the army. That was until Titus bothered him.

'What's up, this is no time to be taking naps Tamar?'

'I wasn't *napping* you fool, can't you tell by now when I am using my magic to help save all of your lives?' Tamar snapped back at the warrior. Titus smiled back enjoying his angered reaction,

'I'm pretty good at doing that myself, if you haven't noticed? Anyway please do enlighten us thick-skulls and retards of your masterful findings; I almost forgot for a moment that I was addressing a god. By what title should I address you by your worshipfulness?' he said mockingly and took a deep bow before him. This seemed to have the effect of lightening his mood rather than annoying him further.

'Listen, I have travelled the spirit world and seen many things. The men of the Aristrian army that we just faced are fragmented and even now the weaker-minded amongst them still flee from this place. The only one who could effectively unite them again is Algar, but he is no longer under the thumb of the Brotherhood's magic and even now he struggles to comprehend his own part in this. He will be of little help to us but more importantly will not stand against us either,' Titus shrugged indifferently to his words, the Su-Katii of this age had showed him little to be impressed about. His eye was instantly redirected behind the magician to a more interesting site, as he noticed Tress bending over to help up a wounded man. Titus's teeth moved over his bottom lip with wanton thought as Tamar regained his attention away from those tight leather leggings with talk of the enemy.

'There is a second Aristrian force several leagues to

the north-east of this hill; they have perhaps six thousand men.' Titus digested the figures and then shrugged again.

'They will be of little consequence against us. Two Su-Katii and a magician with three thousand men in support could crush several times their number,' Titus replied.

'Oh, you fight for the Tanarians now do you? I thought the mighty Titus only thought for himself or for coin.' Tamar suggested with a smirk in return.

'No wizard, I fight for Athene,' he paused, 'Which in turn I guess means that I fight for you and the Tanarian nation; only because I was stupid enough to go along with all this spin about magic swords and the end of the world. You know, I just fight for the little things in life, like living. I have spent long enough in the void to know I don't want to go back. So, where is this God-Queen Soredamor anyway, I bet I could calm her desires to leave this time, why...' Titus's words petered out as he noticed that Athene had returned to within earshot and was giving him a long, dark and disapproving look. Tamar allowed himself a short chuckle at the boastful Su-Katii's words being shut up so quickly and the silence that followed was pleasing to him. During the time earlier as he had meditated and travelled in his spirit form he had viewed the opposing forces that had gathered, he had also sensed the vision of another watching his passing, he had been unable to throw Soredamor's gaze from his presence and had been annoyed with himself for using his magic, it was all too easy for her to find him. He was left with little choice but to return quickly back to his body when Titus had broken his concentration. He knew that Soredamor was now clearly aware of where the last sword was but hoped that she would not make an attempt on it with Athene's nullifying presence at hand. She was their one and only defence against the most powerful magic in the land and as a bonus seemed to also have the power to keep Titus on a tight leash. It was vital that the sword remained safe, but in the chaos of a war it could be very difficult. Amongst the mounting pressure Tamar had yet to work out his final plan of how he would managed to lure Soredamor back into Hadrak's Rift in Cardus and then there was the safety of her unborn child to consider. He had been an infant when the greatest powers had battled in this land, somehow through the protection of others he had survived; now he hoped to repay this debt to his own bloodline. His head ached with the events that gripped the world and he felt daunted with the task before him. A stabbing pain from his healed wound bothered him for the first time.

'Barrad make camp here this night, we will lick our wounds and move out at first light.' Tamar called over to the busy general.

'And which way would you suggest we move come the morning?' the general replied. Tamar scratched at the bristles of his chin.

'I think we will be heading North.'

Chapter 23 – Choices

The two magicians sat opposite one another in Zerch's villa, each man was attentive to the other's every action, yet both men played down their attentions.

'Well Kerric, are you going to drink the wine I poured for you or do you really think that I would poison my guests after I have gone to all the trouble of saving them? Did your master not teach you manners?' Zerch deliberately took a long gulp of his wine and then pretended to choke to amuse himself. The place seemed so dull without Garth about to belittle.

'Well Kerric, it's been a big day, we must rest tonight and then tomorrow we shall talk properly. I trust your room is to your liking, do you need anything? Wine?' Kerric shook his head. 'Women?' Zerch added. Kerric shook his head again. 'A boy perhaps? I can arrange for all sorts here.'

'No,' Kerric added resolutely, he was truly shattered after the battle with Telimus but was still intrigued as to what would come tomorrow. Only one way to find out he thought, but he could sense that the man sitting across from him was waiting for him to ask and would gleefully tell him to wait until the morning.

'Goodnight Zerch,' he rose pausing for a moment, '…And thank you for being there today,' he turned and left for his room.

The loud squawking of birds outside his window tore Kerric away from his vivid dreams of wildly rutting with Soredamor. They were the same dreams that filled his mind with desire every night but they were nothing compared to the real experience. His hands trembled with the very thought of her as he pulled back the blankets of his bed. It usually took several minutes of calming meditation each morning to clear her from his mind enough to focus on the trivial matters of human existence. Today he did not dawdle and found it easier to get going; he wanted to see what the first day of his life without the Brotherhood held, so he dressed quickly and went to meet with Zerch in the common room. Zerch was already there with a bowl of dried fruits on the table for his breakfast.

'Ah at last sleepyhead, please sit and join me in breakfast *Master* Kerric.' He smirked as he spoke the title and the pair sat and made pleasant small talk about the weather and how difficult it was to get fresh fruit with the war upsetting supply routes. The conversation went on for several minutes before reaching the main reason of their conversation.

'Pleasant dreams?' Zerch enquired knowing full well the content of his dreams and their enslaving effects that swept over every Brotherhood magician.

'Yes, thank you,' Kerric replied innocently.

'About Soredamor I presume?' asked Zerch with a raised eyebrow.

'Of course, how did you guess?' the bald magician played along dumbly, knowing full well that Zerch understood that every Master in the Brotherhood dreams of nothing else.

'Then it is time for you to cease dreaming of her my friend.' Zerch stated as if it were possible.

'What if I don't want to stop thinking of her?' Kerric replied distantly, almost as if he were thinking of his queen as he spoke.

'Every living soul who has felt her touch will always crave for more. To join with her brings both power and pleasure an intercourse of more than just body and mind.' Zerch nodded back with agreement, but knew his words were wrong.

'I have also experienced such pleasures but am free to choose my own fate. I have walked a path of destruction, destroying magic wherever it has raised its ugly head. You see Kerric, the old saying is true, power really is corruption - so I have chosen to end this corruption that attempts to spread across our land with its insane ways. I strike back at insanity by destroying the source of power and magic that has killed my family and infested everything precious to me. Only a few remain who command this power.' Zerch sneered as he drew his excited breath.

'Do you mean to kill me then?' Kerric asked flatly. Zerch avoided looking up into Kerric's eyes and replied flatly,

'Not today, but then again that will depend upon you. I am offering you the chance of freedom; if you can break free from her hold over you, once and for all. You see Kerric you were never going to have her all for yourself, even if I were to suddenly become as incompetent at my craft as you and let you destroy me; even then she still would not choose you. I know that even now you will be thinking about trying to finish me off, but that fact that I know your desires alone should be enough to dissuade you. I assure you Kerric, unlike you my soul is untainted by her touch and this gives me the luxury of choice and I choose to reject her. There is only one other certainty …no matter what you do, she will reject you in the end. I on the other hand, am going to destroy her one way or another, I have seen to it. Mark my words, her end will be soon.' Kerric could feel the rising anger in him begin to boil over at Zerch's suggestion, yet he knew it was not truly his own anger, more that of the dark hold that had been induced inside him. The green crystals that lined the room, embedded into the plaster of the wall pulsed with life and Kerric felt himself calming down, something in the villa soothed the anger that threatened to emerge at the mention of killing Soredamor. Kerric sat quietly feeling the anger pass. After a short break of self contemplation Kerric spoke,

'Why did you pick me to live Zerch? I have seen

your magic at work, you could best any one of our Order in single combat, yet you did not destroy me when you had the chance. Now I know you are not soft in the head or heart, so of all of the Brotherhood, why spare me?' Zerch tapped the table with his finger, noting that Kerric had taken the correct line of questioning; there may be hope for him yet?

'OK, Kerric if you really want to know, I'll tell you. It is because you have no real magic inside you of your own. Did you not realise your lack of progression through the ranks of the Brotherhood? Not the fastest was it, huh? I know because I have been following you over your entire career and I tainted your soul long before Soredamor. They simply made a mistake with you, they didn't know it – but they did. Sure you learnt to read magic and could string a few enchantments together but this is no more than any other person who was dropped into their environment could muster. Those with real power are born with it. It is not by chance that only a handful of magicians hold true power, others may only progress as far as their intellect can carry them and I did give you a little help starting out, just enough to fool the other Masters. I'm sorry to tell you this revelation, but you must have felt it yourself? It was not until you joined with Soredamor that she filled you with her dark seed and like a dog carrying lice you have been a host to her power. You have carried this mark like a bad stain on your soul ever since.' Kerric despised his words yet he knew them to be true. He had always been the laughing stock of Bellack's household and the one who was always inept or could not master his teachings. Even the Brotherhood could make mistakes. Zerch knew they did, for it had been him that had selected the skinny runt of a child, claiming that he had witnessed a dormant power inside the child, all those years ago. He had blessed him with just enough magic to fool the other Masters and pass their tests and then like all plants he had encouraged his growth for he had an investment in his future. Kerric had been well placed to progress until Bellack came along and stole the show. Zerch was a master of manipulation and long term planning and he had needed to plant a dud into the Brotherhood at the time; he had grand plans indeed for his Brotherhood jester.

'I'm actually surprised that you even managed to survive for so long in such company, you must complement yourself on your determination – but had I left you to face Telimus alone you would surely be dead now, and how you killed Teon on your own is quite beyond me, perhaps you have impeccable timing or a knack for survival? Now, back to the matter of, do I want to kill you – if Soredamor's power is to live on inside you I can tell you now that I will be forced to slay you Kerric. But we are men of choice and the fact that you lack the power of a true master actually weakens her hold over you, she will make you think that you have no choice, but perhaps you do? We can use that power, the unseen magic that urges you on to do her will. We can track her down and put an end to her once and for all. As even you should know well enough, if she dies so does her hold over you and her magic within you. I don't have to kill you to end the magic of the Brotherhood – just her. You are a cunning and bright man; I'll give you that – so you should have the ability to see past your clouded mind at the moment and my enchantments in this room will assist you. You must block out your desire for her, even though every fibre in your body is telling you that she wants you and needs you. I know you better than yourself Kerric; I know that you have the sense to see it is a lie. She seeks to return to her one true love and will leave you in an instant. Close off the receptors of your body and focus on your mind, let your actions conquer your jealousy for my prey is the most dangerous creature in this world.' Zerch enjoyed watching Kerric's reaction and smiled with a modicum of smugness as he spoke.

'Soredamor also has cunning. This morning she collapsed the cave that leads into her Rift to stop any chance of her return and she has gathered all bar one of the swords that are essential for her return to her lover, you are nothing to her. She has not sat idle whilst I have been saving your arse and dealing with the remainder of her Brotherhood. She has also been systematically destroying anyone with the power enough to challenge her plans. Women huh …they can't come up with their own plans and have to just copy mine.' Kerric did not share his entertained attitude and his head swam with thoughts at the magicians words; Zerch cleared his throat and continued,

'Still perhaps I should have just released her and then left you to it? I would have saved myself a lot of effort. She has busied herself with the destruction of the Clan's Shamans in the Uphrian forests and now that her work there is about done, her gaze will seek us out before finally resting on her brother. She is systematic, I give her that.'

Kerric almost wanted her to appear immediately and end his suffering, even the thought of standing against her brought torment to his mind, but he had to know more.

'What will you do if she comes for you?' Kerric asked.

'Oh, I can evade her, should she find me unprepared if needs be with the Dimesia relic. She ultimately wants the final sword but cannot take it, not whilst Athene is still alive, for the power that released her back into this world also stops her from returning to the world or time that she seeks. Ha, I love the way that life is always like a double-edged sword. She wants it above all else, but she is wise and will bide her time to find the right moment to strike. But she will find that it has already past. We are going to take the only option left to us and also seek the protection of Athene.

Tamar will not welcome us into his camp but he will accept our aid because he knows that he also has no choice, she was always more powerful than him and he will require our help to deal with her. Only together will we stand any chance of bringing her down.'

Kerric still failed to see where he slotted into this apart from being described as a love-sick incompetent, who they could perhaps use to track his queen.

'And me, what do you require of me?' he asked.

'All you need to do is convince Tamar that you are prepared to help us, or on second thoughts, what am I saying - you're incompetent. Keep your mouth shut and let me do the talking, it is that simple. With the last Master of her Brotherhood standing in our camp Soredamor will make her move against us, it will lure her to act instead of waiting, forcing her hand with a false hope. She will come at us, for she will think that she has an ally in our camp. A Master that bettered the most revered of her order.' Zerch let out a slight and nervous laugh then flexed his fingers touching them to his nose in deep thought, whilst Kerric still looked confused.

'Don't worry Kerric, cheer up. I know that in the end you will fail us.

What do you say? Are you prepared to give my plan a go? You really don't have anything to lose, you are a dead man either way – but perhaps you can live?'

After the waves of anger had rippled over his surface the calmness of the real Kerric remained behind. He nodded slowly to the exuberant Master.

'It would seem I have little choice.' Zerch offered him some more fruit in way of celebration.

'Good man, you have made the right choice. Now come, it is time for us to eat some humble pie and visit Tamar. Oh yes and you will need to get out of those damn black robes, the Brotherhood of Keth is no more.

We don't want to get you killed before we can talk just because you decide to wear black, besides it may reinforce the fact that the worm has turned. Wait here, I will fetch you something more suitable.'

Back on the windy hill in Aristria, with the next morning came a second attempt to capture the hill from Tanarian hands, but fortunately the defenders were now better prepared and it had been a half hearted and feeble attempt. After the large Aristrian army had been scattered by the power of Sum on the first day and the slaughter of their Su-Katii commander, they had regrouped as best they could under the command of an Aristrian officer, they just didn't know when to give up. Lord Algar had been nowhere to be found, along with half of their original number – but the Aristrians considered themselves capable enough. The men of the routed army had inadvertently run into the path of the advance elements of a new army marching from the capital. Reinforced with an advanced party of cavalry from their contingent they had rallied and made another attempt at the Tanarians, thinking that their greater numbers alone mattered. By late morning several thousand Aristrian lay dead on the slopes of the hill marking their tragic mistake. The Tanarian army had fought well; led by the two Su-Katii knights fighting side by side and complemented by Tamar's magic, the effects had been devastating. The end of the battle had been induced prematurely once again by Tress's use of Sum, repeating the performance of the day before. She had seen enough unnecessary death that day and despite the Su-Katii's intent on finishing off their enemy she had used the sword in an attempt to stop the senseless slaughter.

In the night before the final battle of the hill, a lone sentry commander had walked between the many sentry posts that surrounded the sleeping hill top camp. Sillic was a junior officer and tonight was a large responsibility for him. He had been passing through the light scrubland of the slopes to check with the men of his next sentry post when a stunningly beautiful woman had stepped out of thin air before him. He had been in awe at her presence and his hand soon dropped away from his sword hilt where the shock of her arrival had instinctively placed it. He recognised her as the woman who had rained fire and thunderbolts against their command post not long before; although now he had little care for such insignificant memories, she looked ravishing. She smiled at him and spoke gently.

'If you desire me I am not outside of your reach, just take my hand now and all my pleasures will be yours.' The screaming faces of Ragnor and Larks filled Sillic's mind as they had died in her projected flames and his fingers began to trace their way back up his sword hilt. Soredamor's eyes fixed with Sillic, they seemed to burn at his soul and he could feel his heart beating strongly in his chest.

'Don't you not want me Sillic? Every man does. I will not refuse you like your frigid wife; I will do anything to please you, come and feel for yourself just how soft and pleasing I can be.' She rubbed her hands over her breasts seductively and pulled her dress to one side exposing a nipple. She was surprised that she had needed to go so far to get this dog to heel.

'Come Sillic,' she sucked her finger and gasped at the young officer as she pursed her fervent lips at him and beckoned him forwards with her glistening wet finger.

'What are you waiting for? Place your hand between my legs and your fingers will soon be as wet as mine.' The moonlight was bright and betrayed her beauty in full. She licked her lips as if she wanted him to taste them. She had been surprised just how resistant this man had been to her charms, her first words alone were normally effective, was the bond of wedlock so binding to these mortals?

'*Come*. Take my hand and I will be your slut forever, you may do with me as you please.' She smiled as she saw the raw conjured images of them together in his mind.

Sillic stepped forwards and reached for her hand, in the blink of an eye both had disappeared.

In the aftermath of the battle Sillic left his post and made his way towards the centre of the hill. He ignored the compliments paid to him by the men of his own troop as they wished him well in passing. His face was distant and his eyes focused only upon the black hair of the lady who stood grilling some meat on a makeshift barbeque. His head tilted to the left as he advanced, General Barrad stood in deep conversation talking to the Magician. His head moved to the right, the other Su-Katii – Titus, sat with his armour removed and at his feet; his bare chest was exposed to cool down after the heat of battle. His back was turned towards him and he appeared busy sharpening his swords; he continued forward as Soredamor's voice replayed inside his mind.

'If you should loose focus on your task, think of me again and feel the weight of my gold in your pocket then remember what is waiting for you on your return. Once you have done as I command and driven your sword through the black-haired woman's heart, hold this stone in your hand and you shall be returned to me.'

He ambled forwards unnoticed, his hand slowly moving to clench the handle of his blade and yet as he neared the woman he felt the release of the force that had controlled him and had guided him so far into this area. He faltered for a moment, seeing Athene as nothing more than a helpless soul, slowing his steps to the woman questioning what he was actually doing here. The memories of his brief yet exhilarating time with

Soredamor flooded back into him, she had been exquisite; in his short time with her he had at last felt like a man, a man that had the urges of a wild animal. As he thought of her his desires grew, there was nothing that would stand in his way of enjoying her again, with his next step he felt the weight of the gold coins and he moved with an instinctive reaction. Sillic's sword withdrew from its scabbard and he quickly raised it to deliver the deadly strike. Athene turned around hearing the approaching steps, thinking Titus had returned for some food, the surprised look in her large green and hazel eyes reminded Sillic of a frightened animal. For a second as he stood there with his sword raised to strike. With Soredamor's suggestions fading fast in his mind he held back the blow, his willpower returning.

A silver sabre appeared from the thin air behind him, slicing through Sillic's raised sword arm like butter. His cry of agony drew everyone's attention and his one remaining hand clutched at and squeezed the very ordinary stone in his pocket. The Sabre of Sum struck again wielded by Tress, smashing through Sillic's collarbone and halfway into his chest. His corpse slid from her blade in a crumpled heap. Tress looked across at the men with her head slightly shaking and her lips pursed into a visible pout,

'You want to take more care of your woman,' she aimed her remark directly at Titus as he came bounding over. Tress had remained in a state of stealth after the battle; there was no point in exposing herself to unnecessary risk as she guarded the sword. In truth she had remained hidden more so from the advances of the Su-Katii General, Barrad, with whom she had the strangest of conversations with the night before the battle, this stranger had approached her out of the blue and invited her to share his tent and had even smacked her bum playfully as he passed her, he turned to her and pronounced,

'I have decided to have a new rule in my army, never have a cold bed.' She had cried out in shock at his playful slap and clenched her fists preventing her natural instinct to lash out at him as he ducked away under the canvas tent flap to retire. What presumptuousness and bravado these rude Su-Katii displayed; how dare he talk to her like that. The general had waited a long time in his bed for her before he realised that she would not be coming. Tress had instead remained hidden since the encounter, keeping herself to herself as she tried to piece together the different parts of the man's brief conversation with her. She was unsure if it was anger or outrage at the General's suggestions and she wondered why his words even replayed in her mind so much. She had spotted the soldier moving towards Athene with a crazed look in his eye; it was frightening how easily he had moved within striking distance of her. For a split second Tress had thought about letting this evil little deed play out, none of them knew that she was even standing there as the last guardian to their cause. The possibilities had stormed quickly through her mind, If Athene was slain, then Titus may turn his attentions to her, after the appropriate amount of time grieving of course. He was a practical man and she had noticed the look of want in his eyes the other day. After all she had been trained to pick up on such reactions from men and use them to exploit her mark. The long string of events that left a bitter taste in her mouth with that particular man were put to one side as her desire overruled her mind. She had quickly dismissed the thought as soon as it had entered her mind; this kind of scheming was not in her true nature and she blamed the dark thought on a combination of her training and Zerch's curse. Light had prevailed and the fact that they needed Athene in the fight against Soredamor had very little to do with her final decision.

'Hey, I look after my women well. Are you alright?'

Titus encircled Athene protectively in his arms.

'I had my eye on him; my throwing knife would have dropped him before he had the chance to strike. …I was just testing you to see if your reactions had improved with your little stay in the Temple. Had you lingered any longer I would have needed to react myself.' Titus gave Athene a tight hug, 'You have nothing to fear now that the hero of Tanaria is watching over you.' Tamar almost choked,

'The hero of Tanaria, ha …I never thought I would hear the day when Titus the killer would call himself by that name. Today must be a very special day indeed; but I think that we must thank Tress for staying alert. This is clearly the first of Soredamor's tricks to put an end to us. Her magic may dissipate in your presence but her beauty and demands can drive a man on to commit foul deeds. We must learn from this and be better prepared in the days to come.' Tamar's voice deepened to a more serious tone with his last words.

'Yes, thank you Tress,' Athene added gracefully. Tress curtsied back in jest trying to lighten the mood of her self-imposed jealousy that had been growing inside her against Titus's lover.

The familiar crackle of a forming transport portal filled the air in the ground beyond where the battle had earlier been fought. The distinctive noise grabbed everyone's attention.

'Soredamor?' questioned Titus; readying his swords. Tamar rolled his eyes upwards at the empty headed warriors suggestion, it was obviously not her – she had mastered far quicker ways of transport.

'No, feeble-minded one – she can travel faster than such antiquated ways that we magicians must use.' The soldiers in the area backed nervously away all the same and looked to Tamar for direction. Two figures walked calmly through the haze of light, hardly displaying the anxiety they felt. The figures cleared the blinding brightness of the light, Zerch in his drab brown cloths and Kerric in a bright mustard yellow robe, it was as if Zerch had prepared such a sickly-coloured robe to humiliate the man on purpose – it even fitted him perfectly. The soldiers raised their spears at the sight of the men as their squad commander challenged the men.

'Halt men, you have entered Tanarian soil; identify yourselves and prepare to submit to my custody.' Zerch looked across at Tamar with his hands held out in a peaceful gesture and called out.

'Bring your dogs to heel Tamar; we are here to join forces with you against a common enemy. Come on man don't look so surprised, we both know this is the only reasonable action; we all want to live and grow old in our world as we know it. Try and put aside my sword master's injuries to you, that wound was meant for her, let us all be adults here.' Kerric whispered into Zerch's ear.

'Why didn't you tell me about this, did your sword master stick Tamar?'

'*Yes*, now shush it,' Zerch said in a low tone.

'Ah, *good*,' replied Kerric with an approving smile.

Tamar stood scratching the blonde bristles of his chin in thought for a moment. Zerch's move was not totally unexpected, but bringing that wretched creature Kerric with him certainly was a surprise. They must have formed some kind of loose alliance; this intrigued him all the more. He also knew that Zerch's powers at least equalled his own and that to fight them both now would weaken them and open a great opportunity for Soredamor to strike; perhaps she even sent them? No, he could believe that of Kerric but never of Zerch – his intentions were clear, he sought her destruction, but there was without doubt more to this than first met the eye.

'It would appear that today is turning out to be a lot stranger than I first thought. *Men*, let them pass.'

Chapter 24 – A Line in the Sand

The group of magicians sat in a circle facing each other. After several heated hours of conversation they had finally reached a decision on how to set their trap for Soredamor. The first element of their action was to distance themselves away from the army; there were far too many problems with staying, an endless supply of victims for Soredamor to corrupt being one of them. Barrad had decided to stay with his men and continue leading his army in pursuit of the fleeing Aristrians; before he departed he had reassured the group that he would be fine, even without any magical protection he was sure that Soredamor would not hunt him or attempt to use him as a bargaining chip, the affairs of men were too trivial for her. He had spent more time with Soredamor than anyone else present as her favourite plaything, so they trusted his judgement on this. Barrad had hoped to have seen Tress's face just one more time before he departed – but it was not to be, even after calling out for her she remained concealed. He understood, she was probably filled with embarrassment and regret with their time together in the forest. He could understand the way of war and tactics but never women. By leading the army away he knew it would aid Tamar's chances of success against Soredamor and the magician was relieved to remove the complication of an endless supply of charmed individuals being used against them. Besides he still had his one man army with him for any sword work …the hero of Tanaria. As long as Athene was with them her shadow was sure to follow and would protect her. Tress on the other hand had frozen in her boots on seeing Zerch come through the Portal and after she eventually found the courage to speak with him, she had turned to Tamar and implored him to cut them loose. Annoyingly Zerch had hardly seemed bothered with her; his words on their re-introduction had been brief to say the least,

'Hello Tress, you are looking well, it looks like you are a free woman now, I guess thing's must be looking up for you these days.' He had sighed and walked off as if the years of hunting her had been nothing but a poor hobby. It had been the major event of her life escaping this man and that was all he could say to her, she was enraged and had to stalk off away from the man to fully vent her anger in private. Tamar ran through a plan of action against Soredamor detailing every piece of information that may be relevant for the battle to come, including the information that she was pregnant. Kerric just managed to contain his anger at the news, turning his back to hide his building rage. Athene sat close by so that their conversation could not be intercepted or eavesdropped by mystical means, their alliance was lose to say the least and it may even be possible that Kerric could be used by her as a two-way conduit to relay their plans.

'You all may as well know, the reason I stepped out foolishly in front of your sword master's blade Zerch, it was to save the unborn life in her stomach, I do not wish to repeat the experience nor see the life of innocents killed in our battle.' Tamar's words sickened Kerric in two ways, the thought of another man's child festering away in Soredamor's belly made him cringe and also the compassion in Tamar to save an 'innocent life' was also a revolting and alien suggestion to him. He attempted to hide his disgust with an uncaring sneer. There were obviously some trying differences amongst their combined group. But before they started the battle that would define their lives they needed to find Soredamor and they had just the man to use, all eyes turned onto Kerric. He was still a conduit of her power and had been spared to use as a tool against her.

'Where is she now?' Tress asked, an edge of worry could clearly be heard in her tone, the task of looking after the sword was starting to take its price on her in worry and lost sleep. Tamar and Zerch each held onto one of Kerric's arms and they concentrated with their eyes shut. Kerric let out a scream more akin to a woman in labour than that of a man and Tamar called out to the others.

'I see her, I see her. She has just slain the last of the Shamans.' The men sat in a state of meditation for several minutes until they returned to their bodies, Kerric returned first followed by Zerch. They begun to shake off the lethargy in their limbs and stood up as they waited for Tamar to open his eyes. Eventually the golden-bearded magician stirred from his sitting position and Zerch regarded him with an air of suspicion.

'You took your time getting back ...is every thing alright?' he questioned in a sceptical tone. Tamar nodded back without comment.

'So it's decided then. We shall travel to Cardus and set up camp there, she knows that Kerric now stands with us, the trap can be set.' Tamar said with an edge of finality. Each man in the group had a different motive and interpretation of the mission before them. The Masters all understood the threat that the goddess represented and knew that she had to be taken down, but should their plans go badly wrong they would have some flexibility in Cardus, for they could utilise the Rift that held Hadrak, as a backup plan. Containment of the problem would be preferable to failure. Unlike the others, Tamar sought to extract the child from Soredamor before her destruction – he was unsure exactly how he would manage this at the moment but he would try. That was as much of the plan that all three men had agreed to - in theory, although he clearly knew that Zerch sought to kill her at the first opportunity and Kerric, well he didn't really know his motives for standing with them, but suspected he would lack the willpower to resist her powers and was sure he would turn against them in the end. Still, even this level of predictability could be of use when there were so many loose ends to deal with. Of all of the Brotherhood Zerch had been the only one to resist Soredamor's ultimate control, how he managed it he didn't have a clew but it was clear that Kerric was not of the same mould; this made him very dangerous and unpredictable. It was almost certain that Kerric would turn on them during the battle to come, as he was still his queen's puppet. He would place him nearest to Athene and Titus so that they could quickly neutralise his magic if needs be. *Ah*, he could suddenly see Zerch's reasoning now; they needed a chink in their armour to make her think that she could succeed against them. Kerric would make the perfect patsy, he wore the mantle of a Spell-master but Soredamor's lack of vision into the world of men over the years would have hid the truth of the string of great victories he had claimed to his queen. Kerric had painted himself to her as a Master of true renown, however Zerch knew that the only power that flowed through Kerric was not his own. The man's trumped-up claims of victory and leadership had little substance in the real world, but his similar reports back in the Rift had only served to further Zerch's aims. It was a very lose alliance but it could still work. Tamar had thought over this situation many times, he could live with Soredamor's death, but her child's would be more difficult to stomach, it was a rational decision to slay her, versus extinction, but as was his way, he was already contemplating a continuity plan of action. He knew well that it would be after they had dealt with Soredamor in one way or another when all hell would break lose between them, too many magicians had turned up dead these last months to think otherwise, Zerch would not stop until every source of magic was stamped firmly out. He thought for a moment, did it actually matter to him if this time line never existed? It may be less bloody if the past could be changed? He and Soredamor were the only people in this world who had walked the earth at the time of their father, he may not be able to recall it, but he was there all the same. By his understanding of the magic that she sought to invoke; the theory went that a person may only travel backwards in time if one's presence was already there. It was written in the most ancient of scrolls that you were not meant to be able to walk through time, just be able to pass your spirit back to its container at an earlier state, replacing what was already there – if the theory was true or not remained to be seen. There had not been a power strong enough to attempt such an event, but with the swords combined and the magic of their father still alive, this could perhaps be a possibility. If this was indeed possible it would mean that with his big sister wanting to travel across time, to depart this world with her lover, it was possible for him to do the same and the move could make him the most powerful man in the future yet to come. This thought was intoxicating to him, who said it was just her that could utilise the power of the swords. Why he could stop every war and plant the seeds of a new society if this time were to pass again with Tamar the magician as its warden, but then they had been her words that had called out to him and halted his return through the mist, just as Kerric and the others had departed back to their bodies, after tracking her earlier.

'*Tamar*, Tamar …are you alright?'   Athene questioned as he staggered and almost fell with his overwhelming thoughts.

'Yes, yes I'm fine. Now Master Zerch let us be going before she is drawn here and we need to be in Cardus before her – the Dimesia if you please, we need to get to Cardus as quick as possible. Zerch pulled out a golden ball from his robes and twisted it in several directions.

'Now let me see. Ah yes, there we go now.'

A shimmering Portal marking the way to Cardus almost instantly opened up before them and the shear cliff-face and circle of power marking the entrance to Hadrak's Rift could clearly be seen beyond. The men stepped through one at a time, Titus hung in indecision whether he should travel before or after Athene, experience had shown him that the order of passing these foul abominations seemed to hold their own challenges. In a split second decision he went before her and thankfully Athene passed through without incident or attack, last of all.

Soredamor looked down at the dead Shaman and the several clansmen that had attempted to stop her rampage through their people; his body was now charred beyond all recognition.

'You have read your last prophesy my pagan friend. How misguided your kind were. You should have submitted to the one true power in this world a long time ago, I would not have shunned you. Oh well I suppose it does not matter for this time line will soon be erased once I have the last sword.' She halted her speech to the uncaring corpse as she felt the presence of magic seeking her location. She closed her eyes and focused on the presence. The image of Kerric appeared from the mist of her mind.

'Mistress, listen to my words my love, I have little time. Your brother seeks to trap you in Hadrak's Rift and Master Zerch has joined with him and wishes to destroy you. They follow my trail to you and will find me soon. We have but seconds.'

Her eyes blazed with anger at Kerric's suggestion and the thought that he had managed to find her so easily.

'The sword Kerric, do they have the sword with them?' She asked with the edge of urgency in her voice. The image of Kerric nodded its agreement,

'Yes, they have it; they also said that I was... oh, no they come. I am sorry that I have led them to you, but I had to warn you – please forgive me.' Soredamor felt the other magician's mystic presence as more eyes watched her from the mist and beyond the reach of harm. Kerric sank back slowly into the mist leaving only his eyes glowing from the swirling mass that surrounded her. Tamar's voice rang out from the hidden veil,

'We have what you want sister; we will wait for you in Cardus where we will meet with you or end this once and for all.' She felt the watching eyes of Kerric and Zerch disappear,

'Brother wait!' she called out to Tamar and she sensed his fading spirit halt its withdrawal.

The Dimesia device had ensured that they could travel quickly to Cardus leaving little time for Soredamor to react; they had hoped that the speed of the powerful device would catch her off guard, equalling her speed of travel. Tress looked across at Titus sheepishly as she remembered the last time she had visited this spot. She had stabbed him just outside the Rift before running off to find the second enchanted sword. She looked away as he subconsciously scratched at his scar on his shoulder. Tamar moved from person to person in turn, explaining exactly where he wanted them placed and Zerch seemed to be relaxed and carefree. Just letting him get on with it.

'Athene, if you and Titus could move out to my right,' he placed them together as he knew it was pointless to attempt to separate them. He moved back to his original position and then cast a short spell of light in order to test where Athene's dispelling aura fell; after three steps to his left the magical glow that hovered before him was suddenly extinguished.

'Perfect, now Tress, if you could remain invisible with your cloak over here near the rift, if it all goes wrong you have the option of putting Sum beyond her reach by jumping into the Rift. I will project a magical image of Sum on the ground over here in order to tempt her in. It will be nothing more than a simple illusion, Delanichi would be proud of me; he used to love his illusions. I don't think she will be able to detect my illusion until she gets up close as the sword gives off a unique magical aura. Hopefully she won't be able to tell without a lengthy inspection and we will make sure that she does not have time for that. Now Kerric, stop lurking about behind me and place yourself over on my left. No, not there, move a little closer to Athene's protection and you Zerch, move to the centre.

Great, now remember these positions for we may have a long wait. Athene, we must rehearse a few movements, you will need to watch me like a hawk a lot will hinge on you. Should I move my hand like this,' he waved his hand in an unmistakable figure of eight, 'Then I will need you to rapidly move towards me about five steps forward or so, Ok?' She nodded back and Titus kissed her neck deliberately distracting her and then he gave a gentlemanly wave at Tamar as he screwed his face up at the over-loving action. Zerch who was further out to their front raised his hands to his lips,

'Shh, don't you hear that?' he said in a loud whisper. An enormous thunderclap reverberated through the air, shortly followed by a growing series of screams that carried their way across the hillside to their ears. Zerch called over to the others.

'Quickly, I fear she has moved quicker than expected, we have not even prepared the magical wards yet and there are signs of her coming. This is good, she has done exactly as I predicted. It's her only logical choice against us when Athene stands ready to nullify her magic. Yes, she has summoned forth Demons to attack us. They are the one thing that will not be dispelled by Athene's aura and they are armed with all the tools to quickly dispatch her, Titus, stand ready, for they will be coming for Athene as their primary target. 'What was the good part in all of that?' Athene questioned. The Su-Katii's swords came to his hands in a flash and Athene went distinctly white. 'I have fought their kind before and as I recall they are pretty tough,' Titus stated.

'Having second thoughts are we, swordsman?' Kerric leered, enjoying Titus's anxiety as he remembered him threatening him in the past, 'There comes a time in every person's life when fear begins to consume you, I see it in your eyes – there is no shame in it Titus,' Kerric's words ended with a faint curl of a smile across his face as he enjoyed delivering them to the man that had brought about the fall of his former masters.

'Fear, ha. You mistake my words you cretin, I meant 'tough' as in 'tough to cut through', like the sinews of your bony little neck Kerric,' he waved his blades at the skinny bald man.

'Now which one of you fine magicians loafing about here can help me with something to improve the effectiveness of my swords against these creatures? Come on don't be shy there must be one amongst you who can lend a hand with this issue? If they are not created by magic it will be just my blades that stand in their way; I can easily take them down if I can cut through them.' Zerch cleared his throat,

'I don't think that last statement is entirely true, we are far from defenceless here. Although I might be able to help, I developed a spell once for Garth it should do you just fine - but once I have used my magic you must stay away from Athene or else you will lose the enchantment. Now come here.' Zerch placed his hands on each sword and chanted his magic drawing an invisible rune above each of the weapons.

'Hurry, I can sense them coming,' Tamar said.

Just as the magician finished his words a low black cloud seemed to roll up the hill towards them. As it closed it became dreadfully apparent that it was not actually a cloud at all, but instead a seething mass of obsidian black bodies slithered over each other in an ever-advancing line. There must have been close to fifty of the creatures from the void clambering up the path and over each other, each one eager to taste with the soft flesh of man or woman.

'Oh my god will you look at that …such power,' mouthed Zerch faintly and Kerric began to back away as the black mist of bodies continued to roll towards them, at first glance, the mass had a smooth appearance, but now as it closed on them it was clearly broken by the jagged edge of fangs and talons. With all eyes fixed on the demon horde they hardly heard the chanting of a spell from Tamar's lips. It took the blast of white energy to pour forth into the horde from Tamar's outstretched hands before the other people snapped out of their defeatist thoughts that flowed through their minds. Titus alone seemed to watch their advance with an eager look of fascination as he edged further forwards deciding on the angle of his first attack.

'Kerric, some protection if you please,' Zerch suggested in a slightly more composed tone, seeming to regain himself once again, after the initial shock at the sheer amount of advancing demons that the Goddess had been able to summon to her will. For the magicians it was back to work as normal as Zerch took the lead.

'Tamar and I will attack, Kerric protect. Titus hang back to protect Athene and deal with anything that gets past us. Titus…' Zerch swung around to find him gone from his position. Tamar rolled his eyes at Zerch,

'You will eventually learn that this one never does as he's told; *now attack before they are on us.*' Titus had broken into a charge forwards to meet the sea of black bodies that had been parted by Tamar's initial blast of magic. From a distance the demons had looked little more than a man's height but now as he leapt amongst them they towered over him as they raised themselves to attack. Titus swords lashed out in an arc of steel as he moved fearlessly into their ranks cutting through their bodies and limbs as he passed. This was not the first time that he had fought their kind, but he was pleased to find that with this encounter his blades moved through their tough hides like soft flesh. As long as he could cut them he was confident that he could anticipate the creature's attack vectors and deal with them. To Titus, fighting was nothing more than working out the possible ranges of movements that the head, claws and tails of the demons could deliver – taking into account the extensive flexible movement of the creature's spine and factoring in the optimal angle of his counter attack. Simple. These were all operations that his brain had repeatedly practised to calculate in a split second over his endless years in training in the Su-Katii Temple and many more in their practical application. His last encounter with a Demon had been in a one-on-one fight and he moved into this encounter relishing the challenge of multiple opponents. Titus spoke to his prey as if they were nothing more than fond domesticated pets; reprimanding them with his blades with perfect execution as they moved at him. His swords burnt with the power of Zerch's runes as they sliced through demon flesh and soon the floor was flooded in their dark blood. Two demons leapt from opposite sides in an attempt to smash Titus between them, but the swordsman had read their movements early as their clawed feet surged with the anticipation of their leap. Titus twisted his body low, ducking under the flying demon to his right, his sword splitting the length of the demon's lower torso to its groin as he narrowly passed under the creature. The two demons collided in mid-air smashing each other to the ground before Titus's sword came back around to end both of the creatures. As the battle ensued, the magicians attacked the creatures to Titus's flanks, firing streams of magic into their ranks. One bolt of power ripped far too close for comfort, impacting next to Titus as he impaled another demon nearby, ducking low under the creature's armpit as its reaching talons snaked out at the space where his head had been a second before. Titus had only the time to return a cold glare back at Tamar, who had thrown the wild bolt of power, before the demons were upon him again. The mass of creatures attempted to bypass the deadly swordsman and several of the creatures attempted to leap forward to rip at the magicians, they sought to reach the prize that stood far behind the three robed men. Kerric stood fast with the men and an invisible barrier knocked the creatures back as they attempted to traverse around it to find a way through to Athene.

Behind the mass of bodies pressed against Kerric's shield, Zerch and Tamar cast new spells of destruction in a vivid display of their powers. The men worked their way through the massed demons, destroying them one by one, with both sword and magic alike. As the tide of the battle turned to their favour none in the group spotted the two demons traversing down the shear cliff-face that backed onto the amber pillars of Hadrak's rift. The creatures moved silently against the distraction of the attacking mob and quickly moved face first down the long drop. The two demons moved closer with face and fang heading downwards to the men's undefended rear. The entire attack had been a distraction for the silent assassins strike from the rear. As the first of the stealthy attackers reached the floor their clawed hands reached for the illusion of the blade, their talons moved through the illusion and scratched into the floor. The real sword of Sum arced out decapitating the first beast, guided by Tress's steady hand as she emerged out from her concealment. The second demon struck out and Tress turned her agile body sideways, long talons reached for her throat, but just missing her and instead ripping into the long cloak that followed her movements behind her. Its claw caught in its folds and ripped and shredded the material like a shark caught in a net. Realising the woman was trapped at the other end of the material it used its entangled arm and began to drag her in closer to its waiting jaws. Athene, who stood just beyond the amber pillars that surrounded the Vortex, swung about at the sound of the struggle; she was shocked at the sudden appearance of a demon so close behind. Tress hacked at the entwined demon in panic and Sum cut through the creature like butter. As they both thrashed about in panic together the dying demon made a last ditch attempt to close in on its intended target and clambered forward towards the other woman dragging Tress along behind it. She was caught up behind it in a tow as it went for Athene. The demon felt the sting of Sum in its back, again and again - its dark life slipped away by the second as it's black blood leaked into the ground. It realised it would not make the final distance to deliver the death strike to the cowering woman it sought. In a last effort it partially raised itself from the ground and smashed it long arms and body into the nearby amber pillars sending great chunks of flying debris into the dark haired woman several feet back. Athene was smashed by a storm of large flying amber debris as the demon fell from its wounds.

Chapter 25 – Showdown

Titus delivered a wicked series of blows to the final demon's chest and neck felling the smooth black-skinned creature before he slumped to his knees with exhaustion. As he sat there panting with his exertions he surveyed the butcher's yard of carnage before him. He quickly recovered and hauled himself up and began to march back towards Tamar, remembering the near miss of his magic. What a fight, just a single claw-scratch to his arm dripped a thin line of blood that trickled down over his knuckles.

'You're bloody inept at your art man; do you know how close that magic came to hitting me? Or were you aiming for me deliberately?' Tamar gave him a dark look in return,

'If you had done as you were told for once and just stayed behind us, then you would have avoided it in the first place.' The men broke into argument before the shouts for help from Tress brought the group's attention to their unprotected rear and their eyes fell upon the still form of Athene lying on the floor. Seeing the dead demons behind them for the first time, each man was confused at how they had managed to get around to their backs; they had assumed this soft spot had been covered by the cliff. The men rushed over, surprised at their presence behind and fearing the worst for Athene.

'Very clever,' admitted Zerch as he regained his breath, 'Keep us busy to the front and then attack from the rear when we think that we have a solid rock face protecting our backs. It would seem that Soredamor still has some tricks up her sleeve.' Titus beat all of the others to Athene's still body as he dashed to her side and barged Tress out of his way to assess her wounds, he had a good appreciation of most types of wounds …usually from the giving end of a sword.

'If you spent more time in stopping Soredamor rather than praising her efforts perhaps we would be rid of her quicker,' Titus snapped at Zerch as the others gathered in,

'Now back off and give me some light – your magic is no good here. As Titus inspected Athene the glow that had filled his swords from Zerch's enchantment faded back to just the plain silver reflection of polished steel. After pulling away her clothing a little to give her some air, he ran his hands through her hair and found little more than a large egg growing on the back of her head and some light blood on his fingers. Head wounds were difficult to judge and could often take a turn for the worst later down the line, but his first impressions were that her wounds were not life threatening. Other than the lump she only sported several light scratches to her head and neck from the flying shards; these were delicate areas but hopefully she would be fine.

'She seems to be concussed, and without stating the obvious - unconscious, no doubt struck by the large debris of the smashed pillars but with time, I think she will recover well enough. Thank you again Tress for looking out for her,' he looked sheepish for a moment and his next words didn't come easy to him.

'I should have remained behind as they said. For once I must admit, I was wrong - I rise to the challenge of battle to easily. If this is the result of my rashness, I swear I will attempt to change my ways.' He looked at Tress and smiled, she was injured herself, the demon had raked at her in its struggle to break free and get to Athene, her leather armour had taken the brunt of its blows and was gouged and scoured with its passing, several lines of blood ran from her forearms where she had instinctively cowered from its blows.

'Here let me patch you up, call me old-fashioned but I still carry some bandage dressings with me.' Titus reached into his pouches and pulled out some linen bandages. He looked across at Tamar with disdain as he pulled out the bandages brushing past him as he went to patch Tress up.

'You know if I were your sister right now, this would be the exact time that I would make my attack – whilst you're all distracted in the aftermath - standing gawping at us.'

Zerch nodded,

'The brute is right, our rest is over - prepare yourselves,' he added. Titus moved closer to Tress to treat her wounds. He reached out and took hold of her arm; she flinched and withdrew from his touch, fearing that even through the pain of her wounds she may enjoy it.

'I'm alright, its nothing really,' she protested at his advance.

'Don't be silly, come here,' he pressed the bandage tight onto her still bleeding forearms.

Tress forgot the pain in her arms as a thumping sound filled her ears, she could feel her heart beginning to pound stronger in her chest as Titus's hands clamped her arms in his firm grip.

'Direct pressure is what you need,' he said as he looked up from his work. His eyes lingered, looking down the fine view of her cleavage that protruded between them, her low-slung leather breastplate was ripped and damaged exposing a generous portion of flesh. As he pressed the bandage to her wounds she was convinced that he had noticed her quickening pulse that rapidly moved her chest up and down with her shallow breaths. She quivered at his proximity. Last time she had been this close to him it had been in Athene's body and at the time she had thought it her inexperience with her borrowed body as to the reason why she had been so overwhelmed by his touch. Now in the familiarity of her own body she knew her pathetic excuses had just been a lie to herself, perhaps to hide the shame of her enjoyment. She pressed herself into the strong grip of his willing hands; in that moment she wanted nothing other of them than to release her wounds and slide over her body. She flushed with excitement; desiring a repeat performance from the only man that had shown her the passions of lovemaking, sadly the memory of Barrad was now long forgotten to her. Tress pulled herself free from his gripping hands with a gasp and she wondered if he had seen the fantasies of lust swimming in her eyes. She came to her senses with Titus's last words about Soredamor striking at any moment, finally sinking in and halting her raging infatuated thoughts. 'What are you thinking, girl?' She reprimanded herself and suddenly realised that she had spoken the words out loud. Titus smirked and turned about to leave her alone in the full stream of her self-embarrassment.

A huge shockwave rippled through the ground knocking everyone from their feet and marking the arrival of Soredamor's next assault. The wave of power faded as it reached Athene yet the debris of the rock and rubble from the surrounding cliff-face fell to the ground close behind the group; she was attempting to bring the cliff down on them. Titus regained his feet first and began to drag Athene away from the dangerous falling rocks. Soredamor walked calmly up the path towards the dazed group; her gown had very little to it and reviled the mesmerising sway of her alluring figure all too well. She stirred a primeval desire in all of the men who watched and it would be very easy to forget the true danger that she represented. They felt her alluring charms even with the aura of protection as they huddled in Athene's presence, for they were not entirely magical induced desires. She reached out and pointed at the group and a stream of fire arched out towards the group. The fire was deflected before its arrival by the invisible barrier that Kerric had earlier created. Its intensity grew and destroyed the barrier as the last of the fire burned about it. Soredamor called out to the group as she approached and the men stepped forwards to have free rein to use their powers against her.

'Give me the sword, that's all I want – you can keep your pathetic little lives. Just give me the sword and I will be gone from this place forever.' Zerch did not waste any of his breath in return and commanded the power of lighting; he projected a powerful bolt of lightning towards Soredamor which she deflected away with a quickly raised hand and a single word of power.

'Kerric, leave these dead men, I will take you with me – come join with me and destroy them, I command you, you belong to me. The Brotherhood magician broke into beads of perspiration as he struggled against her will. The uncontrollable urge to attack the men about him filled his head and he clawed at his forehead as it gripped him with pain as he struggled against her unseen commands. He momentarily questioned why he was fighting his queen's commands? Why? He slowly backed away; barely able to lift his lead heavy feet to where Titus stood over Athene and to his relief he felt the sensations subside. Soredamor stared in disbelief, of all her Brotherhood she had known none more wanting of her pleasures or prepared to submit to her will.

'Now Tamar,' Zerch shouted. They had earlier schemed that Soredamor would be at her weakest if she attempted to focus on her control of Kerric; it was another one of the many reasons why Zerch had spared him. With the magicians' powerful chants signalling their intended attacks their powers gathered in strength, but they soon discovered that like most women Soredamor was a good multitasker. Both magicians opened up on her with everything that they had, pulses of white and orange power stormed across from Tamar and a continuous flow of lighting arched through the sky from Zerch. Their combined powers unleashed a force equal to anything the world had seen before. Soredamor reached for the dagger, Taric, that hung from her belt, pulling the enchanted blade free as she fended off the powerful assault as best she could. Titus held back and studied their art, judging their movements and the timing of the great pulses of magic in their deadly exchange. Zerch yelled across at Tamar,

'Stop holding back, forget the child's life we must finish her,' Zerch had correctly noticed with mounting frustration that Tamar's attacks had been slightly off mark, as if he were only attempting to wing her.

Titus watched Soredamor as she weaved through the arcs of magic that attempted to bring her down; the Greatsword Thulnir was strapped tightly to her back. He was sure that he could quickly traverse the ground between their magical exchanges and introduce Soredamor to his blade. Tress sensed his thoughts and her hand reached out and firmly gripped his shoulder,

'Don't do it Titus. The wizards are prepared against her charms, but once you leave Athene's anti-magic aura you will become her prize and a gift to destroy us all.' He hated the feeling of being useless in a fight, but knew she spoke the truth.

'This battle will be decided by magic,' said Tress releasing his shoulder as she felt him relax in her grip. She looked down at the sabre of Sum in her hand and wondered if she would need to retreat back into the Rift behind them; it was almost beckoning her back in. Soredamor moved the dagger, Taric, before her, deflecting or absorbing the magic that kept on spewing forth from the two Spell-masters. Her defence was aided by the magic in the ancient blade; with its use she just managed to keep her head above the waves of power that crested towards her. With every close impact or near miss from the magician's magic, she called out again in desperation to Kerric for his aid. If she could control her Brotherhood once more, both magicians standing before her would fall easily should an attack come at them from

Kerric from to their rear. Still, Soredamor had more than one trick up her sleeve; with the combined power of the two swords her words began to penetrate the protection of Athene's aura, their powers were not off this world. Kerric's head shot up from the pain that wracked him and the words in his head commanded him to slay Zerch. Tress noticed the mad look in his eyes as he began to move towards the magicians, she reacted, slamming the hilt of her sabre into the back of Kerric's head as he passed. Kerric fell as if pole-axed and the action evidently angered Soredamor more judging by the loud scream that echoed across the hillside. Her screams turned into sounds of pain as a blast of lighting penetrated her defences and she quickly retaliated with a blast of power that threw Zerch from his feet. A pulse of white energy scorched over her face singeing her hair and twisting her around with the shock of the strike. Her voice entered Tamar's head pleading with him in desperation,

'Destroy Zerch with me brother and we can live a new life, a new chance – we are the only ones that can do this. We have a chance for a fresh start; a chance to find our desires. If you go back with me you may even be able to save father? Think of it, you will have the chance to grow anew and mould this world in your vision.' Tamar suddenly halted his attacks as her words struck the right chords of his attention.

'You know our mother destroyed him, she loved him to a point, but it took the touch of another to satisfy her, you know no amount of magic can quell a woman's true desire.' Her voice rang out in his head and she noticed his changing emotions expose the weakness of his mind. Like a true predator she grabbed her chance as he listened, sending a bolt of power from her hands towards him. The bright bolt struck Tamar full on, cart-wheeling him from his feet. Her hidden thoughts had been a two way conduit between their minds, her true intentions had betrayed her as they turned to that of his destruction. Tamar had suddenly realised her trick in the last second, which had left him little chance to raise his full magical defences, only the quickest and weakest spell of protection was brought to bear in time. Tamar spluttered on the ground as the air was knocked from his body, he was winded but still in one piece with the taste of blood on his tongue. Soredamor advanced closer, temping Titus to look at her by calling out his name. She altered he magic probing at Athene's protection; even without magic she could be very persuasive to the opposite sex. Tress had realised the danger and turned grasping Titus firmly, pulling the warrior's face away from the goddess, pressing his face tightly against her bosom to fend it away from her alluring charms.

'Come Titus, forget that skank and look at a real woman; fill your eyes instead with your desires for me,' Soredamor beckoned. Tress held on to him, pressing his face in tight to forestall any rash movements. She knew she would not be able to stop him should he truly desire to go, he was far too strong for her, but her warm body clinging onto him seemed to steady his will to withdraw from her and behold Soredamor. Zerch had rolled slowly on the ground apparently stunned from the blast that had moved him from his feet, but he had used the extra time lying on the ground wisely, as he lay hidden amongst the corpses of the demons he built a new spell with which to attack. He crouched up and unleashed his magic. A stream of raw power flowed out from him as he extracted new energy from the fragments of amber that littered the ground to boost the effects of his already powerful spell. The force flooded over Soredamor knocking her to the ground and dislodging the dagger from her grasp. Tamar spotted the opportunity and calling upon his reserves of energy he threw a large thunderbolt into her stumbling form. She was already enveloped in Zerch's magic and did not see the spell coming. This time his aim did not deliberately miss, he realised that he would only get one clear shot at her - it struck her directly in the head and her body flopped backwards suddenly limp.

'Forgive me sister,' Tamar whispered as he dragged himself to his feet. He looked across at Zerch who nodded back with approval; both men were equally exhausted but pressed forwards to check on Soredamor. Tress released Titus's content face from its comfortable holding place and with the sabre of Sum raised; she advanced cautiously forward towards the magicians, inquisitive about Soredamor's fate. Was it really over she pondered? Tamar reached Soredamor first. She was deathly white and moved only slightly with a groaning pain. She still drew a shallow breath, rapid and like a wounded animal, blood ran from both her ears and flooded down from her nose to cover her chin. Her robes were ripped with the blasts of their magic and Tamar noticed the sword of Thulnir for the first time strapped tightly to her back, the long blade and handle running the length of her spine, the short sword of Taric lay strewn on the ground close by. She had landed awkwardly with the impact of their magic and fallen heavily on the weapon's hand-guard, further damaging her back with the other injuries. Zerch's shadow cast over her as he looked down at the incapacitated goddess.

'And so it ends Soredamor,' a smile grew across his face without reserve as he pressed his foot across her neck and began to assert greater pressure.

'Don't you dare try and stop me this time Tamar,' he commented as he studied the fellow magician's face at his uncompromising action.

'The child still lives, let me save it first that was our agreement,' Tamar replied as he concentrated on the tiny speck of the life-form that emanated from the embryo inside her. Tamar realised it was time to prepared himself; ready to deflect any magical attacks that may come, once Soredamor was dead their alliance would come crashing to its end and he would have seconds to save the child and deal with Zerch. Kerric was of no concern to him, he was still out cold so he squared up to Zerch, it would be better if he could save the child first.

'Wait, let me save the child – you can still have your revenge afterwards.' He had to think on his feet quickly; perhaps he could use Taric to contain the child's soul? It would take some time – but he was sure it could be done?

'I command you Zerch …*step aside.*'

'Now why would I want to do that? I have what I want,' Zerch closed his eyes and uttered two magical words, which were the trigger for his control.

The sabre of Sum burst through Tamar's chest as Tress thrust it through his back with a single well delivered strike; his eyes went wide with disbelief at its sudden shocking appearance jutting though his body. How had he missed Zerch's hidden control in the tangle of her mind? Simple he had been a fool; he had been so easily distracted by the pleasures of her body to read her properly. Tress held onto the blade cutting deeper through the magician's body until his knees buckled and folded. Tress released the handle and Tamar and Sum fell across his sister's body, his head lay upon Soredamor's breast as her eyes rolled backwards in their sockets and her body convulsed in her death throes as Zerch's foot robbed her of her final breath.

'*Ah,* reunited at last, Zerch sneered. Tamar's hand fumbled its way around to his sister's back seeking the sword handle that he knew was there, but his limbs began to weaken as his life force began to slip away. Tress reached down for Sum's handle and tugged to withdraw the sword but Tamar's blood clenched fingers held the sabre tightly in place.

'Tress,' he gasped, 'This is not really you. Only his death can release you from his grasp …I will give you more,' he chanted several further magical words as he struggled for breath and Tress tried to let go of the sword, but she found her hands were stuck fast to the sword's handle. A power began to flow through Tamar's body flooding into her through Sum, she did not know what he was doing but his magic was evident.

'Stop him,' Zerch yelled in panic and taking his foot from Soredamor's limp corpse he slammed his boot repeatedly into Tamar's face, but annoyingly he kept on chanting.

Titus had felt shaken after the siren's magic had called out to him. Thankfully Tress had held him against its overwhelming call. She had released him suddenly and rushed off, he had watched through blurry eyes the drama unfolding about Soredamor's fallen body and even he had been shocked at Tress's unprecedented action. He had wanted to do the same thing to Tamar on several occasions out of frustration with the man, but had never actually considered following through with the action. Although with his personal instinct for survival he was ever aware that a rather drastic change in the balance of the powers of the world had just taken place. One man now held the full reins of magic under his control. He rushed forwards with his swords knowing he must react swiftly in some way, although his intent was still undecided.

Zerch slammed his heel repeatedly into Tamar's face until he was at last silenced. Tress suddenly jerked backwards as the sabre was released from Tamar's body, the glazed look in her eyes suddenly vanished.

'My god what have I done?' she screamed. Zerch replied, his mouth widening to a victorious smile,

'Exactly what you were trained to do,' he glanced to the side and spotted the Su-Katii racing towards him and reacted by pulling the Dimesia relic out from his pocket. He was pleased with the day's work and with his lifelong

349

ambition of eliminating the gods completely, his work here was done. As always his preparation and planning had been deep and exceptional, his powers of control over his sleeper agent had been well hidden underneath the first layer of his magic that erased the memories of her lovers, it had acted as a fine distraction over the years from any inspection of her mind. The use of magic to hide magic had been the perfect solution. Zerch had engineered every aspect of her escape and feigned his years of hunting Tress – it was not through any ineptness on his behalf that he had never managed to track or capture his former slave. It had always been his plan to drive her into the nest of those he sought retribution from, even if she didn't know it. He had spent years perfecting the magic to place in the mind of his Trojan horse and had only to find the right woman at the slave markets to mould as his tool. Tress had fitted the bill perfectly and today many years later he had reaped the rewards of his work. There was to be no sharing of power in the aftermath of Soredamor. Kerric could easily be dealt with after this, even left alone his power as a Spell-master would soon fade with his queen's demise. With the death of the master comes the abolishment of the spell, one of the oldest rules of magic. Zerch twisted the Dimesia. His escape would be swift and he looked down with relief as the magic activated with a single click of the Relic, but to his horror, his hands and the Dimesia had disappeared with the passing sweep of a sabre. In a split-second reaction that only someone with Temple training could produce Tress had swung the sword of Sum up through her old master's wrists. The Dimesia had activated in that same instant carrying Zerch's hands and the relic to the last pre-set location. The whole event which had happened quicker than a blink of an eye, had left Zerch looking down in disbelief at his two crimson stumps. He struggled to mouth words as the searing pain moved through his body. It was near impossible that his slave girl could move with the speed of a Su-Katii? She was fast, but not that fast. Tress nuzzled in close to him and whispered into his ear.

'This is well overdue,' Sum met with his body thrusting up though his chest and into his cold heart. Titus came sprinting over, his swords ready to strike with vengeance, but found only a limp corpse hanging from her sabre. Titus was ignorant of the magicians' scheming ways and oblivious to their powers of control. He was unsure of the events that had just unfolded and maintained his guard, but for all of his run-in's with Tamar, he still had the sense to know that the act of his execution had been wrong. It must have been Athene's over-inflated sense of justice wearing off on him? He would take Tress down for her actions if he had to and moved towards her. A bloody set of fingers raised in the universal sign for mercy as Tamar struggled to hold his shaking hand aloft.

'No Titus. Mercy, my final will is …give her mercy,' he struggled to say the words and his hand fell to the ground as death claimed him and he at last found peace with his sister. Tress turned around after she eased Zerch's body to the ground and their eyes locked; at first it was with fear that she regarded him, at the raised and threatening position of his blades, but soon she saw past the glint of steel as other desires entered her mind and the sword of Sum slipped from her fingers to land on the ground below. She knew the power of the sword and did not want her emotions flooding into the warrior, if she was to have him – it had to be real. She took a single step towards him testing the ground.

'Ah, what the hell, their end was probably for the better,' he said with an uncaring shrug. Tress's hand reached out to grab his chest and she pulled herself in close. Titus's hands instantly moved with many years of reactionary training to her weapons belt and removed the daggers that hung there, disarming her. She felt his hands moving across her body and mistook their real intentions; his words were not those that she had hoped for.

'I think we are all out of trust now, aren't we,' he angled his body so not to expose any indefensible areas.

'Can you believe it Titus, we did it, we really did it,' her head swam with her elated feelings of freedom. She decided to take a chance and spoke what she truly felt, she had nothing to lose, so she just came out with it.

'Make love to me Titus, like you did back in Ubecka; let us celebrate this moment together, I'm so hot for you now, come and feel.' She pulled his head down into her exposed cleavage once more encouraging him to feast upon her. There was no denying that he had enjoyed the lightly-perfumed resting place during the fall of Soredamor and he certainly desired this woman. Everyone whom Tress had targeted with her affections over the years of her forgotten memories had felt the very same sensations. Their wanting desires would rush through their minds at such an offer; yet Titus knew he had already made his choice in life. Perhaps he would live to regret it? He kissed Tress lightly on the cheek and then stepped back.

'You are carried away with the moment Tress, calm yourself down I must tend to Athene and deal with the last wizard. Titus threw one of his swords into the ground with anger when he saw that the laid out body of Kerric was now gone.

Chapter 26 – Always a King

Corvus stood watching on outside the unmoving gate before him, the tall walls of the Aristrian capital, Monumentium, towered above him and his people. He had stood facing the monumental structure for both a day and a night, enduring the continuous stench that the wind carried from the settlement, with only the briefest of sleep. It had been a strange dream that had filled his head as he briefly dozed on the floor.

'Why they not come?' questioned Ievia puzzled. The ranks of Uphrian fighting men were a little thin, but they stood tall, formed up and ready to face anything that might come out from those gates. Their king had only to say the word and they would have followed him into the very gates of hell. A figure moved out to the tall construction of blocks that made up the higher battlements and Corvus squinted up against the bright sky.

'It's a woman,' he said in a confused tone.

Emella Grey looked down at the rabble of gathered Uphrians surrounding the East gate. How had it come to this she thought? The news of the raiders surrounding the city had been vastly over-exaggerated, yet they had still caused great panic and rioting throughout the city. It had taken what few men of the city watch they had left, to contain the troubles from the affluent areas of the capital. She didn't have a clue what had been going on in the poorer regions for none would dare venture into these quarters or cared enough to. There was little point in holding any power in the city if there was nothing left to rule over; the dry rot of the city would consume the place whilst the barbarians merely stood at their gate and sunned themselves. The Aristrian people had never felt the violation of an invader in their backyard before and the people of the capital were further distressed by the lack of their army to defend them. Half of Aristria was now stationed in Tanaria on one mission or another. The leadership had failed them and the chaos and panic that ensued in the streets had never been seen before. She had faced up to the issues and decided on the only logical solution. She had gone to the battlements to make her terms with this rabble. She was sure it would not take much gold before they moved on to bother some other unfortunate soul.

'Name your terms Uphrians,' she yelled down at the small war-band. Corvus scratched his head at the unexpected request.

'Terms, I have no terms, I just want to meet with the commander who led the attack on my people for a one-to-one chat.'

'Oh,' said Emella, 'In that case your terms are more than acceptable to me, but I don't think he will want to come out to you; you see he now holds the seat of command in the city. If only I had come to parlay with you yesterday.' She sighed the final words to herself. 'Well, that puts me in a bit of a position, marauder, I want to give you what you desire but I am in no position to do so. How about we settle this matter with gold? How much do you require for your clan to disappear?' Emella Grey shouted down to Corvus. Her words offended him, yet he had the good sense to realise that if the Aristrians were making them offers of gold, things in the city must truly be in a dire state. Gold was a precious commodity to these people, it was all they understood.

'*Gold*, what use is gold to us when we can take what we want from you already. Gold will not bring back our fallen ones. Your man attacked my people in cold blood; forget about the politics and your high walls, none of these things will change the end result when I come after your. The equation is simple - I will have his life in return. Now, I am a reasonable man, you have until the sun crests the top tower of the wall to present him to me for single combat or else I will lay waste to your city,' he bellowed back up to Emella.

'You speak with bold words; I fear you talk from your heart and not the logic of your mind. I implore you, look at these tall walls before you and reconsider your situation. Be sensible, I would just take the offered gold; our walls are thick enough to repel your pathetic few.' She turned to leave already anticipating his answer and walked directly into a huge chest of a man that blocked her way. She bit her tongue with shock as Corvus towered above her.

'These tall walls cannot even contain a single man, milady.' Emella recoiled with fright into the battlements, almost falling from the tall wall, only the strong arm of the Nordheim King reached out and held her fast, stopping her from falling to certain death below.

'I came up here to be sure that you would know I was serious, and now you know that I am. I could have let you fall, or slain you with my own hands, had I desired it. These hands hold the power of life and death for you,' he released his grip a little as if to drop her and she screamed, clearly getting his point and he continued, 'And as for your city, it stands here for only as long as I let it. But I am no cold-blooded murderer, at least not when I have no need to be. I give you the power of choice, which is a luxury that my people were not afforded by your soldiers. Just make sure he is here.' He placed her back onto a firm footing and in a blink of an eye he was standing on the ground with his people back outside the wall. Emella was visibly shaken by the encounter, but was still faced with the same problem. The people of the counsel would not comprehend the true danger that Corvus represented, she had gone alone to negotiate with him. They would think her mad and have her removed if she explained the true story of what had just happened. She was deflated but not beaten; it appeared that her gold could not solve every problem.

Or could it?

Commander Hermana stood behind the huge gate waiting for it to open. His former comrades at arms and underlings thrust their spears at him from the rear, jeering him onwards to ensuring that he could not return back into the city. Emella Gray had found a use for her gold after all. The men had been more expensive than the marauders outside the city walls but unlike the clansmen, it could buy a solution to all of her troubles. The Aristrian men would sell their own children if the price was right. The gate creaked, opened and a sharp prod in the back forced Hermana out, a sword was thrown further out onto the ground outside, to encourage him forwards.

'Thank you for making us rich sir, you promised us all at the start of the campaign that you would bring us wealth and you have kept your word. You never know sir …you might even beat him?' commented the sergeant from his former command. The door closed tightly behind him and the nervous figure stepped forwards from the shadow of the wall. Emella Gray stood high on her perch looking down at the leaving commander; her usually pursed lips broke their tight seal threatening to break into an amused smile as she enjoyed watching Hermana's nervous gait as he gingerly picked up the sword. Several Uphrian warriors began to rush forward with weapons raised to strike.

'*Stand fast!*' screamed Corvus and the men halted instantly at the command with a disappointed look back at Corvus's stern face. The battlements cresting the wall began to fill with Aristrian onlookers and Emella smiled smugly to herself satisfied with her negotiations and eager to watch the spectacle about to begin. Her wide smile dropped from her face as a shout from one of the men on the wall broke the growing tension of their entertainment below in the surrounding grounds.

'Soldiers to the South,' came the call, declaring that he had spotted a column of troops marching from the south towards the capital. All eyes turned from the spectacle outside the gates to the south road with growing anticipation. A clamber of voices discussed if they were Aristrian or not, the chatter continued until they unanimously decided that they were. More men filed into the view of the watching crowds as the returning soldiers marched back to the safety of their city walls; it was a tactical retreat away from the Su-Katii general and his small Tanarian army. Their dejected mood showed in their depressed dragging steps as they returned home in shame.

Commander Hermana noticed the distant figures as did Corvus, but no returning army was going to rob him and his clan of their vengeance, he had the target of his fury before him. A large crystal axe formed into his hands and the onlookers above were quickly drawn back to viewing the scene of the brief fight outside the wall. The watching crowds winced and looked away within the first moments of its start, as they viewed the rapid slaughter and decapitation of Commander Hermana. Corvus turned victorious to his elated clan, his clothing was blood-splattered from his morning slaughter as the returning army approached ever nearer. Corvus leaned on his axe casually watching their approach as if he were oblivious to the threat they represented. At first the Aristrian commander thought the clan camped outside the city to be Uphrian mercenaries, as it was not uncommon to find a small detachment of these fierce warriors in some of the Aristrian battle groups. The men of the returning army looked up to their home walls as the repeated shouts of warning echoed down at them. After digesting the repeated warnings the commander eventually reacted and four thousand men followed the sudden relayed shouts to prepare for combat, by moving into a hastily prepared shield wall. Corvus reacted in kind raising his axe and shouting out his commands; the Uphrians quickly jumped into action and formed up behind the hulking figure in their own battle formation, a fighting wedge. The Uphrian ranks shouted and screamed their fierce war cries and waved their weapons at the more disciplined ranks that faced them. An uneasy standoff opened between them with more than one insult shouted out at the opposing force, but through the raising chaos the Aristrian commander followed the protocols of war and marched forwards, away from his men under a white banner to talk. Corvus watched his approach and decided to step forwards and listen to what the man had to say.

'Sir, your position is useless, be a good chap and throw in the towel. We outnumber you twenty to one. My men will outflank you in seconds and then it will all be over for you. You must either be insane or incredibly brave to put demands to our city with so few? The world has gone mad. If you insist on standing against us I can only promise you a quick end this day. Surrender your arms now without the aggravation of a fight and you will have my word that you may go on your own way. It is obvious to me that you are not of their kind and as such you may escape their fate. I will take ward of your people and if they comply they will not be harmed, they will simply filter directly into our slave markets and that will be the end of the matter. For their sake and your own, end this stupidity now and throw down your arms.' The blue plume of the commander's helmet jiggled annoyingly as he spoke his declaration to Corvus. The King of Nordheim waited for him to finish and then nodded his head over at the Aristrian corpse by the gate and replied.

'You see him – that corpse over there; he was the last Aristrian commander to talk to me in such a way and now he makes more sense than you. However there is hope for you all yet, the spirits have spoken to me in my dreams and they tell me to save your life today and also that of your wife, Avril, who waits for you in the city. Only by your surrender to me will she continue to live this day. Once first blood is drawn we will not stop outside of this wall, your actions will bring about the death of all within. You have many men, yet I smell the stench of defeat on every single one of them.'

The Aristrian commander was stunned by his bold words,

'What? ...how can you possibly know of my wife?' he questioned to himself angrily. A group of men ran clear of the scrubland behind the Uphrians as they talked. Several men in the Uphrian ranks gave out a loud whooping cry,

'They are of the Red Paw clan,' a clansman shouted in way of explanation to Corvus who looked as confused as the Aristrian commander at their arrival. Another group of men broke out from the cover further down on the ground to their rear.

'Look,' shouted his men excitedly, 'They are men from the Black Eye clan.' The land to the rear of Corvus began to move as masses of Uphrians poured out from every angle onto the potential battlefield,

'Ah, the Arrow Head have arrived,' shouted another man. Thousands of warriors from the mixed clans began to fill the ground behind Corvus.

'The Clans are at your command my king, all the clans have confirmed you as our rightful leader.' shouted out a man, clearly of some rank, within the Arrow Head clan. The shamans were wrong and they paid with their blood as did Kildraken. We follow you now, my Lord.' A large cheer went up from the Uphrian line, their numbers now more than equalled the opposing army, yet their numbers increased all the time as more men continued to stream in. Corvus was surprised and held up his arms victoriously as the Aristrian commander slinked silently back to his men and continued his tactical retreat over to the Eastern gate.

'Open the doors quickly, we are coming in.' he bellowed up and Emella gave an approving nod as the men looked to her for a decision. The creaking doors opened once more and the returning Aristrian army moved through the open gate in double time.

'Do we follow them in and sack the city?' suggested Chieftain Ion above the growing noise of their men as Corvus returned.

'No Ion we don't, I had a strange dream last night and it did not involve the destruction of a city, however we may have some new terms to negotiate. Corvus walked back to the walls of the city and shouted up,

'I believe your situation as changed somewhat, we had better discuss new terms, I am not unreasonable but – I will speak only to the lady, she makes things happen around here.'

Later that night after a day full of hard won negotiations, the Uphrians drank Mallwe in celebration of the new-found independence of their people. It was a historic achievement, restoring their ancestral rights to govern the great forests themselves, Ievia approached Corvus. She looked down at the Mallwe-filled leather cup in his hands and then back up at the celebrating men staggering about beside him, she was an image of the first day they had met.

'You drink and celebrate victory tonight? She questioned in a downtrodden tone.

'Yes, I'm celebrating alright,' she looked away to hide her welling tears as she made to stomp off. Corvus quickly tipped his cup of Mallwe to the floor, he jumped up and grabbed her arm.

'Wait, I'm celebrating with you tonight, come wife, let us go to my tent,' he proudly stated. She looked up at him with big watery eyes and sniffed away her embarrassment.

'We make baby tonight?' she asked tentatively.

'No Ievia, we not make baby tonight,' her face dropped like a stone. 'We make many baby tonight.' he smiled back at her face that had lit up with a loving glow.

Chapter 27 – The Final Stand

A silence surrounded Tagel with the veil of a thick fog that covered the entire area; this kind of weather was not unusual for this time of year and only the tip of the Keep could be seen protruding from the low fog. Several days before, the Aristrian forces had made yet another futile attempt to storm the walls of the Keep. Now after a string of failures they only came at them in surprise attacks rather than large staged assaults, hoping to get lucky with the first show of the morning fog or a night attack. For nearly a month the Aristrian army had remained stuck at the hurdle of the high walls of the castle. Now, without the aid from the Brotherhood's magic they were unable to penetrate the Tanarian defences. Lord Aden had become increasingly frustrated at having to starve them out in a traditional siege and yet that was exactly the tactic he was forced to employ. With each full assault they had made on the Keep, their losses had been too high to sustain and if they fought in this way each day it would be a senseless loss of lives and a huge dent in their combat effectiveness. Lord Aden had already lost one of his precious few Su-Katii knights in the last failed attempt at the wall; the long climb up the ladders and ropes to meet with the battlements left even his best troops exposed to the easiest of pot-shots. The battlements had echoed with elated shouts and raised moral when one of Aden's finest had plunged to his death. The pace of their attacks had slowed down to a crawl compared to the initial successes of the first days of the battle. The best Aden could manage now was the odd surprise attack when the weather permitted or favoured them, attempting to gain the smallest edge with such tactics. The Tanarians had soon learned to stand the men ready on the walls for battle in every storm or moment of foul weather when an unexpected front would come in and envelope the place with impaired visibility. As was exactly the case today; it was the fourth day of morning fog in a row. Lord Thorsden and Lord Mallet met in the Great Hall to discuss their daily orders with their regular meeting. The situation was getting desperate as their supplies of food were running low and the state of sanitation and health of the poor souls stuck outside the castle's walls was in a dire state. These concerns had been raised with regularity in their previous meetings over the last month, but the stakes were getting higher with each day for the overflow of people stranded outside. Last night alone sixteen people had died of the flux and this situation was only getting worse. On the other side of the harbour the Aristrian force sat waiting in the fog for the command to advance once more. Today they hoped to make a difference, for instead of attempting to scale the walls as they had with several failed attempts before they were going to make a consolidated attempt on the main door. They had used their time well and prepared for today's assault, hopefully better than any day before. Their carpenters had been busy, using their time to modify their siege engines into great battering rams to Lord Mako's design. Two rams had been constructed, but only one would be used today – each one was fitted with a formidable heavy iron head that had been smelted from the arms and armour of the fallen men. A reinforced roof was fixed above the contraption to protect them from falling debris and attack; the men really hoped to make a difference today. The design of the roof protection had been personally devised by Mako who had also overseen its construction and the crew operating it had undergone repeated training drills of practice. The heavily reinforced roof had several layers of animal hide stitched together to form several layers of removable blankets that could be stripped off or cut away. Should they become oiled and put to flame by the defenders above, they could cut free the top layers which would give them more time to smash the door. Lord Aden once again felt a level of confidence flow back into the men and even Mako had stopped making the negative noises that he had voiced on his arrival. The order to move forward was silently relayed from man to man and the cloth-wrapped wheels of the battering ram were rocked into its forward motion, dragged and pushed by many pairs of strong hands.

'Good, good.' Aden voiced his approval to Lord Mako as the ram faded silently into the fog. The pathway to the Keep was now clear of the departing tidal waters of the causeway which unfortunately made it a prime and predictable time to attack; but with such dense fog they should make it most of the way to the large reinforced door before they knew about their presence. After what seemed like an eternity of staring into the white wall before them, the loud thud of the ram's first pounding blow carried back through the white shroud to the anxious generals, shortly followed by the undistinguishable commotion of the enraged Tanarian reaction.

'Standby the infantry,' Mako yelled out to the men behind. If they breached the door, the opportunity may be short lived and every remaining Su-Katii including himself would need to rush forward and attempt to hold the entrance open before they had a chance to repel them and reseal the doors. For now he was content as he listened to the music of the slow but repetitive thud of the ram doing its work. On the other side of the wall, the music was not appreciated at all. The walls juddered and the disturbed dust floated through the air, as the strong door creaked and moaned, ejecting the odd split shard of wood from a compressed slat here and there, but to the relief of the men standing behind the iron bindings, the door held fast.

Commander Mallet emerged from the hall into the courtyard shouting out a series of orders in rapid succession,

'I want hot oil and fire raining down on whatever is smashing at my doors by the time I reach the battlements. Every single man to their stations,' he yelled as Tarqin appeared with a shield bearing the standard of the predatory fish for his Lord to buckle on. Arrows and rocks peppered the sheltered men working the ram, the majority of the thrown debris bounced from the reinforced roof above them.

'Come on, put your backs into it,' shouted Alwin who had been selected for the job of leading a squad of men to the rear of the sheltered ram. Alwin, the hero of the wall was selected to lead his battle hardened squad through any breach that may be gained and he had to admit to himself there was apart of him that wished today's attempt would fail, he would rather that he was around to enjoy his plundered loot, but let any man try and stand in his way. It was not long until the dreaded oil and flame came pouring down through the mist upon them and the ram ceased its action as the men attempted to remove the first burning skin above their heads. The designer of the system was now sitting back in the luxury of an acquired town house and had not correctly anticipated the extreme temperatures that the large burning roof could push out, as the operators attempted to cut the holding lines of the first roof-skin, they were burnt and forced back by the extreme heat. A man that stepped out too far from the edge of the structure dropped to the floor as a large rock suddenly flattened his head. Scalding fat seeped and dripped its way down through any crack or crevice finding its own way down to several areas of exposed flesh to scald the men huddled below. With a frantic effort and many curses the skin was finally released and the burning leather was pulled over to one side and cut away, the burning fireball lit the fog to the side of the ram attracting an increased volume of projectiles. Once again, the giant ram begun to beat its solemn tune against the doors of the Keep.

By late morning the fog had started to thin and the process of the roof had been repeated several times, unfortunately they were now down to their final skin. Two crews had taken their turn through the relentless battering of the war-machine and Alwin had been relieved when he was also replaced by a new squad of shock troops. The army was like a machine, always rotating men through it in an effort to keep the fittest and freshest men facing the enemy at all times. Attrition could often be as deadly as facing the enemy. The reinforced door was looking severely battered, yet still the bent and mangled iron of its reinforcements held firm. Lord Mallet was now frantic with his men; he sensed the tenacity of the Aristrians attack and they needed to stop this assault fast. If the ram continued its work they would be in before the setting of the sun. They would have truly known despair had they the knowledge of the second ram waiting out of sight at the edge of the town, but thankfully for now the fog was saving their morale. The option of opening the gate and slaying the men and destroying the ram was passed about the commanders, but as they had now reinforced the doors from the inside with a series of trusses and barricades it would take some time to make the door passable. There was also the constant threat that the last of the Su-Katii lurked hidden in the mist awaiting this possibility, they always seemed to anticipate their every move and so this line of discussion was ended. They would simply hold fast and wear them down.

Under the cover of the mist and with the rising tide, the Black Rose drifted silently into the harbour. The vessel had easily passed the blockade of moored ships unseen in the mist, guided by its experienced commander, Capitan Rizil. They did not, however, know that the harbour was not in Tanarian hands until they closed towards the docks and heard the pounding of the ram and the shouts of men. It was too late to alter course and they had little intention of doing so. Many figures lined the deck of the vessel and they could just about make out the faint image of the ram at work as they eased into the harbour. Both the Tanarians on the wall and the Aristrians noticed the smooth entrance of the vessel drifting in to dock, gracefully guided to within feet of the mooring. Both sides watched with puzzled eyes, both thinking what a difference a full complement of marines on a single sailing vessel could really make to this war? They both reached the same conclusion as the light breeze obscured the vessel in a thick gust of shifting mist – Nothing at all. Lord Mallet knew nothing of Tamar's dream visit to Lord Candis, or the secret mission Candis had in turn sent Rizil out on. Fortunately Rizil was a man of his word and would retire wealthy from the last of 'Candis's gold if he made it past the final hurdle of today. Under the shifting mist Lord Aden did not recognise the vessel as the same ship that had sat in the town's harbour months before. Having little experience of the sea, one ship looked like another to him and he thought it nothing more than a vessel that had made a drastic mistake in the fog. With only the capacity to carry a hundred or so armed men they would be before him in irons before they realised their mistake. He ordered a detachment of men to take the ship and returned his concentration to the reports on the progress on the keeps door. The wind blew away the mist momentarily as the first rays of sun broke through its enveloping veil. Several sailors had jumped to the docks and were securing the vessel, this ship was definitely not preparing for any hurried escape. The mist enveloped the vessel once more. The shouted commands of the troop commander faded back into the mist, no doubt negotiating the terms of the ship's surrender but soon it was followed by the clash of blades. The battle was brief, far briefer than it should have been and nothing but silence once again came from the docks. Moments later a new battle was joined and following the rapid succession of dying screams the pounding of the ram ceased. Lord Aden squinted into the patchy mist, searching for any sign or indication of what had just occurred, Mako reacted immediately with his instincts,

'Stand the entire army to arms now. Every man to his post – I want a shield wall in place and facing that causeway yesterday.' The mist cleared again to reveal the decimated bodies of the men sent to take the ship. A sickening feeling sank through Aden's stomach as he realised that he must have miscalculated a factor in his campaign. Had what destroyed his magicians returned? No, even from this distance he could tell the handiwork of a blade, the clean cut of steel left a body in all sorts of familiar angles with its passing. He scanned back along the track into the town spotting the figures from the ship, they moved towards the town and engaged the first of his men, who were yet to follow Mako's orders.

No, it could not be – he had to double-take his glance …they were children, he strained his eyes on the figures that cut rapidly through his men …not just children but old men were leading them on. Each moved with the familiar movements of a temple-trained warrior, the Su-Katii of the past were leading on the new younger generation who were cutting their way forwards as a single unit of around fifteen combatants. Rizil had followed Lord Candis's orders to the letter and journeyed to the Isle of Cardus where he had found the Rift of the Su-Katii, apparently deserted as suggested. He and his crew had wandered the deserted halls and eventually found the stockpiled bodies of the slain children and old men, the handy work of Titus - they followed his written instructions to remove their bodies from the Rift. It had been stomach-churning work as his crew were not accustomed to the brutal ways of the Temple. One by one the people slain by Titus's rampage the weeks before were returned to life as their bodies met with the air of the real world. Titus had not exacted his warped sense of justice on everyone inside the temple, by dragging them all outside and finishing them - just the particular names on his list. The others that had stood in his way were of no relevance to him and had simply been left to fester in the Temple. The requested price for their freedom was a welcome request. As Rizil had opened Lord Candis's final correspondence he had read out loud the respected Lord's plea for aid. Finding the unmistakable corpse of their immortal god decomposing on the ground outside, the boys and old men of the Temple had found the need to fight.

Lord Aden quickly realised that his men were caught on the back-foot and needed more time to reorganise against such a force.

'Mako and Syska, come stand with me,' the last of the Su-Katii at Tagel went to meet them in battle. The ancient lore of the Su-Katii crossing swords was now forgotten to all.

Mallet had been pleasantly surprised with the arrival of his new reinforcements; Candis had not spoken to him about this, but with the slaughter of the men at the docks and at the ram he was sufficiently convinced that this was no Trojan horse. Unlike Aden he knew well the shape of the Black Rose and as the newcomers began their counter attack he realised that now would be their best chance of success.

'Get every man to the gate, I want it cleared and opened at once, we are going to take the fight to them, lads,' the men went frantically to work and every back was bent.

The Su-Katii old guard and their young students slaughtered the men of the first regiment that had been formed up ready to assault any breach in the Keep; several survivors escaped to spread their panic back into the town.

The three knights stepped forward to block their way, no words were needed to mark the fight about to begin; everyone knew exactly what was at stake here. Mako yelled back at his men with a scowl on his face, *'I said get that shield wall in place now,'* then he turned and took the initiative. Making the first move, he drove straight into the opposing group in an attempt to break their formation and lessen their numbers. His move was almost an exact replay of the one Titus had used against them in the Temple with success and they had learned from that master-class with the experience of their deaths. They sensibly disengaged as one formation, every man or boy holding their position but stepping backwards as one unit, rather than allowing Mako to split their ranks and pick them off individually. Mako soon stopped his wild assault as his blows were repelled and he became in danger of exposing himself to the many counter blows that came back at him from the line of swords. He waited for his companions to catch him up before he would switch tactics and take them apart from their flanks. Aden picked up on his movements and vectored for the opposite flank as Syska watched the middle for an opportunity to strike. One of the old men in the fighting wedge uttered a command and the group moved formations into a fighting circle but not before Mako dashed forwards spotting an opening and took one of the elders that had moved a little too slow in the throat. The dying man's blood sprayed the others around him, reminding them of the deadly reality of their situation. This was no training drill, the slightest miscalculation guaranteed a true death. Until now the combined force of boys and men had only defended against the three masters of their art. But with the first death in their ranks they quickly realised that this tactic would get them picked off one by one. They had talked repeatedly of this possibility during their journey on the Black Rose and the elders who had once been in the shoes of the younger men that they now faced had devised a plan to counter their advantages of strength and youth. It was time for them to die. The old men broke their ranks in an all-out attack, uncaring for their own safety, they threw themselves against the three knights with no thought for defence - a man prepared to die could often be a swordsman's worst enemy. With only attack in their minds, the first two men attempted to impale Syska, but he evaded their wild series of blows impaling each man back in return with his twin blades. However, instead of pulling free his swords from the dying men's bellies they clung on to his arms with their last dying breath stopping their further use and a third old man that followed, impaled Syska through his chest. The tactic was terrible but effective. Lord Aden ducked the man that had launched himself at him, slicing through his neck with a crimson spray as he passed. A young student of the temple rolled forwards across the ground simultaneously going low and hamstrung him, slicing deep across the back of his fine boots. Aden fell to his knees gritting his teeth and plunging his sword through the boys back in return. Enraged by the fall of their comrades, the other boys rushed forward in unison from all sides at their immobile target avoiding the wild trashing of his blades and running him through. Lord Mako kicked back the first greybeard that attempted to rush him, snapping the ribs of the rushing man and his kick knocked the old fellow to the ground. His swords moved quicker than the eye, outpacing the blows of the elders that he faced, dropping one with a blow to the head and wounding the other as he disarmed him. Instead of retreating with the wound the old man came at him again, staggering forward and clinging to his thigh like a dog attempting to hump his leg. The old man reached for a dagger, but his hand was taken off before it could come to bear. The elder man used his body as a weapon and slammed his head into Mako's groin, Mako winced with the pain. He knew that he needed to be free of his dead weight before the others were upon him and slammed his knee into the old man's face sending him flying backwards. These people were insane. The old man quickly scrambled forward to clutch his foot with his one good arm. Mako feigned his injury being greater than reality, doubling over from the blow to his groin and then with a burst of activity killed the young lad that rushed forward to finish him as he panted for breath. A panic spread through the Aristrian soldiers behind, as the lead elements of the gathering army viewed their commander being slain and their finest swordsman doubled over in pain. Had they watched for a moment longer before turning and running they would have seen him recover and continue the fight; but with the line of advancing Tanarians pouring out from the Keep behind, they had decided to grab what plunder they could and leave this place. Mako felt the change in the atmosphere in the air about him; the man was like a snake, tasting the air to gauge events. Slicing the grasping fingers from his boot he faced the four remaining boys and three old men that were licking their wounds and reformed back into a fighting wedge. They did not scare Mako in the slightest; but with the thousands of Tanarians spewing out across the causeway and his army folding behind him, he knew it was time to leave. Mako put his feet to good work and fled the field – Bravery was often a miscalculation in his book.

Over the course of the day the Tanarian army went about their grim work of retaking their town, rooting out any pockets of resistance and dishing out murder and revenge wherever possible. The battle for Tagel would be remembered by very few Aristrians before the war was finally done.

Peta leaned over to pat Brin's clammy forehead with a damp rag. Lord Mallet had been kind enough to grant him a bed in the cramped confines of the Keep. He had been burning with a fever for several nights. How her husband had survived the Brotherhoods magic and transformation was beyond her comprehension, but she was certainly glad of the fact. Brin stirred, disturbed by the sounds of cheering coming through the nearby open window, the sound was coming from the town.

'What is that?' he mumbled weakly. Peta bent over and kissed him on the cheek.

'That my love is the sound of victory.'

Chapter 28 - A Saga Unfolds

After the final battle on the hillside of Cardus, Kerric had came around, stirring from the blow to the back of his head. This was not the first time he had felt such pain and his body was almost becoming accustomed to such rough treatment. The first view that met him as he opened his eyes had filled him with a resounding joy. Seeing Tamar impaled by the woman could not have pleased him more and he soon found his head spinning as he felt the release from the chains of the Brotherhood shudder through him, striping him to his core as Soredamor's breath finally gave out. After spotting what had happened to Tamar and seeing Zerch still standing he took his opportunity to escape; Titus had left him unattended as he sprinted off towards Tress, so he dragged himself to his feet and staggered away as best he could. He knew they had no love for magicians and even less for the Brotherhood, this was only going to end one way for him if he stayed. The warrior had been too busy with Tress to notice his silent departure and as soon as he was clear of Athene's aura he used his magic and teleported as far as his vision allowed. It was of a shorter distance than he had hoped for; probably due to the exhaustion of the battle but it moved him away from harm to the side of the overlooking cliff. He continued on foot and picked his way up around the rising cliff that towered high above the Rift. He sensed that something had changed within him and suddenly realised that both his lust for his queen and his heightened powers were both draining out of him. He could tell with his teleport away that had not been the distance he had desired, he felt that his powers were rapidly decaying away from him. He felt like a leaking vessel as he hurried his pace and yet his soul felt refreshed and much lighter without the burden of Soredamor in his heart. A thought came to him as the greater of his powers were dissipating, the Rift of the Su-Katii still stood, it's amber gates were smashed but the Portal entrance way still remained. This thought offended him and burned in his mind as he made his way ever upwards; this order should not be permitted to remain after the passing of their god; they were an insult to humanity and inside his twisted head he could hear the laughter of the Su-Katii mocking him at the Brotherhoods defeat. He would hinder them if he could with a final use of his departing magic. The cliff above the Rift had already been weakened by Soredamor's attack and the pocket full of crystals and diamonds that he carried would make the perfect catalyst for his final display of magic. He worked his way up the gentle slope to the rear of the cliff face and scattered the stones into the gaps and cracks near the steeper face. He would show them exactly how pathetic and week he was with a grand final display; he allowed himself a quick peek over its edge. Titus and the others had moved out of the area and only the bodies of the dead lay around the smashed entrance to the Rift. A shame, but he would present an appropriate burial for the fallen. He was about to turn away then spotted the body of Zerch amongst the fallen, a brief chuckle gurgled in his throat with amusement – he had been right to snatch his chance at freedom. He selected two diamonds from the last of his mixed stones for his own escape and then tipped the remainder into the cracks of the rock-face. He moved rapidly away traversing the slope and chanting his last words that would carry any great power as he went. The crystals lodged in the cliff, grew and expanded with the power being drawn into them until the point when they could hold no more. It was more through the force of his focused spite and malice than that of his waning magic that caused the sudden reaction in the crystals and rock. The side of the cliff erupted in a great explosion that slew a large portion of the cliff down upon the Rift and the grounds surrounding it. Kerric smiled with the satisfaction of his minor victory, the smaller things in life would need to keep him happy from now on. With his greater powers all but depleted he would need to learn how to live anew; like a bird with clipped wings.

Tress began her sea voyage back to the mainland after leaving Athene and Titus to enjoy each other's company; three was a crowd. For several days she had stayed with them in the small community on the island unsure of her own feelings and coming to terms with what she had unwillingly done. She had wanted to leave their company several times, sickened as Athene leeched her way over the man she desired. Each time she had moved to depart from them she had turned back at the last minute, confused with why she should just give in and let her have him. She could hardly understand herself for that matter, Titus drove her mad with his brainless comments and yet she still wanted him all the same. Seeing Athene with him was a bitter-sweet experience for her each day. Although she understood the laws of magic she had no idea that she now had the ability to remember her new lovers as the curse in her mind was completely lifted with Zerch's passing. As for her past thoughts of that nature, only Titus and the sordid gangbang of the Su-Katii remained in her mind. It was obviously not the best of references to draw upon, but it was all that she had and the majority of her other darker deeds from the past had also thankfully remained long forgotten. She had been presented with a fresh slate, but she just didn't know it. It had only been in conversation after they had mentioned Barrad repeatedly, recounting the battle for the hill that a strange impulse had grown inside her. She only remembered him as the awkward stranger who had propositioned her inappropriately back in the battle camp, but that night she had laid awake thinking about him and by morning her resolution to leave had been complete. There was indeed nothing like a stranger to stir the imagination and if he was propositioning her it was one more proposition than she was getting here, stuck on this slow-paced backwater island. She needed to park the events of her life and just move on. So, finding a vessel departing with the morning tide, she had asked the inn keeper to pass on her farewells to the sleeping couple and rushed off to the harbour to see what adventure may lay before her as she decided to take her chances and seek out this Barrad. Who knows what may happen, he was far from unattractive to her and had proved himself in bravery leading the Army after the enemy to the very gates of their capital. She paused on the deck, catching her breath after her wild dash to meet with the ship before its departure. Her hand went to soothe the pain that shimmered across her stomach and as the boat cast off she began to wretch at the smell of grain that wafted from the dock yard warehouses. It must be the slight motion of the sea that had set her off, she considered briefly. 'How odd,' the smell of stored grain never used to make her gag before? She had no idea of her pregnancy as the ship made its way out to sea.

The gang of children huddled in close around the hooded figure that stooped low over the large open fire; its glowing embers were burning low but it pushed back the surrounding vale of darkness. The story-teller always liked to use a real fire for light when he recounted his tales rather than the power of the crystals, there was always something magical about a real fire. He had finished recounting his story to the children, of how the continents had came to war and how the world eventually came to lose the last of its great magic. Each little face had sat there wide-eyed, listening intently to his fascinating tale of Su-Katii Lords, gods and Wizards and even the smaller children amongst them were still wide awake. The bard relaying the legend pulled his tattered and grubby cloak around him tighter, but it was not the cold night that made him shiver. One of the elder children pulled on his robes demanding an answer to his earlier question about his tales.

'Do tell us, what ever happened to the magic swords?'

'Oh those old things, I don't rightly know – some say they were thrown back into Hadrak's rift before it was buried under the cliff, I have heard others say that only the 'Hero of Tanaria knows where they lie?' replied the story-teller. A little girl stepped forward and asked another question, her large oval eyes looked up inquisitively.

'Did the magician use the power of the sword to save the soul of the goddess's baby?' 'What sort of question is that from a little girl like yourself?' replied the bard.

'But sir …you said before, that if he held onto the swords he had the power to swap souls and if the lady that killed the magician was already with child they could have swapped over their babies, right?'

'How very perceptive of you, I'm going to have to keep my eye on you,' he liked her respectful tone. 'Don't worry yourself about it little girl, it's just a tale – there isn't really any magic left in the world and look how peaceful our lives have all become,' replied the hooded bard thinking that had ended their conversation.

'But…' stuttered the child pulling on the bard's robe with excitement, she pulled too hard and the man's hood fell backwards to reveal horrendous burn marks along the side of his face and neck. The child recoiled slightly at the disfigured burns on the story-teller. Delanichi smiled to himself, he shouldn't really enjoy the children's startled reaction to his disfigurement, but he did, he was always one for a touch of drama.

'Sorry child I didn't mean to startle you. I think that is enough stories for tonight, now off with you children.

Tomorrow I will tell you what happened afterwards to the Hero of Tanarian and his wife; I promise you children it is a tale that will make your flesh crawl.'

THE END

18289683R10202

Made in the USA
Charleston, SC
26 March 2013